Praise for Michelle Shocklee

Writing with gut honesty and transparency, Michelle Shocklee has crafted a multifaceted story full of secrets and twists and turns that won't let you stop reading even as you don't want the story to end. A master at dual timeline novels, Shocklee delivers yet again. *All We Thought We Knew* is everything you want in this genre . . . and more!

> **TAMERA ALEXANDER**, *USA Today* bestselling author of *A Million Little Choices* and *Colors of Truth*

Michelle Shocklee is a master at capturing the heart of her characters and inviting readers right into their journey. In her latest work, she takes us into the Tennessee and North Dakota camps that imprisoned German internees during World War II. I was fascinated by her research even as I felt deeply the losses of the Taylor family. *All We Thought We Knew* is a poignant story about prejudice, family secrets, and both the sorrow and resilience of lives forever altered by war. A powerful time-slip novel.

> **MELANIE DOBSON**, award-winning author of *The Curator's Daughter* and *Catching the Wind*

Memorable and moving, *All We Thought We Knew* is a novel of ordinary people who are tested by two wars that altered America. Through its pages, we journey with characters whose lives intertwine across decades—from a German medical student imprisoned in a Tennessee internment camp to a young woman facing her brother's death in Vietnam and her mother's devastating diagnosis. Michelle Shocklee has woven a poignant tapestry of revelations and restoration, heartbreak and hope.

> **AMANDA BARRATT**, Christy Award–
> *of Sorrow* and *The Warsaw Sisters*

In *All We Thought We Knew*, Michelle Shocklee crafts a compelling family tale focused on faith, forgiveness, and self-discovery. Set in a small Tennessee town in 1969, this intriguing split-time novel will captivate readers and keep them up late, turning pages to discover how Mattie will resolve the issues that have burdened her heart and family for generations.

CARRIE TURANSKY, award-winning author of *The Legacy of Longdale Manor* and *A Token of Love*

All We Thought We Knew is a sweeping tale of generations deeply affected by war and violence and the beautiful way in which God can stitch the pieces back together (sometimes, even using animals to heal the deepest wounds.) Set against the backdrop of two wars and a beautiful horse ranch, this story has so much to grip the reader and hold tight as it wrestles with right and wrong, faith and heartache. This was a lovely, memorable tale with stirring romance to the very end.

NICOLE M. MILLER, author of *Until Our Time Comes: A Novel of World War II Poland*

When you stay up past midnight to finish reading a book, you know it's a winner. Mattie Taylor's journey shines a compelling light on letting go of hurt, healing old wounds, finding a godly purpose, and opening the heart to love. The result is mesmerizing. Michelle Shocklee's brilliance shines again!

PATRICIA RAYBON, Christy Award–winning author of the Annalee Spain Mystery Series, including *Truth Be Told*, on *All We Thought We Knew*

Michelle Shocklee is known by readers as a writer who isn't afraid to delve into the complexities of human relationships. She's brought us another such story in *All We Thought We Knew*. As I read, I found myself empathizing with Mattie as she pieced together the puzzle of her family's history. This deeply emotional novel will capture readers' hearts.

SUSIE FINKBEINER, author of *The All-American* and *All Manner of Things*

A riveting historical romance. . . . Shocklee masterfully weaves mystery and romance in this spellbinding study of the horrors of xenophobia and the bravery of those who stand up to it. This is a timely and expertly crafted tale.

PUBLISHERS WEEKLY on *Count the Nights by Stars*

Captivating. . . . Rich in history and mystery, *Count the Nights by Stars* is a novel that will teach and inspire.

HISTORICAL NOVEL SOCIETY

"That is our mission, dear. To *see* people for who they are beneath the pain. Beneath the sin. To see them as God sees them: a beautiful creation, with plans and purposes only he knows." This is my favorite quote from *Count the Nights by Stars*, a moving historical fiction that explores darkness as well as the beauty that can emerge from it when the right person takes on the purpose of seeing people for who they are beneath the pain.

T. I. LOWE, author of *Under the Magnolias*

In her latest compelling novel, Michelle Shocklee brings to light the long history and hidden forces of human trafficking as well as our country's treatment of immigrants, the poor, and those we view as different from ourselves. *Count the Nights by Stars* is a timely reminder that caring for our neighbor is a privilege that requires our time, patience, and resources, as well as the courage to step outside our comfort zones, freeing our hearts to leap in faith.

CATHY GOHLKE, Christy Award–winning author of *Night Bird Calling*

Shocklee's masterful descriptions thoroughly transport the reader to this unique time and place while bringing to light an issue both historically troubling and heartbreakingly current. *Count the Nights by Stars* is a beautifully written reminder of our need to see—and be seen—by both God and others.

JENNIFER L. WRIGHT, author of *If It Rains*

Experience Tennessee's Centennial Exposition, presented by Michelle Shocklee as a sensuous feast in *Count the Nights by Stars*, then look deeper as two women, one in the late nineteenth century, the other in the 1960s, uncover the lavish celebration's dark, disturbing secret. The story's main setting, the Maxwell House Hotel, is a vivid character itself in its splendid heyday and decline, but it's the heroines who call it home, Audrey and Priscilla, who give this story its true shine, as each seeks to forge a life of purpose, integrity, and love, despite the obstacles she faces. With a mystery that unfolds with irresistible suspense, I predict late nights of page-turning for fans of Michelle Shocklee's books and new readers alike.

LORI BENTON, Christy Award–winning author of *Mountain Laurel* and *Shiloh*

Shocklee beautifully unveils Frankie's past while developing Lorena's awareness of inequality. Though set years ago, this title resonates today, and many struggle with the same issues and questions of racial reconciliation. With its haunting message of forgiveness, this is a must-buy for any Christian or historical fiction collection.

LIBRARY JOURNAL on *Under the Tulip Tree*

Shocklee elevates the redemptive power of remorse and the grace of forgiveness in this moving saga.

PUBLISHERS WEEKLY on *Under the Tulip Tree*

Under the Tulip Tree . . . is an inspiring story of incredible courage in horrific circumstances, of faith, forgiveness, redemption, love, and friendship.

CHRISTIAN NOVEL REVIEW

ALL WE THOUGHT WE KNEW

MICHELLE SHOCKLEE

ALL WE THOUGHT WE KNEW

Tyndale House Publishers
Carol Stream, Illinois

Visit Tyndale online at tyndale.com.

Visit Michelle Shocklee's website at michelleshocklee.com.

Tyndale and Tyndale's quill logo are registered trademarks of Tyndale House Ministries.

All We Thought We Knew

Cover photograph of blue sky by Chris Nguyen on Unsplash.

Cover designed by Sarah Susan Richardson

Edited by Kathryn S. Olson

Published in association with the literary agency of The Steve Laube Agency.

For information about special discounts for bulk purchases, please contact Tyndale House Publishers at csresponse@tyndale.com, or call 1-855-277-9400.

Library of Congress Cataloging-in-Publication Data

A catalog record for this book is available from the Library of Congress.

ISBN 978-1-4964-8416-1 (HC)
ISBN 978-1-4964-8417-8 (SC)

Printed in the United States of America

30 29 28 27 26 25 24
7 6 5 4 3 2 1

For Steve, Chrys, and Gregg.

Thank you for your service to our country.

I'm proud of you!

And in loving memory of James Mark.

We miss you, brother!

The righteous cry out, and the L*ORD* *hears them;*
he delivers them from all their troubles.
The L*ORD* *is close to the brokenhearted*
and saves those who are crushed in spirit.

PSALM 34:17-18

PROLOGUE

November 5, 1968
Western Union Telegram

Mr. and Mrs. Kurt Taylor
Delaney Horse Farm
Route 6
Tullahoma, Tennessee

I deeply regret to confirm that your son Lance Corporal Mark James Taylor died in Vietnam 1 November 1968. He sustained fragmentation wounds to the head and body from hostile mortar fire while participating in a night operation against enemy forces. Please accept on behalf of the United States Marine Corps our sincere sympathy in your bereavement.

L. F. Chapman Jr.,
General USMC Commandant of the Marine Corps

ONE

MATTIE

TULLAHOMA, TENNESSEE
NOVEMBER 1969

The first telegram I ever read shattered my world.

The second arrived a year later and stole what little ground I'd gained over those long, mind-numbing months. It was the sole reason I'd sat on this grimy Greyhound bus for three straight days, terrified of what awaited me at the end of the line.

Your mama is dying. She needs you. Come home.

The brief message came from Dad.

It wasn't a request.

Cool evening air carried the stench of diesel fuel through the partially open, grit-coated window as the bus pulled into the depot, two hours late thanks to an accident on the narrow highway outside of Pulaski. A handful of people stood near the terminal building waiting for a loved one or friend, but an anxious sweep of my eyes confirmed Dad was not among them. Disappointment fought to crowd out the apprehension I'd felt since receiving his telegram. He hadn't included any words of welcome or promise of reunion. The message simply said my mother wasn't long for this world and needed me home.

She needed me home.

Did he?

Passengers gathered their belongings and made their way down the aisle to the exit. I closed my eyes and leaned my forehead against the cool glass, the decision I'd struggled with since boarding in Los Angeles still unresolved.

Do I get off and face everything and everyone I'd tried to forget since Mark's death? Or do I stay in my seat and ride to the next city, effectively slamming the door on ever going home again?

I'd sworn I would never come back to Tullahoma. To Tennessee, for that matter. When I stormed out of the house on a bitter November day one year ago, filled with wrath and grief, I didn't look back. Why would I? Mark was dead. My twin brother had been my world, even when he was on the other side of it fighting a war I refused to condone. Our country was committing a heinous crime keeping soldiers like Mark in Vietnam. How many of our boys had to die before someone put a stop to the madness?

"Miss?"

My eyes flew open.

The gray-haired man who'd taken over the wheel in Little Rock peered down at me from a few paces away. "This is your stop, ain't it?"

I looked past him. The other passengers who'd purchased tickets to Tullahoma were gone. The time to make my decision had arrived.

A glance out the window revealed the sleepy town where I'd grown up. A place I never thought to see again. But I couldn't let Mama down. Not now.

Not again.

"Yes, I'm getting off," I said. "Let me get my things."

The driver nodded and returned to his seat.

I stuffed my sweater and a half-eaten ham-and-cheese sandwich into my duffel while the middle-aged woman across the aisle glared at me, irritated my dawdling would make their arrival in Nashville even later. She hadn't offered a hint of friendliness since boarding in Albuquerque. Her eyes traveled the length of me, taking in my ratty bell-bottom jeans, bohemian style blouse, and long hair in need of a good washing. *"Hippie,"* she'd muttered under her breath when she settled across from me. The bus wasn't overly crowded, giving most of us a row to ourselves, but from the look of disdain she cast my way when our eyes met, neighborly conversation during the long journey was out of the question. It was just as well. I could tell by looking at her she'd voted for Nixon.

More glares were sent my way as I maneuvered the cramped walkway to the set of steep steps. No one offered to help with my bulky bag, not even the bus driver who ignored me as he studied a dog-eared map. My feet hardly touched the pavement when he closed the door behind me, put the bus in gear, and drove off, leaving me in a cloud of black exhaust.

With a cough and a choice word for the driver, I considered my next move. Dad knew I was coming. I'd made a collect call from Memphis to let him know when the bus was scheduled to arrive. It was the first time I'd spoken to him in twelve months. After a long pause he said he'd be at the depot and hung up.

Except he wasn't.

I scanned the parking lot. Two sedans and an old pickup truck occupied spaces, but I didn't recognize any of the vehicles.

Great.

There wasn't anything to do but go inside and ask to use the office telephone since I'd spent the last of my money on the stale sandwich. For a split second I worried Dad had changed his mind.

Maybe he didn't want me here after all. Or maybe Mama had taken a turn for the worse and—

"Mattie?"

The male voice startled me.

I turned to find a tall, jeans-clad man standing near the pickup truck, the open driver's door evidence he'd been inside all this time. A ball cap sat low on his forehead, the bill shadowing his face, and I couldn't determine his identity. Probably someone from high school, but I had no interest in traveling down memory lane with anyone.

"I'm not who you're looking for," I said and continued toward the terminal.

He gave a humorless laugh. "Same ol' stubborn Mattie Taylor."

I faced him again, this time narrowing my eyes to study his features, before my mouth went slack. "Nash?"

"Didn't expect to see me here, did you?"

The question would have been laughable if it weren't for the sharp pain that crashed into my heart with his living, breathing presence in Tullahoma. Last I knew, he was a Marine sniper somewhere in a Vietnam jungle.

How had Nash McCallum returned home from war but Mark hadn't?

Slow steps brought him forward. When our eyes met, I saw the boy who'd been Mark's best friend for as long as I could remember.

"I hadn't heard you'd come home."

A moment passed before he shrugged. "Yeah, well, they don't let you stay unless you have all your limbs intact."

His words, low and grim, sent a chill racing down my spine. My eyes darted to take inventory. Clearly he had both legs and both—

My breath stilled.

The left sleeve of his denim shirt was tucked into his waistband. From a distance, I hadn't noticed it was empty.

"I . . . I didn't know."

"No, you wouldn't have."

Our gazes met again. Was that judgement in his green eyes?

"Your dad was going to pick you up himself, but when we found out the bus was running late he asked me to come." He reached for the duffel bag. "I'm sure you're anxious to get home."

I couldn't miss the sarcasm in his voice.

Was this a huge mistake? Did I really want to face everyone I'd turned my back on at the lowest moment of our lives? Nash's cool greeting was probably the warmest I could expect, considering how I'd shaken the dust of Tullahoma from my shoes a year ago.

He tossed my bag in the bed of the truck, then opened the passenger door and waited. I couldn't see his eyes once again, but I didn't need to. He and Mark joined the Marines on the same day. They'd boarded the same military transport airplane that took them to Vietnam. He and my brother believed in what they were doing. Mark tolerated my liberal views of the war, but they never sat well with Nash.

Now he was home, and Mark was dead.

I didn't say another word and climbed onto the bench seat. Nash closed the door and came around to the driver's side. The engine roared to life, and we headed north. My family's horse farm was ten miles outside of town, a distance I'd covered a zillion times going to school, to a friend's house, or to one of Mark's football games. Today, the miles seemed heavy and endless.

In the fading autumn light, everything out the window seemed oddly foreign yet reassuringly familiar. Homes occupied by people who'd known me my whole life. Pastures dotted with horses or Black Angus cattle. After living in California's big, overcrowded cities for a year, the serene pastoral sight stirred something deep inside me. A longing I'd ignored since running away from everything and everyone.

A longing I knew could never be satisfied in Tullahoma.

I stole a look at Nash.

I hadn't seen him in four years. He'd been a lanky teenager when he and Mark left for Vietnam. War had filled him out with muscle and a hardness to his boyish features. Although he'd always been on the quiet side, his chilly silence gave evidence he had nothing to say to me. I, however, couldn't help but wonder about his presence at the bus depot.

"Why did Dad ask you to pick me up?"

His fingers tightened on the steering wheel as a car whizzed past on the two-lane road. With a jolt, I remembered he only had one hand to drive with. I hadn't noticed a thing different as he shifted gears and steered us toward the farm.

"I work for your parents," he said, his eyes on the road ahead.

"You work for my folks? But you're a—"

I clamped my mouth shut too late.

"A mechanic." He glanced over at me, then back to the road. "Not too many people are anxious to hire a one-armed mechanic. Dale wouldn't even give me back my old job at the auto shop."

I didn't know what to say. I'd heard some soldiers returning from the war weren't welcomed home with open arms. Like a lot of people, I didn't believe they should have been in Vietnam in the first place, but I wouldn't've wanted Mark ill-treated had he returned. Since both gloating that I'd been right about the war or speaking words of sympathy over his injury seemed out of place, silence once again became the best response.

We passed the Allyns' neat farm. I wondered if Paula, Mark's girlfriend, still lived there with her parents. Mama hadn't mentioned her in the handful of letters I'd received since leaving Tennessee. I'd stayed in so many different houses, parks, and communes over the last twelve months, receiving mail wasn't easy. But I knew Mama would worry if she didn't hear from me from time to time, so I'd ask a shop owner or friendly neighbor if I could temporarily use their address. That's how Dad's telegram found me.

Nash slowed the truck and turned off the main road onto a private drive. Tires bumped over gravel and potholes, stirring up a trail of dust behind us and a jumble of nerves in the pit of my stomach. As stars began to dot the sky, gentle hills and autumn green pastures awash in the colors of dusk filled my view. I didn't realize I held my breath until it expelled from my lungs when the whitewashed, two-story farmhouse appeared over a rise.

Home.

Yet it wasn't. Not anymore.

Nash stopped the truck next to the house and cut the engine. Neither of us moved to exit the vehicle. I glanced up to the second-floor window over the porch. Mama's. Muted yellow light shone through the curtain.

Is she truly dying?

I'd avoided that question for four days. Refused to think about it. Even went so far as to accuse my father of lying just to get me home. But here in the yard, gazing up at her bedroom window, I could no longer pretend I didn't know what was happening.

"How bad is she?" I didn't look at Nash, not wanting to see the answer in his eyes I feared would cross his lips soon enough.

He didn't respond right away. A heavy sigh came first, then he said, "Doc doesn't think she'll make it to Christmas."

I sucked in a breath at the sobering truth. I covered my mouth to hold in the cry that rose in my throat.

Christmas was only seven weeks away.

"She's a fighter though," he continued. "She didn't want your dad to tell you about the diagnosis. Not until, well, until it was close to the end."

I turned to him. "Why? I would have come home sooner. How long has she been sick?"

"They found cancer three months ago, but it was already advanced."

I sat, stunned. Three months? Didn't cancer take years to get to the point of death? "Can't they do something about it? Remove tumors. Treat it somehow."

"They tried, but like I said, it was already bad. Chemotherapy might buy a couple months at the most, but there were no guarantees. With the cost and traveling to the hospital in Nashville . . ." He paused. "She wouldn't do it."

I stared at him. "So she chose to die right before Christmas?"

His expression hardened. "Your mom didn't choose cancer, Mattie. She's not choosing death over life. Your father and she discussed their options and settled on the one that seemed best for them."

Anger began to build inside me. "Just like he discussed *options* with Mark about going to Vietnam. Look how that turned out."

The muscle in Nash's jaw ticked. "I know you and Kurt didn't see eye to eye before you left—"

"And I doubt we will now."

He shook his head, exasperation in the movement. "Mattie, his wife is dying. He lost his son. You disappeared. Kurt isn't the same man he was before."

I scoffed. "I've only been gone a year, Nash. No one can change that much."

He gave me a long study. "You're wrong about that." Without another word, he exited the truck and slammed the door behind him. He jerked my bag out of the bed and stomped toward the house.

I blew out a breath.

I sure didn't need Nash McCallum telling me how to feel about my father. He and his own dad hadn't gotten along. Mr. McCallum drank too much and couldn't keep a job. Mark once told me Nash was willing to go to Vietnam just to get away from his old man. I'd adamantly pointed out that wasn't a good reason to throw away one's liberty, but Mark said I didn't get it and walked away.

Heavy dread weighed me down as I climbed from the vehicle and stared at the house. I took in the green shutters, wraparound porch, and Mama's rosebushes, while bittersweet memories flooded my mind. How many hours had Mark and I spent on that porch, playing games, reading books, or dreaming dreams as we sat side by side on the wooden swing? Mama declared us two peas in a pod, but Mark always called us *wombmates*, making me laugh every time.

The remembrance brought a soul-crushing hollowness with it. A deep void I'd endured since the day the telegram arrived, telling us my brother was never coming home. Nothing I'd tried the past year filled it. Drugs and free love masked it for a while. Yoga and Buddhist meditations hinted at peace, but the emptiness was always there. Dark. Dangerous. Pulling me toward a quick end to the pain.

Flashes from the night I'd given in to the darkness sent a shudder through me. If Clay hadn't come into our room and found me . . .

I took a shaky breath.

Someone peered out the kitchen window. I couldn't tell who it was, but they probably wondered if I intended to stand in the yard all night.

Rusty hinges on the back door squealed, announcing my decision. The warmth of the kitchen enveloped me, the welcome hug I had yet to receive. For a moment I felt like a kid again, coming in from feeding the horses with Mark. Mama would be busy baking cookies, canning vegetables from the garden, or preparing dinner, but she always stopped whatever she was doing to fix us a cup of hot chocolate or Kool-Aid, depending on the season. Mark would tell funny stories, making Mama and me laugh, as we snacked on oatmeal raisin cookies.

But it wasn't Mama who greeted me.

Dad stood near the sink, wearing his usual faded blue-jean overalls, yet I barely recognized him. He'd lost weight, and he looked as though he'd aged ten or more years, with grayer hair and a haggardness to his features I didn't remember. As a young girl, I'd thought him the handsomest man in the world, but this gaunt, worn-down version held little resemblance to his former self. I wasn't sure what to make of it.

"Guess you've had a long day."

The stiff words were apparently all the greeting he intended to offer.

I responded in kind. "Three long days."

After a beat, he nodded toward the stove. "We've already eaten, but there's a plate for you."

I shifted my gaze to see the foil-covered dish he indicated. "Thanks."

We stared at each other in silent standoff, just as we'd done dozens of times in the past. I braced myself for the reprimand he'd undoubtedly been itching to give me for a year. I couldn't blame him. I knew I deserved it. I'd abandoned my family in their greatest sorrow. Despite being right about the war and the need to keep Mark safe, I'd done a ghastly thing by leaving home one week after my brother's funeral. Mama's desperate pleas and anguished wails that followed me out the door would haunt me the rest of my life.

Yet the stern words I anticipated never came. His shoulders drooped, as though a heavy weight bore down on him. As I watched my father seemingly struggle for something to say, Nash's statement about him surfaced. *Kurt isn't the same man he was before.* Had he been right?

"Your mama—" His voice cracked, and he pressed his lips tight while his chin trembled. Several ticks from the wall clock above the sink passed before he spoke again. "Your mama's sleeping. Nash told you what the doctors said?"

I nodded, my emotions too raw and confused for anything more.

After another stretch of silence, he said, "I'm sure you're tired. We'll talk in the morning." He moved toward the door to the hallway. "Your room is just as you left it."

In a blink, I was alone.

I wasn't certain what had just happened, but I was glad for it. My brain couldn't have tolerated a lecture, deserved or not. I was disappointed not to see Mama tonight, but that might be for the best too. The changes in my father's appearance were startling. I could only imagine what I would find in the morning when I saw Mama.

I glanced around the kitchen, with its pale-yellow walls and white cupboards. It was odd being in this house again. I felt more like a stranger rather than someone who once belonged. I didn't know what was expected of me. Without Mama's warm embrace and Mark's joyful presence, everything seemed wrong.

Exhaustion stole over me. Sleep was the only thing I craved. Despite having eaten very little the past four days, I had no appetite. Without lifting the foil to discover what was hidden beneath, I placed the plate in the refrigerator, noting it was well stocked, with milk, cheese, and fresh vegetables. I couldn't recall my father ever going into town to shop for groceries, but clearly his appearance wasn't the only thing that had changed.

I turned out the kitchen light and followed the same path I'd taken to my upstairs bedroom from as far back as I could remember. When I came to the closed door to Mark's room at the base of the stairs, however, my feet refused to go any further.

My heart raced as I stared at the wood, the white paint chipped in places. Flickers of memories sped across my mind. I could almost hear Mark on the other side of the door, strumming his guitar or laughing with Nash as they jawed over the football game they'd played that night.

Without thinking it through, I reached for the doorknob.

Faint light from the hallway illuminated the familiar space. A musty odor met my nose, as though the door hadn't been opened in a long time. After my eyes adjusted to the dimness, I found a handful of football trophies and a half dozen favorite books on a shelf in what looked like an ordinary bedroom. Everything that once declared the space as Mark's—his clothes, his record albums, him—was gone.

I took a tentative step inside. Then another. I had almost convinced myself I could do this when I turned to my right. There on the wall above his desk hung a new, large portrait of Mark in his marine uniform. Crisp, dark jacket. Brilliant white hat. Serious, handsome face. Exactly how he looked the day he walked out of this room four years ago.

My undoing came when my eyes fell on the folded United States flag below it, encased in wood and glass. Two medals lay next to it.

My knees gave way then, and I crumpled to the floor, the pain in my heart as piercing as the day the hateful telegram arrived. As excruciating as the moment I understood, with unbearable clarity, I would never see my brother again.

I lay on the hard floor and wept until I had nothing left inside me.

TWO

GUNTHER

NEW YORK CITY, NEW YORK

DECEMBER 1941

Loud banging on the apartment door woke Gunther with a start. Bleary-eyed, he reached for the clock on the small table beside the narrow bed, knocking over a half-empty glass of water in the process, and held the clockface to dim light coming through the lone curtainless window.

Five in the morning.

Who would knock on his door this early?

Gunther sat up, replaced the clock, and rubbed his face. He'd stayed awake well past midnight studying for the anatomy exam he was scheduled to take later that day. He hadn't been asleep for more than a couple hours.

"Who is it?" he called, his voice rough from sleep.

It wouldn't be the first time someone had stumbled home after a night of drinking and gone to the wrong apartment. How he wished he could find a better place to live but rent in the crowded Queens tenement was all he could afford. If his internship with Dr. Sonnenberg came through next semester, he'd look for a flat closer to the hospital. The small stipend the position offered would add to the meager salary he earned at Hofbräuhaus, the German café where he washed dishes in the evenings after classes.

The person in the hall pounded on the door again. "Open up," came a gruff male voice. "Police."

Gunther's empty stomach churned with a pang of alarm rather than hunger.

He'd heard rumors that foreigners were being arrested after Sunday's attack on Pearl Harbor, especially those with ties to Japan. He and some of his German friends had gathered at the Hofbräuhaus the night of the attack and discussed the situation. They'd ultimately convinced themselves they were safe because of their status as students, legally in the country. After all, it was Japan, not Germany, that had attacked the United States.

But what if they'd been wrong?

His gaze darted to the small window, seven floors above ground level. A rusted fire escape offered a way out, but he'd never tried to access it. Would he be able to reach the alley before they caught him? And if he did try to escape and wasn't successful, would it only make matters worse?

"Open up or we'll bust down the door."

Gunther took a calming breath and blew it out.

He hadn't done anything wrong, he reminded himself. Perhaps they'd mistaken his apartment for someone else's.

"I'm coming," he said.

Still fully clothed after his all-night study session, he padded barefoot across the cold linoleum floor of the tiny one-room flat. As he turned the dead bolt, he heard a rat skitter across the counter where dishes and a hot plate sat.

Feeble light from the narrow hallway filtered into the apartment when he opened the door. Three men crowded around the opening. One, a beefy uniformed police officer, held a gun pointed at Gunther.

"Are you Gunther Schneider?" a suit-clad man asked.

"Ja, ich bin Gunther Schneider," he answered, nervousness causing him to slip into German. When the man scowled, he repeated it in English. "I am Gunther Schneider. Is something wrong?"

The man's frown remained. "I'm Special Agent Malone, with the FBI. My colleague, Brock. We have some questions for you."

Gunther's heart pounded hard, and he feared they would hear it and assume he was guilty. Of what, he didn't know. "Please, come in."

Down the hall, a door clicked shut as the men entered the apartment. One of his neighbors must have heard the banging. Most of the residents in the tenement were like him—foreigners hoping to improve their lot in life in America, the land of opportunity.

The room seemed to shrink with four grown men standing nearly shoulder to shoulder. After Gunther handed his identification card to Agent Malone, the man told him to sit on the edge of the bed. The agent studied the card, then took a notebook and pencil from his coat pocket while the other agent and the police officer walked around, rummaging through Gunther's schoolbooks and papers spread over the small table and floor.

"When did you arrive in the United States?" Malone asked, his attention focused on Gunther.

That information was on his ID card, but Gunther didn't want to appear difficult by stating the obvious. "I came in 1937. In May, aboard the SS *New York*. I—"

"Where were you born?"

Unease grew in Gunther's gut. "Krefeld, Germany."

"What is your business in the US?" The other men stopped their prowling and waited for Gunther's answer.

"I am a student at Columbia medical school."

The suit-clad men exchanged a glance before the questioning continued.

"Why did you take an apartment so close to the East River?"

This inquiry stumped Gunther. "It . . . it was the only one I could afford." He didn't confess the river reminded him of the Rhine, where he'd spent time as a boy with his father.

"You speak English surprisingly well for a Kr—" The man paused, smirked, and continued with, "for a *person* born in Germany. Where did you learn English?"

Gunther guessed the man was about to use a derogatory term for people of German descent. He'd heard them all, especially over the last months as Germany continued to raise its iron fist across Europe.

"I was tutored in English and French as a boy. *Mutter* was a teacher. Both of my parents believed education was important."

"What was your mother's maiden name? Is she loyal to Germany?"

Alarm washed through Gunther. Would answering these questions put *Mutter* in danger? She'd lost so much already. He didn't want to bring more trouble to her.

"What does my mother have to do with this? Why are you asking all these questions? I came to this country to study medicine, and I have lived as a law-abiding citizen since my arrival."

"Citizen?" Agent Malone shook his head. "No, Mr. Schneider. You are *not* a citizen of this country. You are an enemy alien. Do you know what that means?"

When Gunther didn't answer, Malone said, "You recall registering last year in compliance with Congress's Alien Registration Act?" He didn't wait for Gunther to respond. "Now that we are at war, we can't have potentially dangerous people roaming free. Therefore, the President and the Justice Department feel it is vital to national safety to remove any threat to our *citizens*."

His brutally candid explanation stunned Gunther. "I am a student, not a dangerous criminal. Besides, the United States is not at war with Germany."

Malone scoffed. "Surely you're not so naive. But because I'm a generous sort of fellow," he grinned, causing the other men to chuckle, "I'll let you in on a secret. We *will* declare war on Germany any day now."

Raw fear exploded in Gunther. "Are you arresting me?"

The man ignored the question and asked one of his own. "What is your brother's name?"

Terrible awareness, fast and swift, surged through Gunther. "Is that what this is about? You think I'm like my brother? That is the furthest thing from the truth. My mother sent me to America to get away from my brother and the things he was becoming involved in. She wanted to protect me."

"What sort of things is he involved in?"

Gunther turned away.

He'd said too much. He needed to be careful. They could twist his words. Twist the truth.

"What sort of things has your brother Rolf gotten himself into back in the fatherland?"

Gunther met Malone's cold gaze. "You already know the answers to these questions. Why waste your time asking them?"

"Your brother, Rolf Schneider, is a member of the SS branch of the Nazi party," the agent said, contempt in his voice. "He joined Hitler's youth program when he was fourteen. Your name was listed directly beneath his on the roster."

Gunther shook his head. "*Nein.* No. That is not true. I never joined. Rolf wanted me to, but *Mutter* would not allow it. She wanted me to become a doctor, like her father, not a soldier."

"Like your father."

Gunther had never been ashamed of *Vater*'s service in the

military during the Great War, but here, in this room where his very freedom was at stake, he buried his pride.

"My father was a good man. He made mistakes, as all men do. He died before I came here."

Malone didn't seem impressed. "Do you have plans to return to Germany?"

"No, I want to stay in America. I hope to apply for citizenship."

"Why haven't you done it yet?"

Gunther thought of the letter he'd received from the German government last year, demanding he return and join the military. It had left him shaken and fearful for his mother's safety.

"It seemed best to wait until the war in Europe was over."

Malone studied Gunther a long moment, an unreadable expression on his face, then turned to the other men. "Search the place. Take anything that looks suspicious."

The men began an inspection of every inch of the tiny apartment, tossing papers, clothes, and dishes to the floor as they went through Gunther's sparse belongings. They looked under furniture, tapped floorboards, and opened the window to examine the fire escape. The policeman retrieved a cardboard box from the hallway, and Agent Brock began to fill it with books printed in German, the handful of pictures Gunther had of his family, and a stack of letters his mother had written to him since he arrived in America. He was tempted to ask to see their search warrant but thought better of it. Things would go easier if he cooperated.

How, he wondered as he watched his home dismantled, did they know so much about his family? Yes, he'd gone to the Astoria post office last year to register as an alien after the law required him to do so, but he didn't recall providing information about his brother other than his name. Rolf was only one year older than Gunther, but they were as different as any brothers could be. Where Gunther was timid and studious, Rolf was loud, arrogant, and mean. He bullied and belittled anyone he deemed inferior, including his brother. When recruiters for Hitler's youth program came to their school, Rolf leaped at the chance to join despite their mother's disapproval of the organization.

Was Agent Malone telling the truth about Rolf's involvement with the infamous *Schutzstaffel*, an elite unit within the Nazi regime? Stories of SS brutality were in the news more and more lately. Rolf had gone into the military after he graduated from the youth program, but Gunther left for America soon after. *Mutter* only said that Rolf was in Berlin, although her last letter revealed her worry over him.

We must pray for your brother, she'd written. *I fear he has forsaken everything I ever taught him about what is right and what is wrong.*

When the policeman picked up the Bible Gunther's mother had given him the day he left Germany, he stood. "That was my father's, given to me by my *Gott*-fearing *Mutter*. Please do not take it."

Agent Malone reached for the book. After thumbing through the pages, he handed it to Gunther. "You may keep it. Pack one suitcase of clothes and any personal items you want to take with you."

Gunther froze. "You are arresting me?"

Brock and the policeman continued tossing Gunther's possessions into the box.

"You're being detained," Malone said. "For more questioning."

Arrested. Detained. What did it matter what they called it? He'd been deemed dangerous, worthy of being locked up, kept away from true American citizens. An enemy to the very country he'd hoped to claim as his own someday.

Minutes later Gunther was told to put on shoes and a coat before he was handcuffed and led out of his apartment. A door down the hall opened on squealing hinges, and Mrs. Kozlowski, his Polish neighbor, poked her head out to watch. She knew very little English, and Gunther had only exchanged simple pleasantries with the older woman since she moved in the previous year. She always seemed to be aware of his comings and goings though, as evidenced now. He thought she might offer a sympathetic nod, but her upper lip curled in an ugly sneer.

"Brudny Nazista," she hissed and spit on Gunther as he passed.

The agents snickered but kept moving.

Gunther had no time to ponder the woman's strange behavior and was driven to the Astoria police station where he was photographed, fingerprinted, and placed in an overcrowded cell with dozens of other German-speaking men, none of whom he recognized. They seemed as clueless about what was happening as Gunther. No charges were read against him, and no explanation was given for his detainment. Despair threatened to overtake him, but he forced himself to remain calm. Surely this was a mistake that would soon be rectified. If he could get word to Dr. Sonnenberg, the professor would surely be able to help him.

Sometime in the afternoon, Gunther and the others were loaded into paddy wagons and taken to New York harbor. A number of similar vehicles with more prisoners were already parked near the docks when they arrived. Gunther followed the man in front of him and carefully climbed from the wagon, his bag of belongings clutched to his chest with his handcuffed hands. Armed guards herded the men like cattle up a gangplank and onto the deck of a waiting Coast Guard ship.

"Where are we going?" someone called out.

A guard standing near Gunther shouted back. "Ellis Island. If any of you try to escape, you'll drown in the bay."

The vessel lurched forward and pulled away from the dock. Any shred of hope Gunther had held on to since his arrest melted away as he looked across the dark water to the small patch of land where he'd taken his first steps onto American soil. Ellis Island was the very place where his dreams of becoming a doctor and living life in peace, far away from the Nazi regime, had taken root. As soon as he'd saved up enough money, he'd planned to bring his mother here, too. Now he was a prisoner of the country he'd called home for over three years. An enemy to the people he'd hoped to provide medical care for someday.

Lady Liberty, with her arm raised in victory, stood in the distance as they crossed the bay. She was a symbol of freedom to every immigrant who arrived in New York from faraway lands, and Gunther remembered seeing her for the first time when he arrived from Germany. Her beauty and everything she represented brought tears of gratitude to his eyes that day. He often visited Battery Park and sat on a bench looking out to her, a reminder that one day soon he would be one of her sons.

But the Lady no longer welcomed Gunther and the men aboard this ship. She'd turned her back and declared them adversaries in an evil war Gunther wanted no part of. A war he'd tried to escape by coming to the land of the free.

The ship pulled up alongside the dock, and a gangplank was lowered. The stately brick buildings on the island loomed above them, appearing more like a prison than a place where he'd heard the Declaration of Independence read in multiple languages when he last stood there.

Something died inside Gunther when he stepped off the boat.

Whether it was his hopes and dreams of a happy life in America, or something that reached far deeper inside him, he knew, beyond any doubt, whatever it was could never be brought back to life again.

THREE

MATTIE

DELANEY HORSE FARM

NOVEMBER 1969

I woke with a start.

Was that Mama's voice I heard?

It took a moment to remember I'd slept in my old bedroom in Tullahoma and wasn't experiencing a drug-induced dream in some dingy California hovel. While that knowledge brought a wave of relief, it quickly faded when the reason I was here crashed over me.

Mama was dying.

With great effort, I pushed myself into a sitting position, feeling as exhausted this morning as when I fell into bed. I'd stayed on the floor in Mark's room for hours before dragging myself upstairs. A new day beckoned beyond the window curtains. Somewhere on the farm, a rooster crowed. The world continued to spin, and life went on, even if I wasn't ready to face it.

Low conversation came from my parents' room across the hallway, and I sat there, listening. Dad's deep murmur, followed by Mama's soft chuckle. The clinking of dishes. So many emotions rushed through my mind.

Grief. Regret. Anger.

Always anger.

I wrapped my arms around my bent knees and recalled Dad's greeting—or lack thereof—from last night. He'd never been much of a conversationalist. Mama always joked that she did enough talking for the both of them. He preferred being with the horses rather than people. Yet despite my father's tendency toward reclusiveness, he and Mama always got along. They weren't one of those married couples who hugged and kissed in front of others, but I'd never worried about them divorcing like so many of the parents of my school friends. As I got older and started to dream about the boy I'd marry someday, I knew I wanted him to be as different from my dad as an apple is from a banana.

My thoughts turned to Mark.

He was the opposite of our father. As the saying goes, Mark never met a stranger. Everyone loved him, and he genuinely loved them back. I'd often wished I could be more like my brother, but I wasn't. I was impatient, headstrong, and opinionated. Those traits served me well in debate class, but in real life . . . not so much. Especially when it came to communicating with our father.

The smell of fried bacon wafted into my room from the kitchen below. I could still hear my parents' muted conversation, making me wonder who was downstairs cooking. Maybe Dad had hired help after Mama's diagnosis.

I hauled myself from bed and shivered when my feet met the cold wood floor. Inching the door open, I found the hallway empty. Careful to avoid the squeaky floorboard, I crept to the bathroom and stared into the mirror. Dark circles. Dirty hair. The same wrinkled clothes I'd worn since leaving California.

What would Mama think when she laid eyes on me?

After I brushed my teeth, I tiptoed out and came face to face with Dad.

"Morning. Your mama's anxious to see you."

His expression gave nothing away.

Was Mama having a good day? Would she tell me how much I'd disappointed her? Was she recognizable or had cancer ravaged her the way life had ravaged my father the past year?

I took a deep breath and walked past him into the room.

Mama lay in bed, propped up by pillows, wearing a powder-blue flannel nightgown with lace around the collar and long sleeves. Where my father looked almost skeletal, Mama's face and hands were unnaturally puffy. For some reason I thought most people with cancer lost their hair, but Mama's simple coif looked as it always had, if slightly rumpled.

Tears glistened in her eyes, and she stretched her arms toward me. "My Mattie. You're home. You're finally home."

I'd told myself to be strong and not fall apart, but her motherly words unearthed every emotion I'd tried to bury over the past twelve months.

"Mama," I whispered and stumbled to the bed. I knelt on the hardwood, took her hand in mine, and buried my face in the soft sleeve of her gown. As I sobbed, I felt her other hand stroke my dirty hair while she crooned, "My girl. My poor, poor girl."

I don't know how long I stayed there, but when my weeping subsided, I looked up to find compassion and love in her eyes rather than the condemnation and disapproval I deserved.

"I'm sorry, Mama," I croaked, the words sincere. I wasn't certain what I was apologizing for, but I knew it was long overdue. For leaving. For coming back. For her diagnosis. For Mark's death. Maybe all of it.

"I know, sweetheart." She sniffled and wiped her nose on a hanky. "We all are."

I searched her face, trying to find my beautiful mother in the swollen flesh. "Why didn't you tell me, Mama? I would have come home. You know I would have."

She squeezed my hand, although there was no strength in her grasp. "I didn't want you to come home for me. I wanted you to come home for you."

It wasn't an answer I would argue with. Not now. There were more important things to discuss. "I'm taking you to the hospital. Today. Let them do what they need to do to get you well."

She removed her hand from mine and caressed my cheek. "I know this is hard to accept, Mattie, but there isn't anything they can do. The cancer spread too much, long before we even knew it was there. They'd have to remove nearly all my innards, and still, they couldn't be sure they'd gotten it all."

Panic surged through me. "There must be something." I heard desperation in my voice.

"You're home now, and that's the best medicine in the world," she said with a soft smile. "Tell me about your trip. I bet you saw all sorts of interesting things."

Mama always changed the subject when she decided the current topic of conversation was played out. I'd humor her for now, but I wasn't giving up on the hospital and doctors. For the next thirty minutes I described Arizona's tall saguaro cacti and the forests of pine trees we passed in Arkansas. I told her about the grumpy lady who boarded in Albuquerque and the bus driver who took a wrong turn in Oklahoma City. Mama laughed the way she used to when Mark told his stories, and although I detected a forced joviality in her smile, I treasured the sweet sound.

"I always thought I'd like to travel and see more of the country," she said, her voice weakening. "But I suppose I'll have to be content listening to you tell of your adventures."

I closed my eyes, but tears escaped anyway. "It's not fair," I hissed. First Mark and now Mama.

"Maybe not, but I'm not afraid. God has his hand on me. On you, too."

When I looked at her again, the expression of peace on her swollen face made me mad. "I can't believe in a God who would fill your body with a vile disease and then sit back and do nothing to help. I won't believe in a God who let my brother die a horrific death, fighting a horrific war that should have never happened. This is all wrong, Mama. Don't you see?"

My raised voice brought my father to the open doorway. "Ava?" he said, concern in the single word as he came forward. He went to the opposite side of the bed and sat on the mattress. He didn't look at me at all.

Mama's lips lifted in a tired smile. "It's good to be together again."

Dad didn't voice his agreement. "You don't want to wear yourself out with too much talking."

"I want to visit with Mattie a while longer." She sounded like a little child, begging to stay up past her bedtime.

"You didn't sleep well last night. It's important for you to rest."

I watched him place a small white pill in her mouth, then he held a glass of water to her lips. After Dad helped her into a comfortable position, Mama reached for my hand again. Her eyelids were already beginning to droop. "Come see me after I've napped a little. We have a lot of catching up to do."

I nodded. By the time I'd gotten to my feet and kissed her forehead, her eyes had drifted closed. I stood and watched her for a long minute while Dad tidied up the bottles of medicines and other items on the bedside table.

"She'll sleep a while now," he said when he'd finished.

I didn't look up. "Why are her face and hands swollen?"

"The medicine."

His answer was woefully inadequate. A dozen questions poured through me. What medicine? What's it for? Why isn't she in the hospital? Why are you letting my mother die? On and on, but I didn't voice any of them. Anything he had to say, I suspected, would not satisfy me.

I turned and left the room without another word.

Despite the desire to crawl back into bed and pull the covers over my head, I trudged downstairs. I wasn't much of a coffee drinker, but I was in serious need of some caffeine or something to keep me going. Ever since my overdose, I'd stayed away from drugs, but I had to admit I wouldn't pass up a line of coke or some LSD right now. The thought of facing my first day back on the farm without something to take the edge off reality terrified me.

I didn't glance at the closed door on my right when I reached the bottom of the steps. When I dragged myself from Mark's room last night, I knew I'd never step foot in there again. What would be the point? His things were gone. He was gone.

The space felt as empty as I did.

I drew to a stop in the kitchen doorway. Nash stood at the sink, scrubbing a propped-up frying pan.

"Morning." He didn't smile but nodded to the table. "There's pancakes and bacon, but they might be a little cold by now. Coffee's still hot though."

Confusion spun through me. "Dad hired *you* to cook?"

He chuckled. "He hired me to help with the farm. The cooking part evolved."

I wasn't sure what to say. Not only was he the farmhand and chauffeur, but he was the housekeeper too?

I moved to pour myself a cup of coffee from the percolator. A hefty dose of cream and sugar lightened the dark liquid. After I took a long sip, I said, "I saw Mama."

He nodded but continued scrubbing.

I heaved a sigh.

Nash and I may not agree on some things, but right now I needed him. He was the only person who would give me the information I required to help me understand what I'd walked into when I came home. Talking to Dad about it was out of the question. "Tell me about her diagnosis." When he glanced over to me, I added, "Please."

Nash stopped what he was doing, toweled off his hand, and motioned me to the table where we both took seats.

"I got back to the States in February, but I didn't come to Tullahoma until the end of March." He paused, his expression convincing me the memory of his homecoming wasn't pleasant. "I stayed in town looking for a job, but I hadn't seen your folks yet." He shrugged. "I didn't know what to say to them. It might sound crazy, but I blamed myself for Mark's death, even though I wasn't there when it happened."

I sat silent. I blamed him too, but now wasn't the time to bring that up.

"When I finally got the courage to come out and see them, they welcomed me. Your dad asked what I planned to do now, and I told him I was looking for a job. Any job. He didn't hesitate. Said I could come work for him."

A soft smile formed on his mouth. "Your mom . . . she's been good to me. I wasn't here long before I noticed she was tired all the time. Ava said it was normal aging and told us not to worry. It was real hot the first week of August, and she collapsed out in the barn. Your dad took her to the hospital, and that's when they discovered the cancer. Doc sent her to Nashville for surgery, but when they opened her up . . ." He grew silent and simply shook his head.

I swallowed hard. Guilt, pain, and regret tightened my throat. "I still don't understand why she won't try to fight it."

He looked out the window, then back to me. "Not every battle can be won, Mattie." He stood and returned to the sink.

I watched him wash and dry dishes, doing it all with one hand. If anyone knew the truth of his statement, it was Nash. Knowing what losses he would suffer, would he still willingly head off to war and take my brother with him? While they'd spent three years fighting the enemy in the jungles of Vietnam, I'd moved to Nashville to attend Vanderbilt and participated in student sit-ins to protest the war. We were beginning to feel like we were making a difference when Mama called with the worst news I could imagine.

Scratching came from the outside door. A loud bark followed.

"That'll be Jake," Nash said. He finished drying off a plate and stored it in the proper cabinet, then strode to open the door. A German shepherd stood on the porch.

"Hey, boy." Nash patted the animal on the head. "You ready for breakfast, too?"

The dog barked again. Nash motioned him in and shut the door.

My mouth gaped. "Dad lets you have a dog inside the house?"

The corner of Nash's mouth lifted. "Your mom's the one who said Jake was welcome. Not much your dad could say after that."

Jake walked with a limp as he slowly made his way into the kitchen. When the animal glanced my way, I was surprised to discover he only had one eye. Furless scars crisscrossed his face, evidence something bad had happened to him.

Nash didn't wait for an inquiry. "Jake is a war dog. He and Gerald, his handler, were both injured by a grenade. The Vietcong target the dogs, hoping to keep them from detecting land mines and tunnels. The powers-that-be up the chain of command were going to have Jake euthanized because of his wounds, but Gerald wouldn't leave Vietnam without his partner. I don't know the whole story, but someone snuck Jake onto the medical transport airplane in a wooden crate, even though it was against regulations. I met Gerald at Walter Reed in Washington."

Nash took a bag from the pantry and dumped a handful of dry dog food into a bowl. Jake hobbled over and began to eat with more gusto than I'd expected.

"Are you keeping Jake for Gerald until he's well enough to come get the dog?"

A shadow darkened Nash's face. "Gerald's dead. He committed suicide. Couldn't stand the thought of being a cripple all his life."

I sucked in a breath. On their own, my eyes darted to his empty sleeve.

"I'm lucky." His tone indicated the exact opposite. "I only lost an arm. Gerald lost both legs. Infection becomes an amputee's worst enemy after he's carried off the battlefield." His eyes narrowed on me. "People back home don't care that not only is the soldier suffering from physical disfigurement, but he's also dealing with depression, hopelessness, criticism from strangers. People out there would rather condemn Gerald for being a soldier in the first place rather than feel any sympathy for what he went through that led him to give up."

Anger laced his words. Was he still talking about Gerald, or had he himself experienced the kind of rejection he spoke of?

"I'm sorry your friend died," I said. "I'm sorry my brother died. But the truth of the matter is, none of you should have been in Vietnam. Certainly not Jake."

He stiffened. "Jake served his country faithfully. That's more than I can say for the cowards who chose to play it safe." He smirked. "I'm sure that includes your *friends* out in California. Sex, drugs, and pseudo peace. Isn't that their motto?"

I wouldn't take the bait. "You, Mark, and even Gerald *chose* to go to war. Jake didn't."

The muscle in Nash's jaw ticked. I braced for a full-on argument, but it didn't come.

"Jake, let's go." Nash grabbed his jacket from a hook by the door and didn't look back as he and the dog left the house.

I watched him through the window as he crossed the yard, his long strides evidence of his anger. Dad must've left the house through the front door after Mama went to sleep, because he met

Nash halfway between the barn and the house. Would Nash tell him about our quarrel? After a minute of conversation, the two disappeared into the big building.

I sat at the table and sipped coffee that had grown cold.

I refused to feel guilty. I'd only spoken the truth. Still, the look on his face when he talked about his friend's suicide . . .

I heaved a sigh.

I didn't want to hurt Nash. He'd been like a brother to Mark for many years. But he'd made his choice four years ago and now had to live with the consequences.

A glance in the direction of the closed bedroom door reminded me we all had to live with those consequences.

After I downed a cold pancake, I put the leftovers away and finished cleaning the kitchen. Upstairs, I peeked in on Mama and found her still asleep. A hot shower and a bottle of shampoo worked magic on my appearance and my mood. After donning an old pair of jeans and a sweatshirt I found in my closet, I made my way outside into a beautiful autumn day. Maybe I'd take Moonlight for a ride. I'm sure my horse had missed me the past year.

Standing on the porch, I inhaled a deep draft of clean, country air. I had to admit the farm held a unique beauty that couldn't be found anywhere else. California had its pretty beaches, deserts, and mountains, but this place . . . These pastures and rolling hills were part of me. They were part of Mark. He and I had covered the two hundred fifty acres countless times, either on foot or on horseback, almost from the moment we learned to walk. We built forts, hunted for arrowheads, and fished in the creek that ran through the back woods. Nash would tag along sometimes, especially on days when Mr. McCallum had been drinking.

Movement near the small guest cottage just past the barn caught my eye.

Jake. He was chasing something. The dog limped along at a quick pace, bent his nose to the ground, and picked up what looked like a red ball. He carried it back to the house, where the door stood open, and disappeared inside. A moment later, a red flash shot through the air into the yard, with Jake right behind it.

Curious, I stepped off the porch and walked in that direction. Jake was just returning with the rubber ball in his mouth when Nash met him at the doorway. They both seemed surprised to see me.

"Sorry. I didn't know you were with him. I saw him from the porch."

Nash bent to retrieve the ball Jake had dropped at his feet. "Sit." The dog did. A moment later, Nash lobbed the ball into the yard, and off went Jake after it. We watched in silence before Nash said, "The vet says exercise is good for him. It may look like he's in pain, but he needs to stay active. Otherwise, his muscles will atrophy."

I nodded. I couldn't help but wonder if the same was true for wounded soldiers.

Jake returned, but instead of dropping the ball at Nash's feet, he plopped down in the dirt, obviously done with the game for now.

I studied the small one-story house. "Do you remember when Granny lived here? She was always so grumpy and didn't smile, but she made the best molasses cookies. Too bad she wouldn't let us have more than one each. Never two."

Nash chuckled. "Then Mark and I would distract her while you snuck in and snitched one for us to share."

"We were quite the team." The memory was bittersweet. "So," I said, needing to change the subject before I ended up in tears. "What does Dad use the cottage for these days? Storage?"

An odd expression crossed his face before his brows rose. "You really don't know?"

I shook my head.

"I live here. Well, Jake and I live here."

I blinked. "Oh. I thought . . . um, I assumed . . ." It was best to simply shut my mouth.

He jammed his hand into his jeans pocket. "Mom moved away after I left. She lives in Chicago now." He looked out to the pastures. "My dad still lives in the same house, but I haven't seen him since I got back."

It seemed Nash and I had more in common than I'd realized. He probably didn't like talking about his relationship with his father any more than I did.

"I'm thinking about taking Moonlight Sky for a ride," I said. "Is she out to pasture?"

"You might want to check with your dad before you ride her."

My spine grew rigid. "If I recall correctly, Moonlight is *my* horse. Just because I've been away for a while doesn't mean I need his permission to ride her."

Annoyance sparked in his eyes. "No one said she isn't your horse, Mattie, but Moonlight Sky is due to foal in the spring. We've been exercising her, but since this is her first foal, Kurt thought it best if she wasn't ridden."

My mouth dropped. "He bred her? Without asking me?"

Nash stared as though I'd gone nuts. "Are you serious? You disappeared after Mark's funeral. Your parents didn't know if they'd ever see you again. You have a lot of nerve getting upset because your dad bred a horse on *his* horse farm."

"And you have a lot of nerve judging me, Nash McCallum," I said through gritted teeth.

"Someone needs to."

We glared at one another until I whirled and stormed away.

FOUR

AVA

DELANEY HORSE FARM

JANUARY 1942

The old farmhouse creaked and moaned in the biting wind, making me wish I'd lingered in bed a little longer. Gertrude said the almanac foretold a hard winter, and I believed it. We'd already suffered two rounds of ice and snow, making life miserable for us and the two dozen horses we cared for. Dark clouds rolling in from the north meant more winter weather was on its way.

I closed my eyes and let the warmth of the coffee mug in my hands seep into the rest of my body. Yet as good as it felt, it couldn't penetrate the frozen despair that had taken up permanent residence deep inside me the day Pearl Harbor was attacked by Japan. Icy fingers of panic clawed at my heart every moment since, with President Roosevelt's words after the attack—a radio address the newspapers called his *infamy speech*—making it worse.

I inhaled a deep breath, fighting tears that seemed to hover just below the surface these days. Despite the terrible national heartbreak, most Americans carried on with life, albeit with sadness and anger, as well as a healthy dose of patriotism. I too would have come through the tragedy intact had it not been for the arrival of a telegram three days later. That lone piece of paper ushered in the chilling truth of the devastation Japan's attack had inflicted upon me personally. The raw terror caused by a handful of typed words destroyed my world just as surely as Japanese bombs destroyed the naval fleet, safe in the harbor . . . or so they'd thought.

Mrs. Ava Delaney,

On behalf of the Department of the Navy, it is my sad duty to confirm that your husband SN Richard Delaney was killed at Pearl Harbor, Hawaii, 7 December 1941. He was aboard the USS West Virginia when it was attacked and sunk by Japanese torpedoes.

My eyes sprang open.

I couldn't spend another day dwelling on all I'd lost. To do so only brought on depression, hopelessness . . . and guilt. Guilt for not loving Richard enough. Guilt for worrying more about my own future now that he was gone rather than cherishing the memories of our brief time together. While some might not blame me, considering I'd only known Richard a total of three weeks before becoming his wife last May, other people—my mother-in-law—saw my paralyzing fear as nothing short of betrayal.

"My son deserves to be mourned by his wife," Gertrude declared just yesterday, her disapproving glare fastened on me as I pulled a batch of peanut butter cookies from the oven. "But here is his widow, baking as though she hadn't a care in the world."

I'd set the tray on the stovetop, stung by the hot pan as well as her sharp words. "I do mourn him. Every moment of every day I wish he were alive."

Which was the truth. I grieved for the life we would never have together, yet I had only been Richard's wife for four blissful days before he left for Hawaii. I hadn't seen him in seven months. His letters were sweet and full of romance, but I'd often felt they came from a stranger. How was I supposed to navigate the loss of someone I hadn't truly known?

But I couldn't tell any of that to his mother.

Gertrude was inconsolable when the telegram arrived. We should have grieved together, but she shut herself in her room. The following day a Navy officer from the recruitment office in Nashville arrived at the farm. She received him, barely acknowledging me as Richard's wife. Although I couldn't blame her, I'm certain the officer wondered why I had little to say in the matter of my husband's death. He'd explained that Richard's body, like that of so many sailors who'd died in the harbor, would not be coming home, breaking Gertrude's heart anew. When the man tried to hand a folded US flag to me, Gertrude stepped forward and accepted it. I realized then we would each bear the burden of grief alone and in our own way. Me with my fear, and Gertrude with her bitterness.

The cookie incident was just one of the many times she'd tried to shame me. I usually ignored her, but yesterday I'd had enough.

"Daniel is leaving tomorrow to join the Army," I'd said, more as a reprimand than a reminder. "Peanut butter cookies are his favorite."

I knew Gertrude had a soft spot for the teenage boy who came to help with the horses. She'd wept when he announced he planned to quit school and go to war now that he was eighteen. After my comment, she huffed and walked out of the kitchen, but the barb she'd launched with her words hit its mark.

I'd only been a real wife a handful of days, yet I would be punished for the rest of my life for not being a good one.

I set the coffee mug down and heaved a heavy sigh.

Something had to change. I couldn't live week after week, suffering Gertrude's disapproval and longing for a happy life that would never be mine. As Richard's widow, I would receive his death benefits, which would be enough for a fresh start somewhere else. But I also knew Gertrude desperately needed financial help to keep the farm running. Richard had joined the Navy to see the world, but he'd also needed a steady income. Every month he sent money home to help keep things afloat. Once his time in the Navy was up, however, he'd hoped to sell the farm—an idea he hadn't broached with Gertrude.

"When she understands I don't want the farm," he'd said. "I'm sure she'll agree to sell."

Yet after living with her for seven months, I wasn't so sure. Gertrude talked of expanding the property once Richard returned home. Of purchasing more horses and breathing life back into things. She dreamed of making the farm what it was before the dark days of the Depression sunk them into debt. The one time I dared to suggest Richard didn't want the farm, she flew into a rage. I never mentioned it again.

Oh, Richard. What are we supposed to do without you?

As difficult as I found Gertrude, I knew she was grieving the loss of her only child. Richard was full of fun and excitement. He'd swept me off my feet quite literally the night we met at a dance at the USO in Nashville. By the end of our third date, he'd declared he loved me and wanted me to become his wife before he shipped out.

"I'll be stationed in Hawaii for a year," he'd said, his green eyes dancing in the brilliant spring sunshine as we held hands and walked around the Parthenon in Centennial Park. "Just think of it, Ava. You can come to the islands as soon as I get our housing approved. We'll go to the beach every day and drink out of coconuts every night." Then he'd grabbed me in a tight embrace, twirled me around, and begged me to marry him.

My eyes filled as the bittersweet memory faded.

I'd been a fool to go along with his plan. I may have been infatuated with the handsome sailor, but I knew I wasn't in love with him. Yet I had no family to speak of and a dead-end job. Richard offered love, stability, and excitement, and I'd embraced it with both arms. Neither of us anticipated the many delays in obtaining housing on base and the need for me to stay in Tullahoma far longer than planned. The last letter I received from him said he hoped to have things worked out by Christmas, promising we'd spend the holiday together. He'd signed it *Mele Kalikimaka, from your adoring husband.*

I stood and moved to look out the window over the sink.

The view never disappointed.

Winter pastures surrounded by white fencing. Tree-covered hills in the distance. Horses grazing on what little they could find. A barn for hay and equipment, and a stable with twenty horse stalls. According to Gertrude, the farm thrived in the old days when people used horses for travel and farmwork. They'd even supplied animals to the Tennessee State Guard horse-mounted cavalry divisions stationed at Camp Peay in the twenties. Sadly, Mr. Delaney died when Richard was a teenager, and he'd taken on the responsibilities that came with running the farm. But raising Tennessee walking horses wasn't Richard's dream.

"I want to see the world," he'd told me on our wedding night, holding me in his arms as we watched the sun set over Nashville from our fifth-floor window in the Maxwell House Hotel. "Being stuck in a small town like Tullahoma was okay when I was a kid, but I'm a married man now. I don't want my wife mucking out horse stalls all her life." He caressed my cheek with his thumb, his gaze intense. "As soon as I'm finished with the Navy, you and me will head to New York City or Los Angeles. Someplace exciting."

It had all sounded so wonderful.

Until it turned into a nightmare.

Floorboards above me squeaked, drawing me out of the past.

Gertrude was awake. She'd be downstairs soon, spouting off a list a mile long of chores that needed tending.

I went to the small refrigerator and took out enough bacon for myself. Gertrude insisted on making her own breakfast despite the many times I'd offered to do so since moving in with her. The fact that she'd never volunteered to make breakfast for me seemed rude at first, but I figured her chilliness would subside as we got to know one another. According to Richard, she was an excellent cook, and he suggested cooking lessons as a marvelous way for us ladies to bond. Unfortunately Gertrude wasn't interested in bonding with me over cooking or anything else. The morning I surprised her with a ready meal, she unapologetically declared it inedible.

"Overcooked eggs and undercooked sausage," she'd muttered as she shoved it away.

I'd just cracked two eggs into a skillet of sizzling bacon when she appeared in the kitchen doorway, bundled in a thick sweater over a faded housedress. Wool socks and sturdy shoes completed the ensemble.

"Good morning." I offered a tight smile. "It's quite chilly today. Coffee's ready."

The eggs snapped and popped, splattering drops of hot grease on the stovetop. I hurried to flip them over, breaking the yokes in the process and causing more flying droplets to dot the stove.

"Your skillet's too hot." She scowled. "I'll have a greasy mess to clean now."

I turned off the flame. "I'll clean it."

She harrumphed and moved to pour a cup of coffee. "We've got plenty to do, what with a storm coming. We sure don't need extra work."

I scraped my breakfast from the pan onto a plate. The sight almost made me cry.

Overcooked eggs and undercooked bacon.

While I ate the paltry meal, Gertrude prepared fluffy scrambled eggs and perfectly crisp bacon for herself. Knowing cordial conversation would not take place, I opened the morning newspaper. Daniel was good about leaving it on the porch when he came to feed the horses. We were going to miss that young man.

Stories about the war dominated the front page, but I had no interest in reading them. I flipped to the local section and scanned articles about a missing cow and the high price of gasoline.

When I turned the page, my eyes fastened on five bold words in the top left corner.

Camp Forrest to Hire Civilians

I stopped chewing the bite of rubbery bacon I'd just taken.

Camp Forrest, located two miles from Tullahoma, needs civilian employees to fill vacancies in the post exchanges, laundry service, maintenance, and administrative offices. Those with experience will be given first preference but all are welcome to apply.

The article gave instructions on where applicants should go and what documentation to bring when they arrived on base. It also declared the salaries being offered were higher than those found at most local businesses.

I swallowed the meat and stared at the newspaper.

Richard hadn't wanted me to work while I waited to move to Hawaii, but I'd held all kinds of jobs since I was fourteen. The years after Mom and Dad divorced filled my memory. Dad disappeared from our lives and Mom remarried a man with three kids younger than me. When her new husband moved the family to Chicago, I begged to remain in St. Louis with her sister until I finished school. Aunt Vy wasn't thrilled but let me stay as long as

I paid my own way. I washed dishes at cafés, scrubbed toilets at hotels, and sold tools at the hardware store. As soon as I graduated high school, I moved to Nashville and found work as a secretary.

I drummed the table with my fingers, my mind alert.

Maybe I could get a job on the military base. Not only would it provide extra income we desperately needed, but it would offer an escape from Gertrude and the farm each day—something my sanity desperately needed. But did I want to work at a large military installation? Most of the soldiers I saw in town were far too rowdy and flirtatious for my liking. Would that be an everyday annoyance I'd have to deal with?

Yet the promise of a good salary chipped at the icy fear encasing my heart.

If I saved enough money, I could give my widow's benefits to Gertrude and leave Tullahoma. I wasn't sure where I'd go, but I knew it would be as far away from Tennessee as I could get. Richard hadn't wanted me to slave away on this farm when he was alive. Now with him gone, there was nothing keeping me here.

I glanced at the clock on the wall. The article said they were taking applications from 9 a.m. to 3 p.m. today. If I hurried, I could be one of the first to—

"What's got you worked up?"

I found Gertrude eyeing me from across the table. How would she feel about my idea? With Daniel joining the Army, the full care of the horses and farm would fall on her until we could find someone to help. Although she was still able to work around the property, the job was more than one woman her age could handle.

I decided honesty was best. "There's an article that says Camp Forrest is hiring civilians. I'm thinking about applying for a job."

I hadn't known what reaction to expect, but the look of sheer panic that filled her sun-wrinkled face was not it. "You're going to leave me here all alone?"

The frantic words shocked me. In all the months I'd spent

with her, she'd never once given the impression she needed me. Or wanted me here, for that matter. She missed her husband and her son, but she'd made it clear I was a sorry substitute. This unexpected vulnerability, however, gave me pause and made me wonder if all her bluster and bravado was a facade, hiding a woman beneath who was just as frightened of the future as I was.

Had I completely misjudged her?

"I would only be gone during the day," I said, hoping to alleviate her worry. "I wouldn't live on base. They're offering good salaries, and you know we need the money."

A moment passed before her expression returned to the scowl I was used to seeing. "An unmarried woman shouldn't work on a military base full of men. You know Richard wouldn't have approved, and neither do I."

I sighed. So much for misjudging her. "Lots of women work on military bases all over the country. While I'm in town, I'll stop at the high school and ask the principal if he can recommend a boy to take Daniel's place."

My firm words didn't sit well with her. We argued for the next ten minutes, but I wouldn't give in. I left her fuming while I changed clothes and applied a bit of makeup for the first time in months. Grabbing the keys to my old Ford sedan, I returned to the kitchen.

Gertrude glared at me from her place at the table, but her eyes were red-rimmed, as though she'd been crying. "I know what you're up to."

Guilt washed over me. Had she guessed my need to get away from her, even for a few hours each day? I was on the verge of making a full confession when she blurted out her accusation.

"You're looking for a new husband, but I won't tolerate it. Do you hear me? I won't allow you to bring men into this house, soiling my Richard's memory."

I stared at her. Had she lost her mind? "How can you even

think I'd be ready to date, let alone marry again? It's barely been a month since he died."

"You only knew my son a week before you tricked him into marrying you. All you'd have to do is bat those lashes at another man and—"

"Stop this." My body trembled with anger. "Richard proposed to me, and I accepted. I wanted to spend the rest of my life with him, but he's gone. We are barely making ends meet. We need more income. I'm going to apply for a job." I leveled a look at her meant to silence any more nonsense. *"A job."*

I left the house without another word.

The Ford didn't start on the first try. Or the second. I fiddled with the gas lever and the choke, then crossed my fingers and tried it again. Thankfully the engine roared to life, and I headed into town. I stopped at the high school and spoke with the principal, who said he knew a couple of boys who didn't live far from us who might be willing to help with farm chores. After leaving my telephone number with his secretary, I made my way to the military base outside the city limits. Even though I'd been married to a Navy man, the sight of armed guards sent a chill racing through me—a reminder that our country was indeed at war.

The young man in an Army-green uniform didn't smile when I rolled down my window.

"Ma'am. What business do you have at Camp Forrest?"

I swallowed. "I'm here to apply for a job. The newspaper said—"

"ID."

I handed it to him. When he returned the card to me, he pointed to one of several two-story, whitewashed buildings located just inside the gate. "The administrative office is on the right, with the flagpole. You can fill out an application there. You do not have permission to go beyond that point."

He took a step back and dismissed me with a motion to move forward. A look in the rearview mirror revealed a number of cars behind me, waiting to enter the base. I thanked him and did exactly as I'd been told. I parked in front of the nondescript structure and, upon entering, found myself in a large room. A dozen or more desks were occupied by women, and the sound of typewriters echoed off the bare wood walls. Two women sat in metal chairs to my left, busy filling out forms.

An older woman approached and offered a pleasant smile. "Good morning. May I help you?"

I nodded. "I saw the ad in the newspaper about civilians being hired at the camp. I'd like to apply for a job."

She smiled again. "I thought so. We've had quite a lot of applicants since the newspaper ad ran."

At my look of concern, she touched my arm. "Don't worry. There are plenty of jobs. Laundry. Cooking. Clerical. What type of work are you looking for?"

While I would take just about any position offered, I thought about what I'd prefer to do if given a choice.

"I was a secretary in Nashville, before . . ." I paused. If this place was to be an escape for me, I'd rather no one knew about Richard. Not yet anyway. "Before I came to Tullahoma."

"We can always use more girls in the secretarial pool." She handed me a clipboard with a sheet of paper attached to it and a pencil. "Fill this out. Someone will contact you in a day or two."

I took a seat and read the bold heading on the official-looking document.

Application for Employment, Camp Forrest,
Tullahoma, Tennessee

As I wrote down my personal information, the tiniest spark of hope ignited somewhere deep inside me.

Hope for today.

Hope for tomorrow.

Despite the devastation in my life and in the world around me, I didn't want darkness and despair to win. Hope didn't make any promises, but it offered a glimpse of happiness, the kind I hadn't known in a very long time.

I could be content with that.

FIVE

MATTIE

DELANEY HORSE FARM

NOVEMBER 1969

Moonlight Sky nickered and nudged my hand from the opposite side of the fence, making me smile, no matter my surly mood. "I know, I know. I've missed you too."

After my argument with Nash, I'd found my horse in the small pasture, closest to the stables. Thankfully she looked good. Healthy. Her chestnut coat shone in the sunshine, and her eyes were bright and clear. If I didn't know she'd been bred, I wouldn't suspect she was pregnant. With this being her first foal, she wouldn't show as early as an older, more experienced mare.

I continued to rub her neck, thinking back to the spring when she was born. A blue-roan colt had arrived the week before, and Mark claimed it as his own, naming it True Blue. Mama woke me when it was time for the next foal to arrive, and I ran to the barn. The moon shone in the inky sky, and a silvery beam, almost heaven-sent, came through the window and touched the white blaze on the newborn filly's nose. I was smitten.

Footsteps drew my attention.

I turned as Dad approached. Moonlight bobbed her head and walked to him. His lips lifted just a hair as he rubbed her neck.

"She's always looking for something sweet."

I didn't respond. Even though I could see for myself Moonlight looked healthy, my irritation with his decision to breed her hadn't diminished.

We stood in silence, watching Moonlight wander off to nibble at a patch of grass.

"I had a good offer from Brooks Farm to breed her with their stallion, Sir Admiral," he finally said. "They lowered the stud fee and want to buy the foal if it's a colt."

I glanced over to find Dad's attention still on the horse. His words were measured in the careful way he always spoke. Never full of emotion and passion, like me, or with humor and ease, like Mark.

He leaned his forearms on the top fence rail and squinted in the sunlight, causing even more wrinkles to appear on his weathered face. "We always planned to breed her. She comes from good stock. Her offspring will fetch top dollar." After another stretch of silence, he said, "You can take her out. Just go slow and easy." Then he turned and walked away.

A long breath pushed past my lips.

I knew I was acting immature. I'd wanted to be taken seriously since I was a kid, but how could I expect anyone, especially my father, to treat me like an adult when I acted like a petulant child?

I decided to hold off on the ride and climbed up and sat on the fence. Moonlight glanced at me, but when I didn't call her over, she continued to graze.

My eyes traveled her sleek, strong body.

I had to admit it made sense that she would be bred now that she was old enough. Her sire, Glory's Blaze, had an impressive pedigree, as did her dam, Midnight Pride. If I were honest, my annoyance at finding she'd been bred came more from the fact that I'd wanted to choose the sire myself. Before Mark died, I'd started to research stallions, some as far away as Colorado. With Moonlight's chestnut coat and lineage, I'd hoped to find a sire that would produce an offspring with buckskin coloring.

A pang of guilt ran through me.

Was it Dad's fault that I'd disappeared for a year? I'd still be in California if I hadn't been summoned home. The business of raising and selling horses had to continue, whether I was present or not.

I glanced at the green-roofed stables behind me.

Dad mentioned the sire, Sir Admiral, came from Brooks Farm, a well-run Tennessee walking horse operation north of Shelbyville. I couldn't remember if that particular horse was on my list of possible sires, but now my curiosity was piqued. What was his coloration? Did his pedigree include names of horses I would recognize?

There were two ways to get the information I sought. Ask Dad, or look in the records stored in the office, located at the back of the stables. Since the latter seemed the path less likely to create conflict, I hopped down off the fence and hurried in that direction.

The stable door sang out as I entered, but a quick glance down the long aisle of horse stalls told me I was alone. I crept to the office. Even though I'd been here too many times to count through the years, I had a feeling of trespassing where I didn't belong.

In the office, I pulled open the top drawer on a four-drawer filing cabinet wedged between the desk and the wall. Various ledgers were stored here. Sales and purchases. Supplies. Employee information. But there was only one I needed now. A familiar thick black binder. Using both hands, I took out the book that held the names and information of every horse associated with Delaney Farm since before Dad married Mama. Stallions. Mares. Foals. Sires and dams. I used to love reading through the names, picturing the horses in my mind. As a girl, I dreamed of working alongside Dad in the family business. I had big plans for the farm in those days.

But then everything changed.

He and I couldn't get along, while he and Mark grew closer. They'd talk about football and things I had no interest in, and Mark started spending more and more time with Dad instead of with me. I resented it. Resented my own father for taking my brother away from me. I once tried to explain this to Clay. He was older and known in our hippie community for having wisdom, and I respected his opinion. But when I claimed my dad was the reason Mark was dead, Clay wouldn't have it.

"It sounds like you were jealous of their relationship," he'd said, while smoke from a joint swirled around his head. "Your brother needed his dad to help him become a man, but you wanted to keep him all to yourself."

The recollection didn't improve my current mood.

I flipped open the ledger. Handwritten notations filled the pages. Although individual files were kept on each horse, the ledger told the history of Delaney Farm. I would have enjoyed reading through the many names and reminiscing, but I wasn't sure when Dad might come back. I didn't want to be caught prowling through things that may not be my business anymore.

I'd just landed on the page with the information on Sir Admiral when I heard a door shut and a low whistle come from somewhere in the building. Should I remain where I was and risk getting caught? The whistling grew louder. I recognized the tune—"Sweet Caroline" by Neil Diamond. Since Dad wasn't into popular music, I doubt he'd know it.

Sure enough, Nash appeared in the doorway.

The whistling stopped.

His brow rose. "Sorry. I didn't know you were in here."

I'm sure I had guilt written across my face. I gave a shrug. "I wanted to find out more about Sir Admiral."

He nodded toward the desk. "Find what you're looking for?"

"Yes." I glanced back to the ledger. "This says he's a bay sabino Appaloosa. That's surprising. His coloring isn't what I expected Dad would want in a sire."

"He's a beautiful animal."

I looked up. "You saw him?"

"Kurt and I trailered Moonlight up to Shelbyville. We weren't there long. Sir Admiral knew exactly what to do."

Even though I'd grown up on a farm, I felt my face grow warm. I returned my attention to the ledger. "His sire was Big John Blue. I've heard that name before."

"He has an impressive pedigree. Having a foal from his bloodline would be good for Delaney Farm. We'd be able to use that in marketing."

It was my turn to be surprised. "I don't remember you ever having an interest in horses. Cars and football were all you thought about in high school."

Nash pointed to a stack of books on the floor next to the desk. "I've been reading up on horse breeding, farm management, bookkeeping. Your dad took a risk hiring me. I want to prove to him that he didn't make a mistake."

I couldn't help but be impressed. "Is the farm doing well? Everything looks good."

Concern crossed his face. "Some of the owners who raise performance horses got wind that your dad was on board with legislation to ban the practice of soring. Granted, not everyone who enters their horses in competitions uses chemicals or chains and stacked shoes to make the horse lift its feet higher, but your dad and others feel it needs to be stopped. There's been some trouble because of Kurt's stance. False accusations. Rumors of abuse here at Delaney Farm. It's hurt business."

My blood boiled. "I'll never forget the first time I saw a horse that had been sored. The poor thing was in horrific pain. He couldn't even stand up. It's a vile practice, and I agree with Dad. There needs to be legislation against it."

His mouth quirked. "I think the American Horse Protection Association is looking for volunteers to go to Washington. You'd be perfect for the job."

His teasing didn't offend me. "Maybe I will." I returned the ledger to the drawer and stood. "So," I said as we moved from the office into the interior of the stables. "What's the routine around here? Is it just you and Dad, or do you have other help?"

I'd seen at least twenty horses in the pastures, with others in paddocks. Between feeding, grooming, exercising, and a plethora of other daily duties, caring for the animals and farm was a big job. Then there were hayfields that needed to be cut, fence and equipment to maintain. Farming isn't for the faint of heart, that's for sure.

"Before I was hired, Kurt did everything himself. Your mom told me he was exhausted, but he wouldn't hire anyone until I came along. It's still a lot of work for just the two of us, but we manage."

We exited the stables into midmorning sunshine. I glanced up to the house. "I better check on Mama. If she's awake, she might be hungry."

We parted, with neither of us bringing up the unpleasantness from earlier. I made my way to the house. Dad was in the kitchen washing out a small bowl.

He glanced at me when I came through the back door. "Your mama would like you to help her get a bath, if you feel up to it."

A tremor of apprehension rolled through me. "Is that okay? I won't hurt her?"

"She enjoys soaking in the warm water. Just be gentle when you help lift her."

I hurried upstairs. Mama sat in a chair by the bedroom window. Her eyes were closed as warm sunshine spilled over her swollen face.

"Mama?"

She smiled when she saw me. "My Mattie. It's so good to have you home."

I took her outstretched hand. "Dad said you'd like to take a bath."

"Your father is good to help me sponge off, but sometimes a good old-fashioned soak in the tub works wonders on my spirit."

I helped her get to her feet. She leaned heavily on me as we made our way to the bathroom in the hallway. The slow steps. The weakness I felt in her body. It all seemed surreal.

"I remember helping Granny when she got to the point she couldn't bathe herself," Mama said, out of breath after the short walk. I closed the lid on the commode so she could sit down. "Granny had always been so independent. It was hard for her to accept help. Especially from me."

Working together, we got her undressed and into a tub of warm, sudsy water. I wadded up a towel and placed it behind her head as a cushion.

"Tell me about California," she said, her eyes partially closed. "Is it as pretty as everyone says?"

Regret choked me as my throat convulsed.

I should have never left. I shouldn't know what California looks like because I should have never been there. Mama'd needed me here. If I'd been home, I would have seen her growing weaker and insisted she see the doctor. Had my selfishness put Mama in jeopardy?

"Mattie?"

I found her gentle gaze on me. Tears spilled down my cheeks.

"If I hadn't gone away . . . if I'd been here, you wouldn't be . . ." Silent sobs overtook me.

Her wet hand found mine. "Listen to me, Martha Ann. No doctor or medicine or procedure could add a single day to my life. God's Word says all our days are recorded in his book before we're born."

I sniffled. "But—"

"No buts, sweetheart." She sank a little deeper into the water and closed her eyes. "Now, tell me about California. What do the beaches look like?"

For the next thirty minutes, I talked about palm trees, the sound of the ocean, and anything else that came to mind. But all the while, guilt settled on me like a farrier's anvil. I'd felt justified in my leaving, with anger at my father the driving force. I'd claimed grief over my brother's death kept me from returning home. He was my twin, after all. We were connected in a way other siblings weren't. How could I go home knowing he'd never be there again?

But being here with Mama now, looking into her eyes and knowing my absence had hurt her, I recognized my actions for what they were: selfishness, pure and simple.

How could I have done that to her?

When the water grew cool, I helped her don a clean nightgown and assisted her back to bed. She panted as though she'd run a marathon.

"I'm as weak as a newborn kitten these days," she said with a slight chuckle. "Who would believe I used to lift hay bales and drive a tractor?"

"You rest, Mama." I fluffed her pillows and tucked her in. "Are you hungry? I can bring up some lunch."

She shook her head, her face pinched. "Your father brought me some soup earlier. Tell him I need my medicine, will you please, dear?"

Before I could answer, Dad spoke from the doorway. "I'm here, Ava."

I stepped back as he moved in close to the bed. With his work-rough hand, he smoothed Mama's puffy cheek. She smiled up to him with such adoration shining in her eyes, I had to look away from the private moment.

"With Mattie's help, I've had a nice bath. Now I'm ready for a nap."

Dad took a pill from a bottle and helped her take it with water. Mama shut her eyes and didn't say more.

"What is that? The medicine, I mean," I asked quietly.

"Morphine." He didn't look at me. "It's a low dose for now. The doctor will prescribe something stronger if . . . if she needs it."

"Is she in a lot of pain?"

He didn't answer right away, his focus never leaving Mama's face. "It comes and goes, but the doctor said it will get worse. She didn't want to take anything for it at first, but . . ." He didn't finish. "Nash made sandwiches. You go eat. I'll stay with her a while."

I left the room, my emotions confused and raw. I'd never witnessed my father like this. Tender. Helpless. He wasn't a man of many words, but I'd never thought of him as weak, either in body or mind. He worked hard from dawn to dusk, maintaining the farm by himself for the most part. Mark had helped, especially during haying season, and we'd both had chores in the barns and stables. I didn't mind helping when I was younger, but after I started high school, time with my friends and special boys was far more important.

That's when Dad and I began to clash.

The kitchen was empty when I arrived, but a plate of chicken salad sandwiches sat on the counter. I took a bite while I stood, and it immediately carried me back to warm summer days, eating lunch here in the kitchen with Mama and Mark. Mama had a secret ingredient that made her chicken salad stand out among all those brought to church potluck dinners: dried apricots from our own trees. Where most of the other ladies used apples or even grapes, the bits of apricot Mama added gave it a unique sweetness the other dishes lacked. I was surprised to taste them now, knowing she wasn't the cook responsible for it.

I poured myself a glass of cold milk, something I hadn't enjoyed since I left home, and settled at the table. Dad joined me a short time later.

"She's resting. Thank you for helping with her bath."

I nodded.

"Doc Monahan or one of his nurses comes out to check her once a week."

Frustration rose in me. "I don't understand why he didn't keep her in the hospital and treat the disease. They're making all sorts of advancements in the medical world these days. Did you get a second opinion? Surely there was something they could've done. I can't believe they would just send her home to die without a fight."

Accusation laced my words. I prepared myself for his angry rebuttal, but he just sat there, looking defeated.

"Doc said we could stay in Nashville and try radiation and chemotherapy, but he warned it would be hard on her. She'd be very sick, and it probably wouldn't change the prognosis." His shoulders lifted in a shrug. "She wanted to come home, so I brought her home."

"And that's it? You simply agreed?" I snapped. "You're just going to sit by and watch her die? Well, I won't. My brother was killed because you wouldn't talk sense into him and keep him from going to Vietnam. Now you won't do everything you can to convince Mama to go to the hospital in Nashville. I can't understand you at all."

He didn't respond.

I wanted to battle things out, make him see I was right, but he remained silent. He stood and moved to the door.

"I'll be in the barn if your mother needs me."

I watched him leave the house, fuming that he would simply give up. The unfairness of the situation made me want to scream. Mama refused to seek treatment. Dad wouldn't make her do it. Mark wouldn't listen to me and went off to war.

Stubbornness, it seemed, ran through our family like a raging river.

SIX

GUNTHER

ENEMY ALIEN DETENTION FACILITY, ELLIS ISLAND, NEW YORK
JANUARY 1942

Gunther had waited four weeks for this day to arrive.

From the moment he was detained, he knew a terrible mistake had been made. But like the hundreds of other men on Ellis Island, he was forced to wait his turn to appear at a formal hearing, certain everything would be made right if he could simply tell his story.

That day was finally here.

At early morning roll call he was ordered to pack his belongings and report to the building where the hearings were held. With tangible relief, he'd hurried to comply.

Now he stood in a long line of detainees, waiting outside a three-story redbrick-and-limestone building. Despite bright sunshine in the clear sky, a bitter January wind came off the dark water of the harbor, sending salty spray into the air as waves splashed over the seawall of the ferry slip. Men hunched into their coats, not saying much to the person nearest them. Like Gunther, they no doubt silently rehearsed the vital information each hoped to convey to the people who would ultimately decide their future.

A ship's horn sounded somewhere in the bay, making Gunther wonder if the detention camp was its destination.

Agent Malone was right. The United States declared war on Germany two days after Gunther's arrest, and detainees had arrived at Ellis Island every day since. Men like him, born in Germany, as well as those from Italy, were rounded up and slapped with the label *enemy alien*. Men who'd come to America with the hope of making a life here. Of starting over for some. He wasn't foolish enough to believe every immigrant came with honorable intentions, but he'd met enough to know the majority simply wanted to live in peace.

Daily he'd watched men called away to attend hearings. None ever came back, leading to speculation as to their fates. Were they released? Shipped back to Germany? Or, according to the latest rumor to sweep the island, they were sent to concentration camps, like those in Germany, in retaliation for what the Nazis were doing to Jews. Although Gunther had not become overly friendly with anyone, preferring to keep to himself, Reinhard, the man who slept on the bunk below Gunther, often shared the day's gossip.

"Those men over there," he'd whispered just last night, motioning to a group of five at the far end of the large room that served as a dormitory. "They are Nazi sympathizers. I heard one say 'heil, Hitler' and the others raised their hands. Fools, every one of them. We're doomed if the Americans think we're all that stupid."

Although there was uncertainty about what would happen today, Gunther prayed things would go well. He had done nothing wrong and had followed the rules since coming to America. No one could say otherwise. Once the men at the hearing understood this, they would see their error and release him. He might even be back in his tiny flat in Queens by nightfall. With a chuckle, he vowed never to complain about his humble home again.

The ship's horn sounded again, but it was farther away now, its cargo not bound for the island.

Sometime after he'd been arrested, Gunther learned that Japanese detainees were also housed there, although they were held in a different building, supposedly for their own safety. Rumor had it most of them were Japanese Americans, born in the United States, causing some of the men in Gunther's group to lose all hope of being released.

"If the government is willing to arrest their own citizens, why would they let us go free?" Reinhard bemoaned. He'd come to America with his family after the Great War, but out of respect to his grandfather, he had never applied for citizenship. Now it seemed not even legal residency would have saved him from being detained.

The line moved at a snail's pace but sometime before noon Gunther was escorted into a sterile room where three men sat behind a long table, cluttered with stacks of files. He was told to sit in the lone straight-backed chair facing them. When asked if he would like an interpreter, he declined.

The man in the center perused a sheet of paper while the other two men looked everywhere but at Gunther. Unease settled on him, but he forced himself to keep his eyes forward. Finally the man laid the paper aside and met Gunther's nervous gaze.

"State your name and where you were born, please."

Gunther swallowed. "Gunther Schneider. I was born in Krefeld, Germany."

A woman tucked in a corner of the room sat at a small table with a typewriter, ostensibly to keep record of what was said. The machine tap-tap-tapped then grew silent as she waited.

"You should know," the man said, followed by more tap-tap-tapping, "this hearing is being conducted not as a matter of any rights you believe you are entitled to, but merely in order to permit you to present information on your own behalf."

Gunther nodded. "I understand."

Once again, he was asked his reason for coming to America, his date of arrival, and his occupation. He answered each question with honesty, but when it came to providing information about his family, Gunther broke out in a sweat.

"Tell us about your brother, Rolf."

Because Gunther knew next to nothing about his brother's exploits over the past four and a half years, he stuck to the facts of their childhood together, explaining the differences between himself and Rolf. They'd never been close, and he needed these men to understand that. "Rolf did not approve of my coming to America."

"Why is that?"

"He thought I should join the army as any proud German would do."

"Are you not a proud German?"

The question was one Gunther had considered many times over the years he'd been in America. With Germany's invasion of Poland, France, and other vulnerable countries, as well as the horrific stories coming out of Europe of what the Nazis were doing to Jews, pride was no longer something Gunther felt for his homeland.

"Germany is a beautiful place, filled with many good people, but I do not condone what the Nazis and Hitler are doing. That is not the Germany I knew."

The man took a folded paper from a file. Gunther recognized it as one of the letters his mother sent him.

"We've translated the letters supposedly written by your mother," he said, his tone casting doubt on the true authorship, "and there is evidence some of the information is written in code."

Gunther's jaw dropped. "That is preposterous. My mother is a simple woman, a teacher and homemaker until my father died.

She went to work at a bakery in Krefeld that was owned by a Jewish family, but when the Nazis forbid Jews to own businesses, she refused to work for the man who took it over. She is a good, Christian woman and does not support the views of the current leadership."

"Maybe she didn't write the letters," said the man on the left, his New Jersey roots as evident in each word as Gunther's German roots were in his own. "Maybe they came from your brother. And maybe you've been writing back to him, giving him all sorts of information about America." His gaze narrowed on Gunther. "Information about New York harbor."

The last sentence, clearly spoken with intent, puzzled Gunther. He couldn't fathom its meaning. What did New York harbor have to do with anything?

A flash of memory from the day he was arrested brought him up straight. He recalled Agent Malone asking why he'd taken an apartment so close to the river.

Did they suspect he was a spy?

The thought sent a cold chill coursing through Gunther.

"I assure you the letters are from my mother and contain nothing but news from home. I have had no communication with my brother since leaving Germany." He thought of *Mutter*'s last correspondence and her worry over Rolf. "My mother fears for him and what he might be involved in, although I do not believe she knows any particulars of what he is doing in Berlin."

The man on the end didn't appear convinced. "Do you know what a U-boat is, Mr. Schneider?"

The chill turned to ice.

German submarines were used in the Great War and were once again wreaking havoc in the deep waters of the Atlantic Ocean. Many merchant vessels and British warships had been sunk by U-boat torpedoes in the past two years.

"I do." There was no sense lying.

"So you understand our concern when a German citizen with known connections to the Nazi party lives so close to our waterways." He paused. "How often do you go down to Battery Park? Do you ever take a camera with you?"

Any shred of hope Gunther had maintained of being released today vanished as reality sank in. He wasn't simply a foreigner, caught up in a situation beyond his control. He was the brother of a Nazi and a suspected spy.

Before Gunther could answer, the man smirked. "I ask because we have a report from someone who seems to think you spend far more time at the park than a German citizen should. It's also been reported that you've taken numerous photographs of the harbor and Lady Liberty, as well as the shipping docks."

Gunther stared at the man, stunned. "Who would say such things? I do not even own a camera." His mind raced with panic. What did Americans do with suspected German spies? He most assuredly did not want to find out. "You can have no proof of such a false claim. The men who came to my apartment to arrest me would have found a camera if I owned one. Pictures as well."

The man in the center chuckled, as though Gunther had told a joke. "New York's a big city, Mr. Schneider. You could have it hidden anywhere."

The suggestion was ludicrous. Gunther shook his head, trying to make sense of what was happening. "I do not understand any of this. Why anyone would say these things. No one knows I sometimes go to—"

Mrs. Kozlowski's angry face suddenly surfaced in his mind.

The day Gunther was arrested, she'd stood in her doorway, spit on him, and said something he didn't understand at the time. The action was shocking, but he'd had more pressing things to worry about. He'd completely forgotten the incident. Until now. Her words came rushing back.

Brudny Nazista.

Although the meaning of the first word eluded him, the second was obvious.

The woman believed he was a Nazi.

Their brief encounters filtered through his mind. Although her broken English was difficult to understand, he always offered a friendly greeting when he passed her in the hallway. Had he mentioned his visits to Battery Park during one of their conversations? It was possible.

"It was Mrs. Kozlowski, wasn't it?" He glanced between the three men facing him. "She is the one who gave you these false reports."

"Why would she do that if it wasn't true?" asked Mr. New Jersey, confirming Gunther's suspicions.

Without warning, guilt—not his own but that of his countrymen—bore down on Gunther. He closed his eyes to the shame that came with his heritage.

"Because she is Polish, and I am German."

The simple statement held a repulsive truth. Great injustices had been suffered by the people of Poland at the hands of Germany. It didn't matter that the acts were carried out by those under the leadership of Hitler, or that German citizens like he and his mother abhorred what was happening. All people like Mrs. Kozlowski knew was that tens of thousands of Poles were killed, injured, or displaced when Germany and Russia invaded their country in 1939. The horror of the brutal murder of so many innocent people shocked the world. Gunther didn't know Mrs. Kozlowski's story—was she one of the many refugees who'd escaped, and did she still have family there?—but he was certain of one thing.

He couldn't blame her for what she'd done.

"Are you calling the old woman a liar?"

Gunther met the man's hard gaze. If he wanted to survive this, he was going to have to fight for his life just as surely as a soldier on a battlefield. "I'm saying she is incorrect. Since I arrived in America, all my time has gone to furthering my education in the medical field. If you contact my professor, Dr. Sonnenberg, he will confirm this. He will tell you of my hope to become an American citizen, like himself. We've spoken of it many times."

The men exchanged whispers before the man in the center dug through a stack of folders and pulled one out. Upon opening it, the other two men leaned in, and more whispers ensued. Finally the lead questioner met Gunther's anxious gaze.

"Dr. Heinrich Sonnenberg?"

"Yes," Gunther said, the tiniest ray of light entering his dark world. If anyone could help him, it would be his mentor. Despite his German beginnings, the older man had taught at Columbia's medical school since 1927 and was over the operating theater at the hospital. It was there Gunther had planned to do his internship next semester. "Dr. Sonnenberg has known me since I arrived in America."

The man's gaze narrowed on Gunther. "I find it interesting that you would willingly connect yourself to Dr. Sonnenberg."

His ominous tone gave Gunther pause. "He is a man of integrity. I am honored that he has taken an interest in helping me achieve my dream of becoming a doctor."

The man continued his study of Gunther. After a time, he leaned his elbows on the table, tenting his fingers. "I'm going to tell you a story, Mr. Schneider. One that, I believe, you are familiar with. However, the ending may surprise you."

Gunther's heart thudded. He didn't know what the man was up to but suffice it to say it didn't sound good.

"Dr. Heinrich Sonnenberg came to our beautiful country at the end of the Great War. He quickly achieved success as a doctor after he set up his practice in a neighborhood swarming with German aliens. His practice grew considerably over the years, and he hobnobbed with wealthy and important German men, including the ambassador to Germany when the man was in New York. Soon he was teaching at Columbia and working at the hospital."

Gunther licked his dry lips. "He has been blessed."

The man smirked. "*Blessed* isn't the word I'd choose. *Positioned* is more fitting." At Gunther's look of puzzlement, he continued. "Who would ever suspect a man in such a prominent position of espionage?"

The room tilted with the loaded word.

Gunther stared, open-mouthed, trying to comprehend the absurd insinuation. "That is even more preposterous than your belief that I am a spy. Dr. Sonnenberg loves America. There is no one more loyal to the idea of liberty and freedom than he. No, I will not believe such lies."

"Would you like to see some of the evidence we have against him?"

"Yes," Gunther boldly declared. "I know there isn't any, just as there is none against me."

The man on the end, who'd been quiet through the proceedings, approached Gunther, papers in hand.

"This is a list of known German spies living in the United States who frequented Dr. Sonnenberg's office."

Gunther took the list. He recognized a half dozen names of men he'd met at dinner parties at the doctor's home. His mind spun, searching for an explanation. "This does not prove anything. Dr. Sonnenberg saw many patients. Even if you are correct that these men are German spies, their association with Dr. Sonnenberg does not mean he is one of them."

"Then there's this."

The man handed a telegram to Gunther, written in German, dated December 8, 1941. Dr. Sonnenberg's name and home address were at the top.

Destroy all files. Abort assignment. No further contact. Stop.

It wasn't signed.

While the brief missive could suggest involvement in something illicit, Gunther refused to believe his advisor was a spy. "This could simply be about private medical records. Dr. Sonnenberg is a good man. He's Jewish. He would not be involved in anything that helped the Nazis."

"You don't find it strange that the good doctor received a telegram the day after Japan attacked the United States and is told to get rid of files?" asked the man in the center.

Gunther had to admit the timing was suspicious. "Who is it from?"

"We can't divulge that information." He glanced at his colleagues, who nodded to his silent question. When he faced Gunther again, he looked grim. "This hearing is over, Mr. Schneider. It is our belief that you should continue to be held as a potentially dangerous enemy alien. You will remain in the custody of the Department of Justice and be transferred to Camp Forrest in Tennessee."

He slapped the file closed, banged it with a rubber stamp, and handed it to the man on the end who added it to a tall stack of similar files.

Stunned by the verdict, Gunther was about to protest when the guard, who'd stood near the door throughout the proceedings, came forward. He held a set of handcuffs.

"Stand up and hold out your hands."

Gunther stared at him.

This couldn't be happening. What right did they have to further detain him? To send him to a different state? What would happen to his apartment and his belongings? His schoolbooks?

He shot a look at the men at the table but none returned his gaze and busied themselves with more files. More hearings where more men would be detained simply because they'd been born in Germany.

"You cannot do this!" His voice echoed in the stark room. No one, not even the woman at the typewriter, glanced his way. "I am innocent."

The guard yanked him up by the arm. "Quiet down, mister." He snapped the handcuffs in place and motioned to Gunther's small suitcase of belongings. "Get your things and follow me." He moved toward the door.

Desperation kept Gunther rooted to the floor. "I am not a spy," he said, speaking more calmly yet with the urgency of a drowning man. The agent in the center finally looked up, indifference on his face. "I came to America to be free from a dangerous government I could not trust. I came with dreams, like millions of immigrants before me—maybe your own ancestors—with the hope of one day calling this country my own. But now I see my trust in America was misplaced. What you are doing to me today, to the others, is shameful."

The man's expression hardened. "Mr. Schneider, your country started the war. Your countrymen are killing innocent people by the thousands, with no end in sight. I think you and I have a different definition of what *shameful* means."

He motioned for the guard, then went back to his files, dismissing Gunther with the action.

"Let's go," the guard said.

Gunther's shoulders sagged in defeat. The vision of freedom he'd felt certain of only an hour ago evaporated as he bent to retrieve his suitcase and followed the military man out a door. Cold air stung his face, and Gunther realized his cheeks were damp with tears.

A boat waited in the ferry slip. Gunther boarded and found it full of men like him—handcuffed, cold, with despair etched in the crevices of their faces. Crushing silence permeated the crowded space, speaking louder than words ever could.

When the boat lurched forward sometime later and moved

into the harbor, Gunther presented his back to Lady Liberty. Never again would he gaze upon her and dream of becoming one of her sons. On land, the men were transferred to paddy wagons that took them to the train station. Gunther was herded onto a southbound train headed for Tennessee, uncertain of what awaited him there. Was he going to a prison camp? Or were the fears of his fellow prisoners correct and a concentration camp awaited them?

The young man next to him, perhaps a year or two Gunther's junior, cried softly into his wool scarf, muttering over and over that he wanted to go home. It was no doubt the sentiment felt by each handcuffed man, forced onto a train that would take them far from loved ones, friends, jobs, dreams.

How long would internment last? Weeks? Months? Years?

As the train pulled from the depot, a devastating truth sucked the air from Gunther's lungs and nearly overwhelmed him.

He no longer had a home.

Not in Germany.

Not in America.

Not anywhere.

SEVEN

MATTIE

DELANEY HORSE FARM

MAY 1965

"Mark James Taylor, where are my hair rollers? I know you hid them."

I stood at the top of the stairs, my loud voice echoing throughout the house, something Mama didn't approve of. But my brother's joke wasn't funny. My shoulder-length hair wouldn't *flip* on the ends without rollers, and I couldn't get up in front of the whole town with un-flipped hair.

"You're going to make us late for graduation," I added, knowing he despised being late for anything. *Mr. Punctual,* I often called him. "You were born wearing a wristwatch," I'd tease, to which he'd reply, "I came out of the womb first and have been waiting on you ever since." I had to admit it was true. I usually left the house with wet hair and shoes in hand most school mornings.

I heard the door to his downstairs bedroom creak open. His

face appeared below me, the blue eyes he'd inherited from our father wide with feigned innocence. "Aw, now, Sis, what would I want with your hair rollers?" He ran a hand across his short-cropped straw-colored hair. "Coach Cooper would make me run fifty laps if he caught me wearing rollers."

A chuckle came from the room behind him.

Nash McCallum had spent the night on the trundle bed in Mark's room again. I never knew the particulars of why Mark's best friend often ended up on the small spare bed, but it usually had to do with the fact that Mr. McCallum was known around town for two things: being drunk and being a mean drunk. Nash's mom often had bruises on her arms when Mama and I saw her at the Piggly Wiggly. Although Nash sported a black eye at school from time to time when he was younger, that changed once he grew taller than his old man and could stand up for himself.

"This isn't funny, Mark." I stomped down the stairs in my bare feet, my bathrobe cinched tight, and stopped on the last step so I could glare at him eye to eye. He stood at least five inches taller than me. Football had added muscle to his body, and I sometimes felt as though he was my older brother instead of my twin. "If I have to go in there and look for them, you'll be sorry." I glanced into the room and found Nash sitting on the bed, fighting a grin. When our eyes met, he had the decency to look away.

"All right, Sis. Don't freak out." He pulled his arm from behind his back, revealing my bag of rollers.

I snatched them from him. "I don't want to hear any complaints if we're late because of this."

He laughed. "You've made us late nearly every day of our senior year. Why would today be any different?"

I narrowed my eyes. "Ha, ha," I said without humor. "It isn't my fault we live so far away from town. Principal Creed should allow us extra time to get to school."

Mama came from the kitchen. She'd dabbed on a bit of lipstick and looked pretty in a new yellow dress she'd ordered from the JCPenney catalog. Unlike me, she'd gone to Wilma's beauty shop in town yesterday and sported a fresh permanent in her fading brown hair.

"What is going on?" Her gaze ping-ponged between Mark and me. "You need to leave in ten minutes if you're going to make it to rehearsal on time."

"Mark took my hair rollers," I whined, holding up the evidence. "You know I can't go to town with my hair looking like this." To emphasize my point, I tugged the ends of a handful of wavy locks. On its best day, my hair curled nicely with little effort. Today, however, was not that day. Unseasonably warm spring weather brought humidity with it, turning my natural waves into a roaring ocean of chestnut frizz.

"Martha Ann, get upstairs and finish getting ready," Mama said without a hint of sympathy. "You should have been dressed an hour ago." She turned to Mark. "And you don't need to play tricks on your sister, especially on an important day like today."

Genuine contrition registered on his face. "I'm sorry, Sis."

"You're forgiven," I said, "but it's still your fault if we're late."

Mama's scowl told me she didn't agree, but she didn't press the issue. "The food is ready to set out as soon as we get home from the ceremony. I expect we'll have forty or so people." She looked past Mark into his bedroom where Nash continued to sit and listen to our family affairs. "Nash, I hope your folks are coming to our little reception. I sent them an invitation."

I glanced at Nash.

"Thank you, ma'am. I'll remind Ma." There was no mention of his father.

I felt sorry for Nash as I climbed the stairs. Dad and I hadn't been getting along lately, mainly because of his wrong ideas about our country's involvement in Vietnam, but I knew I never had to fear him. Mr. McCallum would likely arrive at the graduation ceremony sozzled on bourbon if he came at all. Mrs. McCallum would be there though. I liked her, even if I did think she should have left that no-good husband of hers ages ago. Nash's sister, Suzanne, was three years older than him, but she left town as soon as she graduated high school. When Mark mentioned she'd moved to Florida, I asked if Nash might live with her once school ended. He got a funny look on his face.

"Nash is enlisting in the Marines after graduation."

I'd stared at my brother, mouth agape. "The Marines? Is he nuts? President Johnson is sending more and more troops to Vietnam every day, despite the fact that the United States hasn't declared war. It's outrageous and immoral. How could Nash even think about joining the military now?"

"He doesn't want to stay in Tullahoma with his old man."

"So invading a foreign country and getting himself killed is a better option? What about college? Nash isn't a great student, but I know he's smarter than he lets on. He could do anything he wanted if he put his mind to it. You should talk him into joining us at Vanderbilt. I'm sure he could get in."

A troubled expression crossed Mark's face. "Not everything is as simple as you'd like it to be, Mattie." He'd walked away, leaving me to wonder what he meant.

Miracle of miracles, we made it to graduation rehearsal on time. Rusty Shaw, the star of our Wildcats basketball team, complimented my hairdo, making all the effort to tease and flip my curls into shape worth it. Rusty was headed to the University of California on a basketball scholarship in the fall, and although we'd only dated casually, I was going to miss him.

Graduation went as expected.

One hundred and twenty of us lined up in our black caps and gowns to receive hard-earned diplomas, accepting handshakes of congratulations from Principal Creed and a warm hug of encouragement from Mrs. King, our senior class sponsor. After a round of inspiring speeches and a song from the school choir, Pastor Arnold, who served as an assistant coach and chaplain for the football team, prayed over us, asking God to protect and lead as we ventured into the world. He prayed a special blessing of safety over the boys going to Vietnam and asked the audience members to remember them in their prayers in the coming days.

While Principal Creed closed the ceremony, I snuck a peek two rows ahead of me to where Nash sat. Apparently Mark hadn't been able to talk sense into his friend. Last I heard, Nash was still set on his foolish plan of going to war. Rumors that President Johnson was preparing for American troops to remain in Vietnam indefinitely, despite his campaign promises to do the exact opposite, gave evidence to anyone with a brain that the war overseas would not end anytime soon. An article in the newspaper reported that some young men at UC Berkeley burned their draft notices in front of the draft office building and refused to join the military. I applauded them and thought them very brave.

After the ceremony, I came home with Mama and Dad so Paula Allyn could ride with Mark. "I think she's the one, Sis," he'd said one evening as we sat on the porch swing, listening to night creatures sing their songs. Surprisingly, I felt no jealousy. Paula was a sweet girl, as unpretentious as they came. Even though it was strange to think of us all growing up and moving away from the farm, Paula would make a wonderful life-partner for my brother. Heaven knew he needed a good-natured wife after putting up with a strong-willed and contentious twin sister all these years.

I helped Mama lay out the food as soon as we got back to the farm. Pimento cheese sandwiches. Potato salad. There was even Jell-O in the shape of a graduation cap, made from a copper mold Mama'd been thrilled to find at Kuhn's five-and-ten store. A large, white-frosted cake she'd labored over for two days, with *Congratulations Mark & Mattie* written in blue frosting, sat in the center of the table, while a cut-glass bowl with pink punch and small, matching cups occupied the far end. Blue and white balloons hung from paper streamers here and there, and the radio in the corner was tuned to the old-fashioned Big Band music Dad enjoyed.

People began to arrive. Church friends who'd watched me and my brother grow up. Neighbors. Even clients of the farm who'd purchased horses from us over the years and gradually became like family. All brought gifts for my brother and me. An alarm clock from the Johns. Floral bedsheets for my dorm room from the Pickerings. A new Bible for each of us from Pastor Arnold. There were even envelopes with cash inside. I greeted each guest, genuinely appreciative of their thoughtfulness. Mark, too, accepted handshakes and good wishes.

I'd just thanked our elderly neighbor Mrs. Gaddis for the curtains she'd sewn for me when Rusty arrived in a 1965 fire-engine-red Ford Mustang, a graduation gift from his folks. Some of my friends were with him, turning the gathering into a real party. The brand-new awareness that the world was ours now that we weren't tethered to a brick-and-mortar school building offered a sense of freedom I'd never experienced.

We ate, laughed, danced, and ate some more, celebrating until the sun started its descent behind the hills. By the time stars began to appear in the sky, most of the guests were gone, with only Nash, his mother, and Pastor and Mrs. Arnold remaining.

I floated on cloud nine as I carried empty serving dishes to the kitchen while the adults chatted on the porch. Rusty and I had snuck off to the barn earlier, and he'd kissed me in a way that told me he was going to miss me too. But with him leaving for California in August, and me headed to Vanderbilt, neither of us wanted to commit to a long-distance relationship. We'd agreed to enjoy the summer together and leave it at that for now.

"I'd be happy to drive you boys to Nashville tomorrow."

Pastor Arnold's voice reached me as I made my way back into

the dining room. He must have been speaking to my brother, although I couldn't see either of them in the living room.

My ears perked up.

I'd hoped to go to the city and do some shopping now that school was over. Neither Goldstein's nor Strong's Ladies Apparel had anything worthy of my new status as an incoming freshman at a prestigious school like Vanderbilt. Mark hadn't mentioned taking a trip to Nashville, but if he and Nash were indeed going, I was determined to finagle a way to be included.

"That would be great, Coach. I think both of us would feel better if you were there. It's a big step."

I silently inched to the doorway, making sure to keep out of sight.

"It is, but it's also honorable. I'm proud of both of you."

I heard Nash mutter, "Thank you," before Mark said, "The recruitment office opens at nine. We figure it'll take a little over an hour to get to the city. We'll have all our paperwork ready."

Recruitment office? Recruitment for what? Mark and I were already enrolled at Vanderbilt, but maybe he'd finally convinced Nash to join us. Perhaps they were both planning to try out for the football team, even though Mark hadn't shown any enthusiasm about playing college ball lately.

The screen door slammed.

I heard Mama tell Mrs. McCallum about the upcoming church bazaar as they entered the house. Mama oversaw the fundraiser, and she was always looking for donations.

"Pastor Arnold volunteered to drive Nash and me to the city tomorrow," Mark said.

"I appreciate that, Pastor." This from Dad. "The vet is coming to look at one of the mares first thing in the morning. Otherwise, I'd take them myself."

Even though Dad never attended church services with us, he welcomed the preacher into our home whenever Mama suggested they invite him. I recalled the time I asked Mama why Dad didn't join us in town on Sunday mornings. Granny had recently passed on to her glory, and her funeral was the first and only time I'd ever seen my father inside the church building.

"Doesn't he believe in God?" I asked.

Mama'd caressed my cheek. "Of course he does, sweetheart. Your daddy loves Jesus. He just doesn't feel comfortable around people."

That simple explanation, I'd realized, described my father's entire existence. He had no friends and only went to town if something was needed for the horses. Even at home he was quiet, preferring to listen to our chatter rather than join in. Mama didn't seem to mind, so I'd never let it bother me. That is, not until recently.

Over the last months, he and Mark had grown closer. I'd often see them together while they worked on the tractor or walked the pastures. Many nights after dinner, when Mark and I normally sat on the porch swing and talked, he and Dad went off to the barn, leaving me alone and peeved. I should have been happy my brother was finally bonding with our father, but I felt left out. Neglected. Mark was *my* twin, after all.

Mrs. McCallum's voice drew me back to the present. "It's still hard to believe my son is going off to war."

I waited for someone—Dad, Pastor Arnold, Mark—to speak up and tell Nash he was a fool. That going to Vietnam was the last thing he should do. Not only was it dangerous, but it was also unconscionable. The United States shouldn't be involved in the politics of North and South Vietnam. We were sticking our nose into a civil war we knew nothing about. We certainly shouldn't be dropping bombs and putting our troops in harm's way. Even my US History teacher, Mr. Mott, grimly predicted the war in Vietnam could last for years if we continued traveling the path our country was currently on.

In the silence that followed Mrs. McCallum's statement, I suddenly understood the trip to the city was for Nash. Mark must've volunteered to go with his friend to the Marine recruitment office for moral support. With the serious nature of the trip, I decided not to ask to go along. Shopping seemed rather trivial when compared to one of our schoolmates joining the military.

"God will be with them," Pastor Arnold said. "He'll watch over both of these fine young men as they fulfill their duty. We'll all be praying they're kept safe."

I'd just reached for the bowl of what was left of the punch but paused at his words.

Who was he talking about? Mark had received a scholarship and would attend Vanderbilt with me in the fall. The most danger he'd find there was a frat party gone wild or a pretty girl who wanted to steal him away from Paula.

I tiptoed to the doorway where I could see them standing in a small circle in the center of the living room. Mark's back was to me, so he didn't know I was there when he said, "It's my honor to serve my country, sir. I can't go off to school, knowing my buddy was over there fighting while I played it safe."

I gasped at his words. "No!"

Everyone except Mark turned to me.

Compassion filled Mama's face, while Dad appeared wary of what might come out of my mouth next. The Arnolds and Mrs. McCallum each wore empathetic expressions before they whispered their goodbyes and quietly exited the house. Nash said something to Mark I couldn't make out, then headed down the hall to Mark's room without looking my way.

When my brother finally turned to face me, guilt filled his eyes.

"Sis," he said. His broad shoulders sagged as he slowly moved until he stood in front of me. I searched his face, frantic to see reassurance that I'd misunderstood what I'd just heard. "I need to tell you something. Nash and I are joining the Marines tomorrow."

I stared at him, my breath heavy with confusion. "What are you talking about? You and I are going to Vanderbilt in the fall.

You'll play football. It's already been decided." Anger rose in me. "Did Nash talk you into this?"

"No one talked me into it, Mattie. I've been thinking about it for a while now. I discussed the whole thing with Dad, and—"

"I knew it," I shouted. My angry gaze landed on Dad. "You convinced him to do this. How could you encourage my brother to risk his life?"

"Mattie, stop." Mark grasped my shoulders, silencing me. "The decision to join the Marines is mine and mine alone. It doesn't have anything to do with anyone else. Coach Cooper and Pastor Arnold both think—"

"Everyone knows about this?" We'd been one another's confidant for as long as we'd been alive. We never did anything without first talking it over with the other. "How could you decide this without telling me? Without asking me what I thought?"

"Because I knew what you'd say. I know how you feel about the war. But—"

"But what?" My voice reverberated off the walls.

"Mattie, please understand," Mama said. She crossed the room and tried to take my hand, but I jerked away. "Your brother has to do what his heart tells him."

I gaped at her. "You *want* him to go to Vietnam? What kind of mother are you? How could you want your son to go to the opposite side of the world where he could die in a war we shouldn't be involved in? I expected as much from Dad, but not from you."

"Martha Ann." Dad's stern voice filled the room, drawing everyone's attention. For someone who rarely had much to say, he could be quite commanding when he wanted. "You will not speak to your mother with such disrespect. This is your brother's decision, and we will support him." He paused. "All of us."

Hot tears filled my eyes. It was clear everyone was against me. Mama. Dad. Nash. Even my twin brother.

I'd never felt so alone.

EIGHT

AVA

TULLAHOMA, TENNESSEE

JANUARY 1942

Camp Forrest was enormous.

I slowly drove through Gate No. 1, a heavily guarded entrance, with more nervous excitement than I'd felt in ages. Last week I received a telephone call from the woman in charge of the secretarial pool at the military installation and was offered a job working for the doctor in charge of the station hospital, Dr. Colonel Hew Foster. She'd told me to report to the hospital administration building promptly at "o-seven hundred" Monday morning. I thanked her, hung up the phone, and did a little jig. I had a job. A good job. In that moment, the future didn't look quite as frightening as it had a month ago.

Gertrude's unsmiling face filled my memory as I drove past the plain white building where I'd filled out the job application. She remained resentful that I'd accepted the position.

"You should be here, on your husband's farm, helping your husband's mother. Not gallivanting around a military base with hundreds of men." She had sniffled. "My son's been dead less than two months, but he's already forgotten by his widow."

Nothing I said changed her mind. Even this morning, with her glare following me out the kitchen door, I'd stood my ground. "We need the money, Gertrude," I reminded her for the umpteenth time. "Richard would be proud of me."

The slamming of the door was her response.

Now, with sunshine streaming through the windshield of my old Ford, I drove along streets alive with activity despite the early hour.

I'd received a packet of paperwork in the mail the day after I accepted the job that contained forms to sign, mostly regarding confidentiality, safety, and such. A handbook for Camp Forrest secretaries gave me an idea of what was expected—what I should wear, how to address officers, and the like. Although I'd worked in business offices in Nashville, I had a feeling working at Camp Forrest would be like entering another world.

The packet also included a map of the 85,000-acre installation and instructions on where I was allowed to go as well as areas off-limits to civilians. I'd studied the rendering of the gigantic cantonment for hours, sipping a cup of tea and making notations, praying I never accidentally ventured where I didn't belong. What had once been Camp Peay, a small summer training facility for the Tennessee National Guard situated on a little over a thousand acres, was now one of the largest military camps in the country, thanks to the onset of Hitler's war.

I'd learned that construction began in late 1940. Barely more than a year later, a full-fledged military base had sprung up out of the rich Tennessee farmland. The main thoroughfares were paved, but there were plenty of dirt roads and plank-board sidewalks, filled with men in uniform on foot or in military vehicles. I passed a tall water tower, painted with a checkerboard pattern, and remembered reading the base had its own water plant and sewage treatment facility.

I glanced at the map on the seat beside me. It had hundreds of buildings drawn in technical style, but to see them for myself took my breath. I'd always been good with numbers in school, and the staggering statistics ran through my mind: five hundred two-story barracks to house the soldiers, along with thirty officer quarters. One-hundred-plus mess halls, dozens of day halls, a library, post exchanges, chapels, theaters, warehouses, guardhouses, and even a 9,000-square-foot laundry facility where civilian women were employed. Thousands of Army-green Jeeps, trucks, and even tanks were housed in areas of the base where I was not allowed, all waiting to be shipped overseas. I'd read about acres and acres of training fields, complete with a mock German village, and a huge induction center where scores of young men like my Richard passed through every day, preparing to go to Europe.

I wound my way through unfamiliar streets, looking for the buildings that comprised the hospital complex among the many plain white structures that all looked the same. After two wrong turns, I came to a long line of one-story buildings. Military ambulances, with red crosses on a white background, sat in front. I parked at the far end where I'd been instructed. A glance in the rearview mirror assured me my lipstick was still in place. I'd taken special care with my appearance this morning, another fact that irked Gertrude.

A day spent behind a typewriter doesn't require makeup and a fancy dress.

While her disapproving words were theoretically accurate, I knew a good first impression was vital. I'd never worked in a place as big as Camp Forrest, nor had I made as much money as I'd been promised. This job was key to unlocking the door to my future, and I'd do just about anything to make sure I kept it.

With a gulp of air, I climbed from the car and smoothed my skirt. The dark gray wool gabardine suit I'd purchased the day after I accepted the job made me feel like a professional. Although I preferred brighter colors, I was a widow in mourning. Gertrude hadn't approved of my desire to make a splash on my first day, but I knew she couldn't find fault in the ensemble.

A pleasant-faced young woman greeted me when I entered the building. Like the administration office where I'd completed the job application, the space I entered was spare. Four desks filled the room, with two occupied by young women busy at their typewriters, surrounded by bare walls and plank wood floors.

"I'm Bren Marsh." She smiled. "Colonel Foster isn't in at the moment, but he left instructions for me to get you settled."

She led me over to the unoccupied desk. A typewriter sat in the center, along with a stack of files next to it.

"This is your area. You're welcome to bring a framed photo from home, but I must warn you—your desk will be crammed with paperwork. I wouldn't advise filling it up with too many personal items. The colonel's office is through there," she continued as she pointed to a closed door behind the desk. "You'll work directly with him. You've probably already been told, but Colonel Foster oversees the entire hospital, so you can imagine how busy you'll be. His previous secretary couldn't keep up with the workload, so she quit."

I suddenly felt unsure of myself. "May I ask why you or one of the other girls didn't fill the vacancy?"

"We're just general secretaries. You must have some special skills since they chose you over all the others."

Oh dear.

I thought back to the day I applied for the job. Had I exaggerated my qualifications on the application? I couldn't recall answering any of the questions dishonestly, but now I wondered if I'd overestimated my abilities. I never dreamed I would work for the officer in charge of the hospital. A simple clerk, like Bren and the others, is all I'd had in mind.

"The colonel should arrive within the hour. You might take that time to get your desk organized the way you'd like it. You won't have time later. Let me know if you need anything. Oh, the ladies' room is in the adjoining building."

With that, Bren returned to her own desk and immediately went to work.

The small room echoed with the clacking and clanging of typewriters. After eight months of living on a horse farm in the country, I'd grown used to days filled with peace and quiet. The noise and constant company would take some getting used to.

I took off my pillbox hat and gloves and laid them on the desktop. Seated at the back of the room, I had a view of everyone who might come and go, including my boss. The fact that he was a colonel made me nervous. Visions of a war-hardened man flashed across my mind, silly as it may be. What was Colonel Foster like? Was he so demanding that he ran off the previous secretary? Had I bitten off more than I could chew?

All my questions would be answered soon enough. In the meantime, I took Bren's advice and organized the supplies in my desk. I'd just completed the task when the front door opened, letting in bright morning sunshine. A tall man in an Army-green uniform filled the doorway. The sound of typing immediately silenced.

"Good morning, Colonel," the three young women chimed in unison.

"Good morning, ladies." He closed the door, tucked his hat under his arm, and moved to stand in front of Bren's desk. "Miss Marsh, I have a meeting at thirteen-hundred hours with Major Williams. I'll need the supplies report so I can go over it with him."

"Yes, sir." Bren turned to me and smiled. "Sir, this is your new secretary, Mrs. Delaney."

The man's gaze landed on me, his expression indicating he hadn't noticed my presence until now. For a long, uncomfortable moment, he simply stared at me. Finally, as though remembering his manners, he cleared his throat.

"Mrs. Delaney. Welcome aboard."

"Thank you," I said, a nervous wobble in my voice. "I'm happy to be here."

He didn't smile. "I hope you still feel that way at the end of the day."

The three young women giggled and went back to work.

Colonel Foster made his way to my desk. "Bring a notebook and pen, and we'll get started." He disappeared into his office without another word.

My stomach knotted, but Bren turned to offer an encouraging grin over her shoulder.

"He's really very nice when you get to know him," she whispered.

I hoped she was right. Thankfully I knew exactly where to find a notepad and pen and hurried to follow him. I started to close the door, as I'd always done when meeting with my boss in Nashville, but the colonel stopped me.

"Leave it open."

I did.

"Have a seat." He motioned me to one of two wooden chairs in front of a desk that was covered in neat stacks of files and papers.

I settled in the chair, pen poised to take notes, when he said, "Tell me about yourself."

The request caught me off guard. What did he want to know? "I . . . um . . . I worked as a secretary in Nashville. For an insurance company."

"What brought you to Tullahoma?"

"My husband grew up here." I paused. I hadn't talked about Richard to anyone other than Gertrude, but she suffered her own deep grief and had no desire to understand mine. While I'd rather keep my personal life private, this military man was now my boss and was entitled to know the basics. "He died at Pearl Harbor."

A look of compassion crossed the colonel's face. "I'm sorry for your loss." He looked out the window. "A good friend of mine was killed at Pearl. John and I attended medical school together. He joined the Navy and I joined the Army. He was tending the wounded when a Japanese bomb struck his ship."

Only the sound of typing from the next room filled the space between us. Knowing the colonel had lost a friend reminded me that he was human. It took away some of the apprehension I'd felt since he entered the building. Although he had a commanding presence, I appreciated this small glimpse of his softer side.

He turned to face me again. "As you're no doubt aware, Camp Forrest has only been in operation since the spring of '41. We've had much to accomplish in a short amount of time. In our first month, over one thousand patients were treated here at the hospital. Now, with troops heading to Europe every day, I expect we will begin to receive wounded from overseas soon. My previous secretary was woefully inadequate. She couldn't keep up."

I swallowed.

"What I need, Mrs. Delaney," he leaned forward, his expression stern, "is someone who will work hard, ask questions, and follow orders."

My mouth went dry. "I understand, sir."

"Very well." He reached for a large stack of files and handed them to me. "These personnel files need updating. We've had so many doctors and nurses coming and going, I need to be certain of each person's qualifications and experience. It's imperative we give our servicemen the best care we possibly can, and that means positioning our staff where their skills and knowledge are best utilized."

I nodded in agreement.

"This will be a time-consuming project, but it will also give you the opportunity to become familiar with the hospital and staff. Can I count on you to have it completed by week's end, Mrs. Delaney?"

"You can, sir."

For the first time since our meeting, he offered the slightest smile. "I can be a bit of a curmudgeon at times, but you'll find I'm fair."

He stood, and I did too. "I appreciate the opportunity, sir. I won't let you down."

He inclined his head. "You may close the door on your way out."

I did as I was instructed, then returned to my desk.

Bren hurried over. "How did it go?"

"Good, I think. He gave me these personnel files to update by the end of the week, but I must admit I'm not sure how to go about it."

Bren glanced at her wristwatch. "How about I give you a tour of the hospital complex and introduce you to the principal chief nurse. Captain Leonard is a jewel, and she'll gladly help if she can."

"Thank you, so much, Miss Marsh. I truly appreciate it."

"Call me Bren. And, if you don't mind, we secretaries will call you Ava when it's just us."

We put on our coats and walked out into warm sunshine. Snow was predicted by the end of the week, so it was nice to get outside while we could.

"How long have you worked at Camp Forrest?" I asked.

"I started last summer. My father is retired from the Army, so when he heard Camp Forrest was hiring, he encouraged me to apply. It was a quiet place to work at first, but after Pearl Harbor, everything changed."

I knew exactly what she meant.

We walked to the building adjacent to the administration building and climbed a set of wooden steps. I followed Bren around like a puppy, trying to take notes and remember names and locations, but with sixty-eight buildings and hundreds of staff, I soon gave up.

We saw the operating room, X-ray room, pharmacy, outpatient clinic, a dental clinic, and even a women's clinic. Some of the buildings housed patient wards, with two thousand beds in all. A large kitchen and dining hall occupied a separate building, and Bren laughingly declared the food better than the meals she ate at her boardinghouse in town.

We found Captain Leonard in her office in the last building we visited. The older woman wore a nurse's uniform rather than the military garb I'd expected. Bren introduced me, declared me in capable hands, and bid us farewell. When I explained my mission to the captain, she offered a sympathetic smile.

"My dear, you best get used to this task. Our staff changes with the wind these days."

She took the first file off the stack and pulled out a form with typed information. "See here." She pointed to a box in the top right corner of the page. "This number represents the building where this nurse is assigned. Here is where you'll find the employee's job title—nurse, orderly, doctor, and the like." She handed the folder back to me. "Our staff is quite busy, so it would be best if you tried to limit the need to interrupt their work as much as possible."

I assured her I would do my best and left the office. Back outside, I glanced to my right then my left. Where should I begin? I had nearly one hundred people to track down. How would I find them if I wasn't allowed to make inquiries? More importantly, what if I couldn't complete this assignment by week's end, as Colonel Foster asked?

With the beginnings of panic gnawing my stomach, I opened the same file the captain had used as an example and scanned the information. It was for a nurse working in the surgical building, located at the opposite end of the complex. Was she on duty today? I had no way of knowing.

My shoulders sagged. My feet were already complaining, thanks to the heeled pumps I'd worn to match my "make a good first impression" outfit. The excitement I felt when I arrived on base quickly evaporated into frustration. There was nothing to do but head back to the administration building and hope Bren had some suggestions of how I should go about my task.

One thing was certain.

I couldn't fail at this assignment.

My future depended on it.

NINE

MATTIE

DELANEY HORSE FARM

NOVEMBER 1969

Mama surprised us with a request four days after my return home.

"I'd like to come downstairs for supper," she announced that morning. I had just helped her bathe and was towel-drying her hair. Dad, who hovered nearby, told her it was fine if she didn't overtire herself. He and I hadn't spoken to one another much since our argument over Mama's health. Tension between us was obvious, and I wondered if Mama's desire to join us was an attempt to ease the situation. Later, while Nash helped get the meal on the table, he quietly told me Mama hadn't been downstairs in weeks.

"She's happier now that you're home."

I waited for him to scold me for leaving in the first place, but he didn't.

Memories from last night's supper floated through my mind

while I finished washing the breakfast dishes. Dad had carried Mama down the stairs, a feat which admittedly impressed me. I roasted a chicken with carrots and potatoes and made a salad, topped with Mama's favorite Thousand Island dressing. Although she ate sparingly, she declared it a feast and wore a contented smile when Dad carried her back to bed.

I took the entire evening as a sign that I needed to ramp up my efforts to get Mama to Nashville to see a specialist. Giving up simply wasn't an option in my opinion, which is exactly what I felt my father had done. I understood Mama didn't want to subject herself to radiation and chemotherapy. The horrific side effects of the aggressive treatments were not something I wanted her to endure. She also didn't want to amass thousands of dollars in medical bills, considering the farm hadn't been profitable for some time. Yet if there was even the slightest chance the tumors could shrink and begin to disappear, wouldn't it all be worth it? The cancer would go away and we'd have a healthy Mama again.

I put a coffee mug in the cabinet and slammed the door in frustration.

I couldn't fathom why my father didn't push back. Wouldn't he want to do everything within his power to keep the woman he loved alive? I couldn't bring myself to believe he didn't care about her. He wasn't a man given over to letting others see his emotions, but I'd witnessed enough evidence over the years to feel confident he loved her. He always opened doors for her and helped with household chores. Store-bought gifts were rare but every now and then he'd bring her a bouquet of wildflowers from the pasture or a handful of pretty fall leaves.

Memories of the time I caught them dancing in the kitchen to old-fashioned music floated across my mind's eye. Mark and I were supposed to be asleep, but I'd come downstairs to get a drink of water. Hearing the radio, I crept to the doorway and peeked in. Neither of my parents knew I was there, and I'd watched in dumbfounded fascination as Dad held Mama close and swayed to the ballad. I was at the age where I was just noticing boys, and I wondered what drew Mama to such a quiet, reserved fellow like my father. The saying *opposites attract* certainly described them to perfection.

The back door opened, interrupting my thoughts. Nash and Jake came in with a cold wind. The dog limped over to his bowl, which was empty, and looked at me.

"Sorry fella, I'm not your owner."

Nash chuckled. "Don't let him fool you. He's eaten already."

I noticed his face was red from being out in the chilly weather. Snow was in the forecast, which always made life on the farm harder. "Do you want some coffee? I think there's still some in the pot."

He seemed surprised by my offer. "Sure. That'd be great. The temperature is dropping fast."

I poured the remainder of coffee into a mug and handed it to him. Unlike me, who loaded up the bitter liquid with sugar and cream, I'd noticed yesterday morning that he took it black.

"I came by to let you know I'm going into town. Do you need anything?"

I bit my lip. There were a few personal items on my list but nothing I could ask Nash to pick up. I'd have to go shopping for myself another day.

"I can't think of anything. What takes you to town in this weather?"

"The furnace is out in the cabin. I'm hoping to find parts at the hardware store, but the contraption is ancient. I may be out of luck."

"I don't suppose anyone has used it since Granny passed on."

"Probably not. I didn't need a heater when I first moved in." He downed the last of the coffee and went to rinse the cup then turned to me. "You sure there's nothing I can get for you?"

"Thanks, but I'll probably go into town myself next week." I paused, wondering if I should share my thoughts about Mama's prognosis with him. Last night I'd seen how considerate Nash was to Mama, and she'd treated him like family. Surely he would agree with me about the need to try everything within our power to save her.

"I'm thinking about going to talk to Dr. Monahan. About Mama."

He gave a slow nod. "That's probably a good idea."

His favorable response pleased me. "I'm convinced more can be done. I want him to give me the name of a doctor we can take her to see in Nashville. A specialist in Mama's type of cancer."

He rubbed his chin. "Mattie, I don't know the details, but Doc discussed this with your folks after your mom's surgery revealed the cancer had spread. He doesn't think chemo would help at this point."

"Doc Monahan is a family doctor. He treats kids with broken arms and tonsillitis. He isn't an authority on cancer."

"That's true, but he's been a doctor a long time. I'm sure he's seen his share of cancer patients. I think he knows more about it than you do."

Irritation swam through me. "This isn't about my ego, Nash. This is about my mother. I don't want to lose her a year after losing my brother."

His expression softened. "I get that. All I'm saying is, the decision is your mom's, no one else's."

"That's not good enough for me. And it shouldn't be good enough for anyone who claims to care about her. Would you just let your mother give up and die?"

His jaw tightened. "I'd respect her wishes, no matter how difficult it might be to do that."

"Well, that's where you and I differ. If Mama won't go see the Nashville doctor, then I'll go myself and find out what they think.

With so many advances in medicine these days, it's foolish not to seek out every possible cure."

"I think your mom would tell you life and death are in God's hands, not in medical advancements."

I narrowed my gaze on him. "I never thought of you as a religious person."

"I'm not, but I admit I envy your mom's faith. I've never seen anything like it. But as for me, I have a hard time believing in a God who allows so much suffering in the world."

"For once we agree on something. Maybe you'll come around to my side after I talk to the doctors."

He held my gaze for a long moment. "I hope you get the answers you're looking for. Your parents have been real good to me. I'd never wish anything bad for them."

He whistled for Jake, who'd wandered into the living room while we talked, and I watched the two of them leave the house. Nash wasn't an ally yet, but once I had more information from knowledgeable medical professionals, I felt certain he'd see I was right.

I went upstairs and found Mama bundled in a hand-knit afghan, reading.

"It feels like it's getting colder outside." She glanced out the window. "I wish I could help get the horses settled in the barn. There's always so much to do when a storm is coming. I'm glad your father has Nash to help him."

"Nash had to go to town. The furnace is out in the cabin. He went to find parts."

Concern filled her eyes. "I hope he isn't gone long. Your father will need help before the snow gets here."

I hated for her to worry. "I guess I could go see if there's anything I can do." The idea didn't thrill me, but if it made her feel better, I'd make the sacrifice.

"I know your father would appreciate that, dear." A sweet smile replaced the frown.

Mama was dozing by the time I changed from my hippie clothes into some of the winter things I'd left in my closet and made my way to the horse barn in a bitter wind. With temperatures quickly plummeting, the stalls that were empty only yesterday now held animals in need of care. Some of the horses were left out to pasture, but they were usually the younger ones, with no health concerns, and could withstand the cold better than some of the older animals.

Moonlight poked her nose over the half door to her stall when I approached. "Hey, girl." I rubbed her nose, noticing someone had draped a horse blanket over her. "I guess you're happy to be one of the lucky ones to come in out of the cold."

She knickered and nudged my hand.

"I don't have anything for you this time. I'm here to work."

When I finished petting her, she returned to her feed bucket, hanging where she could easily reach it. I suspected Dad had begun to increase her feed, mixing in a mineral supplement to keep her and her unborn foal healthy.

Thinking about Moonlight's baby brought a twinge of unexpected excitement. Even though I hadn't been able to choose the sire myself, the anticipation of new life lifted some of the dark clouds that hovered because of Mama's illness. Maybe it could do the same thing for her, I realized. Clay always said positive energy could heal anything. That's what Mama needed. An optimistic vibe, not discouragement and hopelessness. Words of life, not death.

I found Dad in the barn, loading rectangular bales of golden hay onto a trailer hitched to his old tractor. Despite the cold, sweat poured down his face.

He seemed alarmed to find me there. "Is your mother all right?"

I nodded. "She's resting." An awkward silence thickened between us. I'd rather eat straw than spend time with my father, but I'd promised Mama. There was nothing to do but push forward. "She thought I should come see if you needed any help, since Nash had to go into town."

His brow rose as he stared at me.

Heavy silence stood between us.

This was a mistake. I shouldn't have come. I was about to walk away when he indicated the tractor trailer.

"I could use a hand with the hay."

Nothing more was said between us.

I went to the storeroom and found a pair of leather work gloves. With my hands protected, I hefted a bale by the wires holding it together onto the trailer. Each one weighed fifty pounds or more, and by the time I'd moved half a dozen, I was sweating as much as Dad. A year in California's hippie communes had made me soft. While some members worked out in the world to support our *family*, which is what Clay always called the group of forty or so people who followed him, the rest of us spent time meditating or listening to Clay teach about how the world needed love, not war. Household chores, tending the garden, and helping with the children in the family were shared by all, but nothing required the muscles I was using now.

By the time we'd loaded the trailer, I was breathing heavily.

"You best go inside and rest," he said, eyeing me. "I'll finish unloading it."

I shook my head. "I'm fine."

He studied me a moment longer, then nodded. I climbed onto the hay and sat on a bale while he drove out of the barn into the cold air. Tiny flakes of snow spit from thick clouds as we made our way to the north pasture where a group of horses trailed us, eager for an easy meal.

Dad stopped the tractor in front of a three-sided shelter. Without speaking, we got to work. Each pasture had similar shelters where the animals could get out of the wind and rain. After we unloaded a half dozen bales, we left the horses happily filling their bellies and headed to the next field.

When we finished and returned to the yard, Nash was there, waiting.

Dad shut off the tractor engine.

"Looks like you two got some work done while I was gone," Nash said.

Dad glanced at me. "Might be best if you checked on your mother now."

I felt dismissed. As though my hard work had somehow been inferior, and he'd had to make do with me until Nash got back.

I climbed off the trailer and marched toward the house.

• • •

Mama sat in an overstuffed chair by the bedroom window. She smiled when she saw me in the doorway, but it quickly faded. "What's wrong, Mattie?"

I hadn't meant to let her see my irritation. After I'd returned to the house, I watched through the window as my father and Nash headed to the cottage, no doubt to work on the furnace. Just yesterday I'd watched them tinker on the tractor, their heads together beneath the raised hood. At one point, Dad laughed heartily at something Nash said and slapped him on the shoulder the way men tended to do. I'd turned away. The scene hurt to watch. They looked like father and son, working side by side, laughing, and enjoying each other's company.

I plopped down on the end of Mama's bed. "I helped Dad like you asked, but the minute Nash appeared, he didn't need me anymore."

Empathy filled Mama's face. "I'm sure he appreciated your hard work, dear." She grew thoughtful. "Nash has had a difficult time since he came home. He refuses to see his father. Wants nothing to do with him. I think his coming here has helped both your dad and Nash. They each carry heavy burdens. I believe God brought Nash to us because he needed your father and your father needed him."

"Dad needed Mark, his *real* son." I shook my head. "I don't understand how you can still think God cares about us. About the details of our lives. If that were true, he wouldn't have let Mark die and Nash live. It would have been the other way around."

"Mattie," Mama said, her voice stern. "God doesn't mind us asking questions when hard things happen, but when we start telling him who should live and who should die . . . well, that simply isn't something we should ever do. Nash survived for a reason, and I'm grateful he did. He's hurting, Mattie, and I don't just mean because of his missing arm. I think it goes back to his childhood, long before the war. Deep inside, he's wounded. If a friendship with your father helps heal that, then I thank God for it."

I wouldn't argue with her. There was no point. The truth is, I didn't wish Nash had died in Vietnam. I just wish Mark had lived.

I noticed the lid to the old trunk in the corner of the room stood open. Mark and I used to prowl through the musty chest from time to time, looking for treasures. What we found, however, was old-fashioned clothing, baby things, and some miscellaneous items I couldn't recall.

"I was feeling nostalgic," she said when she found my attention on the trunk. She reached for something in her lap and held up a miniature nightgown. "You and your brother were such tiny things when you were born. I remember how excited we were to have a boy and a girl."

My throat tightened, and I swallowed hard.

"Neither your dad nor I could recall anyone in our families ever having twins," she continued, not realizing how painful it was for me to listen to her share her memories. "It was such a blessing, especially because I never became pregnant again." She sniffled as she looked at the gown. "Seems like yesterday I was running after the two of you. Two peas in a pod, I called you, but Mark—" Tears filled her eyes as her voice cracked.

I couldn't do this. Not now. Maybe not ever.

"I just remembered I need to take some chicken out of the freezer." I stood, feeling like the worst daughter in the world. I couldn't help it though. Her journey down memory lane was simply too painful for me to join. "You said you wanted soup for supper, isn't that right?"

She wiped a tear that slipped down her cheek. Then she smiled, albeit, not as broadly as earlier. "Yes, soup sounds nice. Especially on a cold day."

"I'll bring your lunch up in a little while." I didn't wait for her response before I fled downstairs. So as not to be a liar, I took out a package of rock-hard chicken and set it in the sink with a *thunk*.

I blew out a breath.

I know Mama wanted to talk about Mark. About his life and his death. But I'd spent the past year doing everything I could to forget. To push the memories, even the happy ones, to the deepest, darkest part of my soul where they couldn't hurt me. Unearthing them now was the last thing I needed. Nothing good could come from reliving that kind of pain all over again. I was on shaky ground as it was, just being back in this house, dealing with Mama's cancer and my rocky relationship with Dad.

I stared out the window at the gray, wintery day.

The way I saw things, I had two choices if I was going to survive: set boundaries and make sure no one penetrated them, or catch the next bus to LA and never look back.

I kept busy in the kitchen, chopping vegetables for soup and baking some corn bread, mainly to avoid going upstairs. When that chore was finished, I threw a load of laundry into the washing machine, folded towels that were in the dryer, and swept the porch despite the frigid breeze. When I couldn't stall any longer, I prepared a soft-boiled egg and toast and carried them to Mama's room. I found her curled in bed, the tiny nightgown clutched in her hands, sound asleep.

Quietly, I set the lunch tray on the side table. I hated to wake her, but the food would be cold soon. I'd wait and see if she awakened.

The lid of the trunk remained open. It looked as though Mama had rummaged through it to find what she was looking for. Seeing the familiar items brought a flash of pain, but I refused to let it settle.

I set about putting the contents of the chest back in order. When I came to a shoebox I assumed held photographs, I was surprised to find it contained an old leather-bound book and two bundles of yellowed envelopes, each tied with string.

I sat back on my haunches and lifted out the book. The edges were quite worn and *Die Bibel* was stamped on the front cover in faded gold lettering. A crackling sound issued from the book's spine when I opened it to the first page. Fancy printed letters repeated the words *Die Bibel* with *Berlin, 1908* beneath them. A handwritten message would surely give a clue as to the ownership, but I couldn't make out the words. It was written in a different language.

"What are you doing?"

Dad's voice startled me, and I dropped the book. I whirled to find him in the doorway, his hard glare fixed on me.

"Mama was feeling nostalgic. She wanted to see some of . . ." I faltered. "She took some things out of the trunk."

His gaze landed on the book in my lap. "Put that away. You have no business looking through things that don't concern you."

Taken aback by his harsh tone, I huffed. "I wasn't being nosy. I was simply cleaning things up."

He stood there a while longer before he turned and left the room.

What in the world was that about?

I picked up the book again. What was so important about the old tome?

With a stealthy glance toward the doorway to make certain he was gone, I studied the cover. *Die Bibel.* If I had to guess, it said *The Bible*, but why would Dad get all worked up about an old, foreign Bible? He'd never shown any interest in religion. Never went to church with us. Never prayed over a meal.

A door banged somewhere downstairs. I heard Dad's voice as he spoke to Nash.

I returned the book to the box, put the box in the bottom of the trunk, and threw a quilt on top of it. With everything back as it was, I woke Mama and helped her with her lunch. All the while, however, my eyes drifted to the trunk.

Something stirred in me.

It was the same feeling I used to get when Mark would suggest we do something we knew we weren't supposed to do, like jump off the loft rafters into a pile of hay or hide a snake in Granny's bed.

Dad said the box and its contents were none of my business.

Exactly the reason I knew I'd make it my business.

TEN

AVA

TULLAHOMA, TENNESSEE
FEBRUARY 1942

I still had a job.

That was something to be grateful for, considering the setbacks I'd experienced in my first week working for Colonel Foster. True to his word, he was a fair man, but I'd seen the look of disappointment in his eyes when I knocked on his office door late Friday afternoon and confessed I had not finished updating the personnel files.

"I'm sorry, sir." I prepared myself to be fired on the spot.

His intense gaze narrowed on me. "What happened?"

Without laying blame on anyone but myself, I admitted I'd had a difficult time locating employees spread throughout the large hospital complex, all while trying hard not to bother anyone. I didn't mention how at least three doctors hadn't been cooperative or that a handful of nurses declared themselves too busy yet found plenty of time to flirt with handsome patients. Some of the files even had the employees' names and ranks incorrect, which took precious time to figure out.

"I still have a dozen or so files to update. If it's permissible, I'd be happy to work through the weekend without pay to complete the task."

The colonel seemed to contemplate my offer. "That's quite admirable, Mrs. Delaney," he said after a lengthy silence. "However, that won't be necessary. You may finish on Monday. But I must warn you, things will only get busier. If you aren't up to it, I suggest you visit the secretarial pool administrator and ask to be reassigned." He'd dismissed me without waiting for my response.

Happily, I delivered the updated files to him early Monday afternoon. He didn't look up from the papers on his desk and simply nodded his thanks. Now, my fingers flew across the typewriter keys, determined not to let the colonel down again. In the past two days, I'd typed dozens of letters, filled out countless supply forms, and taken notes during the two meetings he'd had with various officers. Eight days on the job, and I was finally beginning to feel like I might survive.

"Mrs. Delaney, please come into my office," came the colonel's voice through the open door behind me.

I grabbed a notepad and pencil and hurried to comply. I'd taken two steps into the small, stark room when he said, "You may close the door."

I did.

"There is a situation I need to discuss with you in private. Please have a seat."

After I settled in the chair opposite his desk, wondering what our meeting was about, he motioned to the notepad. "You won't be needing that. What I'm going to tell you will soon be public knowledge, but for now, this is confidential military information."

I nodded. "I understand."

"Two weeks ago, a train full of prisoners arrived at the camp. These men were arrested under the Enemy Alien Control Program and are being housed on base in a restricted and highly guarded area."

I recalled reading about arrests that were made in the days following the attack on Pearl Harbor. People with ties to Germany, Italy, and Japan were rounded up. I hadn't paid much attention to the situation, considering I was dealing with my own grief and fears for the future.

"Why were they brought here?"

"From what I understand, there are thousands of these detainees all across the country." He leaned back against his chair. "Too many to incorporate into our prison systems. The Department of Justice is overseeing the internment program, and several military installations are being used to house the men, Camp Forrest among them. The men we've received are all German citizens."

My heart raced as thoughts of Hitler and the Nazi swastika sped through my mind. "Are they dangerous? Is that why they were arrested?"

"I've been told they were in the United States legally, either working or going to school. None have a criminal history, although it can't be assumed that all of them are anti-Hitler. For most, it seems, their only crime is having been born in a country that is now run by a dictator."

While his comment brought a measure of reassurance, I couldn't help but feel on edge, no matter that the camp was full to overflowing with trained soldiers. The thought of having men with possible ties to Hitler's regime right here at Camp Forrest was terrifying.

"The reason I'm sharing this information with you is because at least one of the detainees will be working in the hospital."

I gasped. "Sir, is that wise? Won't the staff and patients be in danger?"

"I don't believe so. As I said, the men being detained aren't soldiers. This gentleman has indicated he has hospital experience, and according to the DOJ, the detainees are allowed to work while they're here. I suspect there will be others working in various departments around the base. I've been assured an armed escort will always accompany them. That should alleviate any fears."

I gave a hesitant nod.

"Obviously, I will assume responsibility for this man, which is why I thought it necessary that you be made aware of the situation. While I don't foresee the need for you to interact with him, I didn't want you to be taken by surprise when word of the detainees finally leaks out to the staff."

"Are Miss Marsh and the other secretaries aware of the situation?"

He shook his head. "I'd like you to inform them. Just the basic information."

"Yes, sir." I rose to leave, but he stopped me with a question.

"This may not be the best time to ask this, considering the news I've just delivered, but how do you like working at Camp Forrest, Mrs. Delaney? Is it what you expected?"

I returned to my seat. "I admit that after my first day, I was positive I'd made a mistake by accepting the job. But I think that's probably true of any new situation. Thanks to Bren and the other girls, I feel I've settled into the position well." A sudden thought brought a pang of anxiety. "Have I disappointed you, sir, with my job performance?"

"Not at all, Mrs. Delaney. I'm very pleased with your work. I appreciate the efforts you've shown to learn the ropes. The hospital will only get busier as the war progresses, so it will be imperative that we stay one step ahead of things." He smiled. "I think you and I make a good team."

His words of affirmation were a balm to my anxious heart. "Thank you, sir."

I left his office with a lighter step. Bren took notice and came over to my desk.

"Looks like you and the colonel are getting along," she whispered, a sly grin on her lips. "He is quite handsome. And single."

I'd felt comfortable enough with Bren to tell her about Richard. I hoped it hadn't been a mistake. I had no interest in dating anyone.

"It's nothing like that. He simply said I was doing a good job. I do have some news to share with you and the others, though."

Bren called over the other two secretaries, Stella and Ethel, and I passed along the information about the German detainees. However, none of the three young women appeared as shocked as I'd been.

"We've heard rumors about a group of men who are being kept in a fenced-off area of the camp," Bren said. "It's guarded, with towers and ten-foot-high barbed-wire fences, but no one knew who they were."

"Are they Nazis?" Stella asked, her blue eyes wide. "My brother is in Europe fighting Hitler's army. I don't like knowing there are Germans right here in Tullahoma."

"Colonel Foster doesn't believe these men are dangerous. They were in our country legally when the war started, but now the government considers them enemy aliens. The colonel believes the men were arrested because they were born in Germany, not because they are a threat to our safety. But he wanted us to be aware that at least one of them will be working in the hospital."

"I wonder what Captain Leonard thinks about this," Bren said. "Her son is a B-17 pilot. She may not appreciate having Germans working so closely with her nursing staff."

"The Department of Justice is in charge of the detainees, and they've given the men permission to work while they're being held."

The outside door opened, and the supply officer entered the room. Bren hurried to greet him, and Stella and Ethel went back to work. I stayed busy the remainder of the day, but my conversation with Colonel Foster was never far from my mind. When we prepared to leave for the evening, Stella whispered her plan to drive past the detainees' area to see if any of the men were in the yard. Bren and Ethel eagerly said they would follow her. I secretly thought it a foolish idea, considering the area was restricted to military personnel only. The last thing I needed was to lose my job because I ignored the rules. Besides, getting a peek at prisoners considered dangerous enough to lock behind barbed wire wasn't something I was interested in.

I bid them good night. As their vehicles disappeared around the corner, I headed the Ford in the opposite direction, toward the safety of the farm.

• • •

A week had passed since Colonel Foster informed me about the German detainees. Bren and the other secretaries reported no sightings the night they drove past the fenced-off area. They did, however, see dozens of small huts, guard towers, and enough armed soldiers to ensure no one could attempt to escape the area without being caught. After the initial uneasiness regarding the foreign men living on base, the topic faded into the day-to-day busyness of running a military hospital.

I'd just settled at my desk that morning when Colonel Foster brought me another stack of personnel files.

"I'm sorry to assign this task to you again so soon, but we've had another turnover of workers. A group of doctors and nurses shipped out yesterday, while others have joined our staff. These records need updating. I'm afraid this will be an ongoing situation for the duration of the war."

I stood and accepted the folders. "I'm certain it will go faster now that I know my way around the hospital complex."

He nodded, then seemed to study me for a long moment.

"You look very nice today, Mrs. Delaney," he finally said. "I like the way you've done your hair."

His compliment flustered me. "Th . . . thank you," I stuttered, my face growing warm.

I'd swept my shoulder-length pin curls to the side, anchored with a pearl comb, a style I hadn't worn since before Richard died. That the colonel noticed rattled me. Mercifully, none of the other secretaries were in the room, otherwise there would have been no end to their teasing.

The colonel returned to his office, and I donned my coat, gathered the folders, and left the building. The breeze outside was brisk, but it felt good on my warm cheeks.

Colonel Foster's comment regarding my appearance was unexpected, but I had to admit it brought a hint of pleasure. After Richard was sent to Hawaii, I didn't worry much about my hair and makeup, considering I mainly stayed on the farm with Gertrude.

According to Bren, the colonel had never been married and had devoted himself to his patients and military career. The gray around his temples had us guessing his age, which we all agreed must be around forty. But as Bren pointed out the other day, he was indeed a handsome man. It made me wonder why he remained a bachelor.

A pang of guilt washed through me as memories of Richard's ready compliments came to mind. He, too, had liked my hair in this style. From the day we met, he made sure I knew he only had eyes for me. Even his letters were filled with words of love and admiration. He'd looked forward to our future together with hope and excitement.

I heaved a sigh.

How I wished I were in Hawaii right now, with Richard alive and well by my side instead of trying to navigate life on my own. But no amount of wishing would bring him back. I was a widow, which meant I was as single as Colonel Foster. There wasn't anything wrong with receiving—and enjoying—his compliment, I reminded myself.

After an hour of gathering information on the new employees, I came to a name no one recognized. His file contained only one sheet of paper, with minimal information filled in the blanks. His occupation was listed as *Day-Time Orderly*, which meant he could be in any of the sixty-plus hospital buildings, depending on where an orderly was needed at that moment. After searching to no avail, I met one of the nurses who'd helped me locate employees a few weeks ago.

"I'm not sure about the name," she said, continuing with her task of filling pill bottles while we talked. "But I saw a new orderly in the trauma unit a little while ago. There was an accident on the training field."

I thanked her and hurried to the building where specialized care was given to critically injured servicemen. The place buzzed with activity, with doctors and nurses calling out to each other, and patients on gurneys awaiting their turn for medical attention.

Clearly, now was not the time to try to update the file on an orderly.

I'd just turned to leave when I ran into the firm chest of a man wearing a grass-green shirt and matching trousers. Several folders slipped from my hands to the floor.

"Oh, pardon me." I looked up to find intense blue eyes staring at me. "I wasn't watching where I was going."

He simply nodded and stooped to retrieve the items I'd dropped. When he handed them to me, I smiled. "Thank you. I'm Ava Delaney. I work for Colonel Foster."

He dipped his chin. *"Fräulein."*

The single word was so soft I barely heard it, yet it didn't sound like English.

Just then he cast a nervous glance behind him, and I followed his gaze. There stood an armed soldier, unsmiling, watching us.

"Orderly!" came a shout from a doctor across the room. "Get over here. Now." His angry glare was on the man I'd run into.

My heart thundered as the pieces connected.

The reason I'm sharing this information with you is because one of the detainees will be working in the hospital, Colonel Foster had said.

My eyes darted to the name badge clipped to the pocket of his shirt.

Gunther Schneider. Department of Justice Internee.

Here was the orderly I sought.

ELEVEN

MATTIE

DELANEY HORSE FARM

AUGUST 1965

I felt sick to my stomach as I lay on my bed, not caring if my party dress turned into a wrinkled mess. Laughter and music drifted from downstairs, where a group of our friends from school gathered to wish Mark and Nash well before they left for Vietnam in the morning. Two of their football buddies were also headed overseas, so it was a send-off for them too. We'd have a private family dinner later tonight—Mama'd spent the past two days preparing Mark's favorite dishes—before we had to say goodbye.

The whole thing disgusted me.

I folded my arms across my belly.

How could they be in a celebratory mood when my brother and his best friend were trading peace and safety for the frightening evil that awaited them in a place most Americans couldn't find on a map? We should be dressed in black, mourning the death of liberty and freedom, not wearing bright colors as though we had something to celebrate. I'd stayed downstairs as long as I could, a strained smile on my face the entire time before I feared I might erupt. I'd fled to my room to escape the insanity, but now I wished I'd run from the house, saddled Moonlight, and disappeared until everyone was gone.

Mama found me in a foul mood. She looked pretty, with her hair teased in the current fashion older women were wearing. She'd dabbed on lipstick and wore a dress that flattered her middle-aged figure. Who would know by looking at her that her son was leaving for war the next day?

"Mattie, what are you doing up here? Your brother was worried. They're starting a game of charades. You're always so good at it."

I shook my head in disbelief. "I don't understand how you and the others can act like everything is all right." I sat up, frustration swirling. "Mark is going away tomorrow, Mama. We may never see him again. Am I the only one who comprehends what could happen to him when he gets off that airplane in Vietnam?"

I was certain my angry voice carried to the living room below, but I didn't care who heard me. Every single person down there was either completely ignorant of what was happening in the war, or they simply didn't care.

Mama sat next to me and gave me a patient look. "Of course we know the dangers of Mark going to war, but some things are out of our control."

"Mark would have listened if you'd told him not to join the Marines," I insisted. "He would never go against your wishes."

She sighed. "Someday you'll find out for yourself that parents can't always protect their children. I remember when you were a tiny girl, not even three years old, and you were determined to ride a horse all by yourself. You didn't want Dad or me to ride with you. I promised to teach you to ride solo as soon as you were bigger, but that wasn't good enough for you. One day while I was busy in the house, your father hollered from the yard. I'd never heard that kind of fear in his voice. I rushed outside in time to see a horse galloping down the road, with you hanging on to its mane for dear life. We figured out later that you'd opened the gate and climbed up onto the fence. How you managed to mount the horse is still a mystery." She reached to grasp my hand. "You could have been killed."

"I fell off," I said, fuzzy memories of that long-ago day pushing forward in my mind.

"Thankfully you only had a sprained arm. After you stopped crying, you wanted right back on that horse. Nothing I said could convince you otherwise."

"That isn't the same thing as sending Mark off to war."

"In a way it is." She squeezed my fingers. "I learned that no matter how much I want to, I can't protect you and your brother every moment of your lives. There will be times when you make decisions I wish you wouldn't. Do things that could put you in harm's way. If it were up to me, I'd keep the two of you right here on the farm with me and Dad forever, but I know I can't. That's where trust comes in. I've had to learn to trust that you're in God's hands, and that you'll make good choices according to the things we've taught you. I'll pray for Mark every single day, just as I'll be praying for you while you're in Nashville. But I have to let you both go."

"I'm just going to school, Mama. War is different. Every day there are stories in the paper about bombs and Vietcong and American soldiers dying."

"You forget that your father and I weren't much older than you when the war with Germany and Japan took place. We remember how it felt to read about the terrible things that were happening all around the world. We felt powerless then, and in some ways, we feel the same now."

"But Dad—"

She held up her hand. "This is Mark's last night at home for a while, Mattie. We want it to be a happy one. Put aside your arguments and come join your friends."

With little enthusiasm, I trudged downstairs. When I entered the living room, I found Rusty Shaw standing in the middle of the room, gesturing to the ceiling with his fist closed, while tippy-toeing in a circle like a clumsy ballerina. If my mood hadn't been so sour, I might have joined in the laughter with the others as they shouted guesses to his ridiculous clues.

I noticed Paula Allyn sat near the window, away from the group. Her attention was not on Rusty and his antics but was fastened on my brother where he perched on the edge of the sofa next to Nash. Each of them sported a military haircut—flat on top and shaved on the sides—which Mark proudly described as "high and tight, Marine style." I had to admit their heads did remind me of the lid on a jar, hence the nickname *jarhead*. Although neither wore a uniform, two months at boot camp had produced a confidence and bearing in them that hadn't been there before.

Paula looked up when I approached. Telltale redness around her eyes bore evidence that Mark's girlfriend had cried recently.

"You're not playing charades?" I asked, although the answer was obvious.

"I'm not really in the mood for games."

Her quiet answer told me she, too, felt the heaviness of Mark's leaving. I sat on the footstool beside the chair. "I know what you mean."

We watched the game for a while. Mark correctly guessed Rusty's charade—the movie *Mary Poppins*—which meant it was now his turn. With a wink at me and Paula, he took center stage and began even sillier antics than Rusty had performed. Everyone laughed and shouted their guesses, but Paula and I remained grim-faced in our misery.

"I thought he would ask me to marry him before he left."

Her whispered confession didn't surprise me. She and Mark had been sweethearts since junior high. I'd wondered myself if my brother would propose when he returned home from Parris Island last week. Although he hadn't shared his secrets with me lately, I knew he loved Paula.

"Maybe he will."

She shook her head. "He said he doesn't want me to feel obligated to wait for him, in case I meet someone while I'm at Auburn." Tears shimmered in her green eyes. "I told him I loved *him* and that I don't have any interest in dating anyone else, but he thinks it's best if we wait until his tour is over before we decide anything."

Poor girl.

I sent my brother a glare, although he wasn't looking at me. He was pretending to have a huge belly and kept putting something invisible on his head. I knew he was acting out his favorite song—"I'm Henry VIII, I Am" by Herman's Hermits, a band from England that was part of what people called the British Invasion, all started by the Beatles. The inane lyrics cracked Mark up every time it came on the radio, and he'd bust out singing at the top of his lungs. To his great dismay, he'd missed the group's performance of the song on The Ed Sullivan Show while he was in boot camp back in June.

"I'm scared, Mattie." Paula's fearful whisper drew my attention once again. "I'm scared war will change him, and he won't love me when he gets home."

Although Paula, Mark, and I had always been in the same classes all through school, she and I hung out with different friends. She'd been a cheerleader, Miss Tullahoma High, and was voted "Friendliest" girl. I, on the other hand, was secretary for the senior class student council and held a spot on the debate team, a place where I'd honed my arguments against the war over the past year. Ms. Medlin, our sponsor, didn't always agree with me, but she respected my opinions.

I reached for Paula's hand. "Mark loves you. That isn't going to change, no matter what. But I see his point. He might be gone for a long time. You may change your mind."

She shook her head. "I won't. There's no one else for me but Mark."

I offered a supportive smile. "Then think how happy the two of you will be when he finally comes home."

A burst of laughter came from the group when Mark, Nash, and Rusty began prancing about and singing "I'm Henry VIII, I Am" in outrageous British accents. Mark sashayed over and grabbed Paula's hand.

"Dance with me," he hollered over the din, grinning.

Paula's expression instantly changed, from sheer agony to sheer joy, and she eagerly joined in the silliness. I couldn't help but smile, despite my frustration. My brother was a nutcase, but oh, how I loved him.

After everyone was gone, we enjoyed Mama's dinner. Her face shone with pleasure when Mark confessed he was going to miss her home-cooked food. When the meal was over, Mama asked Mark to change into his military uniform so Dad could take his picture. I couldn't believe the transformation when he came out of his room. He looked so mature and handsome. Mama had tears in her eyes as we each took turns standing next to Mark while someone snapped a photograph with Dad's old Kodak Brownie.

Mama shooed us onto the porch once he changed back into street clothes. I guess she knew Mark and I needed some alone time, so we sat on the porch swing, with him gently rocking the wooden bench with his foot. The silence between us wasn't heavy, but there were things I wanted to say before he left tomorrow.

"I know it's too late for you to change your mind about going to Vietnam." My throat thickened with fear. "But promise me you won't do anything stupid, like get yourself shot."

He put his arm around my shoulders. "I promise I won't do

anything stupid, Sis." He tucked me into his side, and I rested my head on his shoulder. "But I need you to understand this is something I feel I'm supposed to do. Like a calling, of sorts."

I jerked out of his embrace and leveled a hard look at him. "People aren't called to war, Mark. They go because some politician or dictator, sitting safely in a fancy office somewhere, decided war was a better option than working things out without bloodshed."

His brow tugged. "That isn't always true, Mattie. Think of King David in the Bible. Taking lives wasn't something he wanted to do, but there are times when war is necessary. I'm not anxious to shoot at someone, but there are innocent people in South Vietnam who need help. I'm proud to be one of the Americans willing to offer it any way I can."

I wanted to argue with him, to tell him he was wrong, but I couldn't. His conviction had never wavered, and I had to admit it was admirable. I just wished he hadn't landed on the wrong side of the debate. Hadn't gone off and joined the Marines.

Hadn't felt it was okay to leave me behind.

I closed my eyes for a long moment. When my gaze met his again, I saw my brother, my twin. My wombmate. The person who knew me better than anyone and still loved me unconditionally. He'd borne my anger, my arguments, my disdain for his decision, yet he'd never fought back. He'd remained steady and kind, the same Mark I'd always known.

My chin trembled and tears filled my eyes.

"I'm proud of you, Mark," I said, my voice wobbly. "I really am. I don't agree with you, and I think it's a huge mistake for you to go to Vietnam, but I'll always love you."

"I love you too, little sis." Moisture shone in his eyes. "Promise me you won't do anything stupid while you're in Nashville, like joining the protests and getting yourself arrested."

I chuckled. "You know me too well."

He reached beside him and picked up a small book. I recognized it as the one Pastor Arnold had given him for graduation.

"The guy who wrote this, Dietrich Bonhoeffer, stood up for his beliefs back in World War II." He ran his hand over the title printed on the cover. *The Cost of Discipleship.* "Dr. Bonhoeffer was a German pastor, and he strongly disagreed with Hitler's regime. He was willing to risk his life to do what was right."

"How could a pastor fight for his beliefs yet join Hitler's army?"

"He didn't join the army. He wasn't a soldier. At least not the kind you're thinking of. He fought the lies being told to the German people by speaking truth. He was called to spread the gospel in a time and place where it wasn't welcome. And he made a lot of enemies doing so, including Hitler."

"He sounds like someone I would like to meet."

I thought my little joke would make Mark smile, but he didn't.

"Unfortunately, that isn't possible. He was arrested in 1943 and was eventually murdered in one of Hitler's concentration camps just before the allies liberated it."

This revelation stunned me. "How awful."

"The thing is, he'd come to America to teach. He could've stayed here, safe from Hitler and the Nazis, but Bonhoeffer chose to return to Germany."

"Why?" I asked. "Who would choose to live under a government run by a murderous tyrant when they could stay in the Land of the Free?"

"A man who felt called to minister to his countrymen. He knew they needed help. He once told a friend that if he'd stayed in America and didn't suffer the trials of war along with the rest of Germany, then he would have no right to participate in the reconstruction of Christianity when the war was over."

I recognized the point Mark wanted to make. "If you're trying to be a modern-day Bonhoeffer, there are better ways to do it than going to Vietnam. You're going as a soldier carrying a gun, not a preacher carrying a Bible."

"Can't I be both?"

His question startled me. "I've never heard you mention anything about being a preacher. It's always been football, football, football. You wanted to play and then coach."

He gave a slight shrug. "I still love football, and maybe I'll coach someday, but right now, I'm a soldier. That doesn't mean I can't share the gospel with people though. Pastor Arnold once said we don't need to go to seminary to talk to others about Jesus. The disciples were regular guys—fishermen, mostly—and they went out and changed the world by spreading the Good News. I figure I'm a pretty regular guy too. I want God to use me, like he used them, if he's willing."

I suddenly felt ashamed of the hard time I'd given him since he joined the Marines. "I guess I can't argue with that."

He handed the book to me. "I want you to keep this while I'm gone. I think you'll like it." He grinned. "You wanna know something else I have in common with Dietrich Bonhoeffer?"

"What?"

"He had a twin sister. Her name was Sabine."

"Really? What happened to her?"

"Her husband was Jewish, so they escaped to England with their children once Hitler came into power."

I studied the cover of the book. "I wonder what Sabine thought about Dietrich putting himself in harm's way, especially after he died because of it." I looked up. "There isn't anything wrong with safety, you know. People can still speak up for what's right without putting themselves in danger."

"I know." He took my hand and locked fingers with me. "But sometimes, someone has to do the hard things and make sacrifices to make sure the people they care about are safe."

Later, when the house was dark and still, I lay in bed, thinking about what he'd said. I knew on a certain level he was right. For centuries, men and women had fought for what they believed in. Freedom, religious rights, family. But Mark's going to Vietnam was different. There was no fear of that country's communistic government taking over the world the way people feared Hitler and the Japanese Empire would during World War II. I knew China was allied with the Vietcong, and that President Johnson was adamant in his support of the South Vietnamese, but I didn't agree with him regarding the use of American servicemen like Mark to police the tiny country.

Why couldn't Mark see that I was right this time?

I must've fallen asleep sometime in the wee hours of morning because I woke to the smell of fried bacon. A glance at my wristwatch told me it was a little before seven. Mark needed to be at the bus station at nine.

Tears rolled down my cheeks into my hair.

This was really happening.

My brother—my twin, my other half—was leaving to go to the opposite side of the world. We wouldn't see him for a year or more. I recalled what Paula said last night about the possibility of Mark being different when he returned from war. Would her worries come true?

By the time I made my way downstairs, Mama, Mark, and Dad had finished eating and were sitting at the table, drinking coffee, and talking about a horse Dad wanted to sell.

"Good morning, Miss Sunshine," Mark said with a grin. It was his usual greeting, especially on school mornings when he'd be up and dressed and ready to go before I even dragged myself out of bed.

Mama stood. "Do you want some breakfast, Mattie? There's time before we need to leave for town."

My stomach was in knots. The thought of food made me nauseous. "No, thanks."

She gave me an empathetic nod.

The next hour flew by, with Mama making sure Mark took this item or that. Dad didn't go out to the barn after breakfast, as was his custom, but stayed in the kitchen, a solemn look on his face. I was still frustrated with him, but it was too late for arguments.

By eight thirty, we were loaded into Dad's pickup truck. Mark sat on his big green duffel bag in the bed, with his back up against the window. Mama sat in the middle, which allowed me to watch Mark rather than the passing scenery.

Was he going to miss me as much as I would miss him? We'd never been separated for very long. Since the beginning of our existence, we'd been together nearly every day. What would I do without him?

Too soon, we arrived at the bus station. Nash stood outside the terminal building, a duffel bag identical to Mark's at his feet. Neither his mom nor his dad was with him.

We piled out of the truck. Dad went inside to the ticket counter and came back with a one-way ticket to Atlanta. He didn't smile when he handed the ticket to Mark, and I wondered if he might finally regret Mark's decision and his role in it.

Paula and Pastor Arnold joined us as we waited. Pastor offered a prayer for Mark and Nash just as a bus rolled into the terminal, spewing black exhaust into the warm morning air.

Nash thanked my parents for everything they'd done for him through the years. Dad shook his hand and Mama gave him a motherly hug.

When he faced me, he said, "Take care of yourself, Mattie."

"You too."

Then it was time to say goodbye to Mark.

As he folded me into a fierce embrace, I couldn't stop the tears. "I love you, Mark," I whispered. "Please come home."

"I love you, too, Sis. Write to me, okay?" he said, his voice choked with emotion.

I could barely watch as he hugged our parents, then kissed Paula goodbye as tears streamed down her cheeks.

He boarded the bus with one last wave.

The driver closed the door, put the big vehicle into gear, and carried away the most important person in my world.

I knew life would never be the same again.

TWELVE

GUNTHER

CAMP FORREST, TENNESSEE
FEBRUARY 1942

Gunther knew he should be grateful to have a job as an orderly in the military hospital at Camp Forrest, but there was no pride in the position. He was essentially a prisoner of war, with little choice but to comply with his captors. From the moment he was arrested, he'd tried to gain back the freedom stolen from him, but to no avail. Since arriving in Tennessee, he and the others were told they were not being held on criminal charges, but reality said otherwise.

The evidence declared they were dangerous inmates.

High barbed-wire fences surrounded the small huts where they lived, six men crammed into a space barely fit for three or four. Armed soldiers stood guard at the gate and in watchtowers twenty-four hours a day. Gunther and his fellow internees had neither the freedom to move about the camp nor access to legal help to fight for their release. Even now, a soldier carrying a rifle walked behind Gunther, watching while he pushed the wheelchair of an injured young man to the building where the X-ray machine was housed.

The chair bumped over a rough place on the wooden walkway, causing the young man to curse.

"Watch where you're goin'," he said, his southern accent thick. The man glared at Gunther over his shoulder. "My leg's already broken. I don't need some lousy German makin' it worse."

Gunther clenched his jaw. "My apologies."

He continued to push the chair forward until they reached the building. The ramp to the door was steep, requiring Gunther to pull the chair up backwards. Once again, the wheels hit an uneven plank.

"I don't know why the Army lets you people work on base," the patient bellowed. Foul words followed. "Every one of you should be shipped back to Germany."

Gunther's grip on the handles tightened. He wished he could dump the chair over the side of the ramp with the rude soldier in it. He glanced at the armed guard. Clearly, he'd heard the cursing and callous remarks, yet even though he outranked the patient, he obviously had no plans to intervene.

When they reached the landing, Gunther shoved the chair through the door, ignoring the complaints of the young man. He parked him in the crowded waiting area and turned his back, fighting to suppress his anger.

How he longed to tell the arrogant soldier exactly what he thought of him and his fellow Americans. How the "land of the free" wasn't free to everyone. But Gunther knew if he spoke his mind, he would likely lose his job. And although being an orderly was a menial and thankless position, it provided an escape from the barbed-wire prison.

After a minute or two, his hot anger cooled.

The insults were nothing new. Some of the guards on Ellis

Island had the same opinion of Gunther as this man did. It didn't matter to them that he'd done nothing wrong. It didn't matter that he'd been a student, studying medicine, with the hope of becoming a doctor. A doctor who could tend to this man's broken leg.

None of that was important to Americans like him. The only thing they knew about Gunther was that he was German. And that made him the enemy.

The main door opened, and an attractive woman entered.

Gunther recognized her as the young woman who'd bumped into him the other day. He couldn't recall her name, but he would never forget her smile. Sadly, it had disappeared the moment she realized he was one of the German detainees. She hadn't said anything, but he'd seen it in her hazel eyes.

Gunther watched her now as she walked to the receptionist's desk. The two women were chatting when a nurse arrived and called for the patient with the broken leg. The woman turned, and her gaze met Gunther's.

Her brow lifted, but after a moment, she offered a small nod, indicating she remembered him. Gunther returned the gesture.

"Don't you have ears, Fritz?" the soldier in the wheelchair hollered. "The nurse called my name. Get movin'."

The woman's eyes widened, and embarrassment washed over Gunther. He wished she hadn't been there to witness his shame.

"Can't you hear me, Fritz? I said, get movin'!"

The patient's loud voice silenced the crowded room. Everyone's attention focused on them.

Gunther took hold of the chair's handles and began to push. He kept his eyes downcast as they neared the desk.

"Sir? May I have a word with you?"

Both Gunther and the patient turned to look at her.

"You talkin' to me, pretty lady?" the young man drawled, then grinned. "I've gotta get this leg of mine tended to, but after that I'll have all the time in the world for you."

The woman, however, didn't smile. "I wasn't speaking to you." She focused her attention on Gunther, and her expression softened. "It's Mr. Schneider, correct?"

Gunther nodded, stunned that she knew his name.

"We met the other day. I'm Ava Delaney. I work for Colonel Foster. I'm updating personnel files." She held up a small stack of folders. "Yours is one of them. When you're finished here, would it be possible for me to ask you some questions?"

Gunther stared at her, at a loss for words. The young soldier, however, had plenty.

"Ma'am, this fella ain't American. He's one of them enemy aliens the Army brought in. You best keep your distance. He could be a Nazi, for all we know."

Gunther thought Miss Delaney would realize the mistake she'd made by approaching him, but she leveled a severe look at the soldier, not Gunther.

"Colonel Foster does not tolerate disrespect in his hospital. To anyone." She turned to the armed guard. "It is your duty to see to it that this man treats *everyone* with respect. Do I make myself clear?"

"Yes, ma'am," the man said.

The patient's face grew dark. "I'm a soldier in the United States Army. You got no right to tell me—"

"That's enough, soldier." The guard moved to stand between him and Miss Delaney. He looked at Gunther. "Get this man into X-ray. When you're finished, you can meet with the lady."

Gunther nodded.

A quick look at Miss Delaney told him she agreed with the plan.

He pushed the chair forward. The angry patient remained sullen until they reached their destination. Gunther and a nurse helped him from the wheelchair onto a raised padded table, with a metal contraption hovering above. When the nurse stepped out of the room, Gunther turned to follow, but the young man grabbed his arm and yanked him back.

"You better watch yourself, Fritz," he said in a low voice, his lips curved in a snarl. "No broken leg is gonna stop me from teachin' you a lesson next time we meet."

Gunther jerked his arm from the man's grip and left the room without a backwards glance.

Miss Delaney was waiting for him when he and the guard returned to the reception area.

"I'll try not to take up too much of your time." She offered a cautious smile.

"Thanks to your government, I have nothing but time on my hands."

An uncertain expression marred her face, and Gunther wished he could take his terse words back. His anger with the injured man had gotten the better of him, and he shouldn't take it out on her.

"I thought we could talk in the mess hall next door," she said to both Gunther and the guard. "That will afford us more privacy."

With it settled, the guard led the way. Lunch would be served soon, and aromas from the kitchen greeted them when they entered the long building. Rows of tables and chairs filled the space.

Miss Delaney sat at the nearest table. Gunther took the seat opposite her, while the guard remained near the door.

"I must apologize, Miss Delaney," Gunther said. "I was rude a moment ago when you were merely being polite by offering not to take too much of my time."

Her serious gaze studied him. Gunther wondered what she saw. The enemy?

"You don't need to apologize." She gave a slight shrug. "I don't actually understand why you and the others are being detained."

"Nor do we."

She seemed surprised by his response. "Didn't they tell you?"

Gunther saw her earnestness, so he answered without sarcasm. "The authorities arrived at my apartment in New York City and took me to Ellis Island, where I was held for a month before I was given a hearing. No charges were brought against me. Only questions," he said, shaking his head. "But they didn't listen to my answers. They didn't care that I was innocent of whatever it was they thought me guilty of. The other detainees have similar stories."

Sympathy shone in her eyes. "I'm sorry. I had no idea."

The guard approached. "Ma'am, I need you to finish with this man so he can get back to work."

Miss Delaney nodded. "Yes, of course." She opened a brown file folder and took out a single sheet of paper. With pencil in hand, she looked up at Gunther. "State your name and where you were born."

For a moment, Gunther's mind flashed back to the interrogation in New York. The government men who came to his apartment asked the same questions. Had Miss Delaney been sent here to trick him? Perhaps they hoped his responses would be different if a pretty woman asked them.

"Gunther Schneider. I was born in Germany."

He watched her closely to gauge her reaction, but she simply jotted down the information.

"What is your occupation?"

"I was a student at Columbia medical school, studying to be a doctor, before I was arrested."

Her brow rose. "A doctor? That's wonderful."

Gunther glanced at the guard, then back to her. "It was, but now the question is, will I be allowed to return to my studies?"

Three men in military garb came through the door, chatting as they entered. They glanced at Gunther and Miss Delaney but continued to the long counter at the far end of the room where lunch foods were set out, filled their plates, and took a seat at one of the tables.

Miss Delaney returned her attention to Gunther. "We better hurry, before the room fills with hungry personnel."

She proceeded to ask more questions. His age. His religious background. His family. Gunther provided the answers, although he didn't elaborate on Rolf or his military involvement in Germany.

"That's all the information we need." She returned the sheet of paper to the folder.

Gunther stood. "Thank you, Miss Delaney."

"It's actually Mrs. Delaney."

"My apologies."

She nodded and seemed about to say something when a ruckus arose from the table where the soldiers dined.

"Help!" one of them hollered.

Gunther turned to see a man lying on the wood floor, with the other two gathered around.

"Someone help him. He isn't breathing."

The guard hurried to the group. He conferred with the men, then approached Gunther and Mrs. Delaney. "I'm going for a doctor," he said. He gave Gunther a hard look. "You stay here. Understand?"

At Gunther's nod, the guard ran out the door.

"I hope that young man will be all right."

Mrs. Delaney's worried voice brought Gunther back to the situation. The two men continued to hover over their friend, but no one was doing anything to help him. If he truly wasn't breathing, Gunther knew these minutes were vital.

"He needs chest compressions and air to his lungs." Mrs. Delaney's wide eyes met his. "He won't make it if the doctor doesn't arrive soon."

Her frightened gaze darted between the man on the floor and back to Gunther. "Can you help him?"

A memory flashed through Gunther's mind.

He'd watched Dr. Sonnenberg perform a lifesaving technique

at the hospital with positive results, but he'd never attempted it himself. "Perhaps."

Before he knew what was happening, Mrs. Delaney took him by the arm and tugged him with her. The two worried soldiers looked up.

"This man can help your friend until the doctor arrives," she said. "Move aside."

The men looked skeptical as they eyed Gunther's green prisoner uniform, but they finally stepped away to make room for him.

Gunther knelt next to the man. He felt for a pulse and listened for breathing, finding neither. Planting his palm in the middle of the man's chest, he began to administer quick pushes, ten or so, before he blew into the man's mouth. He repeated the procedure two more times, then listened for a heartbeat.

Gunther had just begun another round of chest compressions when two things happened. The unconscious man gasped for air, and a horde of medical personnel and the guard rushed into the building.

"What are you doing?" The doctor who'd yelled at Gunther earlier now gave him a hard shove, causing him to lose balance and land on his backside. "Get away from this man."

The guard grabbed Gunther by the arm and yanked him up. "I told you to stay put," he growled. "I oughta lock you up—"

"Stop this." Mrs. Delaney's shout gained everyone's attention. "Mr. Schneider has studied medicine. He was trying to save this man's life."

Right on cue, the patient groaned and opened his eyes. The doctor's attention shifted to him.

"It's true," said one of the men who'd been dining with the soldier when he collapsed. He met Gunther's gaze. "You saved Joe. He wasn't breathing until you started working on him."

In the next minutes, the patient was loaded onto a stretcher and carried away. His buddies went back to their meal, but not before each of them thanked Gunther for what he'd done for their friend.

"Let's go," the guard said. He didn't smile, but he also didn't seem as unfriendly as he'd been before.

Gunther turned to Mrs. Delaney and found her watching him, her eyes shining.

"That was amazing, Mr. Schneider. You truly did save that man's life."

Her praise embarrassed him. "Anyone could have done it, given the correct training."

She offered her hand. "It's been a pleasure meeting you, Mr. Schneider."

Gunther stared at her. It took a moment to recover, and when he did, he gently grasped her soft hand. "The pleasure was mine, Mrs. Delaney."

She gave a shy smile.

Gunther followed the guard out the door. Sunshine poured over him as they crossed the grounds and headed for the hospital, but it was Mrs. Delaney's smile that filled him with genuine happiness for the first time in weeks.

THIRTEEN

MATTIE

DELANEY HORSE FARM

NOVEMBER 1969

Tomorrow was Thanksgiving Day.

I sat at the kitchen table with a small box that held Mama's recipes, each written on an index card in her neat handwriting, looking for inspiration. The special meal had always been Mama's favorite. She'd cook a feast and invite friends to join us. I felt obligated to continue the tradition. Not because we had anything to celebrate, but because she couldn't come downstairs and prepare the meal herself.

Memories from last year's dinner drifted over me.

It had been a disaster.

I'd come home from school the day after the hateful telegram arrived, telling us of Mark's death. It took the military two weeks to get his body back to Tennessee. Mama wanted her son buried near home rather than the national cemetery in Nashville or faraway Washington, and a service was planned, complete with a seven-gun salute. We'd laid Mark to rest on a Wednesday the week before Thanksgiving, and it felt utterly wrong to go forward with a meal that was meant to remind us of our blessings. Mama had insisted Mark would want us to, but when Pastor Arnold referred to Mark as a hero during grace, I lost control.

"Mark isn't a hero!" I screamed in response, drawing everyone's shocked attention.

I'd spent the wee hours of the morning in my room, crying and consuming an entire bottle of Jack Daniel's. My head throbbed, and my stomach rebelled at the aromas, but I'd let Mama coax me downstairs.

That was a huge mistake.

"Mark is a victim. You all killed him." I staggered over to Dad and dared him to look me in the eye. "You sent him to war. You had no right to encourage my brother to go to Vietnam. To sacrifice him on the altar of politics and money. I will never forgive you for what you've done."

Mama'd hurried to pull me from the room and escort me back upstairs. I saw disappointment and sorrow in her eyes as she stood in the doorway, but I ignored it.

"Mattie, you aren't the only one who loved Mark. We all miss him," she said, sniffling.

To my shame, I slammed the door in her face. The following morning, I boarded a bus for California.

A howling wind rattled the kitchen window, bringing me out of my miserable thoughts. The thermometer on the porch said the temperature was thirty-three degrees, but I suspected the windchill was in the twenties. Dad left the house early this morning to check on the horses. I'd caught glimpses of him and Nash coming and going as they cared for the animals. The disagreeable weather was yet one more reason we should forget Thanksgiving Day. I'd rather eat bologna sandwiches and call it done.

I glanced in the direction of the stairs, just out of sight from where I sat.

Mama wasn't doing well. She'd been in terrible pain the past week, which meant more medicine. While the tiny white pills took the pain away, they took Mama away too. She'd sleep for hours, and in the short periods she was awake, her speech was slow and difficult.

I thought back to my meeting with Dr. Monahan. It hadn't gone as I'd hoped. He had, just as Nash predicted, told me the same thing he'd told my parents: the cancer was too far advanced. New medicines and treatments were on the horizon, but they would come too late to help Mama. When I pushed back, declaring the need to take her to a specialist in Nashville, the man who'd tended my birth spoke bluntly.

"Mattie, there comes a time when we have to accept that life and death are not in our hands. We in the medical profession do our best, but we aren't God. If I thought the doctors in Nashville could save your mom, I would've taken her there myself. The best thing you can do now is spend time with her and make her as comfortable as possible."

I left his office and cried all the way home.

With a sigh, I closed the lid on the recipe box and stood.

Why bother with Thanksgiving? What did we have to be thankful for? Mark was gone, and if the doctors were right, Mama wasn't long for this world. Although Nash volunteered to go to town yesterday and came home with all the usual fixings, the very idea of preparing the meal without Mama's help made me want to chuck Tom Turkey in the garbage and forget the holiday.

I made my way upstairs and tiptoed into Mama's room, but she wasn't sleeping. Her eyes were glassy, and I guessed she'd taken another pill. It wouldn't be long before she was asleep again.

"There's my girl." Although her voice was rough from disuse, her smile was genuine.

"Can I get you anything, Mama? Some water or something to eat?" I came forward and sat on the edge of the bed.

She reached for my hand. "You're all I need. Stay and talk a while."

I curled my fingers around hers, swollen to nearly twice their size. Dr. Monahan assured me the swelling was a side effect from the medicine and showed me some massaging techniques that might help. I used one of them now while we chatted about the weather, the horses, and, finally, the upcoming holiday where I confessed I felt inadequate for the job.

"I remember the first Thanksgiving dinner I cooked after your father and I married," Mama said, her eyes half-closed and a soft smile on her lips. "Granny had moved out of the main house into the cabin and declared it no longer her responsibility to cook the meal. I'd never roasted a turkey before, but I was willing to try." She gave a weak chuckle. "As you might guess, it didn't turn out very well. I didn't know you had to baste the bird often to keep it from drying out."

I gently rubbed her arm up and down. "Granny was always so mean to everyone. She didn't even like Dad, her own son."

Sadness washed over her features. "Mattie, there are things you need to know. To understand. Our family . . . it isn't what you've always believed."

I stopped massaging her arm, trying to make sense of what she was saying. "What are you talking about?"

She closed her eyes, her face squinched in the way that told me she was hurting inside. When the episode passed, she looked at me with such urgency in her gaze, it set me on edge.

"I want to show you something." She motioned to the trunk in the corner. The same one she'd been rummaging through the day she dug out our baby things. "There's a box with some letters in it. Can you find it for me, please?"

I knew the box she meant. Although I'd rather not travel down memory lane by going through the trunk's contents, the task seemed important to her.

The hinges on the lid of the trunk creaked when I opened it. I knew exactly where to look for the old shoebox and soon placed it on the bed beside her. However, she didn't open it right away. She ran a hand over the top, as though it held something valuable.

"So many memories," she whispered as her eyelids drifted closed.

I waited for her to continue, but when she remained still, I said, "Mama?"

She struggled to open her eyes. "I'm so tired, dear. Take this." She pushed the box toward me. "Read the letters. You need to know who you are. Where you come from. You won't understand everything in them but read them. All of them. I'll explain later."

The strange request puzzled me. What could a box of old letters have to do with me? And then there was my father's reaction to seeing me with it the day Mama prowled through the trunk. "Are you sure Dad won't mind me looking at these things?"

Her eyes closed. "He might, but it's time for secrets to come into the light."

She fell silent then. Her breathing told me she was asleep. I waited a full minute to be certain she didn't wake up before I quietly left the room. I carried the box across the hall and set it on my desk. When I lifted the lid, the contents were the same as they'd been the day I'd returned it to the trunk. The old Bible lay on top of two stacks of yellowed envelopes, each tied with string.

What secrets was Mama talking about? How could knowing them help me understand who I was?

The letters apparently held the key, but a more important question was, did I *want* to unlock what could amount to a closet full of family skeletons? Would it even matter, especially if Mama didn't get any better? I'd purposefully avoided thinking about what I would do if she died, but I knew one thing for certain. Staying in Tullahoma was out of the question. The mysteries this shoebox held, therefore, were irrelevant.

I closed the lid to the box and shoved it under my bed.

Hopefully Mama would forget she gave it to me.

I had no intention of reminding her about it.

• • •

I awoke Thanksgiving morning to find three inches of snow on the ground, with more coming by the looks of heavy clouds in the sky.

"Great."

I crawled out of my warm bed and looked out the frost-covered window. The scene outside was ideal for the front of a cheery Christmas card but little else.

A shiver raced through me as I threw on an old sweatshirt with *Tullahoma High School Debate Team* printed on the front, and a pair of bell-bottom jeans I'd brought with me from California. While the furnace in the basement did a decent job of heating most of the farmhouse, a draft from the old coal-burning fireplace in my room did its best to turn me into a block of ice every winter.

When I came out of the bathroom, the door to my parents' bedroom was open. I tiptoed over to peek in. Mama was tucked snuggly in bed, asleep. I'd heard her and Dad stirring during the night, their voices slightly raised, but I hadn't been able to make out the words. It had almost sounded as though they were arguing about something, which was unusual. Not only was it an odd time to have any kind of discussion, but the truth is they rarely argued. At least, not in front of Mark and me.

I went downstairs and found Dad and Nash sipping coffee at the table. Jake lay on a rag rug near the heating vent in the floor, his head on his paws and his lone eye on me.

"Good morning."

The men responded likewise. I assumed they'd already eaten,

since a clean frying pan and two plates sat in the dish rack, drying. Nash was good about cleaning up after himself, which I appreciated.

"I guess I'll get started on the dinner preparations," I said with little enthusiasm. Between the foul weather and the daunting task of fixing a huge meal by myself, there wasn't much about this day I was going to enjoy.

I'd just opened the refrigerator to take out the turkey when Dad cleared his throat in a way that meant he had something to say. I glanced at him and waited.

"With the roads iced over, I doubt the Arnolds will be able to make it out to the farm today." He met my gaze. "I know the meal is a lot of work, especially without your mother to help. If you'd rather not go to the trouble, we can make do with simple fare."

I straightened.

Both his offer and his understanding of how overwhelmed I felt surprised me. I glanced at Nash, who nodded his agreement.

"What about Mama?" I said. "She always looks forward to Thanksgiving. Won't she be disappointed if we skip it?"

Dad stared into his coffee mug for a long moment. "Her disappointment is that she can't prepare the food herself. Being surrounded by her family and friends was always more important than what we ate. Cooking was her way of showing us love."

I knew he was right. Mama genuinely loved people. Even though it was just the four of us after Granny passed, she made every day special. Neighbors and friends from church often graced our table through the years. Fourth of July cookouts at the farm were lively events. Everyone brought a dish to share, but Mama's barbecued beef brisket was the star of the show.

A twinge of shame pricked me.

It would be easy to simply ignore the holiday—that's what I'd wanted to do from the get-go—but now, after Dad's reminder about Mama's heart for people, I suddenly felt differently, way deep inside. More . . . charitable, I guess, which admittedly wasn't something I came by naturally.

Maybe there was a tiny bit of my mother's goodness in me, after all.

"Let's have the big dinner," I said, surprising the two men as well as myself. "For Mama."

Dad pressed his lips together and nodded.

"After we get the horses settled, I'm happy to help," Nash said. His lips curved in a lopsided smile. "I can't promise it'll be edible, but I'm willing to try."

I shrugged. "I'm not making any promises either."

"Well, I will," Dad said, a rare glint in his eyes. "I promise to eat whatever you two come up with."

Even I had to chuckle at that.

My dark mood lifted, although the heavy clouds outside did not. After the men bundled in coats and gloves and left the house, I sat at the table with my own cup of coffee, amazed at what had just taken place. I'd come downstairs, depressed, and dreading the day, yet a surge of unexpected excitement and anticipation rushed through me now. Not about cooking a huge meal, but because I knew it would please my mother. And, if I were honest, my father, too.

That truly was a Thanksgiving miracle.

With a completely different mindset, I began preparations for the meal. Tom Turkey was in the oven, filled with Mama's famous sage stuffing, by the time Nash returned to the house. A blast of cold air came in with him. Earlier, he'd asked if Jake could stay in the kitchen with me, voicing concern for the dog's arthritic bones in the cold weather. Now, Jake slowly stood and ambled over to Nash, his tail wagging.

Nash bent to pet the dog. "I appreciate you letting him stay inside. It's brutal out there."

I sat at the table, peeling a mound of potatoes. "He slept the whole time. I didn't even remember he was here until just now."

Nash moved to the sink where a stack of dirty pots and pans filled the basin. "I'll take care of these," he said. He ran water and added soap, but when I glanced his way again, I noticed the cuff of his flannel shirt was getting wet.

I frowned.

Should I volunteer to roll up his sleeve? I didn't want to offend him. From what I'd noticed since arriving back in Tullahoma, Nash was stubbornly independent. He wouldn't let having one arm prevent him from accomplishing whatever he set his mind on.

But a wet sleeve would be uncomfortable, especially when he went back outside.

I stood and walked over to him. "Let me roll up your sleeve so it won't get soaked."

Surprise registered in his eyes before he removed his hand from the soapy water, patted it on a dish towel, then extended it toward me.

"Thanks."

I nodded and set about folding the damp material until it reached the bend in his arm. I couldn't help but notice how muscled his forearm felt beneath my fingers, with his biceps bulging above. Because he had to do everything with this one arm, it needed to be strong. I'd become so used to seeing him go about his work without slowing down, it was easy to forget he'd lost an arm in the war.

With the task taken care of, I returned to the table without looking at him. I didn't want to make a big deal of it, but the nervous quiver in my belly after being so near him had me confused. I'd never been attracted to Nash. Never. He was simply Mark's friend. I'd lost touch with Rusty Shaw after graduation, which hadn't left me heartbroken in the least. And even though I'd been with Clay the past six months, he'd made it clear marriage wasn't something he was interested in.

We worked in silence. When the dishes were washed and put away, he asked, "What's next?" He glanced at the stove. "The turkey already smells good. Should I baste it?"

I'd completely forgotten about the basting.

"Shoot!" I huffed. "Mama just told me a story last night about the first time she cooked the Thanksgiving meal. She didn't know she was supposed to baste the turkey and it turned out awful."

Nash grinned. "We don't want that to happen."

He dug around in a drawer of cooking utensils and pulled out a strange looking tubelike item with a bulb on one end. I couldn't remember ever seeing the thing before. I watched as he slid his hand into an oven mitt, opened the oven door, and proceeded to squeeze turkey juices over the top of the big, browning bird.

"How do you even know how to do that?" I asked, impressed.

"I used to watch my mom every year." He closed the oven and removed the mitt. "We never had much, but every Thanksgiving, Mom would splurge and get a turkey. My sister and I always wanted to be present when she opened the oven to baste it. I can still remember how good it smelled."

Regret came with his words.

I couldn't remember ever watching Mama do such a thing. Where had I been all those Thanksgivings while she was in the kitchen, cooking for hours on end?

Nash went to the cellar to retrieve a couple jars of Mama's canned green beans while I started on the dough for her mouthwatering yeast rolls. We planned to eat around four o'clock in the afternoon, so there was plenty of time to let the dough rise in the warm kitchen.

He'd just returned when we heard Mama call from upstairs. My hands were covered in dough and flour, so Nash volunteered to check on her. When he returned, he said she was awake and needed my help with the bedpan we'd begun to use now that it was getting difficult for her to walk to the bathroom in the hallway.

As I washed my hands, I glanced at Nash, who was already cleaning up my floury mess. "I don't think I've told you this, but . . . thank you." My throat tightened, and I couldn't say more.

He met my gaze. "I'm the one who's grateful. Your folks took me in and gave me a purpose when I didn't think I had one anymore."

I nodded, then made my way upstairs.

After I helped Mama use the bedpan, I sat in the chair next to her. "We have the turkey in the oven, stuffed and filling the house with delicious aromas."

She offered a weak smile. "I can smell it. Don't forget to baste it," she said with a wink.

I told her about Nash and his memories of his mother cooking the holiday meal. Then I confessed my own regret about my lack of such memories.

I reached for her hand, finding it icy. "I'm sorry I never helped you, Mama."

"I was always happiest in the kitchen, cooking for my family. You kids had better things to do, like build forts and ride horses and enjoy God's beautiful world."

She wanted to hear all about the meal preparations. After I'd told her every detail, she changed the subject.

"Have you read the letters from the box yet?"

I hedged. "I haven't had time, what with Thanksgiving and everything I needed to get done."

She nodded then winced. "I believe I need one of my pills, dear."

I hurried to comply.

After she'd settled again, she closed her eyes. "Your father doesn't know I kept them after all these years."

I knew she was talking about the letters. "What's this about, Mama? Why are the letters so important?"

Her eyes remained closed. "You need to know. Mark too. He shouldn't go to war without knowing."

I frowned.

Was the medicine messing with her mind? "What should I know?"

But she didn't respond.

I waited to see if she would rouse, but the pill had already taken hold. Dr. Monahan had prescribed a stronger dosage after Dad called him on Tuesday to let our family physician know Mama's pain was increasing with each passing day. I'd used my share of drugs while I was in California, with the desire to leave reality behind, but the little pills Mama took removed her from me. I didn't like that at all.

To our disappointment, Mama slept through most of the day. Pastor and Mrs. Arnold braved the cold and the icy roads and arrived right on time. I hadn't seen them since last Thanksgiving, when I'd been drunk and angry, yet they both greeted me with a warm hug and seemed genuinely happy to see me.

The dinner turned out better than I'd expected, with juicy turkey and lump-free gravy. The two empty chairs, however, reminded me holidays would never be the same. I missed Mark intensely. I could almost hear him cracking jokes about my cooking or challenging me to see who could eat the most rolls. Mama's absence, too, felt heavy, especially knowing she was upstairs in a drug-induced oblivion.

I'd just served everyone some of Mrs. Arnold's pumpkin pie when her husband brought up the war, a topic the rest of us had avoided.

"I read an article in the *Reader's Digest* the other day about the many POWs being held in Vietnam, and how we can help them." He wore a pained expression. "I can't imagine what those men are going through."

Everyone but me gave a solemn nod. Not because I didn't care about the men being held in a foreign country halfway around the world, but because providing them help should have come years ago. Back when the decision was made to send them there in the first place.

"Thankfully President Nixon has promised to withdraw our troops as soon as possible and bring all of our boys home."

I stared at him, stunned. "Are you kidding me?"

All heads turned in my direction, but I kept my focus on the pastor. "Nixon got up in front of TV cameras and told the nation a bunch of lies. He has no intention of ending the war anytime soon."

"Mattie," Dad said from his place at the head of the table, warning in the one word.

I faced him, frustrated. "It's true. Nixon couldn't care less about *our boys*. The coward admitted he wouldn't bring them home right now because it would be 'the first defeat in our Nation's history' and that it would hurt Asia's confidence in American politics. What he's saying is that he cares more about Asia's confidence than he does the thousands of Americans who put themselves in danger over there every day. Including those poor POWs."

I glanced at Nash to see if he would join the conversation. We hadn't talked about it since I arrived home, but surely his views on the whole Vietnam issue had changed since he left for war. He'd lost an arm and his best friend to the madness.

But he didn't speak up. He simply stared at the pie on his plate.

"I believe President Nixon cares about all our military personnel overseas," Pastor said, keeping his tone even and calm. "But he has to think of the broader picture, and the repercussions of what will happen to South Vietnam if the United States pulls out. The polls show that most Americans approve of the way President Nixon is handling the war."

I shook my head with disgust. "You sound just like him and all the other Washington politicians. Nixon had the audacity to refer to people like me as a *vocal minority* because we won't stay silent like the rest of you sheep. In fact, I—"

Dad stood with so much force, the glassware on the table rattled. "That's enough." His voice echoed off the floral-papered walls. "We know how you feel about the war, but that's no reason to be rude to our guests." He looked at the pastor. "I'm sorry, Reverend. Mattie is too quick to share her opinions."

My face flamed.

Dad retook his seat.

Pastor Arnold didn't look angry. "I don't blame Mattie and the young people like her for speaking out for what they believe. You and I," he turned to me, "want the same thing. We want the war to end. But neither of us has been to Vietnam and seen firsthand what's going on over there." He faced Nash. "What do you think, son? Is it time for the United States to pull out?"

My eyes fastened on Nash, willing him to tell Pastor Arnold the truth.

After a long silence, he cleared his throat. "I think mistakes have been made since our involvement in Vietnam began," he said, giving me hope. "But I also think it would be a mistake to remove all US presence from the country right now." He glanced at me. "The people of South Vietnam need help. They're as much prisoners of the Vietcong as our boys in those prisons are. Until the job is finished and the South Vietnamese army can protect the people, we're needed there."

He held my gaze, almost in challenge. My throat tightened with angry tears, but I wouldn't give any of them the satisfaction of seeing me cry.

I stood, snatched up the plate with my half-eaten pie on it, and stomped into the kitchen.

If they all thought of me as an ignorant child, I might as well act like one.

Low voices came from the dining room, but I didn't care if I was the subject of their conversation. One of these days, when it was too late, they'd have to acknowledge I was right. Even Nash.

Mrs. Arnold came into the kitchen, a look of empathy on her face.

"The meal was delicious, Mattie. Your mother would be proud." She walked to the sink and deposited the three plates she carried into the sudsy water.

She could have said so many things to me, but her kindness worked to loosen the grip anger had on my tongue.

"Thank you." I heaved a sigh. "I suppose I should apologize for speaking my mind."

She faced me. "It's never wrong to express an opinion on something you feel passionately about." She laid a gentle hand on my arm. "You and your family have suffered a great loss because of the war. I don't think anyone can blame you for feeling so strongly about how things are being handled in Washington."

I appreciated her understanding. "Does your husband know you don't agree with him?"

"Oh, I agree with him, for the most part." At my confused look, she continued. "We live in a wonderful country where we enjoy the kind of freedom millions of people in the world don't have. Communism strips citizens of the right to choose for themselves. Those living under it are little more than pawns. The North Vietnamese government has done terrible things under communism. If South Vietnam falls to them, they will suffer the same fate."

"But it isn't right to send our young men over there to police what is essentially a civil war," I said, keeping my voice lowered so Dad wouldn't hear.

She gave me a patient look. "Would you have said the same thing about the war in Europe? President Roosevelt kept the United States out of that war far longer than he should have, in my opinion. Hundreds of thousands of innocent lives were lost before our troops crossed the ocean."

I saw her point. "But the war in Europe was different. Japan attacked us, and Hitler wanted to rule the world."

"I don't think the people of South Vietnam would agree with you. War looks the same, no matter the circumstances. Innocent people are suffering because of the Vietcong's determination to rule the entire region."

Pastor Arnold entered the kitchen then and our conversation ended. The couple went upstairs to visit Mama before they took their leave. I carried up a plate of food, and although she ate a small helping of the special meal, I could tell Mama was in pain. Another white pill soon took her away.

Exhaustion—both mental and physical—rolled through me. I was more than ready to end this day. Nash and Dad had gone back to work in the barns after the Arnolds left, and it was dark when they returned, with Jake leading the way. I noticed Nash carried a bundle of personal belongings and Dad carried a dog bed.

"The furnace is out again in the cabin," he said at my silent question. "It's too cold without heat. I told Nash he could sleep in Mark's old room."

I stiffened. "Mark's room?"

Mama called from upstairs just then, and Dad hurried away, leaving Nash and me alone. I stalked to the sink and took a pot from the drying rack, banged it loudly, and slammed the cabinet door as I put it away. I repeated the process until the rack was empty, then wiped the already-clean counters with vicious swipes, all while Nash stood and watched.

"You have a problem with me staying in Mark's room?"

My jaw clenched, and I met his gaze. "I didn't say a word."

He scoffed. "You didn't have to. I can see it in your face."

I hurled the washrag into the sink and folded my arms. "All right. I do have a problem with you staying there. It's *Mark's* room. Dad had no right to . . . to . . . give it away."

"He didn't give it away, Mattie. He offered to let me sleep there rather than being out in the cold. Would you prefer I stayed in the cabin without heat?"

I scowled. "Of course not. But you can sleep on the couch in the den until the furnace is fixed."

He took a step toward me and leveled a hard look into my eyes. "Mark doesn't need his room anymore, Mattie. He's dead."

Before I knew what was happening, my palm connected with his cheek with a loud *thwack*.

Shock filled his eyes, and Jake let out a fierce growl.

I stared at Nash in horror, and then, much to my humiliation, burst into uncontrollable sobs.

I expected Nash to walk away or haul me over the coals for such outrageous behavior, but he didn't. I felt his arm go around me, and he tugged me into his chest.

I clung to him and bawled like a newborn baby.

FOURTEEN

AVA

TULLAHOMA, TENNESSEE
FEBRUARY 1942

The hospital staff continued to buzz about Gunther Schneider's heroic actions.

Although I hadn't seen him since the day he walked out of the mess hall under guard, I heard nurses, orderlies, and even a handful of doctors discussing the case. *How did he know what to do?* was the common question. I didn't have answers for them, being that the personal information Gunther shared with me about attending medical school in New York was private. In all honesty, I was as amazed as everyone else that he'd saved a life right before my very eyes. Just yesterday the soldier who'd collapsed was released from the hospital. I never heard what caused him to stop breathing, but I hoped he counted himself lucky that Gunther Schneider was nearby when he did.

Colonel Foster approached my desk when he returned to the

office later that afternoon, a serious look on his face. "I need to have a word with you, Mrs. Delaney."

I hurried to follow him into his office, where he closed the door. Nervous butterflies whirled in my stomach. Had I done something wrong? I was still learning about supply lists, medical terms, and the like, and it was easy to make a mistake.

He motioned for me to take a seat, then settled in his own chair. "I had a lunch meeting with some of our doctors today." He tented his fingers while his elbows rested on his desk. "It seems you were involved in an incident last week, along with one of the German detainees. Is this true?"

I swallowed. "Yes, sir."

"Would you care to explain why you were in the company of this man?"

I blinked. "You gave me his file to update, sir."

The colonel frowned. "I gave you his file?"

I nodded.

After a long moment, the scowl on his face eased. "I apologize, Mrs. Delaney. That was an error on my part. You should not have been put in the position of interacting with one of the internees."

My tense shoulders relaxed. "He was very polite."

Colonel Foster leaned back in his chair. "I understand he saved a man's life."

"It was extraordinary." I couldn't hide my awe. "Mr. Schneider was a student at Columbia medical school when he was arrested."

"Ah. That answers some of my questions." He met my gaze. "What else did Mr. Schneider tell you?"

I suddenly felt a strange sense of protectiveness over the conversation I'd had with Gunther about his arrest and detainment. Although he hadn't elaborated on his life, he had trusted me enough to vocalize his confusion over the situation he found himself in. While Colonel Foster oversaw the hospital, I didn't know if the private details Gunther shared with me were relevant to his job.

"He hopes to return to medical school someday to become a doctor."

The colonel looked thoughtful. "Tell me what you witnessed Mr. Schneider do that day."

I described the situation as best I could. I also had to confess it was my idea to involve Gunther in the first place. "I'm not a doctor, but I can't help but wonder if the soldier would have survived if Mr. Schneider had not acted as he did. It's a shame he's locked up, unable to continue his studies. At least he's able to work as an orderly until he's released."

A pensive look crossed the colonel's face. "Major Tyson doesn't agree. He refused to let Schneider return to the hospital after the incident."

"But why? Mr. Schneider *saved* that soldier's life."

"The major doesn't believe an orderly should have performed a medical procedure. Especially not an orderly who is a German detainee. Schneider could have killed the man." He paused. "I agree with Major Tyson. We can't have unskilled personnel acting without supervision."

"But Mr. Schneider isn't unskilled. He was training to become a doctor before the government arrested him."

The colonel gave me a patient look. "We don't know anything about Mr. Schneider, other than the information he himself has provided. I don't think it wise to find him trustworthy just yet."

"But is it fair to *mis*trust him simply because he's German?"

A slight smile lifted the corners of his mouth. "Touché." He tapped his finger on the desk. "Perhaps I should meet Mr. Schneider before I decide on whether to let him continue to work in the hospital or not. Please set up an appointment for him to come to my office tomorrow."

I couldn't help but grin. "Yes, sir."

He chuckled. "I believe your skills of persuasion are wasted as a secretary, Mrs. Delaney. You should be an attorney."

I returned to my desk and checked the colonel's schedule for the following day, determining the best time for Gunther to meet with him. I wasn't sure how the German man would feel about this, or if he even desired to continue working in the hospital, but I also couldn't help but believe he had skills that shouldn't go to waste.

After several unsuccessful attempts to contact the guardhouse at the detainment area by telephone, I decided to go in person. I hadn't ventured beyond the hospital complex since I began working on base, and I felt nervous as I drove along unfamiliar streets.

The internment camp was located farther away from the main sector than I realized, yet I knew when I reached it. Surrounded by forest, the entire area was enclosed in high, barbed-wire fencing. Guard towers were visible where armed men watched over the inmates. Row after row of small, identical huts with pointed roofs—exactly as Stella and Ethel described—filled my view as I inched toward the gated entrance.

An unsmiling soldier exited a guardhouse and approached when I rolled down the car window.

"Ma'am, this is a restricted area. You'll need to leave."

I swallowed my nerves. "I work for Colonel Foster. He has requested a meeting with one of the internees."

The young man eyed me suspiciously. "Which internee does the colonel wish to see?"

"Gunther Schneider. He works as an orderly in the hospital."

The guard walked back to the small building where another soldier stood, watching me. They conferred, then the first man returned.

"Where does the colonel want the prisoner brought, and what time?"

My shoulders stiffened. "Mr. Schneider is not a prisoner. None of these men are. They're being detained by our government because of their birth origins. Some of them aren't even aware of the charges brought against them."

The soldier appeared unmoved.

I gave him the location and time for the meeting tomorrow, then turned the car around and headed back to the office. However, I couldn't help but study the internment camp as I drove alongside the barbed-wire fence. Although most of Camp Forrest's buildings were new construction and had little embellishment, the huts Gunther and the other internees lived in seemed especially austere. Maybe it was simply that I knew it to be a prison of sorts, but I found myself outraged that men like Gunther Schneider were forced to reside here.

When the day came to an end, I bid Bren and the others good night and drove home. The beauty of the countryside always lifted my spirits, and I turned up the radio when Jimmy Dorsey's "Blue Champagne" began to play. Richard had loved to dance to this song, and I smiled, remembering how he'd twirled me across the dance floor at the USO in Nashville.

I turned off the paved road and crested the hill to the farm, grateful that memories of Richard didn't hurt as much as they had right after we learned he'd been killed. I still missed him and wished things had turned out differently, but the tiniest hints of peace were beginning to replace the fear and aloneness I'd felt in those first weeks.

A strange sedan sat in front of the house when I arrived. I cut off the engine, curious who'd come to visit Gertrude. In the time I'd lived on the farm, she had never invited guests. In all honesty, I wasn't sure she possessed any friends or family.

High-pitched laughter greeted me as I came in the kitchen door. A young woman with midnight-black hair, styled in the latest fashion, and ruby-red lips sat at the table with Gertrude.

"I told him he had another think comin' if he thought I'd go on a second date with him," she said with a southern twang. A loud cackle followed.

I closed the door. The sound drew Gertrude's attention.

"It's about time you got home. We've been waiting."

I drew to a stop, confused by her angry tone. "I'm sorry. Did you ask me to come home early today?" I glanced at the young woman sitting with her. Her dark eyes gave me a once-over, seeming to sum me up from head to toe.

Gertrude waved her hand in the air. "Never mind. Come meet Ivy Lee Culbertson."

I set my purse on the counter and stepped toward the stranger. She didn't rise, so I offered my hand. "It's nice to meet you, Miss Culbertson. Are you a friend of Gertrude's?"

She looked at me as though I'd said something ridiculous. "I'm your new boarder, silly." Her eyes traveled around the kitchen. "I wasn't sure I'd like livin' out here in the boonies, but now that I'm here, I think I'll enjoy the country." She waggled her perfectly plucked eyebrows. "You got any cowboys out here? I've never met one before."

I stood silent, baffled by the conversation.

Ivy Lee referred to herself as our boarder, but Gertrude hadn't mentioned anything about taking in renters. With few motels or rental properties available in town, I'd heard people were opening their homes to the wives and families of servicemen, as well as those who came to work at the military installation. I'd never considered allowing a stranger to move into the farmhouse, mainly because Gertrude valued her privacy too much. I'd tried to respect that in the months I'd been here, often retiring to my room right after supper, so she could have the parlor to herself to read or listen to one of her favorite radio programs. It was totally out of character for her to open her door to a young woman neither of us knew.

But when I looked to her for answers, she wouldn't meet my gaze.

"Miss Culbertson." I forced a smile. "Would you excuse Gertrude and me for a moment? There's something I need to discuss with her. We won't be long."

I didn't wait to see if Gertrude followed and headed for the bedroom at the foot of the stairs. It had once been Richard's, but now it was where I slept. When she appeared a moment later, I closed the door.

"Would you care to tell me what's going on?"

She sniffed and jutted out her chin. "I rented a room to Ivy Lee."

"I gathered that," I said, folding my arms across my belly. "Don't you think you should have consulted me first?"

"This is my house. I can do what I want." She gave a blasé shrug. "Don't need your permission."

I took a deep breath to calm my rising ire. "I'm not saying you do, but this is my home, too. It would've been nice to at least have some warning that you intended to allow a stranger to move in."

"You were a stranger to me when you first got here," she said, challenge in the words. "That didn't stop you."

I stared at her. "I was your son's wife. Your daughter-in-law. Surely you see the difference."

She turned away. "Well, it's too late. I've already told her she can have the room."

"Which room?"

She rolled her eyes. "The one upstairs. I wouldn't give away your room without telling you first."

Her answer didn't make me feel better.

"May I ask what you know about her? Where did you meet her?"

Gertrude proceeded to impart the tale of how she'd gone to town to the market—"Since you aren't around to help me anymore"—and ran into Clara Bontrager. Clara, a widow in her seventies, had taken in boarders, but her home was full and couldn't accommodate Ivy Lee, whose friend was staying at Clara's house.

"The poor child had no place to go," Gertrude said, her sympathetic expression unpersuasive.

The account sounded factually correct, but I wasn't convinced Gertrude had done this solely to help the young woman currently seated at the kitchen table.

"How much is she paying you for room and board each month?"

Gertrude's scowl told me she didn't want to divulge that information, but when she finally said the amount—far more than I'd expected—I knew I'd discovered the reason Ivy Lee was moving to the farm.

"You're always saying we don't have enough money," she huffed. "If you don't like Ivy's being here, *you* tell her she can't move in."

I heaved a sigh. "I just wish you would have discussed this with me before offering to rent a room, that's all. But you're right. We can definitely use the extra income."

I followed Gertrude back to the kitchen, but Ivy Lee wasn't where we'd left her. A noise came from the parlor. When we reached the doorway, we found our new boarder rifling through the drawer of the desk in the corner.

"Ahem," I said.

The nosy woman startled. When she looked up, she sent us a sheepish look. "I was lookin' for a pencil."

My gaze dropped from her unapologetic expression to the holder on the desktop, filled with half a dozen perfectly fit writing instruments.

"Oh, how silly of me," she said when she glanced at them too.

Whether she was truly that scatterbrained or had just given us evidence of her untrustworthiness, I wasn't certain, but it served to put me on edge.

"Why don't we sit down and get to know one another." I proceeded to settle on the sofa without giving her or Gertrude the opportunity to decline.

Once we were seated, I asked, "When would you like to move in?"

"As soon as possible. I'm staying at a motel over in Shelbyville, but I start my new job at Camp Forrest tomorrow."

"I work at the camp, too," I said. "What department are you in?"

"It's top secret, hon. You know how that is."

I forced myself not to roll my eyes. "What about your family? Where are they?"

"All my kin are in Memphis. That's where I grew up. Daddy's an important politician, and Mama is a member of the DAR *and* the Daughters of the Confederacy."

I nodded, pretending to be impressed. "I'm sure they'll miss you."

Her gaze landed on a framed photograph of Richard on the mantel. "He sure is handsome. Who is he? One of your boarders, I hope."

Her coquettish grin rankled. I glanced at Gertrude to see if she would put the girl in her place, but she just stared at the black-and-white picture, taken right after Richard joined the Navy.

"That is my husband, Richard. Gertrude's son." I met the young woman's curious gaze. "He died at Pearl Harbor."

Ivy Lee took in a gulp of air, and, for the first time, she spoke with sincerity. "I'm very sorry. I didn't know."

I stood, indicating our meeting was over.

Ivy Lee followed. It was decided she would move in tomorrow evening after work, and she bid us goodbye.

Gertrude and I ate leftover meatloaf in silence. I volunteered to wash the dishes, and Gertrude disappeared upstairs. Although I had more questions about Ivy Lee and how we would handle a boarder, they would have to wait until morning.

I started in the direction of my room, turning out lights as I went. In the parlor, I stopped in front of Richard's photograph. Ivy Lee was right. He truly was handsome. All the girls at the USO in Nashville thought him dreamy, and more than one looked at me with envy when he asked me to dance.

"I wish you were here," I whispered. "Everything is so different without you."

Unfortunately, wishes like that don't come true.

I flicked off the lamp and retreated to my room where I readied for bed. Beneath the cold sheets, I stared into the darkness.

Suddenly, a man's face appeared in my mind, his eyes brilliant blue, but it wasn't Richard.

I fell asleep thinking about the German internee, Gunther Schneider.

FIFTEEN

MATTIE

DELANEY HORSE FARM
NOVEMBER 1969

I couldn't believe I slapped Nash.

And I couldn't believe he let me get away with it.

We sat on the sofa, dim light from the kitchen giving shadowy illumination to the room. I'd cried until my body couldn't create another tear. I honestly couldn't say what prompted them. Embarrassment. Grief. Mental exhaustion. Yet throughout my sobbing, Nash's arm stayed wrapped around me, tucking me against his side like one of the footballs he'd carried across the end zone during high school.

When my hiccups subsided and I felt I could speak, I whispered, "I'm sorry I hit you."

He chuckled. "I have to admit I didn't expect it." He worked his jaw, as though making sure it functioned properly. "I'm just glad it wasn't a right hook. I might've lost some teeth."

I groaned. "It isn't funny, Nash." I sat forward, sniffling. "I'm a horrible person."

He removed his arm from my shoulders. "You're not a horrible person." His mouth quirked. "A bit temperamental and overly sensitive, but not horrible."

Considering what I'd done, I appreciated his humor. He had every right to bawl me out, but instead he tried to make *me* feel better.

"Mark used to call me *Fourth of July* when I'd get angry with him. He said I was like a bundle of Black Cat firecrackers, ready to take someone's arm off."

Nash grinned. "I remember."

I studied him for a long moment, seeing the boy Mark and I had known most of our lives. "You were a good friend to him. He loved you like the brother he never had. I sometimes used to think it would've been better if I'd been his identical twin rather than a fraternal twin. He would've been happier with a brother, I think."

"Don't say that. He loved you more than anyone else."

"I loved him more than anyone else, too."

The grandfather clock in the hallway chimed ten times into the stillness.

"It's getting late," I said. "We better turn in." Yet neither of us moved.

"Can I ask you something?"

I nodded but added, "You may not like the answer."

My forthrightness didn't deter him. "Why have you always been angry with your dad?"

The question wasn't what I expected. "I haven't always been mad at him."

"You have. At least from what I remember. Even when we were young, you'd act like he was the worst person in the world, usually because he was working and wouldn't stop to do whatever it was you wanted."

I gave him a hard stare. "That's because he was *always* working. He never took time off to do anything with us. Mama did all the parenting. He didn't help with homework or come to any of our school plays or go to church with us, no matter how many times we asked." I shook my head. "I don't have a single memory of him playing with me. No piggyback rides. No dancing with my feet on his shoes. No bedtime stories. No nothing. On rare occasions he'd take Mark down to the creek to go fishing, but I wasn't invited. When they'd return, I'd ask Mark what they talked about, and he'd say they didn't talk at all."

Nash seemed thoughtful. "Maybe it isn't fair to compare, but I would have rather had a dad like yours than one like my old man. At least your dad wasn't a drunk who beat up his wife and kids. My old man couldn't keep a job, so he didn't go to work. He stayed home and drank." He looked away. "Count yourself lucky your dad didn't show you the kind of attention mine showed my sister when she turned thirteen."

I didn't know what to say. Mark had told me stories about Nash's father over the years, but either I hadn't truly been listening or life had taught me that nothing in this world is good. Not even fathers.

His revelation now, however, hit me in the gut. I reached for his hand. "I'm sorry, Nash," I whispered.

His grip tightened as he met my gaze. "If it hadn't been for your folks letting me stay over here so much, I don't think I would've survived."

We sat in silence a long time, our fingers locked. The enormity of what he was saying, what I believed he was confessing, reminded me that everything would have been different without Nash.

The way it was different without Mark.

"I guess I just wish I knew why Dad is the way he is, you know?"

"Someday you need to ask him. His answer might surprise you."

His words reminded me of my conversation with Mama about

the shoebox she insisted I look through. I told Nash about it, adding, "I'm not sure I can handle the revelation of family secrets right now. I'm barely hanging on as it is."

"It sounds like it's important to your mom. She wouldn't have asked if it wasn't."

I heaved a sigh. "I know you're probably right, but—" I paused, trying to articulate the angst and confusion churning inside me. "I think I'm afraid. What if these secrets take me to an even darker place?"

Nash's hand tightened on mine. "If you want, I'll go through the box first, see what's in it, and then you can decide from there."

I didn't think I had any tears left in me, but here they came again. "Why are you so good to me? I don't deserve your kindness after the way I've treated you."

He shook his head. "No, you don't," he said, dodging when I pretended to slug his shoulder. "But that's what friends are for."

Nash had always been Mark's friend. That he considered me his friend now warmed me to my very core.

I bit my lip. "Would you want to look through the box now? I know it's late, but I can't promise I'll have the courage to do it tomorrow."

"Let's do this."

I tiptoed upstairs, not wanting to disturb Mama and Dad. No light came from the crack beneath their door. As I slid the box out from under my bed, I took a deep breath and blew it out.

"I don't know what secrets you hold," I whispered into the chilly air, "but please, be something good. I can't take any more bad news."

I returned to the living room. Nash had turned on the lamp, but he was nowhere to be seen. I'd just settled on the sofa when he came in from the kitchen, holding two mugs of hot chocolate with his one hand.

Doggone it. More tears sprang to my eyes.

"Thanks," I said, accepting one of the mugs. "I can't remember the last time I had hot cocoa. The weather in California is usually so pleasant, it's not something you think about making."

He sat next to me. "Where did you live?"

I stirred the chocolate, my mind going back to the day I left Tullahoma, determined never to return. "I spent the first four or five months in LA. Then I met a group of people who were headed to San Francisco, so I tagged along. That's where I met Clay." I glanced at Nash. "He's my boyfriend." But even as I said the word, I realized I hadn't missed him at all. Hadn't thought about him, really. I'd given Clay my parents' telephone number, but he had yet to call to check on me or ask how Mama was doing.

"Clay has a following. A family, they call themselves. He's their father, their mentor, their teacher, their preacher. I became part of them. We moved around a lot. Sometimes we lived in houses, but mostly we camped in parks or up in the hills."

Nash stared at the cup in his hand. "Did you like that kind of life?"

The answer to that question was complicated. "I think I *needed* that kind of life. I couldn't deal with all of this," I said, indicating the room, the house, my family. "I had to escape."

After a long moment, Nash nodded. "I understand wanting to escape. That's why I went to Vietnam."

If he had made that statement just yesterday, I would have lit into him about how ludicrous it was to believe going to war was an escape from anything. But I didn't argue with him now. I'm not sure why, but I suddenly got what he was saying. I may not agree with his thinking, but I realized Nash and I had something in common I hadn't recognized before.

"We're quite the pair, aren't we? Going off in all directions, only to come back to what we were trying to get away from in the first place."

We sipped our cocoa in silence until Nash set his empty cup on the coffee table next to the shoebox. He opened the lid and took out the old Bible.

"Dad wasn't pleased when he found me with that the other day." I set my empty mug next to his. "Maybe it's really valuable or something."

Nash carefully thumbed through the delicate, yellowed pages. "Looks like it's written in German."

"Or maybe Russian."

He closed it and set it aside, then reached for the first of the two bundles of letters. After untying one of the ribbons, he scanned the envelopes.

"They're all addressed to Ava Delaney." He squinted at the smaller handwriting in the top-left corner of the first one. "These came from someone in the military in Hawaii. The postmark is from 1941."

I sat forward to get a closer look. "That's strange. Mom's maiden name is Robinson. Granny's family were the Delaneys. She was so proud of her family name, she wouldn't change the name of the farm to Taylor Farms."

He turned to me. "Are you ready to find out what this is all about?"

My gut warned that the answer to his question was *no*. But Nash was right. Learning the secrets these letters held was important to Mama. Why, I couldn't begin to guess.

"I'm as ready as I'll ever be. I hope you'll stick around to pick up the pieces when I fall apart."

He didn't smile at my half-hearted joke. Instead, he gave me the most intimate look I'd ever seen.

"Always."

Nash silently read the first letter while I held my breath, afraid of what it contained.

When he came to its end, his brow furrowed. "I'm confused."

I blinked. "By what?"

He pointed to the signature on the second page. "It's signed *Aloha from your loving husband, Richard.*" He faced me. "Is your dad's name Richard? I've always known him as Kurt."

I reached for the letter and studied the name. "Not that I know of. Are you sure these are to my mom? Maybe there was another relative named Ava, and Mom kept her letters for some reason."

Nash opened the second letter.

"Read it out loud," I said. "Please."

"June twenty-second, 1941. Pearl Harbor, Hawaii. My dearest Ava, I can't tell you how much I miss you. The guys are already making fun of me because this is my second letter to you in a week. But I told them they can tease me all they want. I plan to write to my wife as often as I can."

"Wife." I repeated. "Obviously this letter wasn't written to Mama. Dad's name isn't Richard, and he never joined the Navy or went overseas."

Nash continued to read, but the remainder of the letter was news about Pearl Harbor, the ships, the town, and Richard's hope that his Ava would join him soon. It was signed in the same manner as the first letter.

"I don't know much about Dad's side of the family. He never talked about them. Neither did Granny. Maybe that's what this is all about. Maybe these belong to some Delaney relative that shared the same name as Mama." I punctuated the comment with a huge yawn.

"Do you want to read the others? I'm not sure you'll be able to stay awake," he said with a grin.

"I guess they can wait until tomorrow. It doesn't appear they hold any deep, dark family secrets like I feared." We stood. "Don't mention this to Dad. Mama didn't think he'd approve, although I have no idea why not."

Jake rose from his place near the heating vent in the corner.

I'd completely forgotten he was there and that he and Nash would spend the night in Mark's old room.

As though reading my mind, Nash said, "I'll sleep out in the cabin, but Jake would be warmer here in the house if that's okay with you."

I glanced down the hall. Although it was out of my line of sight, we had a room, empty and unused, with a comfortable bed and warm blankets. More importantly, we had a friend, a family member, in need of it.

"In some ways, that room is more yours than anyone else's." My eyes locked on his. "I really am sorry I got upset when Dad offered it to you. Mark wouldn't want you to sleep out in the cold."

"To be honest, I was feeling kind of weird about sleeping in there. You know, without him."

"That's how I've felt from the moment I stepped into this house. But it wouldn't make sense for you to stay in the cabin without a heater."

Nash took Jake outside while I rinsed our mugs. I tidied the living room, picked up the shoebox, and turned out the lights as I heard them come inside.

I waited at the base of the stairs in front of the closed door to Mark's room. When Nash opened it, Jake walked in and curled into a dark ball at the foot of the bed.

The emotional evening left me feeling vulnerable, yet I needed to be truthful with him too. "Tonight was good. Well, except for the part where I hit you."

He grinned, then shoved his hand into his pants pocket. "Good night, Mattie."

"Good night."

As I quietly climbed the stairs, Mark's bedroom door closed, a sound I'd heard a million times. Although my brother would never sleep in his room again, somehow knowing Nash was under our roof brought a sense of normalcy my life had lacked for over a year.

At the upstairs landing, I tiptoed to the window that overlooked the farm. Stars twinkled in the midnight sky, visible now that the storm had moved south, and everything was beautiful and still.

Peaceful.

"Good night, Mark," I whispered.

Good night, Sis, my heart heard him say.

SIXTEEN

GUNTHER

CAMP FORREST, TENNESSEE

FEBRUARY 1942

Nervousness swam through Gunther as he sat in a metal chair in the reception area of a building at the far end of the hospital complex. Three young women seated at desks pretended to keep busy with their work, but Gunther felt their curious looks as he waited to meet with Colonel Hew Foster, the man in charge of the entire hospital.

Why did the officer want to meet with him?

That question had run through his mind ever since a guard found him in his hut yesterday afternoon and told him about the appointment. He could only guess it had something to do with what happened the day the soldier collapsed in the mess hall. He'd been a fool to let Mrs. Delaney talk him into administering chest compressions on the unconscious man. That it had turned out well seemed not to matter. The angry doctor who'd arrived at the scene had chewed Gunther up one side and down the other when the dust settled, then banned him from ever entering the hospital again.

He glanced at the closed door with the colonel's name on it. Fear roiled in his stomach.

Would he be deported back to Germany because of his reckless actions?

The very thought sent an icy chill down his spine.

While he would enjoy seeing his mother again, he had no desire to live in Nazi-ruled Germany. He, along with the rest of the world, heard horrifying news coming out of his home country. Jews murdered by the thousands. People arrested and shipped off to work camps if they didn't conform to the Nazi regime.

Mutter had seen this coming.

"You must go to America," she'd told him two months before his eighteenth birthday. Rolf wasn't home, giving Gunther and his mother the freedom to speak their minds without his brother's condescending censure. "Hitler is building his army, and I fear you will be forced to join."

They'd had this conversation before. From the time Hitler became chancellor in 1933, his racist ideals frightened her, and that only grew once Rolf joined the Hitler Youth.

"You know we cannot afford to send me to America," Gunther reminded her. "Besides, I will be studying medicine in Munich. Hitler himself says he wants more doctors and scientists in Germany."

His mother sat across the table from him, a grave look in her eyes. "Son, listen to me. Hitler is an arrogant man. He will not stop until he has what he wants: a Germany free of the people he deems unworthy to be German." She rose and retrieved a book from the drawer. "I found this in your brother's room."

She handed it to Gunther. "*Mein Kampf* by Adolf Hitler. I have heard of it, although I don't know what he means by *my struggle*. Rolf tried to get me to read it, but I said I was too busy with schoolwork."

"I'm glad you didn't read it, but now you need to know what it says. Hitler talks about his plans for transforming Germany into a perfect society based on race. He says Jews, people with dark skin, and those with mental problems poison society. According to Hitler, the only solution is to remove them . . . permanently."

Gunther stared at her. "Surely the government would not allow such extremes."

"Hitler *is* the government, son. Terrible things are coming to Germany." Terror shone in her eyes and laced her voice. "I have lost one son to him. I cannot lose you, too."

She pulled a leather pouch from her apron pocket.

Gunther gasped when she removed a wad of reichsmark banknotes. "Where did you get that money from?"

"I sold the car." She passed the bills to me. "I want you to purchase passage on a ship, bound for America. Go, study medicine in a place where you will be free, and I'll know you are no longer in danger."

Yet Gunther was now a prisoner of the very country where she thought he'd be safe. How he'd hated to write a letter to her, informing her that the freedom they both dreamed of had turned into a nightmare.

The door to the colonel's office opened. Expecting to see a uniformed man, Gunther was confused when Mrs. Delaney walked out. Her gaze met his, and a slight smile touched her bright red lips.

"Good morning, Mr. Schneider. Colonel Foster will see you now."

Gunther suddenly remembered she said she worked for a colonel. Did she have something to do with this meeting?

Colonel Foster rose from where he was seated at his desk when they entered and offered his hand. "Mr. Schneider, thank you for agreeing to meet with me."

Gunther nodded, unsure how to respond. As far as he knew, he hadn't been given a choice.

The man motioned Gunther to one of two chairs in front of the desk. Behind him, the door clicked closed, and he assumed Mrs. Delaney exited the room. However, a moment later, she quietly took a seat in the chair next to him, a notepad and pencil in hand, and her attention focused on the colonel.

"I've heard various accounts of what happened in the mess hall last week," he began, casting a quick look at Mrs. Delaney, then back to Gunther. "I don't know if you're aware, but the man whose life you saved is doing well. He apparently has a heart anomaly, which he was unaware of until he collapsed. He's been medically discharged from the Army and was sent home to his family, thanks in part to you."

The man's praise and cordial tone wasn't at all what Gunther had anticipated. "I'm . . . glad to hear it, sir."

The colonel studied Gunther before saying, "I understand you were a medical student before the war started. What school did you attend?"

Wariness crept over Gunther. He'd answered these same questions over and over after his arrest. "Columbia, sir."

Colonel Foster's brow rose. "Impressive. I understand they have an excellent program."

Gunther remained silent.

"Please describe what happened with the soldier in the mess hall, and why you chose to administer a medical procedure only a qualified doctor should employ. Considering your position here at Camp Forrest, it doesn't seem as though it was the wisest thing to attempt."

Gunther contemplated how to respond. While there was no reason he shouldn't be truthful, honesty had not served him well with US government officials lately.

He glanced at Mrs. Delaney, but she stared at the pad of paper in her lap, pencil poised to begin writing. There were already notes on the page. Was she recording everything he said?

He faced the colonel again. "Mrs. Delaney asked me to meet with her so she could complete a . . ." He struggled to remember the word she'd used.

"Personnel file," she quietly supplied.

Gunther nodded his thanks when she looked up. "Yes, a personnel file. We were finished with our conversation when someone called out that a man was not breathing. The guard told us he would get help, but I felt it took too long."

"So, you decided to intervene, despite the fact that you're not a doctor?"

Gunther met the man's gaze. "I decided I did not want to watch a man die, especially if there was something I could do to prevent it."

"Even though he was an American soldier, training to fight Germans?"

"My professor at Columbia, Dr. Sonnenberg, teaches there should be no prejudices in medicine."

Colonel Foster gave a slow nod. "Well said." He leaned back in his chair. "Tell me about your training."

Gunther gave the basics of his admission into Columbia and the subjects he'd studied. He also shared how Dr. Sonnenberg, a fellow German, took him under his wing. "I had hoped to begin an internship with him this semester." There was no need to explain why it hadn't happened.

"And the method you used on the unconscious man." Colonel Foster said. "Had you performed it before?"

Gunther gripped the armrest. Should he answer honestly? If he did, he could soon find himself on a ship bound for Germany.

"I had not, sir. I only watched as Dr. Sonnenberg used it to revive a patient." He paused. He'd probably already sealed his fate, so he finished by saying, "Dr. Friedrich Maass, a *German* surgeon in the 1890s, advocated using chest compressions rather than ventilation alone. I believe his technique has been used around the world to revive thousands of patients."

A bemused expression crossed the colonel's face. "Perhaps you are correct." He leaned his elbows on the desktop and tented his fingers. "In the meantime, however, I need to decide what to do with you. Mrs. Delaney," he smiled at her when she looked up from her notepad, "believes you should be given another chance to work in the hospital."

Gunther turned to see her face grow a becoming shade of pink.

"After speaking with you, I'm inclined to agree."

Gunther couldn't believe what he was hearing. "You're not sending me back to Germany?"

The colonel frowned. "Is it your wish to return to your homeland?"

"No," Gunther said, too quickly and too loudly. He composed himself before saying, "What I mean is, I came to America to study medicine. That is still my wish."

"I'm glad to hear that. While I can't offer you the same type of internship you would have received in New York, I believe you can be useful in the dispensary. Soldiers with minor ailments and such are treated there rather than taking up beds in the hospital. Major Gridley oversees the unit. He's a fine man. I'm sure he would welcome the help."

Gunther sat speechless.

He wasn't being deported. He wasn't even being punished for acting irrationally and putting the patient in danger. He would be allowed to work in a medical clinic. Not as an orderly, simply there to lift patients or clean up messes, but to be of use to the ill and injured.

For the first time since his arrest, Gunther felt as though someone cared about him as a human being. If people like Colonel

Foster and Mrs. Delaney could see him as the man he was and not some foreign enemy alien, then perhaps others could too.

"Thank you," he finally said. "I appreciate your willingness to trust me."

The colonel stood. Gunther and Mrs. Delaney rose too.

"You're welcome, Mr. Schneider. I'll look forward to hearing a good report from Major Gridley in the coming days."

He offered his hand once again, and Gunther accepted it with a new respect for the man. He turned and followed Mrs. Delaney from the office. His ever-present guard sat on the corner of a desk and flirted with the young woman seated behind it. When he saw Gunther, he leaned down and whispered something to her, causing her to giggle.

Gunther turned to Mrs. Delaney.

"How can I ever thank you for this?" he said, dumbfounded how things had worked out. "I thought for certain I would be sent back to Germany."

Her hazel eyes shone. "I simply told Colonel Foster what I saw that day. It's something I'll never forget. You should be allowed to continue your studies and become a doctor. You have a gift from God that shouldn't go to waste."

"Let's go, Schneider," the guard called. Gunther turned to find the armed man near the door.

When he faced Mrs. Delaney again, he lowered his voice. "You have given me hope. And for that, I will be forever grateful."

With her warm smile tucked away in his memory, Gunther followed the guard outside.

He didn't even mind that it was snowing.

SEVENTEEN

MATTIE

DELANEY HORSE FARM
NOVEMBER 1969

I awoke the morning after Thanksgiving to bright sunshine streaming through the lacey curtains of my bedroom, providing a bit of warmth to the otherwise chilly air. It was half past nine, much later than I'd intended to sleep. Unlike most mornings, I couldn't recall having any dreams during the night. The strange images usually kept me tossing and turning, making me groggy, but today I felt rested.

While I showered, I heard the telephone ring downstairs. By the time I dressed in jeans and a flannel shirt, ready to start the day, an unfamiliar female voice came from Mama's room. I crept across the hall and found Dad chatting with a woman I didn't recognize. A glance toward the bed told me Mama slept through it.

"Mattie, this is LuAnn Bradford," Dad said when he spotted

me. "She is a nurse. Dr. Monahan thought it best if we had someone come help a little every day."

Although this news caught me off guard, I nodded politely. "It's nice to meet you, ma'am."

The older woman smiled kindly. "It's good to see you again, Mattie. You probably don't remember me, but I worked in Dr. Monahan's office when you were a little girl. My family and I moved to St. Louis some years ago, but now we're back in Tullahoma. I'm what they call a *home nurse* now. I make house calls, like in the olden days."

I nodded again, but I wondered why we suddenly needed a nurse. Dr. Monahan visited Mama last week, but I hadn't heard him mention it. Was there something he wasn't telling us about her condition?

The nurse moved to Mama's bedside. "Your father says you're doing a fine job taking care of your mother," she said to me, then focused on Mama. "She looks good, considering all that's going on inside."

While she gently lifted Mama's hand to take her pulse, I glanced at Dad, but his attention was on the nurse's actions. It surprised me to hear that he'd sung my praises to the woman. He certainly never voiced his approval to me.

After listening to Mama's heart, chest, and stomach with a stethoscope, LuAnn returned to where Dad and I waited in silence.

"I was telling your father that Dr. Monahan suggested I visit each morning and assist with bathroom and bathing needs, and generally relieve some of the burden you both have been carrying. I don't live far from here, so it's not a problem."

"Why didn't Dr. Monahan tell us about this when he was here?" I asked. "Mama sleeps a lot and hasn't been very hungry lately, but I haven't noticed any big change."

LuAnn's eyes offered sympathy. "The doctor just wants to be sure you and your father, as the caregivers, aren't overwhelmed. I've tended to many patients in the final stages of life. There are signs the body is beginning to slow down, like sleeping more. Although that can be attributed to the pain medication in part, it's also a natural occurrence. So is loss of appetite, becoming forgetful, and losing an interest in the world beyond these walls. Unfortunately, our bodies aren't meant to last forever. Thankfully, we get new ones when our life here on earth is over."

I stiffened.

Religious platitudes about death being the beginning of something wonderful was the last thing I wanted to hear just now.

Dad had a question about one of the medications the doctor prescribed, and he and LuAnn rounded the bed to discuss the various bottles on a small table. I went to Mama and studied her pale features. Her cheeks remained puffy, and her lips held a slight bluish tinge around the edges, but she was still as beautiful as she'd always been.

"I'm happy to stay with her, dear, if you have something you need to do this morning," LuAnn said when she and Dad ended their conversation. "I'll leave around noon, then be back each morning at eight o'clock. We can adjust that schedule as needed."

Dad agreed, but I kept quiet. While it would be good to have an extra pair of hands to help lift and move Mama, especially when Dad and Nash were busy, I couldn't help but feel everything was about to change.

And that wasn't something I wanted to think about.

I left them and made my way downstairs. Nash and Jake were in the kitchen. I noticed dishes containing leftovers from our Thanksgiving meal were spread across the table.

"Good morning," Nash said, pausing from his task of placing a scoop of stiff mashed potatoes onto a plate that already contained a lump of dressing and a pile of green beans.

"I know our dinner yesterday was good, but is that what you're having for breakfast?"

Nash chuckled. "No. I'm going into town to pick up some feed for the horses. I thought I'd check on my buddy, Fred. He doesn't have family in the area anymore, so I figured I'd take him a plate of food. Your dad said it was okay."

"That's thoughtful of you."

I moved to pour myself a cup of coffee from the percolator. After dousing it with milk and a couple squares of sugar, I leaned against the counter and watched Nash add slices of turkey to the heaping plate, then cover everything with congealed gravy.

Footsteps from the room above reminded me of the nurse's presence.

I heaved a sigh.

Nash looked over. "Something wrong?"

"I wasn't expecting to wake up and find a strange woman in the house."

"Nurse Bradford," he said with a nod. "I met her. Seems like a nice lady."

"I'm sure she is, but I wish Dr. Monahan would've mentioned his plan to have her start coming every day."

"You don't think it's necessary?"

I wrapped my fingers around the mug, letting its warmth seep into me. My emotions suddenly felt raw and exposed, yet after last night, I believed Nash understood me a little better.

"I'm sure she'll be a lot of help. It's just that," I lifted my shoulders again, "I guess I'm still in denial. If things stay the same, with Mama simply napping a lot and us taking care of her ourselves, it feels like we could do this indefinitely. But having a nurse, a professional, come every day means . . ." I pressed my lips together. If I finished the thought, I'd end up in a heap on the floor.

He gave a slow nod. "I understand."

We didn't say more.

He finished filling the plate and carefully wrapped it with a piece of foil. Watching, I was struck that his lack of a second hand never slowed him down, no matter what he was doing. Whether it was helping Dad with the horses, or working on the tractor, Nash was as capable as any two-armed man.

He returned the dishes of leftover food to the refrigerator, then took his heavy coat from the back of a chair and shrugged into it. Jake rose from where he'd been laying on a rug, stretched, and hobbled to the back door.

Nash picked up the plate, then let his gaze meet mine. "Do you want to come to town with me? Might be good for you to get out of the house, after working so hard yesterday."

The offer, while unexpected, sounded like the perfect escape. "Let me get my jacket."

I hurried upstairs and told Dad and LuAnn our plans. Bundled against the cold morning, I met Nash at the truck parked in the yard. Jake was already settled in the middle of the bench seat.

"I hope you don't mind if he tags along," Nash said. "Fred, my friend, likes it when I bring Jake with me."

We headed toward town. Thankfully the roads were clear, with melting snow pushed off to the edges of the pavement. It took a while for the heater to begin to warm the chilly air in the cab, but it felt good to get outside after being cooped up in the house.

We passed the Allyn farm. "I wonder if Paula is still around. Do you ever see her?"

Nash took his time answering. "She and I have talked a few times since I got back. She quit school and is staying with her grandparents in Lynchburg. They're getting older, and her grandfather has dementia."

"I always liked Paula," I said. "I hope she finds someone to love again someday."

Nash kept his attention on the road.

When we reached the outskirts of town, he steered the truck to a neighborhood of neat homes on good-sized lots. Trees filled the yards, with red and yellow leaves clinging to limbs that would soon be bare. We passed the remnants of a snowman, his straw hat lopsided and his stick arms drooping.

Nash stopped in front of a stately redbrick house and cut the engine. A wreath of plastic pink and purple flowers hung on the front door, looking out of place in the wintry world around them.

"Is this where your friend lives?" I asked.

"Mr. and Mrs. Graham live in the main house, but they're out of town for the holiday. Fred lives out back." He paused, his expression solemn. "Fred is a couple years older than us, so I didn't know him when we were growing up. His homelife was about like mine, and he quit school and joined the Army as soon as he was eligible. He was on his second deployment to 'Nam when he stepped on a land mine. He woke up in the hospital, paralyzed from the waist down."

My heart sank hearing the sad tale. "I'm sorry."

Nash nodded. "He's had a hard time since he got back to the States. Mr. Graham was wounded in World War II and received a hero's welcome when he finally made it home. Now he works with vets like Fred and me. He says it's his job to make sure those of us who went to Vietnam know that our service was just as important as his."

His words weren't meant as a rebuke on my stance against the war, but I felt chastised, nonetheless.

"How did you meet them?"

"Someone at the VA in Nashville told me about the Grahams. They open their home every week to a group of us. It's a safe place to talk about what we experienced in 'Nam." His mouth quirked. "I'm not too keen on sharing personal stuff with strangers, but after I got back to Tullahoma, I decided to give it a try. I met Fred here. Since he doesn't have family, the Grahams offered to let him live in their guesthouse."

We exited the vehicle, with Jake leading the way up a concrete driveway toward the backyard. After a couple steps, however, I hesitated.

"Maybe I should wait in the truck. Your friend may not want a stranger showing up unannounced."

Nash slowed his progress and faced me. "I wouldn't've invited you if I thought you weren't welcome. But I'll understand if you'd rather not go in. Seeing Fred in a wheelchair can be a little unnerving."

"I'm not afraid to meet him. I just don't want him to be uncomfortable meeting me."

"He knows about you and Mark. How we grew up together, and how Mark and I went to 'Nam on the same day. He'd probably enjoy seeing a face to go with the name."

I wasn't sure I liked the idea of Nash talking about me and my brother, especially since there was no telling what he might say about me and my liberal ideas. But we were part of Nash's childhood, same as he was part of ours. Our story wouldn't be complete without him, and vice versa.

We continued to make our way around the house. A charming cottage stood in the corner of the backyard, with a wide, brick path going from the patio of the main house to the front door of the small dwelling.

Jake sat in front of the closed door, but when he saw Nash, he began to bark. Before we'd even reached the house, the door swung open.

"Jake, my boy." A moment later, a man in a wheelchair appeared in the opening and reached to pet the dog where he stood, waiting. Uncertainty flashed across Fred's face when he spotted me with Nash.

"Hey, buddy," Nash said when we approached. "This is my friend, Mattie Taylor. We thought we'd bring you a little turkey and stuffing."

I couldn't quite read Fred's expression as we shook hands. He almost seemed embarrassed.

"Come in." He used both hands to make the chair wheels roll backwards into the house.

Jake happily followed. Nash sent me an encouraging smile before we entered.

The small home was cozy, yet I noticed there weren't a lot of furnishings. A small sofa, a television set on a rolling cart, and a table with two chairs occupied the living/kitchen/dining area. A wide, open doorway led to what I assumed was the bedroom.

Nash put the foil-covered dish on the stovetop, then took a seat at the table. I wasn't sure what to do, so I quietly sank onto the sofa.

"I guess the Grahams are glad they went to Florida to visit their daughter and missed this cold snap," Fred said.

While he and Nash chatted about the weather, I surreptitiously studied Fred as he slowly ran his hand up and down Jake's back. Jake, for his part, sat completely still, with his eye half closed, enjoying the attention.

Although Nash said Fred was only a couple years older than us, his face looked as haggard as Dad's. Thin and balding, I would've guessed him to be much older. It didn't seem fair that he'd suffered so much in his life. Without family to help care for him, I wondered what the future held for the man.

"I heard Kenny Beckman was killed last week." Fred's voice held a grim tone. "You probably don't remember him, but he played tight end for the Wildcats back in the day. Left a wife and two kids."

I felt out of place as the two former soldiers discussed the situation in Vietnam. They talked about battles and officers and places I'd never heard of, forcing me to acknowledge that maybe I didn't know as much about the war as I liked to think. Sure, I read news articles and listened to speeches given by leaders at protest rallies, but being in a room with men who'd been there was eye-opening in a way I hadn't anticipated.

Their conversation switched to the farm and preparations for winter.

"Now that the sun's finally out, the horses that have been cooped up in their stalls will need some exercise." Nash glanced at me, as though inviting me to join the discussion. "Right, Mattie?"

"Yes," I said, smiling when Fred glanced my way. "I've always loved riding in autumn. The air is crisp, and the hills are covered in fall colors."

Instead of returning the smile, Fred grew solemn. "I used to ride when we'd visit my grandparents in Kentucky. They had a small place, but it was out in the country. My cousins and I would saddle up and be gone for hours." He turned away. "Guess I'll never do that again."

I glanced at Nash, feeling as though I'd said something wrong.

He quickly changed the subject to the furnace in the cabin, asking for Fred's opinion on gas versus electric since the heater would need to be replaced. But my mind stayed on the previous conversation and the sad fact that Fred would never ride a horse again.

In the year I'd been away, I'd missed the freedom I experienced every time I took Moonlight out for a ride. Big city living was exciting at first, but even though I'd tried to forget my life in Tennessee, the longing to fly across the green hills on the back of a horse never left me. I couldn't imagine living the rest of my life without ever being astride a horse again.

I peeked at Fred.

I'd never known someone who couldn't walk and had to use a wheelchair. I had no idea what it was like to wake up every morning and face the limitations and confinement of a situation like his. It must be a daily struggle to endure the challenges and disappointments of living life without the use of your legs.

Although I believed things would be far different if he hadn't gone to Vietnam, my opinion on the war wasn't important to Fred. He had far greater issues to deal with.

I tapped my finger on the armrest.

Nash was obviously a good friend to Fred. Jake was too, from the looks of it. He'd curled up at Fred's feet and snored softly while the men talked. And even though I didn't know the Grahams, it sounded like they truly cared about Fred and the others.

What about me?

I'd just met the man, yet his story had touched me in a way I hadn't expected. For more than a year, I'd been drowning in my own grief and loss. I hadn't come up for air yet when Dad's telegram found me. The thought of losing Mama was unbearable.

Yet meeting Fred, hearing his pain, reminded me that I wasn't the only one with scars.

I tapped my finger again.

I may not know as much about people and the world as I'd thought just that morning, but what I did know about was horses. Tennessee walking horses, to be specific. With their smooth, easy gait and pleasant personalities, our Tennessee walkers could easily adapt to each rider's specific needs. I'd seen young children, elderly people, and everyone in between learn to ride on the docile animals. It's why the breed was so popular.

"Why not?" I said out loud before I'd thought through the idea swirling in my head.

Both men looked at me.

"Why not, what?" Nash asked.

I moistened my lips, hoping that what I was about to say wouldn't offend the man in the wheelchair. "Why can't you ride a horse again?"

Nash shot me a look of warning, but Fred's eyes narrowed when our gazes met.

"I think it's pretty obvious."

I swallowed hard. There was no turning back now. "I've been around horses all my life. I could barely walk when I started riding. Mama likes to tell the story about when I was a toddler and climbed up on a horse all by myself. Scared her half to death when I went tearing down the road on its back."

Neither man smiled at the endearing tale, so I plunged on.

"What I'm saying is, if a child who can't reach the stirrups can ride a horse, why can't someone who's full grown but can't walk do the same thing?"

I glanced at his legs for the first time since entering the house. Bony and toothpick-thin beneath his jeans, I could only guess his muscles had deteriorated since his injury. But if he could just get in the saddle—

"Mattie," Nash said, drawing my attention. He didn't look happy. "I don't think you understand Fred's situation." He glanced at his friend. "I'm sorry about this. Maybe we should go."

Fred's narrowed gaze, however, remained fixed on me. "Do you really think I could ride again?"

His question demanded honesty. "I don't know. This isn't something we've ever tried on the farm. But," I glanced between him and Nash, who now wore a look of cautious curiosity, "when Dad was teaching Mark and me to ride, he put thick leather belts around our waists. He'd hold on to it while he walked beside us, keeping us steady in the saddle. Granted, we were just kids, but, in theory, the principal could apply to an adult with limited mobility."

They both stared at me. Admittedly, the idea sounded crazy.

"You know," Nash finally said. He scratched his unshaved jaw, a half grin inching its way up his face. "If we rigged up some type of back support to attach to the saddle and used the belt, like Mattie was talking about, it just might work."

I stared at him.

Was Nash saying he approved of my wild idea?

"How would I mount the horse?" Fred asked. "I may not weigh much these days, but I don't think anyone could lift me into a saddle."

Nash and I looked at each other. "A platform," we said at the same time.

"We could build a platform that's level with the horse's back. You'd be able to roll onto it in your chair, then mount the horse with some help." I looked at Nash, who nodded in agreement.

Fred's gaze bounced between Nash and me, his expression reminding me of a kid on Christmas morning. "You'd be willing to go to all that trouble, just so I can ride again?"

Looking at this man who'd suffered so much, the answer was easy.

"Absolutely."

EIGHTEEN

AVA

CAMP FORREST, TENNESSEE
MARCH 1942

The month of March blew in like a lion, but that didn't stop spring from arriving. Wildflowers and budding trees lined the two-lane road that led to Camp Forrest, and herds of Black Angus cattle happily grazed on bright green grass despite strong winds swirling around them. Tennessee truly was beautiful year-round, but after all the sorrow we'd suffered this past winter, the rebirth that came with the warmer weather was more than welcome.

Brilliant morning sunshine peeked over the horizon as I drove through the main gate and made my way to the hospital. I'd begun arriving earlier lately. At first it helped me stay caught up on my ever-growing responsibilities, but in the last week or two, I realized I was using work as an excuse to escape the farm.

There were two reasons for that.

Ivy Lee and Gertrude.

In the short time since Ivy Lee moved into the farmhouse, the two women had become fast friends. Which was confounding, considering Gertrude hadn't spoken a friendly word to me since I arrived last summer. While I generally got along with most people, Gertrude's obvious dislike of me was something I didn't understand and couldn't overcome, no matter what I did to alleviate the situation. Now, watching her laugh and gossip with Ivy Lee every evening, I felt completely left out in my own home.

I parked the Ford in my usual place and carefully made my way across one of the plank sidewalks strewn throughout the camp. Rain had turned the grounds into a muddy mess, and I'd nearly lost a shoe to the abyss yesterday. We could only hope the skies would stay sunny the rest of the week and dry things out.

I glanced toward a building at the far end of the complex.

I hadn't seen Gunther since he began working in the dispensary. I'd hoped to find an excuse to visit him and see how he was faring, but none of the never-ending personnel files took me to the building where the clinic was located. He seemed like a pleasant young man, with a bright future as a doctor if given a chance.

I let myself into the office only to find Colonel Foster engrossed in work.

"Good morning, sir. You're here early."

He looked up. "Good morning, Mrs. Delaney. I might say the same about you."

"Can I get you some coffee?"

He motioned to the mug on his desk. "This is my third cup. I better quit before I start running laps around the camp."

I smiled, then looked at the mound of paperwork on his desk. "Is there anything I can do for you?"

His expression turned serious. "The first group of wounded soldiers from Europe arrive later this week. They're currently being treated in English hospitals but as you can imagine, there are more wounded than England can handle. We need to be certain the hospital is well stocked and well staffed before they get here."

For the rest of the morning, we went over supply lists, requisitions for more beds, the number of ambulances required, and dozens of other details that needed attention. I heard Bren, Stella, and Ethel in the outer office as they came through the door, chatting, but they went right to work, their typewriters singing a familiar song.

By noon, my back ached from sitting in the hard chair.

"I have a lunch appointment at headquarters." Colonel Foster looked at his wristwatch. "Let's meet back here at fourteen-hundred hours."

He greeted the secretaries as he passed through the office and headed outside.

Bren turned to me after he closed the door. "Boy, whatever you're working on must be important."

I filled her and the others in on the imminent arrival of wounded soldiers from Europe. They would receive work related to the influx of patients soon, so knowing ahead of time would help prepare them.

"I think I'll take a break and get some lunch at the mess hall," I said.

We usually ate our sack lunches at our desks, but I'd been in a hurry to leave the house this morning before Ivy Lee and Gertrude came downstairs and started their chatter. I still hadn't figured out what Ivy Lee's job was, but her hours were different from mine, which worked out fine. It kept me from feeling obligated to share a ride with her.

As I walked outside to a breezy but warm day, guilt niggled me.

I didn't want to be unfriendly to Ivy Lee. It wasn't her fault Gertrude preferred her company over mine. I knew I wasn't jealous. I'd come to understand long ago that Richard's mother simply didn't like me and probably never would. It hurt at first, because I hadn't had a mother figure in my life for a while. Mom lived with her new family in Chicago and seemed to forget me altogether. Aunt Vy once told me I reminded Mom of my dad, which wasn't a good thing. Richard had hoped his mother and I would become friends. He'd be disappointed to see us now.

The hospital mess hall was crowded when I entered, with medical personnel, soldiers, and even patients well enough to get out of bed. The aroma of fried chicken and yeast rolls made my mouth water, and I eagerly joined the line.

With my tray in hand, I searched for an empty seat in the packed room. There, in the very back corner, was a small table with only one occupant. As I approached, however, I realized it was a man, and he wore the grass-green uniform of a DOJ detainee.

I was about to turn around when he glanced my way.

"Mrs. Delaney." Gunther stood. "It is good to see you again."

"And you. I must admit I've wondered how you've been. Do you like working at the dispensary?"

He waved to the empty chair opposite him. "You're welcome to join me, and I will tell you about it."

I accepted the offer. "Is your guard not with you?"

A slight smile creased his eyes. "Happily, I am allowed to move about without him. He takes me to the dispensary in the mornings and returns to drive me back to the internment camp at the end of the day. Colonel Foster's orders, as I understand it."

This news pleased me. "I imagine you've been kept busy."

"I have, for which I am grateful. It keeps my mind occupied."

His English was heavily accented but quite good. I wondered how he came to learn it.

"I have been enjoying the warmer weather," he said.

"Yes," I agreed, perhaps a bit too eagerly. "I'm glad winter is behind us."

He nodded. "When I was a child, I took pleasure in the snow.

We would go sledding and build snowmen. But now, I do not care for it so much."

"Do you miss Germany?" I hoped the question wasn't inappropriate, but I couldn't help but be curious about the foreign man.

He seemed to ponder his answer. "I suppose there are things I miss about my homeland, like the food and the music, but I was glad to come to America. My *Mutter*, she wanted me to become a doctor, like her father."

"I'm sure she's proud of you."

He looked down at his plate. "I fear her dream for me will never come true."

I heard defeat in his voice. "Don't give up." His face lifted, and blue eyes met mine. "I don't know what will happen, with the war or with you and the others, but I'm learning we must stay positive and hope for the best."

"That may be easier for you than for me. Everything has been taken from me. Even my freedom. I cannot see a future for me in America, nor do I wish to return to Germany. Not while Hitler and the Nazis are in power."

I debated whether I should tell him my story, but somehow it felt right. "I know the feeling of losing everything. My husband, Richard, died at Pearl Harbor. We hadn't been married for very long. I was supposed to go to Hawaii to be with him, but there was a delay in obtaining our housing."

Genuine sorrow filled his face. "I am very sorry, Mrs. Delaney. You have surely suffered a greater loss than I have."

I offered a sad smile. "We've both suffered. War is so awful. I don't know why some leaders are bent on power at any cost."

"Let us hope the Allies win soon, so it will all come to an end."

I picked up my glass of water and held it up. "Cheers to that."

A smile formed on his lips, and he did likewise. "Cheers."

We ate our meal, with easy conversation between us. A glance at the clock above the main doors, however, reminded me of my duties.

"I best get back to the office." I stood and reached for the lunch tray, but Gunther took it from me.

"Please, allow me."

It had been some time since a man showed such chivalry toward me. "Thank you, Mr. Schneider."

We walked to a window-sized opening where an unseen person took the trays, then made our way outside. Some of the servicemen watched us with curiosity, no doubt wondering what a civilian employee was doing with one of the enemy aliens. Thankfully no one questioned us and we stepped into a glorious afternoon. Even the wind had died down, making the afternoon truly pleasant.

"I enjoyed speaking with you, Mrs. Delaney."

I smiled. "And I you."

He glanced toward the dispensary, then faced me, regret in his eyes. "I hope I will see you again."

A warm tingle spread up my arms. "That would be nice."

I turned toward the administration building, wondering if he was watching. I forced myself to face forward until I reached the wooden steps. When I glanced in the direction I'd come, my heart skipped a beat.

He stood in the same place where we'd parted.

He lifted his hand to wave goodbye.

Only when I returned the gesture did he turn and walk back to the dispensary.

• • •

Gunther and I *accidentally* met at noon the following day, and the day after that.

I purposefully didn't bring lunch from home, ensuring the need to make the trek to the mess hall, the same time I'd gone that first day. When I spotted his green uniform at the table in the back corner, I had to keep my bottom lip clamped between my teeth to hide my grin.

We talked about all kinds of things. The hospital. The internment camp. The war. Although neither of us delved too deeply into the subjects, considering our positions at Camp Forrest, by the end of our third meeting, I knew I'd found a friend.

"Where did you learn to speak English so well?" I asked. We'd both finished eating our fried fish and coleslaw, with Gunther bemoaning the lack of sauerkraut on the menu at American mess halls. My lunch break only lasted forty-five minutes, so we filled every second with conversation.

"After my father died from the effects of the mustard gas he was exposed to during the Great War, *Mutter* went to work as a schoolteacher to support us. She was fluent in French, and when one of her fellow teachers asked her to tutor his daughter, *Mutter* in turn asked the man to tutor me in English." He paused, as though remembering that long ago day. "She always hoped I would come to America to study medicine."

"What about your brother? You said he's older than you."

Gunther's brow tugged into a frown, and he didn't answer right away. "Rolf joined the army as a youth. I have not heard from him directly in many years."

His stiff answer reminded me that our friendship was new. Although I hoped he knew he could trust me, I would understand if he remained cautious regarding the information he divulged about his family and his life in Germany.

We followed the same routine we'd begun the first day. He carried my tray to the counter, then waited for me to reach the office steps before he waved. I'd just raised my hand in return when I heard Colonel Foster's voice behind me.

"Is that Mr. Schneider?"

I nearly jumped out of my skin and whirled to find his attention focused on Gunther's retreating back. When he looked at me, I felt like a child caught doing something naughty.

"Yes," I said, attempting to sound normal. "I ran into him at the mess hall."

Which was true, for the most part.

He didn't say more, so I turned and entered the building. He followed and went directly to his office and closed the door.

Bren peeked over her shoulder at me. "Where have you been?" she whispered. "This is the third day in a row you haven't eaten with us."

I rolled a sheet of paper into the Underwood typewriter on my desk. "I haven't been to the PX this week, and Gertrude doesn't want me to take leftovers for lunch anymore. She says Ivy Lee is paying rent, so she gets first dibs."

Again, that was true. Gertrude had indeed told Ivy Lee she was welcome to make her lunch from anything she found in the refrigerator. She'd also insinuated that I could have whatever was left, which was usually bologna.

However, I didn't want anyone—not Bren, the other secretaries, or especially Colonel Foster—becoming suspicious about my friendship with Gunther. Tomorrow I'd let him know we would need to limit our lunches to twice a week. But I'd also had an idea spring to mind today when we were together, and I wanted to talk to him about it as soon as possible.

That conversation had to wait.

Gunther didn't come to the mess hall the next day, then I had to work through lunch on Friday to process a rush requisition for supplies. When the clock struck noon on Monday, I practically ran from the office to the mess hall, anxious to see if he was there.

Relief washed through me when I spotted the familiar green in the corner.

I hurried through the line, not even caring that the meal today was chipped beef on toast with a side of peas. When I reached the table, I was out of breath.

"Mrs. Delaney," he said, concern in his blue eyes as he stood. "Are you all right?"

I laughed. "Yes, but I was worried about you. Why weren't you here last Thursday?"

"There was an emergency at the dispensary. I came the following day, but you were not here. I too worried."

We shared a grin. "Aren't we a couple of sillies. But," I said, sobering, "I think it best if we limit our lunch meetings." I glanced around, and although no one seemed to take notice of us, I felt nervous. "I wouldn't want anyone to get the wrong impression."

Gunther's gaze passed over the large room filled with military and hospital personnel. When we settled in our seats, he leaned forward and spoke in a low tone.

"I do not wish to bring trouble to you. I will understand if you would rather not come again."

"I don't want to stop meeting," I hurried to say. I couldn't help the smile that came to my lips when I added, "I enjoy our time together."

My reward was the light that came into his eyes. "As do I."

I looked down at the unappetizing food on my plate. "I think I'll probably do more talking today than eating."

He laughed. "It tastes gooder than it looks."

His use of the incorrect word reminded me of my idea. "I want to ask you about something. You said a friend of your mother's tutored you in English, and it certainly shows. You have a wonderful command of the language, considering it's not native to you."

His attention on me never faltered. "Thank you. Sometimes, though, I struggle with how to pronounce English words correctly. I know my German accent is difficult to understand for some."

"Would you like to continue to study English? I could help. I'm not a teacher, but—"

"Yes."

His quick answer made me smile. "I hoped you'd say that."

"How would we accomplish this?" He glanced around the noisy room, then faced me again. "It is difficult to hear your voice even now."

He was right, of course.

I mulled over ideas for a quieter place to meet rather than the loud mess hall. The library or one of the recreation halls would work well, but Gunther's status as an enemy alien prevented him from leaving the hospital complex. My office was out of the question, too, since I didn't want to raise questions about why I was spending time with him. Even though our friendship was completely innocent, I knew some people might misunderstand or disapprove because Gunther was German.

The door opened as someone entered, letting in midday sunshine.

"We could meet outside now that the weather is warmer," I said. "There's a bench behind the dental clinic, but it's in plain view from the windows. Captain Jones, the dentist in charge, takes his breaks there so he can smoke a cigarette."

We discussed the plan, deciding it would be best for me to bring sandwiches for both of us on our study days. It would save time, plus we could bypass the mess hall all together.

When our lunch came to an end and we walked outside, Gunther turned to me.

"May I ask you something, Mrs. Delaney?"

When I nodded, he said, "Why do you wish to help me? Most Americans believe I am their enemy. I cannot fault them, considering what is happening in my homeland. But you," he shook his head in wonder, "you see me differently. You see me for who I am, not where I come from."

"My grandmother used to tell me to treat people the way I want them to treat me. The day you saved that soldier's life, I knew you were trustworthy. I've never had many friends. I keep people at a distance, mainly because I'm afraid they'll abandon me, like my dad and then my mom." I hoped he didn't think I was some crazy American woman making a pass at him. "I want to be your friend, Gunther."

His eyes widened at my use of his given name, but soon a slow smile lifted his lips. "*Danke*, Ava," he said softly. "I want very much to be your friend, too."

We parted with the promise of meeting again at the bench behind the dental clinic. When I reached the office steps and turned, he was there, his hand lifted in farewell.

Lunchtime on Wednesday couldn't get here fast enough.

NINETEEN

MATTIE

DELANEY HORSE FARM

NOVEMBER 1969

Nurse Bradford was gone by the time Nash and I returned to the farm. I learned from Dad that Mama'd had a sponge bath and had eaten some oatmeal before the woman departed. Even though I enjoyed spending the morning with Nash and Fred without worrying about Mama, I couldn't shake the feeling of no longer being needed.

It's not surprising, then, that I spent the entire afternoon with her.

"Now it so happened, that, in spite of Emma's resolution of never marrying, there was something in the name, in the idea, of Mr. Frank Churchill, which always interested her. She had frequently thought—especially since his father's marriage with Miss Taylor—that if she were to marry, he was the very person to suit her in age, character, and condition."

I glanced up from the book in my hands to be sure Mama hadn't fallen asleep again. Although she'd read Jane Austen's *Emma* countless times through the years, she'd asked me to read it aloud to her today. I was pleased to see her eyes open, watching me.

"Emma wouldn't have been happy if she'd married Mr. Churchill." She gave a languid smile. "Nor would he have been happy with her. They were each meant to marry someone else."

My gaze drifted to the framed black-and-white photograph on the bureau of her and Dad. It was taken on the farm before Mark and I were born. While Mama smiled into the camera, Dad's expression was his usual solemn frown. Even as a little girl, I'd often wondered why my father was so unhappy.

"How did you know Dad was the man you were supposed to marry?"

She, too, looked at the photograph. "He needed me, and I needed him."

That didn't sound very romantic. Maybe that's why she enjoyed novels like *Emma*. Mr. Knightley was the epitome of manly excellence. Handsome. Rich. Kind. Honorable. It made me wonder if such men only existed in fiction. I had yet to come across one.

I read for another thirty minutes before she drifted to sleep. Closing the book, I walked over to the photograph and picked it up. Mama was so pretty. Not much older than I was now, she looked young and vibrant. Happiness radiated from her face.

My eyes studied Dad next.

Tall and handsome, I could see why Mama was attracted to him. But unlike Mr. Knightley, Dad's hero-like qualities ended there. He wasn't a mean drunk, like Nash's father, nor was he lazy, but I couldn't find anything in his character that clued me in to why Mama had married him. Other than the one time I'd seen him dancing with her in the kitchen, I couldn't recall witnessing marital affection between them.

I set the picture down, snuck one last peek at Mama, and

tiptoed from the room. It was too early to start dinner, so I headed to my bedroom. On the way home from town, Nash and I had discussed the possibility of helping Fred ride a horse once again.

"Are we sure this is a good idea?" The moment we left Fred's cottage, I'd started to doubt the certainty I'd felt just minutes before. "I would hate to get his hopes up only to have it fail. Or worse. He could fall off the horse and get hurt."

Nash glanced over to me. "Did you see his face when you suggested it? I've never seen Fred that excited." He focused on the road again. "The fact that you would consider trying to help him get on a horse was enough to breathe life back into him."

We'd brainstormed designs for the type of platform we would need to build to get Fred level with a horse's back. A sturdy harness or belt of some sort would also be required. Nash said he'd run the idea of Fred coming out to the farm past Dad, but I couldn't see any reason why he would disagree. We made plans to get to work on the platform tomorrow morning while Nurse Bradford was here. By the time we reached home, my mind was spinning with the concept of helping a paralyzed war veteran ride a horse. I couldn't help but chuckle, thinking about how shocked my brother would be if he were here.

"You sure like to keep me guessing, don't you, Sis?" he used to say when I'd share my latest wild pipe dream.

Back in my room, I felt restless. My gaze landed on the shoebox of letters on my desk. Mama'd said they held secrets that needed to be revealed, yet after Nash and I read some of them last night, I'd found them harmless.

Settling on my unmade bed cross-legged, with the box in my lap, I took out the bundles of letters and read the addressee's name. *Ava Delaney.* The scrawled name on the envelopes of both bundles were the same. The returnees' names, however, were different. The first batch was from SN Richard Delaney. The second group came from someone named Gunther Schneider.

I studied the envelope in my hand.

Why would Mama have letters written to a woman named Ava Delaney? Did they perhaps belong to *her* mother? I couldn't recall my grandmother's first name. I'd only met her once. Had she been a Delaney too, like Granny?

Memories of the time Mama, Mark, and I took the train to Chicago when he and I were about five years old floated across my mind. I vaguely remembered meeting a woman with graying hair. She wasn't mean or grumpy, like Granny. She simply wasn't interested in us, her grandchildren from Tennessee. We didn't stay long, as I recall. Maybe a couple days at most. She'd passed away when Mark and I were in high school. Mama went to the funeral alone.

Laying the letters aside, I reached for the old book.

Die Bibel.

As I thumbed through the pages, I was convinced my first assumption was correct. It was most likely written in German, and it was unmistakably a Bible. But why it was in Mama's belongings, however, remained a mystery.

I leaned back against the pillows and turned to the front of the book. There I found neat but faded handwriting.

Für meinen Sohn, Ehre Gott immer. Ich liebe dich, Mutter.

I spoke the strange words aloud, no doubt destroying the correct pronunciation. Could the first sentence be *For my son*? Possibly. The next words completely stumped me, but I felt certain *Mutter* was Mother. We'd once had an Amish family purchase a horse from us, and the cute little boy, dressed like his father in black pants, white shirt, and straw hat, had called his mother *Mutter*. If my guess was right, then it stood to reason that someone's mother gave them this Bible many years ago.

Again, the question I'd asked earlier returned.

Why did Mama have it?

I yawned, my eyelids suddenly heavy. After I returned the book and the letters to the box, I lay back against the pillows. Maybe

Nash would have time this evening after dinner to read more of the letters with me. The mystery regarding Ava Delaney was starting to bug me. I wanted to know who she was and why Mama had her letters.

I awoke an hour later. The sky out my window still had light, but it was dwindling quickly. When I walked into the hallway, Mama's bedroom door was closed, but I could hear Dad speaking quietly.

I reached the kitchen to find Nash at the stove, frying hamburger patties.

"I'm sorry," I said. "I just meant to close my eyes for a minute or two, but I fell asleep."

"It's no problem." He flipped the sizzling meat. "I cooked a lot of burgers when I was a kid. Mom worked at the Dairy Bar drive-in, and she'd bring home ground meat the owner was going to throw out."

As I helped chop onions and slice a tomato, I thought about Nash's mom. I hadn't known Mrs. McCallum well. She kept to herself for the most part. Mama'd tried to become friendly with her when the boys began to pal around, inviting her to come for lunch or join us at church. But Mrs. McCallum would politely decline, usually with some kind of excuse. If Mark and Nash ever talked about it, I didn't know the details. Nash's mom lived up north now. I hoped she'd found some happiness there.

Dad arrived in the kitchen, and we sat down to dinner.

"Nash says you offered to let his friend come out and ride," he said after a stretch of silence while we dug into our food.

I glanced up, trying to judge his tone and facial expression. The disapproval I usually saw when I expressed an opinion on a subject, however, wasn't there.

"I don't know if it will work, but I think we should try." I glanced at Nash. "I may not agree with the reason Fred was in Vietnam, but that doesn't matter now. He's home, he's injured, and he needs people in his life who care about that. You and the Grahams are doing your part." I gave a slight shrug. "I'd like to do mine."

Dad nodded. "I told Nash his friend is welcome here, anytime."

Long after we'd each finished eating the simple yet delicious meal, we sat at the table and discussed the details of teaching a paralyzed man to ride a horse again. Dad had a lot of great suggestions. He reminded us that Fred hadn't walked in nearly a year. His balance, therefore, wouldn't be the same as it was when both his legs functioned. There was also the fact that riding a horse typically required the rider to use pressure from their legs to guide the animal.

"He'll need a horse we can retrain." He rubbed his jaw. "Moonlight would have been good, but I don't want to take any risks with her. Dawn's Rose is our smallest mare. Her gait is smooth and won't jostle him."

"I was thinking about her too." I felt unusually pleased to find myself in agreement with my father. It didn't happen often. "Do you remember the belts you used when Mark and I were little and learning to ride? You'd hold on to the back of it while you walked beside the horse. I thought we could do something like that for Fred."

The corners of his mouth lifted, and he nodded. "I remember."

With plans in motion, Nash and I cleaned the kitchen while Dad took some soup to Mama.

"Thank you for offering to help Fred," Nash said as he scraped a leftover beef patty into Jake's bowl. The dog sniffed it, then gingerly picked it up with his teeth and carried it over to his rug to enjoy in comfort.

"It's the right thing to do." I met Nash's gaze. "I know it's hard for you and Dad to believe this, but I only wanted what was best. For our country. For Mark. Even for you. Going to fight a war on the other side of the world wasn't best. For anyone."

"And you may not believe this, but I agree with you."

I blinked. "What?"

"War is never *best*," he said, "but sometimes it's necessary."

I narrowed my eyes. "If I ask you something, will you give me an honest answer?"

"Always."

"If you could go back to the summer of '65, knowing what you know now, would you do anything differently? Would you still go to Vietnam?"

He didn't respond right away. When he did finally answer, his words weren't what I expected to hear. "I'd do everything differently."

"What do you mean?"

He glanced out the window to the stars in the inky sky. "I wouldn't tell anyone I was joining the military. Not even Mark. Especially not Mark. I'd just catch a bus to Nashville and disappear."

"I don't understand. You'd still go to war?"

"I would, but I wouldn't take Mark with me." He shook his head, anguish in his eyes. "If I hadn't talked about becoming a Marine—hadn't bragged about doing my duty—Mark wouldn't have gone to 'Nam. He would've gone to Vanderbilt with you. He would've played football and married Paula." He turned away. "He wouldn't've died over there. It's my fault he isn't here."

Stunned, I could only stare at him.

For four years, I'd blamed Nash for everything he'd just confessed. I'd been convinced my brother would still be alive if it wasn't for him. In the months I lived in California, I'd hated Nash. How many times had I wished it was him who'd come home in a body bag instead of my brother?

But now, here in the stillness of the farmhouse, I knew I'd been wrong.

And Nash was wrong too.

"That isn't true," I said. When he looked at me, I offered a feeble shrug. "I used to think it was true. I was so angry at you. I was certain you were responsible for Mark going to Vietnam. For taking him away from me." Tears blurred my vision. "But the truth is, he would've gone anyway. He wasn't the kind of person to let someone else's decision sway his. He was determined to be a modern-day Dietrich Bonhoeffer."

Silence stood between us for a long moment.

"Are you saying you forgive me?" Nash asked, his voice full of emotion.

Was I?

Nash wasn't my enemy, I realized. He was a casualty of war, same as Mark. He'd gone to Vietnam whole and come back broken. So had Fred and countless others. I would still speak out against the wrongs done by our government and military leaders, but I could no longer hate the soldiers. Men who weren't much different than my brother and his best friend.

"I guess I am."

His expression eased. "Thank you."

We didn't say more on the subject.

When the kitchen was clean and the house quiet, I said, "I thought I'd go through more of those old letters of Mama's. I could use some company."

Nash smiled. "Sure thing."

We settled on the sofa after I went upstairs to retrieve the box. The door to my parents' room was closed. No sound came from inside. I hoped Mama was resting comfortably. I even hoped Dad could get some rest, too.

"I still think it's strange that the letters are addressed to someone named Ava Delaney." I took a folded sheet of paper from one of the envelopes that came from Hawaii. Like those we'd read yesterday, this too was signed *Your loving husband, Richard.*

We took turns reading out loud as we went through the stack of correspondences, all similar in content. It was clear Richard loved Ava. His anxiousness for her to join him in Hawaii was evident. When we reached the last one, I looked at the postmarked date on the envelope.

"This was mailed on December fifth, 1941." I glanced at Nash. "Wasn't that just a couple days before Pearl Harbor was attacked?"

Nash nodded. "I wonder if Richard was there."

"There aren't any more letters after this one."

When I finished reading it, I put it with the others. "Ava Delaney must've been a relative. That's why Mama has her letters."

"But didn't your mom say the letters held some sort of secret she wanted you to know?"

"She did, but so far I don't see anything out of the ordinary about them. I've never heard of Richard Delaney."

I picked up the second bundle of envelopes. "Then there are these, from someone named Gunther Schneider. I've never heard of him either. There aren't as many of these as there are from Richard, but from the dates on the postmarks," I said, thumbing through the right-hand corner of the stack, "they were all written in 1943, '44, and '45."

Nash nodded as he stifled a yawn.

I chuckled. "I better let you get some sleep. The mystery can wait. We'll read these tomorrow."

I bid him and Jake good night and quietly made my way upstairs. After my impromptu nap earlier, I wasn't ready to turn in yet. I'd enjoyed reading the letters with Nash, so I didn't want to start on the second bundle alone.

I took the old Bible from the box and stretched out on my bed.

Memories of attending church with Mama and Mark floated through my mind.

Even as a little girl, I'd always been one to ask questions during Sunday school. While the other children sat quietly and listened to the teacher share stories about Moses, David, and Jesus, I wanted to know details.

Why did God let baby Moses live while other baby boys died?

How could David kill a giant with one stone?

What happened to the little boy who gave his lunch of five loaves and two fish to Jesus? I bet he couldn't believe it when Jesus fed a big crowd with it.

On and on. I'd wave my hand in the air as soon as something popped into my head and keep waving until the teacher reluctantly called on me. Mark teased me about being so inquisitive, but I didn't care. I wanted to know why I should believe the stories. More than one teacher grew weary of my interruptions through the years.

Why don't you ask your mother when you get home, they'd say when they'd had enough. Then they'd finish the lesson using flannel board cutouts of Bible characters, palm trees, and plain-looking houses we were sometimes allowed to play with when the class ended. On the drive back to the farm, I would pepper Mama with questions, and she would patiently give the best answers she could.

I ran my fingers over the cover of the foreign Bible.

Why had I never had a childlike faith in the tales found in this book? Mark easily accepted everything it said, but I don't think I ever did. I believed in God, mainly because it seemed illogical not to, considering the world around us. But like young Mattie in Sunday school class, I still had many questions.

Why does God allow evil to exist?

If he loves his children, why do people like Fred suffer?

Where was God when my brother died?

No, I couldn't just blindly believe like Mama and Mark. I needed logical answers, and so far, I had yet to get them.

I turned page after page, studying beautiful illustrations when I came to them. I knew the names of the books in the Bible. We'd had to memorize them in Sunday school. But with no understanding of the language this Bible was written in, it was pointless to continue perusing it.

I'd just thumbed through the last book—*Das Buch der Offenbarung*—when I discovered a small, brown cardboard sheath stuck to the inside cover. It looked like the kind that held our grade school class pictures, with a flap to keep the photograph from getting scratched.

It didn't take much effort to free it from the back cover without doing damage to either the book or the case. Curious to see what it contained, I was mildly disappointed to find a black-and-white image of a woman standing with each arm around the shoulders of two school-age boys. The group stood outside, next to an old-fashioned, dark vehicle. There was no writing on the back to give clues as to who they were.

Could the woman be Ava Delaney? Maybe. It would make sense, being that the Bible was in the same box as the letters. But I still didn't know why Mama was in possession of the mysterious Ava's belongings.

I yawned.

I returned the photograph to where I'd found it and closed the book.

With everything we needed to do to get ready for Fred before he came to the farm this weekend, I didn't have time to waste on supposed family secrets.

TWENTY

GUNTHER

CAMP FORREST, TENNESSEE
MARCH 1942

Gunther watched the clock on the wall in the dispensary like a hawk looking for a mouse in a cornfield.

One hour until he and Ava were to meet at the bench behind the dental clinic.

Concealing a grin, he forced his attention back to the medical instruments he was cleaning. A soldier had come in earlier with a deep gash on his forehead after falling from a high wall on the training field. The wound required ten stitches, and Major Gridley allowed Gunther to perform the procedure under his supervision. It was the second time the doctor asked Gunther to take charge of a patient since he'd begun working in the dispensary a month ago.

"I'm a Columbia medical school alumni," the older man said the first day Gunther arrived at the small clinic. "After Colonel

Foster assigned you to me, I called an old friend at Columbia and asked him to look into your records. They're impressive. I'm happy to have you on board."

The affirming words were a balm to an open wound. His work in the dispensary helped Gunther feel like a normal person rather than an enemy alien. To know the major found him worthy to continue to learn and practice medicine, despite his German roots, buoyed him in a profound way. He still wasn't certain what would happen when the war ended, but the major's confidence in Gunther's abilities made him think that perhaps his dream of becoming a doctor wasn't dead after all.

The officer proved to be a considerate, knowledgeable man, and Gunther found himself looking up to Major Gridley in the same way he'd looked up to Dr. Sonnenberg. The men were complete opposites in many ways—Dr. Sonnenberg was a small, serious, Jewish man, and the major was overweight, loved a good joke, and kept a Bible on his desk—yet their skills as doctors shone through in everything they did.

He appeared in the doorway of the back room while Gunther was putting away the sterilized instruments.

"How is your patient doing, Mr. Schneider?"

Gunther was pleased by the inquiry. "He has a concussion, but his X-ray showed no fractures to the skull. After a day or two in the hospital, he should be fit to return to his unit."

The major nodded. "I must say, you have quite a talent for stitching. Perhaps you've chosen the wrong profession. You'd make a fine tailor."

The quirk to the man's mouth told Gunther he was teasing. "My *Mutter* taught me how to use a needle when I was a boy. It was for the purpose of patching my clothes, but I believe she would be happy to know I'm putting it to use patching people."

The man looked thoughtful. "You did well. I have never seen such neat stitches. That soldier owes you, as I doubt he'll have any scarring at all. Although, some of these boys don't mind a scar or two. They think it helps with the ladies."

Gunther returned to his work after the man left.

His mind drifted to Ava. He didn't think she was the kind of woman who would be impressed by scars. What *would* get her attention, he wondered? He'd been surprised when she told him she was a widow. She was far too young to have gone through something like losing a husband. But with war raging across the globe, there would be thousands of women like Ava by the end of it.

His mind returned to their last lunch together. She thought it best if they weren't seen together too often, as she didn't want anyone to grow suspicious. They'd decided to meet on Tuesdays and Thursdays at noon. Although their purpose in meeting was innocent, Gunther knew she was right to be concerned, yet he wished they could meet whenever they pleased.

He made his way back to the main room of the dispensary.

Limited space caused it to feel crowded, with two examination stations, each complete with a folding chair and a cabinet with supplies, plus a long examination table shoved up against the far wall. A wooden bench just inside the door acted as the waiting area.

Luckily, there weren't any patients in the clinic now. He hoped none would arrive before lunchtime, thus stealing away his time with Ava.

He picked up the book she'd brought to him last week. *Emma* by Jane Austen. She explained it was her favorite novel. She'd read it so many times, she said, she had parts of it memorized.

"I know it may seem strange to ask you to read a romance novel that was first published in 1815," she said when she handed it to Gunther, "but the language Miss Austen uses is pure and free of slang and American terms. I thought it would be a good place to begin our English lessons."

Gunther had, of course, heard of the novel and its author. The book was translated into many languages through the years, including German. But he'd never once had an interest in reading it . . . until now.

"I'm sure I will enjoy the story."

The happy smile that filled her face was worth the teasing he would no doubt receive from his cabinmates when they found him reading such a book.

When the hands on the clock were straight up on twelve, Gunther let Major Gridley know he was going to lunch and left the building. The dental clinic was located on the opposite side of the hospital complex, and he walked as fast as he could. Although the weather had turned warm, he'd put on the lightweight black jacket he'd brought with him from New York to help conceal the bright green of his internee uniform.

As soon as he saw her waiting for him on the bench, he slowed his pace.

She smiled when he approached. "Hello."

"Hello."

She held up a brown paper bag. "I brought chicken salad sandwiches today. They're quite good if I do say so myself. I use a secret ingredient."

Gunther settled on the bench, keeping an appropriate amount of space between them. "I will be able to pay you for the lunches soon. Major Gridley said I am to earn a small wage."

"That's wonderful, but you needn't worry about reimbursing me. You'll want to save every penny so you can go back to school as soon as the Hearing Board reviews your case again and realizes there's been a terrible mistake."

Gunther sighed. "*If* they review my case again. I have not heard of anyone being released once they leave Ellis Island."

They ate their sandwiches and enjoyed a lively discussion on the character of Emma. Gunther declared her spoiled, but Ava defended Emma's independent personality. When Gunther began to read the third chapter aloud, Ava stopped him periodically to correct his pronunciation of this word or that. Her instruction was never done in a patronizing way but always with kindness and a genuine desire to help him learn.

"Qua-drille," she said, sounding out a word unfamiliar to Gunther. "It's a type of dance they did back in those days."

Gunther repeated the word several times before she was satisfied.

"There was a club in New York where my friends and I would dance the jitterbug on weekends," he said, thinking back to the days before his world imploded. So easy and carefree. "*Jitterbug* is easier to say than *qua-drille*."

Ava laughed. "I imagine it's easier to dance, too. Four couples are required for the quadrille, and there are many steps to learn. The timing and pace is important."

"I don't z'ink my friends an' I would enjoy such a dance. It sounds more complicated zan fun," Gunther said.

He immediately realized he'd lapsed into what he called "lazy English," letting his pronunciation of certain words announce to the world he was German. It usually happened when he was tired or relaxed, as he was becoming in Ava's company.

"*Th*ink. *Th*an. It sounds more complicated *th*an fun," she corrected. "Try not to use the *z* sound when pronouncing words that begin with *t-h*."

Gunther slowly said the sentence again, once again conscious of his tendency to let his German accent overpower the English words. "I hope a day will come when my English is so good," he said, emphasizing the *d* sound rather than saying it as a *t*, "no one will know I am from Germany."

He thought the comment would please her, but Ava looked troubled.

"There is nothing wrong with being German. It's part of your heritage, your story. You shouldn't be blamed for the terrible things the leaders of your country have done any more than I should be blamed for the wrongs done in America."

He considered the wisdom in her comment. "I agree, but unfortunately, not everyone else does. I worry what will happen if Germany wins the war."

"Do you think you'd be sent back?"

"I do not know, but sometimes I fear staying more than I fear returning. If I remain in America, I could be a prisoner for the rest of my life. The truth is, I no longer have a home. Not in Germany. Not in America."

Her expression revealed her empathy. "Then we need to pray that Hitler will be defeated. I can't imagine a world where he is in power over all of Europe."

They sat in silence for a while, each deep in thought, before Ava glanced at her watch.

"I better get back to the office." She gathered the empty lunch wrappers and stuffed them into the bag.

They walked to the front of the dental clinic. Two soldiers were just leaving, but neither took notice of Gunther and Ava.

"I will practice my qua-drille when I return to the internee camp," Gunther said in jest, hoping to lighten the mood. "So the next time we meet, I will be proficient at it."

The grin he'd hoped for spread across Ava's face. "I can almost picture you and your housemates dancing tonight." She gave a low curtsy. "Kind sir, may I have this dance?" she said with a laugh.

When she met his gaze again, all humor faded as he stared into her hazel eyes. "It would be my honor to dance with you one day, Mrs. Delaney."

A slight flush filled her cheeks, but she didn't look away. "I'd like that, Mr. Schneider."

They parted. As was their custom, just before she went around the corner, Ava turned and Gunther lifted his hand. After she returned the gesture and he started back to the dispensary, he realized two things.

He was falling in love with Ava Delaney.

But along with that awareness came a bitter truth.

They had no hope of a future together.

None whatsoever.

TWENTY-ONE

AVA

CAMP FORREST, TENNESSEE
MARCH 1942

Gertrude and Ivy Lee were in the kitchen when I arrived home.

The delicious aroma of chicken soup and corn bread filled the air, making my mouth water. While rumors of impending rationing continued to dominate the news, just this week we enjoyed Gertrude's meatloaf, pot roast, and even a vanilla cake. As far as I knew, Gertrude hadn't complained even once about preparing meals for our boarder the way she used to complain about cooking for me.

Ivy Lee hadn't gone to work that morning. Whether she had the day off or had taken it off, I didn't know, but I now saw the reason for it. She'd obviously gone into town to the beauty shop. Her hair was teased and combed high, and her nails sported a fresh coat of red polish. A new dress hugged her curves, and she looked ready for a night on the town. Although I still hadn't warmed to our new housemate the way Gertrude had, I did attempt to be more friendly when we were together.

"You look nice," I said, pushing a smile to my lips. "Is there a special occasion?"

Ivy Lee and Gertrude exchanged grins before she looked at me again. "I should say so. Yours truly has a date with a *colonel*."

I might have guessed. The young woman constantly talked about the men she pursued and those who pursued her. On a military installation as big as Camp Forrest, there were certainly plenty of eligible bachelors to keep a girl like Ivy Lee busy every weekend.

"That's nice."

Ivy Lee cackled. "Nice? Honey, I'm not talkin' about some wet-behind-the-ears private. Colonel Paxton is a *man*. He's been in the Army for ages and oversees the entire trainin' facility." She winked. "If I play my cards right, I might be quittin' my job and gettin' married soon."

From the stove where she stirred the soup in a large pot, Gertrude said, "I hope he won't want to wait until the war ends. No telling when that might be."

A sly smile curved Ivy Lee's ruby lips. "Oh, he won't want to wait too long. I know how to give a man just enough to keep him interested without givin' him the keys to the house, if you know what I mean."

Poor Colonel Paxton. Did he know what he was getting himself into?

I wondered how Ivy Lee met the officer but didn't ask. I still didn't know what her job was on base, but it apparently put her in a position to meet plenty of men. She'd had a dozen dates since she moved to the farm.

The woman's gaze fell on me then, giving me a critical once over. "What about your colonel? I hear he's available. Maybe we could double-date sometime."

I frowned. "I work for Colonel Foster. He isn't interested in me romantically."

"I bet we could change that with a little makeup and a trip to the dress shop in town." She tilted her head and examined me. "You do tend to look a bit frumpy. I'd be happy to help you find an outfit that suits you better. Then you'll have to fight off all the men wantin' to take you to the USO."

I offered a stiff smile. "It will be some time before I'm ready to date again."

The not-so-subtle reminder of my widowhood hung in the air.

"Oh, of course," she said, looking contrite. "I'm sorry. I . . . forgot." She cast an apologetic glance to Gertrude, but the older woman stared into the pot.

We sat down to dinner, although Ivy Lee declared she couldn't eat much since she had a date later. The conversation moved from eligible men to the war.

"The newspaper says we're sending fifty thousand of our boys over to Europe every month now." Gertrude shook her head as she buttered a piece of corn bread. "It ain't right. Our young men shouldn't have to fight that German madman."

Ivy Lee nodded in agreement. "And to think, over two hundred German Nazis are right here in Tullahoma, livin' on base. It's positively terrifyin', I tell you. They'd no doubt kill us all if given the chance."

My shoulders tensed. While I couldn't speak for every one of the internees, I knew Gunther's story. "I don't believe all the German men being held at Camp Forrest are Nazis."

"How do you know?" Gertrude's eyes narrowed. "Anyone who hails from Germany is certain to be loyal to Hitler."

I thought of Gunther and what he'd told me about his mother wanting him to come to America to become a doctor. "From what I understand, many of the men being detained came to America to work or go to school. They aren't soldiers. Some of them don't want to return to Germany."

"That's exactly where they need to go," Ivy Lee said. "It isn't safe to have those men in our country. Some of the soldiers I know think they're spies, pretending to be innocent victims yet all the while gathering information about us and sending it back to Germany. I'll ask Colonel Paxton about them when we go to dinner tonight." A dreamy expression replaced her scowl. "He's takin' me to a late supper at the Minor's Restaurant at the Hotel King. He promised we'd have caviar and champagne."

Thankfully, Ivy Lee continued to gush about the colonel, veering far from the topic of the German internees. I'd already said too much. I certainly didn't want to accidentally divulge anything that would make Gertrude suspicious about my growing friendship with Gunther.

When we finished the meal, I washed dishes while Ivy Lee freshened her makeup and left the house. Gertrude retired to her room upstairs, leaving me alone with my thoughts. Flicking off the kitchen light, I went to the parlor and turned on the radio. Jimmy Dorsey's voice filled the small room as I settled on the sofa, my legs tucked beneath me. He sang of glowing sunsets in summer skies, and the gleam of love in his sweetheart's lovely eyes.

I sighed.

Songs like that always brought regret to the surface, although it was never far away.

I glanced at the photograph of Richard on the mantel as the song continued. "I wish I'd loved you the way you loved me," I whispered.

Bittersweet memories of dancing to Big Band music with Richard at the USO brought tears to my eyes. "We did have fun together though, didn't we? If things were different and you were here, I'd try every day to be the wife you deserved. We would've been happy."

But even as I said the words, part of me wondered if they were true. How could I be the wife I'd promised to be without truly loving my husband? I'd cared for Richard, yet genuine love hadn't taken root in my heart. Not even during the handful of days when I was his wife in every way. I'd held on to hope that love would grow once we were together in Hawaii and started our life as a married couple, but that chance was stolen from us by the cruel hand of war.

The song ended.

It wasn't good to dwell on the past. I couldn't go back and change the choices I'd made. I needed to look forward. Make plans as best I could. I'd already managed to save some money since I began working. I hated to admit it, but the rental income Ivy Lee brought with her had helped with the bills. It also helped me see that Gertrude didn't need me to stay. She'd never thought of me as her daughter-in-law. Seeing her enjoy Ivy Lee's company allowed me to consider leaving the farm without guilt. Richard had always planned to sell it and move away, so it didn't make sense for me to remain much longer.

Another ballad began to play. For reasons I couldn't understand, Gunther's image appeared in my mind's eye.

It would be my honor to dance with you one day, Mrs. Delaney.

Warm tingles raced up my arms, remembering his soft words. They'd felt like a caress, and I'd wanted to fall into his embrace right then and there.

I shook my head and forced my eyes open.

"You're being ridiculous," I chided myself. I switched off the radio and left the light on for Ivy Lee before going to my bedroom.

Yet as soon as I crawled beneath the covers, and the world was quiet and dark, Gunther invaded my mind once again.

With a huff, I rolled onto my side and stared out the window to the night sky.

"Gunther Schneider is a German enemy alien," I said to the

stars, knowing they would keep my secret. "I shouldn't be thinking of him at all."

Yes, he was handsome.

Yes, he'd been a gentleman every time we'd been together.

Yet none of those things mattered most. The fact is, I had no firsthand knowledge of why Gunther had been arrested and remained under the government's supervision. Ivy Lee and Gertrude believed the detainees were all Nazis simply because they came from Germany. While I couldn't bring myself to believe Gunther had anything to do with the Nazi party, I also had to admit I couldn't be certain. Was he even now gathering intelligence about Camp Forrest and everything going on at the military installation and somehow relaying it back to Germany?

I rolled over again and stared at the dark ceiling.

Was I a fool to spend time with him? Was it a mistake to help him with his English? He'd expressed a desire to speak the language so well, no one would know he was German. Why? Did he hope to hide his identity and go unnoticed in society should he be released?

Suspicion swirled through my head, but my heart refused to join in. I wouldn't—couldn't—believe Gunther was a spy or had any nefarious reasons for spending time with me. Tutoring him in English was my idea. And the truth is, I enjoyed his company.

My spirit settled as my eyes drifted closed.

I would continue to befriend Gunther. But I would also keep my wits about me and not let silly romantic notions about the German man prevent me from seeing something amiss. Should he do or say *anything* that led me to suspect he wasn't the man I believed him to be, I would report it to Colonel Foster.

Immediately.

TWENTY-TWO

MATTIE

DELANEY HORSE FARM
DECEMBER 1969

Mild autumn weather returned after Thanksgiving, making it feel more like October than December. Frosty mornings gave way to glorious sunshine and cloudless blue skies before the breakfast dishes were even cleared from the table. Most of the horses were put back into the pastures, giving them the freedom to run and stretch their legs after cold days stuck in their stalls. I'd taken Moonlight out for some exercise, although I was cautious not to run her. It felt good to be in the saddle again.

"How is the platform for Fred coming along?" Dad lingered over his coffee, a sure sign he had something on his mind.

"Good," Nash said. "We finished the main structure. Today we need to figure out how steep to make the ramp. It will need rails for safety, too."

Nash and I spent three afternoons together in the hay barn working on the project, taking a prerequisite rest on Sunday at Mama's insistence. I hadn't had a clue where to begin, but somehow Nash knew intuitively what to do. I helped him cut lumber into pieces and held them in place while he hammered nails into them, enjoying easy conversation as we worked side by side. Every so often I'd run across the yard to the house to check on Mama. "We make a good team," Nash said at the end of the first day. The comment pleased me.

Dad sipped his coffee, his eyes squinted over the steam. "You will need to get Dawn's Rose used to someone mounting her from the platform. When will Fred come to the farm?"

"I told him we'd try for Saturday, if the weather holds." Nash smiled. "Mrs. Graham said Fred has started doing his exercises again, working on his upper body and core strength. He hasn't done them since he got out of the hospital."

"Good," Dad said. "Balance and strength will be important if he is to be successful." He glanced at me. "I'll stay with your mother after Nurse Bradford leaves so you can help Nash finish the platform."

With plans for the day set in place, the men headed out to do chores while I tidied things up and checked on Mama.

Laughter greeted me when I reached the upstairs landing.

"I could never keep up with those two." Mama's voice, weak but clear, came from the room. "Twins have such a special connection, and they outwitted me more times than I can count."

I pressed my lips together to keep from chuckling.

It was true. Mark and I nearly always knew what the other was thinking. We communicated with our eyes and hands when we didn't want anyone else to know what we were talking about. Unsuspecting teachers at school were unaware of the silent conversations we had from across the room.

"My mother was a twin," Nurse Bradford said. "Sadly, her sister was stillborn. Mother often talks about how much she misses her sister, even though she never knew her."

A lump formed in my throat.

I knew the feeling of loneliness for my twin. Nurse Bradford was wrong though. Her mother and her twin had definitely known each other the months they were in the womb.

I moved into the room. Mama's eyes brightened when she saw me.

"Mattie, I was hoping you'd come see me before you went out to help Nash."

Nurse Bradford rose from where she was seated in a chair next to Mama's bed. "I think I'll get a cup of coffee while you ladies chat. Ava, can I bring you a soft-boiled egg when I come back?"

Mama grimaced. "I don't think so. Maybe just some hot cocoa to warm me up."

The nurse left us alone. Mama studied my face.

"You look more rested than you have since you got home."

I settled in the chair after Nurse Bradford vacated it. "I've slept better the last couple nights."

A gentle smile lifted the edges of her mouth. "I'm glad. Now tell me about the platform for Fred. When will it be ready?"

I attempted to describe the structure we'd built, adding that it still needed a ramp with rails. "All in all, I think it's going to work. We'll know Saturday, anyway."

She reached a hand toward me, and I grasped it. Her fingers weakly squeezed mine.

"I'm so proud of you, Mattie." Tears filled her eyes. "I know how strongly you feel about the war, yet what you're doing for Fred . . ." Her chin trembled. "Mark would be proud of you too."

I fought to maintain control of my emotions. When I felt I could speak without bursting into sobs, I said, "Fred and Mark and even Nash are victims of the war. I may not agree with their decision to go to Vietnam, but they don't deserve my hatred. Or anyone else's, for that matter." I sighed. "I felt so sorry for Fred, you know. He'll never walk again. You should have heard him talking about riding horses when he was growing up. If we can get him in the saddle, I'm hopeful we can have him riding again."

"That's my girl. You've never been one to quit once your mind is made up."

Mama wanted to know which horse we planned to use with Fred, how we'd keep him in the saddle, and so on.

"I wish I could be there to help," she said, her eyes drooping. "LuAnn mentioned that she's heard of using horses for therapy with people with disabilities, although she's never seen it done."

"Really? I didn't know it was a thing."

"You should talk to her about Fred. She might have some suggestions."

I sat with Mama after she dozed off, my mind whirling.

I'd never heard of using horses to help people, especially those like Fred who no longer had use of their legs. Nash had proven that losing an arm couldn't slow him down, but to lose the ability to walk would be completely life-altering. Yet the moment Fred mentioned horseback riding in his youth and his obvious disappointment that he would never do so again, the idea of helping him wouldn't let me go.

I hurried downstairs and found LuAnn in the living room, looking through an old issue of *Life* magazine. She glanced up when I came in.

"Mama's asleep. Do you have a minute? I'd like to talk to you about something."

She laid the magazine aside. "Of course. Do you have questions about your mother?"

"No," I said, then changed it to, "well, yes, but that's not what I wanted to talk to you about right now. Mama said you've heard of using horses to help people like Fred."

She smiled as I sat in the armchair. "I was so pleased when Ava told me what you and Nash are doing for his friend. Poor man. I've known people through the years who've become paralyzed, usually after some terrible accident. Many of them simply give up or end up in a nursing home far sooner than they should."

"But what about using horses to help them? How does that work if they can't feel their legs?"

"I read an article in a medical journal not long ago about a doctor in Canada who started a therapeutic horseback riding program. If memory serves, his first patient was a woman who is quadriplegic."

My mouth fell open. "Doesn't that mean she's paralyzed from the neck down? How could she ride a horse?"

"I don't know much about it, I'm afraid." A thoughtful look crossed her face. "But I'm sure I still have the journal with the article in it somewhere. I'd be happy to hunt it down. Apparently, horse therapy has been used for centuries for all sorts of physical and mental challenges. Which makes perfect sense, considering God created those beautiful animals. Surely they have a greater purpose beyond carrying people here and there or pulling wagons and such."

Her comment mirrored my own beliefs. "I've always thought so too. When I take Moonlight out for a ride, I feel better, way down deep."

"I believe Fred will too, once he gets the hang of it."

Nurse Bradford went to make a cup of hot cocoa for Mama while I went out to the barn.

I found Nash already at work, measuring wood for the ramp. He'd removed his jacket and wore a ball cap backwards, with the bill facing the back of his head. His dark hair curled over the rim of the cap, longer than I could ever remember him wearing it in high school. He and Mark were both on the football team, so Coach Cooper's rules on hair length had always prevented them from letting their locks get too long.

With his concentration on the lumber he'd purchased in town, Nash hadn't noticed me yet. I stayed in the shadows and took the opportunity to study him, watching how he used his one hand to do the job of two. I never realized how much I took having two functioning arms and hands for granted until I started helping him build the ramp. To compensate for his missing limb, he used his body—hips, knees, and even his booted feet—to aid him in maneuvering the heavy wood.

I thought about other soldiers like Nash. Young men who'd come home from war without an arm. Some without both arms. How were they coping? Hopefully their homelife was better than Nash's, and they had people who loved them helping them adjust, but I knew not everyone was that fortunate.

Nash straightened and glanced my way. "Hey, I didn't know you were there."

My face heated at being caught spying on him. "I was trying to picture Fred in his wheelchair, going up the ramp," I fibbed. I came forward and stood next to him. "We can't make it too steep, otherwise Fred won't be able to get up it by himself."

"I've been thinking about that too." He reached for a sheet of paper lying on a bale of hay, torn out of a spiral notebook by the looks of the shredded edge. A simple technical drawing of the platform was on it. "I figured we'd make the ramp in two sections, each about six feet long, with some kind of connector underneath that will allow us to dismantle the ramp easily." He eyed the finished structure nearby. "We kept the height of the platform at two-and-a-half feet, so a ramp that's approximately twelve feet long should keep it from being too steep."

I stared at him in amazement. "How is it you can figure all this out? You were awful at math in school."

He chuckled. "I don't mind math, but grades didn't mean anything to me back then. No one at home cared if I went to school or not. It probably would've been easier for my mom if I'd quit and worked full time. I kept going because of Mark. Anytime I talked about quitting, he'd give me the rundown of all the reasons I needed to stay and graduate."

"I didn't know you wanted to quit."

He nodded. "I didn't need to go to school to be a mechanic. I was always good with engines and fixing things. But Mark argued I shouldn't be satisfied just working in an auto shop. He thought I should be the owner of one, and to him, that meant I needed to stay in school."

I smiled, even as bittersweet memories of Mark's enthusiasm for life brought a pang of sadness. "He was the most positive, upbeat person I've ever known. I used to say that he got all the goodness of Mama and I got all the sourness of Dad."

Nash gave me a look. "You aren't sour, and neither is your dad. You both just see the world differently than Mark did. But you're right. He was a glass-half-full kind of guy. I needed him way more than he needed me."

My throat tightened. "I did too."

We set to work on building the ramp, following Nash's specifications. Dad came by midmorning and seemed satisfied with all we'd accomplished.

"As soon as it's ready, let Dawn's Rose get used to it. I don't know if Fred's wheelchair will scare her or not, so you might also find something, like a wheelbarrow, to roll up and down the ramp while she's near it."

"That's a good idea," I said, impressed at his insight.

After lunch, we attached the ramp to the platform.

"We still need to add rails," Nash reminded as I walked up the incline to test its sturdiness, with Jake following behind. The dog had dozed in the corner of the barn the entire time we'd been working but now came to investigate the contraption.

A sense of accomplishment washed over me. "I think this is going to work." I glanced back to Nash where he stood watching me. "You're a pretty good craftsman, Mr. McCallum."

His mouth quirked. "And you're a fine apprentice, Miss Taylor."

"I'm anxious to see what Dawn's Rose will think about it."

"I'll get her saddled and bring her over."

While I waited for Nash, I swept up as much of the construction mess as I could. I'd just put the broom and dustpan away when he returned, leading not just a fully saddled Dawn's Rose but Moonlight as well. She knickered when she saw me.

"Why did you bring her?" I asked, coming forward to pet her.

"I thought Dawn might like a friend nearby when we introduce her to the platform." He paused. "I also thought you and I could go for a ride after we're done, since we've been working so hard."

A warm tingle ran through me. "You are full of surprises today."

"How about I lead Dawn to the platform and you mount her from it. After she gets used to it, then we can take your dad's advice and roll the wheelbarrow up and down the ramp while she waits."

The plan sounded good.

Dawn's Rose seemed unbothered by the new way to mount her. She stood patiently while I walked up the ramp to the platform and climbed aboard.

"Maybe you should lead her, like we'll do when Fred is here Saturday. That way she'll associate the platform mount with being led around the corral instead of riding freely. At least until Fred gets confident enough to take her out on his own."

Nash glanced at me. "I hope this works."

I heard the doubt in his words. "It will." I told him about the article Nurse Bradford read about using horses for centuries to assist people with disabilities. "We may not know what we're doing, but Dawn's Rose does. She'll do what she was born to do."

Nash led us around the barn while Moonlight stood watching.

I dismounted when we reached the platform again, walked down the ramp, then came back and did it all over again.

By the fourth time around the barn, I said, "I think she's going to be fine with Fred mounting her from the platform. Let's see what she thinks about the wheelbarrow."

As I suspected, Dawn's Rose wasn't concerned with the wheeled cart in the least. I even sat in it to mimic what it might look like when Fred was in his chair, but she simply stood and waited patiently, no doubt wondering what our strange behavior was all about.

"I'm satisfied she'll do great on Saturday." I climbed from the saddle for the last time.

"I am too." Nash rubbed Dawn's neck, then turned to me. "Do you feel like riding?"

My smile was my answer.

Nash used the platform to mount Dawn's Rose while I climbed up on Moonlight. He told Jake to stay, and we headed out of the barn into waning afternoon light.

"Where to?" Nash asked.

"Let's go to the creek," I said, a sense of inner peace I hadn't felt in ages settling over me. I wondered if Fred would feel the same way when he sat in the saddle again.

We didn't speak as we walked the horses to the far end of the farm, but the silence wasn't uncomfortable. The beauty of this land never disappointed, even as nature prepared to usher in winter. Trees with almost bare branches served as reminders that new beginnings would come again someday. Rest and restoration must take place during the cold, hard months before fresh life could appear. Mark loved the lessons nature taught. I could almost hear what he'd say about my deep reflections today.

New beginnings, Sis. Be brave and reach for 'em.

When we came to the creek, we stopped, listening to the sound of water rushing over rocks. I couldn't count the number of times

Mark and I had come down here, sometimes on foot, sometimes on horseback. In the summertime, he would fish while I read a book. When it was cold, we'd build a campfire. It was our private sanctuary, and although I couldn't recall Nash ever accompanying us, being here with him today felt right.

"Do you believe in heaven?" I asked, my voice quiet so as not to disturb the peacefulness of the place.

Nash didn't seem bothered by the question. "I'd like to think there's a place better than this world. No wars. No disease. Just this." He gazed at the beauty around us.

I nodded, suddenly wishing I knew for certain if heaven was for real. Were Mark and Mama right about God and everything they believed? Or were they fools, clinging to made-up fairy tales?

The sun began its quick descent, and we headed back to the barn as the air grew chilly.

"I'll take care of the horses," Nash said after we'd both dismounted. Once again, he used the platform, and I realized it was as beneficial for him as it would be for Fred.

"Thanks for suggesting we go for a ride." I handed Moonlight's reins to him. "It was nice."

His eyes took on a mischievous look. "The first time I ever met you, you were on the back of a horse."

"Really? I don't remember."

"It was the summer when we were eight years old. My family had just moved to Tullahoma, and I wandered away from our house and got lost. Your dad and Mark were coming from town and found me walking along Highway 55. I couldn't tell them where I lived, so they brought me here, to the farm."

He glanced out the barn door to the corral across from the entrance. "You were in there, riding a big black horse."

"Midnight Pride. She was Moonlight's mama."

"I couldn't believe this little girl was sitting up on that big ol' horse and wasn't a bit afraid. Your hair was wild and for some reason you were wearing a red winter scarf, and I couldn't help but be awestruck." He met my gaze. "I'll never forget that day."

I watched him lead the horses away, a sudden awareness of being known, really *known*, by another living soul. Nash McCallum had been in my life longer than anyone who wasn't blood kin. He'd seen the best of me . . . and the worst. He'd known Mark. Deeply. Brotherly. In the best possible way.

Why had I never taken notice of Nash before? He'd practically lived at our house during high school when things at his own home were bad. I'd dated a few boys over the years, and I'd been Clay's girl while I was in California, but I'd never seen Nash as anything other than Mark's friend. Something about him now—the man he'd become and how he was determined to overcome what life had thrown at him—made me wonder if I should take a closer look.

I left the barn and headed for the house. I'd visit with Mama before starting dinner. Dad was just coming down the stairs, carrying a load of soiled bedsheets.

At my silent question, he said, "She had an accident." Sadness shone in his eyes. "LuAnn warned it might happen more frequently as your mother's muscles begin to weaken."

I swallowed past the lump in my throat. "Can I help?"

"It's taken care of." He glanced up to the landing. "She will be happy to see you."

Mama sat in the chair with a crocheted afghan wrapped around her, staring out the window when I arrived in the open doorway. She didn't respond when I spoke until I walked across the room and touched her arm.

"Mattie, I didn't hear you come in."

"You looked like you were far away." I settled on the floor at her feet.

A shadow crossed her face. "I was remembering the first time I saw the farm. It was spring, and everything was fresh and new. I had such hope for the future."

It didn't sound like a happy memory. "Was that after you and Dad got married?"

She met my gaze, a troubled look in her eyes. "Have you read the letters from the box?" she asked rather than answering my question.

I nodded. "The ones that came from Hawaii, but I don't understand who they're written to or who sent them. Is Ava Delaney a relative of Granny's?"

Mama's brow tugged into a deep frown. "Will you do me a favor? Go to the cottage and look in the bottom drawer of the bureau in the bedroom. You'll find a photo album. Bring it here, and I'll explain everything."

The strange request baffled me, but I complied. Crossing the yard, I saw Dad and Nash tinkering with the tractor. Only Jake, lying nearby, took notice of me.

I found the album where Mama said it would be. On my way out of the bedroom, I stopped short. There in the corner of the tiny living room was an easel with an unfinished painting on it. A small table with tubes of oil paints, brushes, and a can of turpentine sat next to it. I couldn't recall Granny ever being interested in painting, nor did it seem likely that the art paraphernalia belonged to either of my parents.

That left only one person as the mystery artist.

Nash.

I took a closer look at the image on the canvas. Clearly it was of a horse's head, but light pencil sketches here and there revealed something or someone else was planned to join the animal. The room was too dim for me to make out what they were intended to be, but the surprising discovery of the painting floored me.

Nash was an artist.

I left the cottage, hoping he and Dad wouldn't notice me hurrying away from it. I didn't want Nash to feel as though I'd invaded his private space. When I returned to Mama, she was staring out the window again. This time, however, she heard me enter the room.

Her eyes fell on the album in my lap when I retook my seat on the floor. "There are so many things I need to tell you, Mattie. Things that should have been revealed a long time ago." She grimaced, as though in pain.

"Mama, do you need your medicine? We can talk later."

She shook her head, becoming agitated. "I must tell you now. You need to know."

"All right, Mama." I reached for her hand. She clung to me the way a person clings to a life preserver when they've fallen out of the boat.

When she'd calmed, she looked at me with such intensity, I immediately knew I wouldn't like what she was about to say.

"The letters were written to me. I'm Ava Delaney."

I stared at her, trying to fit the puzzle pieces together in my mind, to no avail. "I don't understand. The fellow who wrote them, Richard Delaney, signed them *Your loving husband*."

She didn't respond.

A shocking thought suddenly exploded in my head. I blurted it out before I'd had time to think it through. "Were you married to someone else before you married Dad?"

Her slow nod was in stark contrast to the thundering beat of my heart.

She indicated the album. "Open it."

With shaky hands, I did as she bid. Images of a woman holding a baby met me. She looked like a younger version of Granny. A man I didn't recognize stood with them, in front of what was unmistakably our farmhouse.

"Richard was Granny Gertrude's only child. Her husband died when Richard was in high school, so he took over the farm."

I looked up from the black-and-white photographs, my mind spinning. "This farm? But I thought Granny was Dad's mother."

She shook her head. "I don't believe I ever lied to you and Mark, but I also never told you the truth about who Granny was to you."

"She wasn't my grandmother?" I asked, stunned.

"No, she wasn't," Mama said, regret in her eyes.

I thought back to the small, elderly woman Mark and I had secretly dubbed Grouchy Granny Gertrude. She'd never been affectionate to us the way most grandmothers were with their grandchildren, but she'd bake us cookies and let us look through her stacks of *Life* magazines on occasion. I hadn't cried when she passed away, I recalled, although tenderhearted Mark had.

"I met Richard in Nashville when I was twenty years old," she began, her eyes on the album. "He was handsome and full of life. He'd joined the Navy to see the world and wanted me to go with him."

Dazed, I sat in silence as the shocking story spilled forth.

"He was sent to Hawaii shortly after we married. While I waited to join him, I came to live here on the farm, with his mother, Gertrude."

I couldn't believe what my ears took in. "What happened to him?"

She squeezed her eyes shut, either to block out the pain of the memory, or the pain from the disease ravaging her body. "He was killed in the attack on Pearl Harbor."

I gasped. "Oh, Mama."

I looked back at the picture of Granny holding a baby boy. My mother's first husband, I realized. Granny must've been devastated when she lost her son.

A thousand questions tumbled through my mind.

When had Mama met Dad? I couldn't recall ever hearing the details of their courtship. I only knew they'd lived in the cottage when they first married, but after Mark and I were born, Granny moved out of the big house into the smaller dwelling.

"I was barely twenty-one years old, but I was a widow. My family, as you know, weren't close, and I didn't want to move to Chicago. I stayed here and helped Granny with the farm. I took a job at Camp Forrest, the military installation that was here during the war."

All I could do was stare at her. The woman I'd known my entire life suddenly seemed like a stranger. "I can't believe you never told me about this. Why did you keep it a secret?"

Tears pooled in her eyes. "I don't have a good answer to that question. I suppose it was because it was my past, and I didn't want to burden you or Mark with it. Granny didn't have family, and even though she didn't show it, I believe she loved you kids."

A sense of betrayal lurked inside me despite her rationalization. "Why tell me about it now?"

Sadness washed over her face. "Because I won't be here much longer, and I don't want you to discover things—about me, about your father, about yourself—without explaining them."

I wasn't sure what she meant and was about to ask when the sound of the back door closing echoed through the house. It was probably Dad and Nash, coming in for supper.

Panic filled Mama's eyes. "Mattie, take the album to your room. I don't want your father to see it."

"Why?"

"Please, just go."

I didn't question her again and hurried across the hall to my room as Dad came up the stairs. "I'll be down to start dinner in a minute," I said, using the door to keep the album out of sight.

"Nash is going into town, so it will just be us. We can keep it simple. Maybe pancakes or sandwiches."

"That sounds good."

He disappeared into the master bedroom while I hid the album under my bed, next to the box of letters.

Mama'd been married before she met Dad!

I felt completely blindsided by her revelation. But now with the mystery about the first bundle of letters solved, my curiosity about the second packet from someone named Gunther Schneider rose exponentially. Who was he and how did he play into the startling history unfolding?

I arrived in the kitchen as Nash poured dry dog food into Jake's bowl. He'd changed into a crisp, white button-down and wore a pair of jeans with shiny black boots I'd never seen before.

"You look nice. Got a date?" I joked.

He didn't smile. "Naw, just meeting a friend in town for dinner."

"Dad's letting me take the night off since you won't be here. Pancakes or sandwiches."

He nodded. "I won't be gone too long. Do you need anything from town?"

"Nothing I can think of." I glanced down the hall to make sure Dad hadn't come downstairs without me hearing him. I lowered my voice. "When you get back, I've got some crazy news to tell you about the letters and Mama's past. And we need to go through the other letters, the ones from the guy named Gunther."

"Sounds like a plan." He grabbed his denim jacket and left the house.

I heard his truck roar to life as I got out the ingredients for pancakes. Jake whined at the closed door as Nash drove away.

"He'll be back soon," I said. "Then we'll both get to spend the evening with him."

While I poured batter onto a hot griddle, I realized I looked forward to Nash's return nearly as much as Jake did.

TWENTY-THREE

GUNTHER

CAMP FORREST, TENNESSEE
MAY 1943

Gunther's hands were covered with wet, white plaster when Major Gridley found him in the back room of the dispensary. The soldier who'd come in with a broken arm a short while ago had talked nonstop from the moment he stepped through the door, even while Gunther took X-rays, set the bone, and led him to the back where plaster supplies were stored in a cabinet next to a large porcelain sink. Topics of his one-sided conversation ranged from the war overseas to the young woman he met at the USO in town. He never paused long enough for Gunther to reply before he moved on to a new subject.

"Sure am glad I didn't break my leg," he said, laughing. "Wouldn't want some other fella to steal my gal. Say, did you know—"

"Ahem."

Gunther and the patient turned to find Major Gridley standing in the doorway.

"Major." The young man saluted the officer with his good arm.

The major nodded but his attention focused on Gunther. He wore a serious expression, which was unusual, considering the man was typically upbeat no matter the circumstances.

"Mr. Schneider, please come see me in my office when you're finished here."

"Yes, sir," he said, wondering what had the man looking so grave. He hoped there hadn't been another accident on the training field. Not long ago, a soldier was killed and others injured when a truck flipped over during a nighttime exercise.

"You must be a pretty good doctor," the young man said after the major departed. "I heard all the Kra—" He paused, looked sheepish, then continued. "I heard the Germans who live in the internment camp are members of the Nazi party. I don't guess they'd let a Nazi work in the hospital unless he was a real good doctor."

Gunther continued to wrap the man's arm with plaster-coated strips of cloth. He'd heard the rumor dozens of times over the past year and a half he'd worked in the infirmary. "I'm not a Nazi. I'm also not a doctor."

"For real? Boy, you could'a fooled me. You speak good English, too. I once met a man who could talk Spanish and he . . ." The young man launched into another outlandish story while Gunther finished with his cast. The soldier was still talking when Gunther walked him to the door and sent him on his way.

"I feel sorry for his bunkmates," he said to the nurse on duty, who giggled in response.

But the young man's compliment of Gunther's English pleased him.

Ava had tutored him for fourteen months now. They'd read and discussed dozens of books she checked out from the Camp Forrest library, including *For Whom the Bell Tolls* by Ernest Hemmingway. She'd been disappointed with the ending—"Was Robert Jordan killed or does he miraculously survive?"—but Gunther thought it a perfect way to leave the story. She also brought newspapers to help him stay informed on what was happening in the world, and they discussed the war and Hitler without Gunther fearing his words would be mistaken or used against him.

After washing his hands, he went to the major's office.

"Come in, Mr. Schneider." Major Gridley waved to a chair in front of his desk. Once Gunther was seated, he asked, "How is your patient?"

"His arm should mend well, as long as he doesn't do anything reckless in the next six weeks." Gunther chuckled. "When a soldier comes in with the same injury, the nurses call him a *repeat customer*."

He expected the major to smile at the joke, but instead the frown on his brow deepened. "I'm afraid I have some bad news."

Gunther waited.

He hoped this wasn't about his mother. He hadn't heard from her in months, despite his many letters. She'd written shortly after he informed her of his new address in Tennessee, but there had been silence since then. He guessed mail delivery into Germany from America was halted by the Nazis, and vice versa, but still, he longed to hear from her soon.

"I've been informed that a large group of German POWs will arrive soon. Most of the men were captured in Africa."

Relief washed over Gunther. This wasn't about *Mutter*. POWs had begun arriving at Camp Forrest months ago. A few more was nothing to be concerned about.

"I don't know where they'll sleep," he said, thinking of the cramped quarters in the internment camp. "We're already six or seven men to a hut built for four. The lines at the mess hall and showers are long. I can't imagine what it will be like when more POWs arrive."

Major Gridley heaved a sigh. "You misunderstand. To make room for the prisoners, all the DOJ detainees will be transferred to a different camp."

The news, while disappointing, wasn't so bad. "As long as I can continue working in the dispensary, it doesn't matter where I bunk at night."

"I'm sorry to say, the camp you're being transferred to is in North Dakota."

Gunther wasn't familiar with the location. "Is that in Tennessee?"

Major Gridley shook his head. "North Dakota is a state in the northern part of the country, near the Canadian border."

Gunther gasped. "Canada? Why would they send us there? Why not send the POWs to that camp instead of moving us?"

"I don't know." He offered a sympathetic shake of his head. "It makes no sense to me, but I'm not in charge."

Panic surged through Gunther. "Is there anything you can do? I want to stay here, at Camp Forrest, and continue working in the dispensary. I've learned so much from you, sir."

"I wish there was something I could do. You've been an excellent apprentice, and I've come to rely on you. I spoke with the commander and told him how well you've done here, but they won't make exceptions. All the internees will be transferred by the end of the week."

"So soon?" Gunther's heart sank.

How would he tell Ava? Did she already know?

"I'll send Mr. McCoy, the commander of the new camp, a recommendation for you to continue working in the hospital at Fort Lincoln." He gave Gunther an intense look. "This war will end one day, Mr. Schneider. God has given you a special gift. I expect you to become a great doctor someday."

Gunther exited the office, defeat rising inside him despite the man's commendation. A glance at the clock on the wall told him he'd have to wait a little over an hour before he met Ava.

Leaving Camp Forrest and his job at the dispensary was disheartening, but the thought of never seeing Ava again filled him with desperation.

For one wild moment, he wondered if he should escape before he and the others were loaded onto northbound trains. Two men tried to sneak through the fences of the military installation last month. Both were caught. Gunther's job, however, gave him special privileges to move about without a guard. It wouldn't be difficult to hide in one of the many delivery trucks that came and went through the gates.

But what would he do if he were successful? He couldn't put Ava in danger by asking her to help him. And if he couldn't continue to see Ava, there was no point risking an escape.

When both hands on the clock reached twelve, Gunther dashed out of the dispensary and practically ran for their normal meeting place.

She was already there.

When she turned to him, her face told him she'd heard the news.

"You know." He joined her on the bench.

She nodded. "Colonel Foster told us this morning."

Gunther heaved a sigh. "I foolishly believed I would remain at Camp Forrest for the duration of the war. It never occurred to me they would move us to make room for POWs. Even after the Japanese internees who'd arrived from Hawaii were relocated last year, I didn't think we would be next."

Ava worried her bottom lip. "I don't know much about North Dakota, other than it gets very cold there in the winter."

"I hope the housing they provide is better than the huts here. The concrete floors are always damp, and gaps in the wooden walls allow the wind to pass through, especially when it blows from the north."

They sat in silence for a time before Ava reached for the brown paper bag next to her.

"I brought roasted turkey sandwiches. Gertrude found a wild turkey trapped in one of the barns yesterday and managed to grab it. The meat is a little gamey, but with beef and cheese and other items now being rationed, I suppose we should be grateful for anything extra we can get."

Gunther accepted the sandwich, but he had no appetite.

There was so much he wanted to say to her, but he wasn't certain he should. Ever since they'd begun their lunch-tutoring sessions, he'd held out hope they could have a future together once the war was over. His training under Major Gridley convinced him he could return to medical school and become a doctor, a profession that would allow him to take care of her in the manner she deserved. Although she had never indicated her feelings went as deep as his, she enjoyed his company as much as he enjoyed hers.

But with this morning's news of his imminent transfer from Camp Forrest, all hope of a future with her seemed lost.

They didn't discuss the latest book they'd been reading. Lessons in English seemed futile now. Instead, Gunther peppered her with questions about the farm, her dreams—personal topics he'd avoided until now. With their time together limited, he wanted to know everything about her. She in turn asked about his life in Germany, and for the first time, he admitted that his brother was a Nazi and his fear for his mother.

"When the war is over, I will bring *Mutter* to the United States," he said, determined. "There will be nothing left of Germany when the Allies are finished. The country she has always known no longer exists. She will need a new beginning."

Ava smiled, although there was sadness around the edges of her bright red lips. "You are a good man, Mr. Schneider. A good son. You don't deserve any of the hardships that have been forced upon you. I'll always cherish our friendship."

Her words were not what his heart wanted to hear, but he treasured her friendship too.

They met the following three days at their usual time and place. A sense of urgency hovered over their conversations, although Gunther restrained himself from professing his love and admiration for her.

"There is a going-away gathering for the internees in the camp mess hall tonight. Cake and dancing, from what I'm told." He'd practiced this speech numerous times that morning, but his nerves nearly choked him now. "Major Gridley said personnel from Camp Forrest who worked with many of us will be in attendance, including himself." He swallowed and met her gaze. "I hope you will come."

"I'll be there."

Her soft, shy response emboldened Gunther. "I would be honored if you would save a dance for me."

Her eyes, beautiful and shining, gave him his answer before she spoke. "I'd like that."

When they stood, she took a book from the lunch bag and handed it to him. Gunther recognized her dog-eared copy of *Emma*.

"I want you to have this, to remember me by."

Their fingers brushed when he accepted it. "I could never forget you."

With slow steps, they followed their usual path one last time. When she turned, it was Ava who raised her hand first. Gunther returned the gesture, his arm like lead.

She was the sole reason his internment at Camp Forrest hadn't crushed him.

How would he survive in North Dakota without her?

TWENTY-FOUR

AVA

CAMP FORREST, TENNESSEE

MAY 1943

I left the office at the end of the long day and sped home. I needed to change clothes and fix my hair before the farewell gathering for the internees.

"I want to thank the German men who helped in the hospital," Colonel Foster said as he, too, exited the building and informed me of his attendance at the gathering. "I can't imagine what they must be feeling, being shipped off to a new camp."

Gertrude and Ivy Lee sat in the parlor listening to the radio when I came out of my room. I hadn't worn the midnight blue cocktail dress since before Richard died, but it felt right to put it on for Gunther's going away.

"My, my, look at you." Ivy Lee's southern accent drew out each word as she inspected me from head to toe. "You must be meetin' someone special for dinner."

Gertrude eyed me with suspicion.

"It isn't like that," I hurried to say. "I'm going to the base for the send-off for the internees. Colonel Foster thinks it's appropriate for those of us who knew and worked with the men to attend."

Ivy Lee grimaced. "Good riddance, I say. Those Germans always gave me the creeps, lookin' like a passel of green beans in their ugly uniforms. I'd bet my last nickel they're here to spy on us. But we'll have even more after all those POWs arrive."

"POWs?" Gertrude said, her eyes wide. "I hadn't heard anything about prisoners of war being brought in."

Ivy Lee puckered her ruby lips. "Oops. I wasn't s'pposed to let out that top secret information yet. Calvin—Colonel Paxton, I mean—said the men comin' were captured in Africa, of all places. I didn't even know there was fightin' goin' on over there."

I restrained the urge to shake the young woman. Her lack of understanding about what was happening in the world never ceased to exasperate. This wasn't the first time she'd shared classified information with Gertrude.

"I don't think Colonel Paxton would be pleased to learn you'd divulged things meant to remain secret."

Ivy Lee huffed. "I don't see why Gertrude shouldn't know what kind of people are livin' on the other side of town." Her lips curved in a devilish grin. "You might be surprised at the secrets I've kept. All sorts of things, including *clandestine romances*."

I took my hat from the antique hall tree in the corner. "It isn't wise to listen to camp gossip."

The other woman smirked. "Oh, this ain't gossip. I know all about your foreign fella. About lunch dates and sharin' books." Her eyes swept my gown. "My guess is the dress is for *him*."

I froze, suddenly feeling exposed.

How did Ivy Lee know about Gunther? We'd always met on the bench behind the dental clinic, out of sight from the general population of Camp Forrest. Captain Jones, the dentist in charge of the clinic, asked me about my meetings with Gunther early on. When I explained I was helping Gunther with his English so he could continue his medical training after the war, the older man nodded with approval. The next day I noticed the blinds on the window facing the bench were closed and remained so to this day. Whether it had anything to do with Gunther and me, I didn't know, but it did afford us a bit of privacy from nosy patients having their teeth cleaned.

Gertrude glanced between me and Ivy Lee. "What are you talking about?" Her narrowed attention settled on me. "Have you been stepping out with someone?" Anger tinged her words.

"Of course not." My face grew hot under her scrutiny. "Ivy Lee is speaking of the English lessons I've been giving to one of the internees. He hopes to continue his studies in America to become a doctor after the war. I offered to help."

The older woman sneered. "Why would you do that? Those men are our enemies."

They'd had this discussion many times over the past year. Both Gertrude and Ivy Lee felt the men and women who'd been declared enemy aliens should have been deported immediately, even those born in America.

"Most of the men who've been held at Camp Forrest aren't like the POWs. Mr. Schneider and the others were already in the United States when they were arrested. They didn't carry a weapon and shoot at our boys. I'd be more worried about the incoming men than I would the ones being sent to North Dakota."

Gertrude scoffed. "Not all enemies carry a weapon. He could be a spy for the Nazis for all you know. I don't like that you've been helping one of them. Ivy Lee is right. Good riddance."

I refused to continue the argument. "I don't know what time I'll be home. Have a nice evening."

I fumed all the way back to the base.

Like many people in America, my mother-in-law and

housemate passed judgement on thousands of people without knowing anything about them other than they were considered enemies of the United States. Yet after getting to know Gunther and hearing his story, I was convinced that, like him, most of the internees throughout the country were innocent victims of government bureaucracy. It wasn't right to hold them against their will indefinitely, disrupting their lives and families, on the small chance one among them could be a spy.

When the guard at the entrance to Camp Forrest approached my open car window, he grinned. "Good evening, Mrs. Delaney. You sure look nice."

"Thank you."

He waved me through, and I wound my way through the vast cantonment to where the internees were housed. A guard I wasn't familiar with checked my credentials while another man looked in the back seat of the vehicle. When they were satisfied, the young soldier told me where to park and allowed me to enter the area I'd only seen from outside the high barbed-wire fences.

Army jeeps and sedans filled the dirt parking area in front of the mess hall. In the distance I saw rows of small, identical huts, and remembered Gunther's comments about the poor quality with which they'd been built. I hoped the accommodations in North Dakota were an improvement, especially with the frigid weather that part of the country was known for.

Music drifted through the open door of the building. Two soldiers stood at the entrance, rifles in their hands, but neither looked at me as they chatted. I moved past them and entered.

The large room was crowded with men wearing green uniforms that told the world they were DOJ detainees. Officers stood off to the side in deep discussion with a group of internees. Tables and chairs were pushed to the edges to create space for a dance floor where couples, each comprised of a man in green and a civilian woman, danced to the fast-paced song coming from a Victrola.

They shimmied, laughed, and appeared to have what looked like a good time despite the gloomy occasion.

I scoured the room for Gunther but didn't find him. He hadn't changed his mind about coming, had he?

A long table occupied the far wall and held a large punch bowl and slices of sheet cake. I made my way to it, needing a distraction.

The young woman serving the refreshments smiled and handed me a cup of pink punch. "Do you know one of the fellas leaving for North Dakota?"

I nodded, not relishing small talk just now.

"I do too," she said. "I work in the laundry with some of them. They're nice men. We're going to miss them."

"Yes," I said, grateful to find someone else who had positive things to say about the foreign men. "I'll miss my friend too."

The young woman moved to serve someone else, and I stepped out of the way. When I turned to face the room again, my heart stilled.

Gunther stood a few steps away. Although he wore the same green garb as the other men, he stood out, tall and handsome.

He closed the distance between us.

"Good evening, Mrs. Delaney." His eyes filled with appreciation as he took in my hair, my dress, me. "You look lovely."

"Thank you," I said, breathless.

We watched as more couples moved onto the dance floor.

Gunther turned to me and grinned. "The jitterbug."

I chuckled. "Much easier to dance than the quadrille." I sobered. "I hope you will continue to practice your English. Read out loud to your bunkmates. They'll enjoy the story."

His eyes held mine. The music and dancers faded.

"I will miss our time together."

"I will too."

We stood silent, our gazes locked. There were so many things I longed to say. I wanted to tell him he'd been the best friend I'd ever had. That our lunch dates were the highlight of my week. That I'd come to care for him and didn't want him to leave.

"Would you—" he began.

A deep voice startled us both. "Mrs. Delaney."

I turned to see Colonel Foster. He wore his dress uniform, with medals pinned to his chest. "Colonel Foster, hello."

His glance took in Gunther. "Mr. Schneider."

"Colonel."

"I hope I'm not interrupting," he said.

Gunther took a step back, widening the space between us. "I was just telling Mrs. Delaney how I will miss working in the dispensary. Major Gridley has been very kind and taught me much."

Colonel Foster gave a solemn nod. "He and I have both written letters to the camp commander at Fort Lincoln, recommending you be allowed to work in the hospital or clinic there."

"I appreciate that, Colonel."

Major Gridley joined them, as did other personnel from the hospital, each thanking Gunther for his work. I moved away, giving them more room. Every so often Gunther's gaze found me, and I'd offer an encouraging smile or nod. It pleased me to see others value Gunther and his work, but I wished we could be alone one last time.

The evening went by all too quickly.

"This is the last dance, folks," the soldier operating the Victrola announced.

The opening strains of Glenn Miller's "Always in My Heart" filled the room. Couples moved onto the dance floor, swaying slowly to the sound of the orchestra.

My heart thrummed when I found Gunther's gaze on me, despite the major speaking to him.

"Excuse me, gentlemen." He stepped out of the circle of men. "Mrs. Delaney, would you do me the honor of dancing with me?"

Although I knew Colonel Foster and the others watched, I nodded. "Yes, Mr. Schneider."

He took my hand and led me onto the crowded floor, yet all I knew was the feel of his arm around my waist and my hand clutched in his as we began to move to the music. Soon, a man's voice joined the instruments, telling a sad tale of being far away from the woman he loved, and reminding her of the songs of love they sang when they were together.

Gunther's hand on the small of my back moved me closer to him, and I went willingly. I closed my eyes, memorizing the feel of him, the smell of soap clinging to his skin, his warm breath on my cheek.

The vocalist continued his story of love, promising that one day, even though the skies are gray, the sun *will* break through, and he and his lover will meet again. Until then . . . "You are always in my heart."

The music ended, yet Gunther didn't release me.

"I will miss you, Ava," he whispered close to my ear. "May I write to you?"

I gripped his fingers, fighting tears. "Yes."

When we drew apart, his eyes shone with moisture. "Thank you. For everything."

I nodded, not ready to say goodbye. "I'll come to the train station tomorrow."

"I would like that."

Movement reminded us we weren't alone. People began to leave the mess hall, offering good wishes to the internees as they departed. When I stepped away from Gunther, I found Colonel Foster's gaze on us.

His frown eased when he approached and shook Gunther's hand. "I appreciate your hard work over the past year, Mr. Schneider. You've been a fine addition to the dispensary staff. When the war ends, I hope you will resume your studies."

"Thank you, sir," Gunther said.

The colonel turned to me. "Let me walk you to your car, Mrs. Delaney. It's dark out."

I couldn't refuse. "Thank you." I turned to Gunther. "Good night, Mr. Schneider."

"Good night," he said, including the colonel in his farewell.

As I drove home, tears flowed down my cheeks, the feel of Gunther's arm around me fresh and sweet.

I was in love with Gunther Schneider, I finally admitted. I think I had been since the day he saved the soldier's life in the mess hall. But he was leaving for North Dakota tomorrow, his future uncertain.

My heart ached with a bitter truth.

At long last, I'd fallen in love, but the man my heart chose was the enemy.

TWENTY-FIVE

MATTIE

DELANEY HORSE FARM
DECEMBER 1969

I sat on the sofa in the living room, a fire in the fireplace sending out warmth and comfort into the quiet house, when Nash returned from town. Jake wagged his tail from where he lay in front of the hearth, but not even Nash's presence was enough to entice him from his cozy spot.

"How was dinner?" I asked as he settled on the opposite end of the couch. The light scent of his cologne wafted over, and I inhaled.

"Good." He didn't elaborate. "So what's the big mystery you discovered about your mom? Does it have anything to do with the letters?"

I reached for a stack of envelopes next to me and handed them to him. "These are the letters from the guy in Hawaii to Ava Delaney." I tapped my mother's name.

Nash nodded, squinting his eyes. "And?"

"Ava Delaney is my mom. This guy," I said, moving my finger to the return addressee, "is her *first* husband."

I let that news sink in.

"Wow." His brow rose. "You and Mark didn't know your mom was married before?"

"Not a peep was ever said about it."

He looked at the letters again. "What happened to him?"

"He was killed when Japan bombed Pearl Harbor."

"That's heavy."

The fire popped and crackled as we processed the shocking realities of the unfolding tale.

"When did your mom meet your dad?"

I shrugged. "It was during the war, but I don't remember the details. I just know they lived here, on the farm, after they got married. Mama was too tired to finish telling me everything and said I needed to read the other letters. The ones from the guy in North Dakota. But I have to admit, I'm kind of nervous about what I might learn from them. I mean, she's got letters from two men, but neither of them is my father."

A startling thought rocketed across my mind, and I gasped. "What if—"

I couldn't finish the question.

"What if what?" Nash prompted.

I met his gaze, my heart racing as my imagination took off in a direction I didn't want to go. "What if my dad *isn't* my dad?"

Nash stared at me. "Do you think that's a possibility?"

I fell back against the couch cushion, stunned by the wild implications. "I honestly don't know. I would have never dreamed Mama'd been married before, but it's true. Who knows what other secrets she might have kept all these years."

I heard accusation in my voice, but I couldn't help feeling

betrayed by my own mother. Why hadn't she told Mark and me the truth about her past?

"I think we should read the other letters." Nash's calm words slowed my whirling thoughts. "We might be jumping to the wrong conclusion."

He was right. "Thanks for being here with me."

I opened the first envelope in the stack from Gunther Schneider.

"Dear Ava," I read aloud, a tremor in my voice. *"I arrived at Fort Lincoln, North Dakota yesterday, a place I had never heard of but now find it is my home. The internment camp is much like the one at Camp Forrest, although it is no longer a—"*

The rest of the sentence was blacked out.

"Looks like military censors didn't approve of what Gunther wrote," Nash said.

"I didn't realize they did that back then."

He nodded. "There were a lot of spies around the world, and most of their communication was written. The government censored just about everyone's mail."

I continued reading.

The barracks are made of red brick. They tell us the temperatures during winter can drop to forty below zero. I hope they are wrong. There are many Italians here as well as Germans. I have been assigned to the hospital and look forward to beginning my duties. I appreciate Colonel Foster's recommendation.

I miss our English lessons and your chicken salad sandwiches. I am ever grateful for the time we shared together. It is bold of me to ask, but I hope you will write to me. It would brighten my day.

Sincerely,
Gunther Schneider

I finished reading the letter but didn't return it to the envelope. "I wonder what he means by the *internment camp*?"

"When we were in school, I remember Mr. Mott talking about German POWs at Camp Forrest during the war," Nash said. "Maybe he was a POW."

I gaped at him. "A POW? I know Mama worked at Camp Forrest, but why would she befriend the enemy? Especially after her husband was killed in the war."

"The Germans weren't responsible for Pearl Harbor." He took the letter from me and read, "Gunther wrote, *I miss our English lessons*. It sounds like your mom was a tutor or something."

"That's definitely something she would do, even for the enemy." I reached for the next envelope in the stack. "Maybe the other letters will shed more light on their relationship."

I read the next letter and the next, but they were both similar in content to the first, with descriptions of the camp, the weather, and Gunther's appreciation for the note Ava sent him.

"It doesn't sound as though they had a romantic relationship," Nash said. "These letters were written after her husband died, so she might've been lonely. He may have needed a friend and found one in your mom."

"Possibly, but why would she want me to read these if they didn't have anything to do with me?"

"I can't answer that."

The clock in the hall chimed midnight.

"We better turn in." I counted the remaining envelopes. "There are six more letters. We can read them later. If you want to, that is."

His eyes met mine. "I want to."

The softness of his voice, along with the intense way he looked at me, stirred butterflies in my belly. I swallowed, tempted to move closer and sink into his strong embrace.

I forced myself to look away.

Nash was a good friend. Anything beyond that was a bad idea. Staying in Tullahoma wasn't in my future. It wouldn't be fair to either of us to start something that couldn't be finished.

I stood and he followed suit. Jake slowly rose from his spot near the fireplace where embers glowed.

"Hopefully Mama will tell me who Gunther Schneider is when I see her tomorrow."

I bid Nash good night and carried the letters upstairs. His recollection about POWs being housed at Camp Forrest during the war, along with his earlier math calculations, reminded me that although he hadn't been a good student, barely passing most of his classes, he'd obviously paid attention in school. I found it sad that his parents hadn't cared whether he did well or not.

Dad had always stressed how important it was to get an education, making sure Mark and I did our homework and brought home A's. He'd wanted us to attend college, too, but the war in Vietnam changed things for Mark.

And for me.

My thoughts drifted to the mysterious Gunther Schneider.

Who was he and what had he meant to my mother? The fact that she'd kept his letters was significant. That she wanted me to read them even more so. Nash didn't believe Gunther and Mama had a romantic relationship, but I couldn't shake the unsettling possibility that he'd been more to her than a friend. Even though Dad and I didn't have the greatest bond, he was my father.

My gut churned.

Or is he?

I closed my eyes, forcing my mind to halt that line of thinking.

I'd get answers from Mama tomorrow. Until then, I wouldn't let my imagination run wild.

But it was many hours before sleep finally came.

• • •

Nash was waiting for me when I came downstairs early Saturday morning.

"I'm going to pick up Fred around ten o'clock," he said from his place at the table.

I nodded. "I'll have Dawn's Rose saddled and ready."

He met my gaze over the coffee cup he held. "I stopped by his place yesterday while I was in town. I've never seen him so excited about anything."

"I hope it works out the way we all want it to. I'd feel horrible if he was injured or disappointed."

Nash stood and carried his mug to the sink. "The fact that someone cared enough to see him and offer more than mere sympathy, or worse, apathy or disdain, means more to him than you know."

The back door opened. Dad and Jake came inside. The dog immediately went to Nash where he received a scratch behind his ears.

"Looks like the weather will be nice for Fred's riding lesson," Dad said. His voice held a touch of excitement, and I realized he anticipated the special visitor to the farm as much as Nash. "I have the leather belt ready, as well as a strap to help keep him steady in the saddle. It might help him feel more secure until he can figure out how to stay balanced."

"I appreciate everything you two have done for Fred." Nash glanced between Dad and me. "Whether or not this works out, just knowing that someone cared enough to try is huge."

Dad nodded solemnly. "Mark would want us to help the boys returning from war in any way we can. I would have wanted someone to do the same for him, had he come home."

My throat convulsed.

I'd never heard Dad talk about Mark since he died. In the days after we received the telegram, informing us of Mark's death, Dad had kept his grief hidden in the busyness of making arrangements, fielding the many phone calls, and comforting Mama. I knew he loved Mark, but his lack of outward emotions had incensed me. He hadn't even cried at the funeral but stood stoically grim next to Mama and me as we wept. By the time Pastor Arnold made his unfortunate comment about Mark being a hero rather than a victim a week later, I was an erupting volcano, unable to stop the flow of hot, angry words before I stormed out of the house for good.

Nash left to pick up Fred.

"I'll get Dawn's Rose saddled," Dad said. "I'd like to help, if that's all right with you."

His comment surprised me. He certainly didn't need my permission. But then I remembered the farm had belonged to Mama's first husband's family, not Dad's, as I'd always assumed. A dozen questions rolled through my mind, but now was not the time to voice them. I needed to talk to Mama first.

"I'm sure Fred would appreciate you being there. I don't really know what to expect as far as his ability to stay in the saddle. It might be best to have both you and Nash on either side of him while I lead Dawn's Rose."

With the plan in place, I hurried upstairs to put on my boots. Nurse Bradford was just coming from the bathroom, carrying a hand basin and a load of towels.

"Good morning," she said, her normal cheery smile in place. "Your mother has just had a shampoo and sponge bath. I'm sure she'd love to visit with you."

I thanked her and made a detour to Mama's room. She sat in the chair by the window, wrapped in a fuzzy blue robe with a pair of Dad's wool hunting socks on her feet. Her body sagged, as though she had no strength to keep herself upright.

"There's my girl," she said, her words slow and weak.

"How are you today, Mama?" I knelt beside her and took her hand. Her fingers were icy cold.

"Tired of all this."

Mama never complained, so it was unsettling to hear her admit her frustration with her illness.

"Do you want to get back in bed? Nurse Bradford shouldn't have left you here by the window."

She patted my cheek. "I'm fine, Mattie. Just a bit worn out."

"Maybe I should stay with you instead of helping Nash with Fred today."

"Absolutely not. LuAnn is here all morning. You go on. I want a full report this afternoon."

I promised I'd tell her every detail and left her after Nurse Bradford returned.

Wearing boots and a light jacket with my jeans and sweatshirt, I headed outside. Dad was just leading Dawn's Rose from the horse barn, saddled and ready to ride.

"Mama seems especially tired today," I said when I approached.

He gave a slow nod. "She doesn't sleep well. The pain is getting worse."

The two of us hadn't discussed Mama's condition since I arrived home. Now wasn't the best time to bring it up, but I had questions. "Why didn't you tell me Mama was sick when she was first diagnosed? I would have come home sooner if I'd known."

He didn't look at me and kept walking. "She didn't want to burden you."

His answer wasn't good enough. "I understand her reasoning, but didn't *you* think I should know? She needed me."

He drew to a stop and met my gaze, sorrow in his eyes. "She needed you after your brother died."

The words, said without malice, were a gut punch.

The sound of Nash's truck crunching over gravel, however, prevented me from uttering a response, although there wasn't anything I could say that would make what I'd done a year ago go away.

While Dad greeted Fred, I tried to compose myself.

I knew I'd abandoned Mama. I left home a week after Mark's funeral, my anger burning hot. But once it began to simmer, crippling guilt soon replaced it. What kind of daughter forsakes her family after suffering such a tragic loss? Outwardly I pretended it was Dad and his mistakes that kept me from coming home, but deep inside I knew I was ashamed of my own behavior. I'd done everything I could to bury it, but no amount of drugs and free living could ever fully remove the stain.

Now, to hear it put so bluntly from my father, left me wrecked.

After Fred settled in his wheelchair, Nash came over, his keen eyes studying me. "You okay?"

I shook my head. "Not really." When he gave me a questioning look, I said, "I'll tell you later."

He nodded, but I could see concern on his face.

We joined the others. Fred eyed Dawn's Rose while Dad held her steady.

"I don't know about this," Fred said. "She's a lot taller than I expected."

I heard fear in his voice. I couldn't blame him. Although I'd never been afraid of horses, I'd experienced more fear in the past year than I had in my entire lifetime. I still had a long way to go to overcome it, and I suspected Fred did too. We were on different roads, with different circumstances holding us prisoner, but fear, no matter what it looked like, would eventually destroy us if something didn't change. Conquering Fred's self-doubt was a step in the right direction and had to be accomplished before he could successfully ride again.

What did I need to help me overcome mine?

I wished I knew the answer.

"Come see the platform Nash built for you," I said, forcing a smile. "He's quite the carpenter." I glanced at Nash, with a small nod toward Fred.

He took the hint. "It's a thing of beauty, if I say so myself." He got behind Fred's chair and wheeled him toward the barn while Dad and I walked behind them with Dawn's Rose. Nash pushed Fred up the ramp, chatting all the while about the wood, the design, the possible improvements. Technical things that had nothing to do with the size of the horse or the question of whether Fred could ride her or not.

Dad led Dawn's Rose over, letting her head come even with Fred. I noticed the leather belt and strap were draped across the handrail of the platform, ready and waiting.

"Give her a rub," I said to Fred. "She loves attention."

He reached a tentative hand to pet the horse's neck.

"Dawn's Rose is one of my favorite horses. She's very gentle and has one of the smoothest gaits of all the horses here on the farm."

My speech reminded me of Dad's sales pitches when potential buyers needed a little push to complete the transaction.

Fred eyed the saddle. "How are we going to do this?"

As Nash explained the plan—he and Dad would walk with Fred on either side of the horse, holding on to the belt he'd wear—I gauged Fred's reaction. While he didn't appear as uncertain about it as he had in the yard, he also didn't seem convinced.

"What if she bucks or takes off running? I'm a goner."

I patted Dawn's Rose. "This girl has never bucked a rider. Besides, I'll be leading her. She won't have a chance to run. We'll be in the corral where she's used to walking."

Fred took a deep breath. "All right. Let's give it a try. Even if I fall off, I don't guess I could get hurt worse than I already am."

Nash and I exchanged a look, communicating with our eyes. We desperately wanted this to succeed.

It took both Dad and Nash to get Fred settled in the saddle. I held Dawn's Rose steady, but she never flinched and stood patiently awaiting my instruction. While Dad held Fred by the shoulders from atop the platform, Nash came down the ramp and placed each of Fred's feet in the stirrups.

"I ain't gonna lie." Fred gripped the saddle horn with both hands. "It's pretty scary up here." Panic filled his widened eyes.

"We won't do anything until you're ready," I assured. "Nash is going to put the belt and strap on you now."

When all was in place, with Dad on the right side of the horse and Nash on the left, we waited for Fred to decide what was next.

"How do you feel in the saddle?" Nash asked. "Comfortable? Secure?"

Fred's grip on the horn loosened just a bit. "Good, I guess."

"Would you like to walk around here in the barn first?" I asked.

Fred swallowed, staring at Dawn's Rose. "Yeah, but real slow."

"Okay. Here we go." I made eye contact with Nash and Dad. "Nice and easy."

Both men held on to the belt while the strap across Fred's lap anchored him to the saddle. I led Dawn's Rose into a slow walk, and we made a circle, ending up back at the platform. I think we were all holding our breath, as no one said a word.

I looked at Fred. "How was it?"

He continued to grip the saddle horn, but the tension in his face had eased. "Not bad. Can we go again?"

"We sure can."

We repeated the process two more times.

Fred appeared a little more confident with each turn around the barn. "I think I'm ready to try the corral," he said.

I led Dawn's Rose the short distance across the yard. Dad and Nash both encouraged Fred as we made our way to the fenced area. After we'd completed two full circles, Fred declared he'd had enough for today. His body trembled by the time we got back to the platform where Nash and Dad helped get him into his wheelchair.

I worried we'd overdone things, but once Fred was seated and had a sip of water from the thermos Dad thoughtfully provided, a slow grin inched up his face.

"I would'a never thought I'd ride a horse again, but sure as shootin', I did it."

We all smiled at that.

"You did really great," I said, pleased with how well everything had gone.

"I didn't fall off." Fred gave a short laugh, then sobered. "But I felt like I could've there at the end."

Nash laid an encouraging hand on Fred's shoulder. "Your core muscles will get stronger each time you ride. Keep doing your exercises in the meantime."

Fred's chin quivered, and he shook his head. "I can't thank y'all enough for doin' this for me."

Dad stepped forward and put his hand on Fred's other shoulder. "And we can't thank you enough for your willingness to fight for freedom. This is the least we can do, but we're very happy to do it."

Fred nodded, obviously emotional. "I bet a lot of guys comin' back from the war all beat up would like to do what I did today. I'm a lucky fella to have such good friends."

"Do you want to come up to the house for a cup of coffee or a soda before I take you home?" Nash asked.

Fred declined, thanking us again, and bid me farewell. While the men got Fred settled in the pickup, I led Dawn's Rose to the barn and unsaddled her. I had just begun to brush her when Dad found me.

"Fred would like to come out again next weekend."

I glanced up to see a look of satisfaction on his face. "That's great. He did really well."

He nodded.

I thought he would leave, but he lingered, watching me run a stiff brush over Dawn's Rose. After a long silence, he cleared his throat.

"I'm proud of you, Mattie. You gave Fred a gift today. One that will have a long-lasting effect on his life."

He sounded sincere.

I couldn't remember hearing words of praise from my father that weren't directed at Mark. I wasn't sure how to respond.

"Thank you," I finally said.

He left me alone then. I didn't know what just happened, but it felt monumental. Like a shift in the galaxy or something. Dad was a man of few words, so to hear him say he was proud of me—especially coming on the heels of his soul-wrenching reminder that I'd abandoned Mama when she needed me most—completely caught me off guard.

I finished grooming Dawn's Rose, but I wasn't ready to go inside the house. I needed time by myself to sort through the morning's events.

I walked to Moonlight's stall. She put her nose over the half door and nudged me.

"How about we go for a ride, girl?" I said, rubbing her strong jaw.

Ten minutes later, we headed out of the barn into glorious sunshine.

TWENTY-SIX

AVA

DELANEY HORSE FARM

JUNE 1943

I wept the day Gunther boarded a train bound for North Dakota.

To my great disappointment, I wasn't allowed to bid him farewell. Armed soldiers flooded the area and kept all non-military personnel far away from the depot, fearful someone might attempt an escape. Desperate to see Gunther one last time, I drove to a railroad crossing and waited an hour before the train pulled away from the station and began the long journey north.

As it picked up speed, I stood alongside the Ford, straining to catch a glimpse of Gunther in any of the railcar windows, but to no avail. By the time the red caboose rattled past, its rear deck occupied by two soldiers with rifles, tears flowed down my face.

Gunther was gone.

The days and weeks dragged by after that. Bren and the other girls noticed my melancholy and tried to entice me to join them at the USO on the weekends, but I declined. I had no interest in dancing with anyone other than Gunther.

I arrived home after a long day. Several hundred new German POWs had arrived at Camp Forrest. Each was given a full physical, and their records were kept in a locked filing cabinet in Colonel Foster's office. He'd asked me to take charge of them, making sure the information was complete and remained confidential.

"A letter came for you," Gertrude said when I entered the house. "Who do you know in North Dakota?"

I gasped.

It had to be from Gunther.

Before I could answer, Ivy Lee entered the room, dressed to the nines. She obviously had a date with her colonel.

"What about North Dakota?" She picked up the envelope from the table. "That's where all those German spies were sent." Her blue eyes landed on me, a smirk on her ruby lips. "Don't tell me you're correspondin' with that fella you snuck around with. What was his name? Adolph something?"

Heat filled my face. "I didn't sneak around with anyone. I helped Mr. Schneider with his English."

"Why would he contact you?" Gertrude's scowl deepened. "It isn't appropriate for a German prisoner to write to an American war widow. Did you invite him to correspond with you?"

I refused to be questioned by these women. "I'm tired. It's been a long day, and I'd like to lie down. I'll make a sandwich later."

I didn't wait for a response.

I snatched the envelope from Ivy Lee and hurried down the hallway to my bedroom. In the waning light, I leaned against the closed door, the letter clutched to my heart. When my breathing grew normal, I moved to the window. With trembling hands, I opened the envelope, taking care not to rip the edges. A single sheet of folded paper slipped out.

Dear Ava,

I arrived at Fort Lincoln, North Dakota yesterday, a place I had never heard of but now find it is my home. The internment camp is much like the one at Camp Forrest . . .

Although I could tell military censors read my letter before it reached me, I devoured every word. When I came to the last paragraph, my heart skipped, and I had to reread each word to be sure I hadn't misunderstood his meaning.

I miss our English lessons and your chicken salad sandwiches. I am ever grateful for the time we shared together. It is bold of me to ask, but I hope you will write to me. It would brighten my day.

Sincerely,
Gunther Schneider

I pressed the back of my hand to my lips to keep from squealing with joy.

Gunther hadn't forgotten me. He missed our time together and wanted me to write to him.

I read the letter again, and again, memorizing each detail he shared. He'd been assigned to the hospital, for which I was pleased. While not the same as attending medical school, he would continue to gain experience and knowledge, preparing for the day when the war ended or he was released, whichever came first, and he could return to his studies.

I had to send a reply right away. It had taken several weeks for his letter to reach me, whether that was due to his position as an enemy alien or wartime mail service, I didn't know. I worried he might think I wasn't going to write back.

Settling at the desk with paper and pen, I stared at the blank page for a long time. There were so many things I wanted to say to him.

I miss you.

I wish you were here.

I love you.

Yet it was too soon for such revealing sentiments. The future too uncertain. Knowing an official at Fort Lincoln would no doubt read my words before they reached Gunther, I needed to be careful.

I kept my reply lighthearted and general, filling him in on the arrival of the German POWs, news from the farm, and my hope that he stays well.

When I came to the closing, however, my hand hovered over the paper.

How should I sign it? He'd used the word *sincerely* in his letter, but I wanted something less formal and more meaningful. Best wishes? Kindest regards?

His friendship meant more to me than he knew, so I chose to acknowledge it.

Your friend, Ava.

I sealed the envelope, resisting the desire to stamp it with a red lipstick kiss.

"Good night, my dearest," I whispered, looking out the window to the twinkling stars. *Were the skies in North Dakota clear tonight?* I wondered.

Although Gunther was a thousand or more miles away, I suddenly didn't feel quite so lonely.

TWENTY-SEVEN

GUNTHER

FORT LINCOLN, NORTH DAKOTA
AUGUST 1943

Gunther repositioned the bare light bulb above the examination table, hoping to get a better look at the gash on the back of the German sailor's head.

"You'll need stitches," he said, speaking in his native language.

Since arriving at Fort Lincoln three months ago, he'd found that most of the inmates of the internment camp didn't speak English. Especially those who remained loyal to the Nazi party and vocally promoted their anti-American sentiments. Whether the men couldn't understand the language or chose not to use it, Gunther didn't know and didn't ask.

"You're lucky," he continued. "I don't believe you have a concussion."

The man grimaced as Gunther cleaned the wound. "I would

have been luckier if I hadn't fallen off a table in the casino and cracked my head open."

Gunther kept his concurrence to himself.

In the weeks since he'd been assigned to the hospital, he'd attended to numerous patients with minor injuries received in drunken antics or brawls at the detainees' canteen, the small building next to the mess hall where inmates were allowed to drink beer, wine, and play cards after dinner. The colorfully decorated establishment also offered cigarettes, paper, pens, candy, and basic hygiene items for purchase. However, it took only one visit to the noisy watering hole for Gunther to discover a hierarchy existed in the camp.

He'd barely taken his first sip of dark beer when a burly sailor filled the seat across from him.

"You're new. You need to know how things work around here."

He was one of over two hundred German seamen—many who worked for Standard Oil—who'd arrived in May and June of 1941. The sailors were detained while docked in New York after Germany invaded western Europe. Their merchant ships and tankers were seized and the men taken to Ellis Island before being transferred here. Gunther remembered hearing about the seizures but assumed the men in question were Nazis, thus leading to their arrests. Unfortunately, neither Gunther nor his friends took the aggressive act as a warning of things to come.

Although Gunther found that most of the sailors were amiable, there were some who believed they were in command. They called themselves the Schlageter in honor of an early Nazi hero who was executed by the French, and they had a deep disdain for the enemy alien internees. The group of twenty or so men viewed Gunther and the others as traitors to Germany because of their presence in America when the war erupted. Gunther quickly learned to avoid this group of men when he saw them in the mess hall or the casino.

He sent the stitched-up sailor on his way, warning the young man to return to the hospital should he feel unwell. It had been a long day, and Gunther was more than ready to return to his barracks. Dr. Lipp, the local physician contracted to provide medical services for the inmates, was too busy with his private practice in town to come to the camp the last couple days, leaving the care of patients with Dr. Ludwig, the medical officer from one of the oil tankers. That man, however, was difficult to work with and held clear biases against anyone who was not pro-Nazi.

Gunther finished straightening the examination room, putting supplies away and sterilizing the instruments he'd used. He'd just turned out the lights when a ruckus arose down the hall.

"Get out. I won't have a Jew tend to me," a patient bellowed in German, followed by a string of foul words.

Two civilian nurses stood outside an open doorway, whispering, and peering into the room as though they were afraid to enter.

"What is the problem?" Gunther asked in English, his voice lowered.

The older of the two, Nurse Roe, huffed. "A new doctor arrived today. Mr. Schmidt isn't pleased the man is Jewish."

Gunther groaned inwardly.

Wolfgang Schmidt. One of the leaders of the Schlageter. The sailor had suffered a ruptured appendix last week, and although Dr. Lipp performed lifesaving surgery, the man had a long way to go to full recovery. His demands on the hospital staff and surly disposition were taxing on everyone.

The unknown doctor murmured something Gunther couldn't make out, to which Wolfgang responded with more foul words. There were only three or four Jewish prisoners at Fort Lincoln, but they kept to themselves to avoid problems with the Schlageter. The fact that the new doctor's background was already creating drama could prove troublesome in the long term.

The nurses returned to their duties while Gunther peeked into the room. A partially drawn curtain around the bed allowed a view of Wolfgang's blanket-covered feet and nothing more. The new doctor remained out of sight.

Gunther had just turned to leave when the man spoke again.

"You may refuse treatment," came calm and gentle words, "but you will put yourself in danger. There is still a great risk of infection."

Gunther paused.

The voice. It sounded familiar.

"I'd rather die than have a Jew touch me," Wolfgang snarled.

"As you wish. I will make a note, asking Dr. Ludwig to look in on you. Good night, Mr. Schmidt."

A small, bespectacled, suit-clad man emerged from behind the curtain. He was thinner than Gunther remembered, but there was no mistaking his old professor.

"Dr. Sonnenberg?"

His mentor's eyes widened. "Gunther Schneider," he said, clearly as astonished to see Gunther as Gunther was to see him. "I could not have wished for anything so wonderful as to find my favorite student here in North Dakota."

The two embraced.

"How long have you been here?" the older man asked when they parted.

"I arrived in May," Gunther said. "Before that I was in Tennessee, and before that, Ellis Island."

Dr. Sonnenberg opened his mouth to respond, but Wolfgang's loud voice interrupted their reunion.

"Schneider, don't tell me you're a Jew-lover as well as a traitor," he shouted. Gunther couldn't see the riled sailor's face, but it didn't matter. He'd witnessed Wolfgang's anger plenty of times in the past three months. "I always knew you couldn't be trusted."

Gunther ignored the remark and motioned for Dr. Sonnenberg

to follow him. He led the man to an empty room at the far end of the hallway where they could talk in private.

"I cannot believe you're here." Gunther spoke in hushed English, astonished at finding his beloved professor so far from Columbia medical school. "When were you arrested?"

"In the spring. My longtime position at the university kept me safe for a while, but I knew it was a matter of time before they came for me." He gave a helpless shrug. "They accused me of being a spy."

"Were you given a hearing?"

Dr. Sonnenberg shook his head. "I was charged with passing vital information to the Gestapo. There was supposedly evidence but nothing was ever presented. I was held at Ellis Island until three days ago."

A memory surfaced in Gunther's mind. "When I was questioned on the island, they showed me a telegram you received, with instructions to destroy files after America declared war on Germany."

He gave a solemn nod. "I suspect my nurse was a spy. I don't know what secrets she passed while working in the clinic, but I believe her associates sent the telegram to me to throw the authorities off her trail."

Gunther's stomach roiled at the injustice. "You are a renowned doctor and professor at Columbia medical school. It is obscene the way you've been treated."

"I am a German in their eyes. Nothing more, nothing less." His keen gaze studied Gunther. "Tell me about yourself. Are you practicing medicine these days?"

Gunther filled his mentor in on the work he'd done at Camp Forrest, giving the doctor credit for demonstrating the lifesaving technique he'd used on the soldier in the mess hall. He told how Colonel Foster assigned him to the dispensary and recommended him for the hospital at Fort Lincoln when they learned of his transfer.

Gunther left out the part about Ava's help and how she'd become someone dear to him. He'd been disappointed she hadn't come to the depot to see him off. The one brief letter he'd received hadn't given him hope she felt more than friendship, and he'd deliberated the wisdom of continuing the correspondence. Ultimately, he decided he would rather have Ava as a friend than not have her in his life at all. He'd sent another letter and now awaited her response.

"What barracks are you assigned to?" Gunther asked as they made their way outside.

The small medical building was located on the west end of the internment camp, just beyond the ten-foot cyclone fence surrounding the complex. Only authorized personnel were permitted in and out. Should someone attempt an escape, as Gunther had heard happened before he arrived, patrolmen positioned in the seven steel guard towers strategically located along the fence were armed and ready to stop the desperate inmate from getting far.

The sun had just disappeared below the treeless horizon when they were escorted through the gate. Although afternoons could get hot on the North Dakota prairie, evenings were comfortable and pleasant. All that would change once winter arrived, he reminded himself daily.

As it turned out, Dr. Sonnenberg was housed in the same red-brick building as Gunther but on a different level. The man sharing Gunther's small, dormitory-like room volunteered to switch with Dr. Sonnenberg when he heard of their long friendship, allowing Gunther to delight in deep conversations with his mentor once again.

If not for the ugly detail of being held prisoners of the American government, Gunther might have thoroughly enjoyed the experience.

* * *

By September, Gunther and Dr. Sonnenberg had firmly reestablished their teacher-student relationship, with the older man giving wise instruction to Gunther as they worked side by side in the hospital. Medical procedures, thoughts on various medications, and all manner of lively scientific discussions helped lift the depression each of them had carried since their arrests. Although they continued to remain hopeful their internment would not last the duration of the war, having a friend one could trust was life-giving while they awaited freedom.

Two events, however, reminded everyone of their status as enemy aliens in America.

On a mid-September evening, Gunther and Dr. Sonnenberg were making rounds at the hospital when the roar of loud voices came from the enclosed camp.

"That does not sound good," Gunther said. He rushed to a window and looked out across the yard. A large group of internees—too many to count—made their way toward the main gate, shouting, and brandishing sticks and anything else they could use as a weapon. "It looks like a riot."

His grim pronouncement drew Dr. Sonnenberg to the scene. "Let us hope this does not end badly."

Gunther opened the window, and they listened as the men chanted in German, although the distance between the hospital and the mob was such that Gunther couldn't make out all the words. Freedom seemed to be the main theme. Armed guards and border patrolmen arrived from all over the camp and took up positions on the opposite side of the fence. Boyd, one of the guards who often escorted Gunther and Dr. Sonnenberg in and out of the enclosure, ran past the hospital toward the group, carrying a submachine gun over his shoulder.

Gunther and Dr. Sonnenberg exchanged grave looks.

"We best prepare the staff for an emergency," the older man said as he turned from the spectacle.

Over the next three hours, they readied bandages and various medical supplies needed should the riot erupt in violence. Even Dr. Ludwig came to help, his demeanor unusually solemn and cooperative. Every so often Gunther glanced out the window to see if the situation had changed. Although the men continued shouting and singing in German, and the guards stayed in their positions with guns raised, things remained tense but controlled.

At ten o'clock, the curfew whistle sounded throughout the camp. Tonight, with fear and unrest swirling in the dry, cool air, the long, eerie blast was especially unsettling as it reverberated across the Missouri River bottomland. Would it trigger violence if the men did not disband and return to their barracks?

Thankfully the group slowly began to disperse until only the guards remained. Later, Gunther wasn't surprised to learn the Schlageter were responsible for instigating the riot. Seven of their comrades were locked up after beating an internee who mocked their pro-Nazi ideals. That the entire camp came to their defense left Gunther wondering what his fellow detainees—those who were moderate in their political beliefs—would do if forced to choose sides. Would they align with the Schlageter? The thought was frightening, considering he and Dr. Sonnenberg were already at odds with the sailors who made up that notorious group.

Things had finally begun to settle when the camp was once again plunged into turmoil after one of the newer internees became the first to successfully escape, four weeks after the near riot.

Gunther and Dr. Sonnenberg huddled around a furnace in the hospital as a howling, bitterly cold November wind swept across the barren landscape with brutal force. Dr. Ludwig soon joined them and launched into the tale of how one of his frequent patients, Heinz Fengler, walked away from the railroad gang he was assigned to and disappeared.

"Fengler often came to the hospital with bouts of depression or insomnia. He complained of headaches and seemed a troubled sort of fellow." The doctor chuckled. "But I would have never guessed he had the nerve to escape. I heard he has a woman friend in a nearby town. I suspect she assisted him."

Rumors circulated for weeks about where Fengler would go, who had helped him, and what would happen to him if he were caught. Mr. McCoy, the camp commander, and his staff ramped up security, including posting an armed guard inside the hospital and restricting civilian visits. Everyone was thoroughly checked when they entered the building and when they exited.

Between the riot and the escape, the mood around camp felt like a tinderbox ready to ignite. While some internees applauded Fengler and his ingenuity to break free and hoped he wasn't caught, others argued both the escape and the nighttime uprising had made things worse for the rest of them. Tightened security, activities canceled, earlier roll calls, stricter curfew checks. Guards who'd been friendly and relaxed before the incidents now held guns at the ready, casting suspicious looks at everyone. Even Hooch and Waven, the two German shepherds used to patrol fence lines, growled and bared their teeth when Gunther and Dr. Sonnenberg walked past on their way to the hospital.

It was January, however, when the unrest became personal.

Late one night, a loud banging sounded, followed by scuffling feet in the hallway. Groggy, Gunther clicked on the light and found someone had slid a note beneath their door. By the time he peeked into the hall, the culprit was gone.

"Death to all Jews," Dr. Sonnenberg read the brief, hate-filled message aloud. The image of a swastika served as a signature.

"This is outrageous." Gunther paced the wooden floor of the small room, his frustration and his voice rising. "I don't understand why McCoy won't rein in the Schlageter. He is the officer in charge, yet he allows them to put up a monument to the Nazi party and hang Nazi flags in their rooms. They greet each other with their ridiculous 'heil, Hitler' and salute one another. They terrorize anyone who doesn't agree with their vile way of thinking. Those men should be separated from the rest of us. *They* are the real enemies."

The older man sat on the edge of his bed, his thinning gray hair wild. Gunther couldn't help but notice his mentor seemed more frail, more vulnerable, there in his pajamas in the middle of the night, holding what was essentially a death threat.

"Mr. McCoy is busy with the hunt for Fengler." Dr. Sonnenberg shrugged. "Dealing with the Schlageter is not a priority."

Gunther scoffed. "McCoy is more worried about how the escape looks to his superiors rather than what is going on here in camp. Heinz Fengler was allowed too much freedom after he volunteered for the railroad gang. It isn't surprising he simply walked away."

"I cannot fault him for wanting to leave this place."

"Neither can I, but his selfish decision has affected everyone. While all the attention is on finding him, the sailors think they can get away with their bullying without anyone noticing." He indicated the contemptable note. "We need to report this. I doubt anything will be done about it but at least McCoy and the others in charge will know what kind of hate is being perpetrated against you simply because you are Jewish."

His words echoed in the quiet dormitory. Someone in the room next door thumped on the wall and shouted for Gunther to be quiet.

Dr. Sonnenberg studied the note. "It has always been this way for my people," he said sadly. "An unpleasant note is nothing compared to what my fellow Jews are experiencing in Germany. Arrests. Concentration camps. Death chambers. More horror than I can imagine, I'm certain. I'm honored to stand in solidarity with them here, across the ocean."

Gunther sank down onto his own bed, sobered by his friend's words. He thought back to Dr. Sonnenberg's first day at the hospital. "How did Wolfgang Schmidt discover you were a Jew?"

"When he heard my name, he asked if it was Jewish. I told him the truth. I am not ashamed of my heritage."

While they'd never discussed either of their religious beliefs during his time at Columbia, Gunther had always known Dr. Sonnenberg was Jewish. *Mutter* was a devout Christian, placing her faith firmly in Jesus Christ, and she taught Gunther and Rolf to do the same. He couldn't say for certain whether his brother accepted what the Bible said, but Gunther did. Yet he could never hate someone simply because their views were different from his.

"Why don't your people believe Jesus is the Messiah?"

The question came out of nowhere, but it somehow seemed appropriate tonight.

"Jews do not believe that Jesus satisfies the prophecies concerning the Messiah," Dr. Sonnenberg said in the thoughtful, unhurried manner he'd always used while giving lectures at Columbia. "The verses in the King James Bible that Christians most often reference, claiming they prove Jesus is the long-awaited One, are, at times, misinterpreted in my opinion."

An idea formed in Gunther's mind. "I'd like to learn more about the differences between Jews and Christians. Perhaps you and I can study those passages together. I have the Bible my *Mutter* gave me when I came to America."

A slow smile lifted the corners of Dr. Sonnenberg's mouth. "Ever the student," he said with a chuckle. He laid aside the hateful note. "I do not believe I will be able to return to sleep. Shall we begin now?"

TWENTY-EIGHT

MATTIE

DELANEY HORSE FARM
DECEMBER 1969

Mama's cry woke me.

The sky outside my window was black, shrouding the farm in dark shadows. The glowing hands on the small clock on the bedside table told me it was half past four.

Should I see if Mama needed something?

The murmur of Dad's voice sounded. Their door creaked open, and I heard his soft footfalls as he padded to the bathroom. Running water, the click of the bedroom door, and then all was quiet again.

Despite closing my eyes, sleep wouldn't come. With a sigh, I sat up and turned on the lamp. Blinking until my eyes adjusted to the sudden brightness, I contemplated what to do. It was too early for breakfast. A cup of hot cocoa would be nice, but I didn't want to go downstairs and make noise.

My gaze drifted to the old shoebox on the desk.

Nash and I hadn't finished reading the letters. An emergency arose with one of the horses, and he and Dad spent hours in the barn working with a gelding that had injured its leg. I stayed with Mama, but she dozed most of the time. In her sporadic wakeful moments, she wanted to hear about Fred's accomplishments or what we'd had for dinner. Delving into her mysterious past would have to wait.

I tiptoed to the desk, avoiding a loose floorboard, and retrieved the box. Although I'd rather read the letters with Nash by my side, now was as good a time as any to go through the remaining notes from Gunther. Then I'd be ready to talk to Mama about them once the sun made its appearance.

Settled with the stack on my lap and my feet tucked beneath the covers, I picked up an envelope. The postmark was from Bismarck, North Dakota, dated January 1944.

Dear Ava,

Thank you for your letter. I'm glad to hear all is well on the farm. Your descriptions make me wish I could have seen it while I was in Tennessee.

Dr. Sonnenberg and I are studying the New Testament in the evenings while the other men play cards or chess in the casino. I am learning much about Jewish traditions, but I fear I am not a very good teacher when it comes to explaining why I believe Jesus Christ is the Messiah. It has made me want to spend more time reading God's Word. I can only pray that he will overcome my inadequacies and bring understanding to my friend.

We experienced our first blizzard last week. We could not leave the hospital for three days. Snowdrifts reached the eaves and covered doorways, and icicles more than six feet long still hang from the roof. I am grateful for brick walls, furnaces, and wool socks.

I hope your new year is full of blessings.

Your friend,
Gunther Schneider

I returned the letter to its envelope and reached for the next one in the stack. The content was much the same, only this time hints of spring gave Gunther hope that frigid weather would come to an end soon. A third letter told of his disappointment that Dr. Sonnenberg was no longer allowed to work in the hospital, but they continued their religious studies at night.

A long breath pushed past my lips.

There was nothing in Gunther Schneider's correspondence that made me believe he was anything more to my mother than a friend. Not one word of admiration or hint of attraction was exchanged, at least on his part. The missives were friendly, newsy, and nothing more.

I glanced at the three remaining envelopes.

I'd wait to read them with Nash, but I felt confident now that Mama hadn't had a romantic fling with the foreign man. Why she felt I needed to know about him was still unknown, but I was satisfied I had nothing to fear.

With that settled, I tossed all the envelopes back into the box. I was ready to carry it to the desk when my eyes fell on the partially hidden cover of the old Bible. I lifted it out.

Die Bibel.

The faded gold lettering and leather binding told me it had once been lovely. With gentle care, I opened it and read the handwritten inscription.

Für meinen Sohn, Ehre Gott immer. Ich liebe dich, Mutter.

I sounded out the strange words as best I could. "Fur meanin' Sohn. For my son."

The next words, however, still stumped me. "Air Got immer. Ick liebe ditch."

I had no clue what any of it meant.

The last word drew me. "Mutter. Mother."

If I were correct about the translation of the first line—*For my son*—then it would make sense that someone's mother had given him the Bible. The rest of the message was probably something sentimental only a mother would write.

Why was the book in Mama's possession? Had it belonged to the German prisoner Gunther Schneider?

My father's reaction at seeing the old book the day Mama dug through the trunk floated across my mind. Clearly he had not been pleased to see me with it. He'd never cared about anything associated with religion as far as I knew, but his unhappiness at seeing the old book that day was obvious. Was he angry Mama kept it all these years? Did he know about her correspondence with Gunther, and could he be jealous?

So many questions. Not enough answers.

Soft morning light began to fill the sky.

Nurse Bradford would be here soon. Even though I hadn't been thrilled when she started coming to help Mama, I now saw the wisdom in it. Her calm presence allowed us to maintain a normal daily routine despite the gravity of Mama's illness. I still found it impossible to believe Mama was dying. That terrible reality was something I simply couldn't dwell on for any length of time. Normalcy and busyness distracted me enough to make it through each day without completely falling apart.

The door to Nash's room was closed when I came downstairs. I guessed he was sleeping in after a late night in the barn, but he appeared in the kitchen after I started the coffee percolator. His shoulder-length hair was damp, telling me he'd already showered in the tiny downstairs bathroom Dad added on to the house when Mark and I were teenagers. A family of four adults couldn't share one bathroom, he'd declared.

"Morning," he said. "You're up early."

"I was going to say the same about you, considering you were out in the barn past midnight. How is the horse?"

While I poured each of us a cup of coffee, he filled me in on the horse's injury and prognosis. "The vet should be here soon to check on him, but your dad feels confident the leg will mend well."

I took a careful sip of the steaming liquid. "Now that I know Dad isn't Granny's son, I wonder how he learned so much about caring for horses."

"Maybe his family raised horses too."

"It's strange not knowing about my own grandparents. I mean, why would he and Mama let Mark and me think Granny was our biological grandmother? I would have rather known she wasn't, especially since she never really liked us."

He looked thoughtful. "I think it would've been hard for Granny to see your mom married and having a family with someone else. Didn't you say her son was her only child?"

His logic made sense. "Yeah, he was. Richard. And you're probably right. Granny no doubt mourned her son the rest of her life." I sighed. "Now I feel bad for playing pranks on her."

Nash grinned. "You and Mark did come up with some crazy ideas. I'll never forget the look on Granny's face when she came running out of the cottage after she found a baby skunk in her bathtub."

Later, Nurse Bradford arrived, followed by the veterinarian. Dad came downstairs and left the house with Nash, while I went upstairs with the nurse.

Mama was awake and greeted us with a weak smile.

"Hi, Mama." I bent to kiss her forehead. "Are you hungry? I could make you a soft-boiled egg and toast."

She shook her head. "Maybe in a bit." Her words were slow and slurred.

I stepped aside as Nurse Bradford came forward to check Mama's pulse and listen to her heart and lungs. "How did you sleep, Ava?" she asked as she glanced at her watch.

"Not well. I had a terrible headache."

Nurse Bradford kept up a one-sided conversation about the weather while she helped Mama sit up and lean against a mound of pillows. "Let's get you freshened up for the day. Do you need to use the bedpan?"

Mama looked confused. "The what?"

"Do you need to empty your bladder?" Nurse Bradford clarified.

Mama shook her head then looked at me. "Are you a nurse too?"

The question startled me. I shot a look at Nurse Bradford. Concern filled her face.

"Ava, can you tell me your whole name?"

Mama blinked, her brow furrowed. "Ava . . . Delaney."

Fear surged up in me. "What's wrong? Why is she so confused?" I whispered.

Nurse Bradford kept her attention on Mama. "Ava, do you know where you are?"

A long silence lapsed as Mama slowly gazed around the room. "The farm."

"That's right. And who is this young woman?" she asked, pointing to me.

Mama stared at me, her face blank.

"It's me, Mama. Mattie," I said, desperate for my mother to return to her normal self.

"Mattie," she repeated. Whether or not she knew I was her daughter, I wasn't sure.

"I think you should take a little rest now, Ava," Nurse Bradford said. "We can tend to your bath later."

By the time the nurse had her tucked beneath the covers, Mama was asleep. Nurse Bradford motioned me into the hallway.

I didn't wait for her to speak. "What's wrong with Mama? I've never seen her this confused. She didn't even know me."

Nurse Bradford's usual gentle smile and calming words were gone, replaced with a grave look in her eyes.

"I can't be certain, but I suspect the cancer has reached your mother's brain."

I gasped and covered my mouth.

"I'll call Dr. Monahan and let him know. He'll want to examine Ava, but without an X-ray, there's no way to be sure."

She hurried downstairs to use the telephone. I stood in the doorway to Mama's room, tears clouding my vision.

"Please don't take her," I whispered, not realizing I was praying until the words were out of my mouth. I didn't stop. "Don't take her," I hissed. "Not like you took Mark. I need her."

Mama groaned and tossed her head back and forth on the pillow.

I hurried to her. "Rest easy, Mama." I smoothed her cheek. "I'm right here with you."

She quieted for a time. I thought she'd fallen asleep when she stirred again. This time she mumbled something unintelligible.

"What, Mama? What did you say?"

Her eyes sprang open. Fear filled her face, and she reached for my hand.

"Gunther," she said, panicked. "Where's Gunther? I need him."

My heart felt as though it came to a screeching halt as I stared at her in horror.

Mama wasn't calling out for Dad.

She was calling out for Gunther Schneider.

• • •

"Brain metastases occur when cancer cells spread from their original site to the brain," Dr. Monahan said as Dad, Nash, and I sat silent in the living room. Nurse Bradford remained upstairs with Mama so the doctor could deliver his devastating prognosis after his examination. "As the metastatic tumors grow, they create pressure on the brain, changing the function of surrounding tissue. This causes symptoms like headaches, personality changes, memory loss, and even seizures. Although we don't have conclusive proof that is what's happening, I've seen it before. There isn't any other reason why Ava would suddenly be forgetful of her environment and the people around her."

I couldn't breathe. Couldn't look at anyone.

This shouldn't be happening. Not to my beautiful, gentle mother. She believed in God. Prayed. Went to church. The entire town knew her to be one of the kindest, most giving people.

"I'm sorry I don't have better news." Dr. Monahan sighed. "It will be important to keep her pain medication continuous. As the tumors enlarge, her pain level will increase. Nurse Bradford and I will discuss the use of an intravenous drip should it become difficult for Ava to swallow medication." He paused. "Do you have any questions?"

Neither Dad nor I spoke.

"What will happen next?" Nash asked.

I sent him a look of appreciation. I couldn't voice the query, but I needed to know the answer, no matter how much I hated it.

"Ava will steadily decline. She may have periods of lucidity, but she will grow increasingly confused. You mustn't become upset or try to reason with her. Keep her as calm and comfortable as possible."

Dad nodded. "Thank you, Dr. Monahan. We appreciate you coming so quickly."

His voice sounded normal, yet I had a feeling my father was struggling to keep himself composed. His hands trembled, and his jaw clenched and unclenched.

"You're welcome. You, Ava, and the kids," the doctor said, including me in his gaze, "are practically family. I wish there was more I could do."

Dad walked the doctor out while Nash and I remained in the living room.

"Are you okay?" he asked.

I shook my head, fighting tears. When I trusted my voice, I said, "She doesn't deserve this, Nash."

"No, she doesn't."

"Then why is God doing this to her?" I said, my voice hard. "If he's as real as she believes, why would he do this to one of his most faithful followers?"

I didn't expect an answer. That same question had no doubt been asked through the ages.

Dad returned. His face looked ashen as he retook his seat. "Dr. Monahan said he would come by tomorrow. LuAnn will call him if we need him before that."

I knew there were things we should discuss—end-of-life things—but I couldn't handle them right now.

I stood. "I'm going to see if Mama is hungry. She didn't eat any breakfast."

Dad simply nodded.

When I reached the upstairs landing, relief swept through me when I saw Mama sitting up in bed.

"There's my girl." She still sounded groggy, but at least she knew who I was.

"I thought I'd come see if you were hungry."

Nurse Bradford rose from the chair next to Mama's bed. "We were just talking about that. I'll go downstairs and heat some broth."

I settled in the vacant seat. There were so many things we needed to talk about. It seemed surreal that time was running out. Dr. Monahan said she would become more and more forgetful as the tumors grew. Just this morning I concluded her friendship with Gunther Schneider wasn't important, but after hearing her call for him, I didn't know what to believe.

"Mama," I began but faltered.

Should I simply leave the past in the past? Her secrets would be buried with her when the time came. Yet she'd wanted me to know. To understand something about her that she felt was important.

"Mama, can I ask you a question?"

Her gaze was fixed on the window where sunshine spilled into the room. When she turned to me, she seemed like she was a million miles away. "You look so much like your father."

The comment surprised me. I'd always been told I resembled her. We had the same coloring, the same shape to our faces.

"He was so handsome," she continued, her voice soft. "I knew I'd always love him, even when everyone told me I shouldn't."

"What do you mean? Who said you shouldn't love him?"

She rubbed her temple, grimacing. "My head hurts again."

"Mama," I said, urgency in my voice. I reached for her hand, drawing her attention back to me. "Why weren't you supposed to love him?"

The question seemed to draw her back to the present. "I never told anyone. Only Gertrude knew, but she promised to keep our secret."

"What secret, Mama?"

"We kept it from you and Mark to protect you."

My mouth went dry, and icy fingers of fear gripped my thundering heart. "Mama, what secret?"

She closed her eyes for a long moment before she met my gaze.

"Your father was a German prisoner at Camp Forrest," she whispered. "His name is Gunther Schneider."

TWENTY-NINE

GUNTHER

FORT LINCOLN, NORTH DAKOTA
JUNE 1944

Gunther found Dr. Sonnenberg reading a book in the foyer of the dormitory, waiting for him when he returned from a long day at the hospital.

"You look tired," his mentor said as he placed a scrap of paper between the pages to keep his place. When he closed the cover, Gunther saw it was a copy of Mark Twain's *The Adventures of Huckleberry Finn*. Residents of Bismarck had generously donated books to create a small library for the internees, many classics among them. With nothing beyond dreary weather, barren landscape, and long boring hours to look forward to day after day, an escape through a good book was much appreciated.

Gunther dropped onto an empty chair. "Dr. Ludwig had me

cleaning bedpans and mopping floors again today rather than helping with patients."

Sympathy showed on the older man's face. "I'm sorry. You suffer because of your friendship with me."

Outrage washed over Gunther. "It is ridiculous that McCoy gave in to the Schlageter's demands and removed you from the hospital. You are far more qualified than a man who made his living tending to drunken sailors on an oil tanker."

Dr. Sonnenberg gave Gunther a patient look. "Now, now. Accidents and illnesses arise on ships when they're out to sea, same as on land. Having a doctor onboard could mean the difference between life and death."

Gunther scoffed. "From what I've seen, I'd take my chances rather than have Dr. Ludwig attend me. The man is a clown. He nearly broke the X-ray machine today. One of the levers was jammed, and he beat it with a hammer. Thankfully Nurse Roe intervened before the machine was destroyed."

"Dr. Lipp will not be pleased when he hears about this."

Gunther shook his head. "He's as frustrated as the rest of us with Dr. Ludwig's antics, but McCoy won't listen. I think he fears more what the Schlageter will do if they don't get their way than the complaints against their doctor."

Dr. Sonnenberg looked thoughtful. "I don't believe Mr. McCoy is afraid of the Schlageter, but I do believe he will go to any length to keep peace in camp. He's in a precarious position if you think about it. We aren't prisoners of war, and while the regulations set by the Geneva Convention do pertain to us, they weren't specifically written for our situation. Most of us are not American citizens, so the rights stated in the Declaration of Independence don't apply either. Although, as we've seen with Japanese American internees, the government has treated them as badly as they've treated us." He looked at Gunther. "I'm Jewish, and the Schlageter hate Jews. Neither of those facts are going to change."

"That may be true," Gunther said, "but the behavior of those men only gets worse when McCoy gives in to their demands."

As the sun disappeared below the horizon, they made their way to the mess hall for dinner. Delicious aromas and noise met them when they entered. Most of the men had already eaten but remained in the great room to socialize. Gunther had to admit one positive thing about Fort Lincoln was the food. Unlike at Camp Forrest, where they ate the same American fare as the soldiers, Mr. McCoy had assigned German cooks to prepare food for the internees. They enjoyed authentic German dishes like *Schnitzel* with mushroom gravy, *Spätzle*, and *Apfelkuchen* for dessert. It made him long for *Mutter*'s cooking.

His mind was still on her when they carried their trays to an empty table near the back of the crowded room.

"You look troubled," Dr. Sonnenberg said.

Gunther noticed his friend's plate held only vegetables, and he remembered their discussion about Jewish practices regarding food and food preparation. Dr. Sonnenberg did the best he could to keep to his traditions without starving.

"I was thinking about *Mutter*. I haven't heard from her since I arrived at Fort Lincoln." He lowered his voice so only his friend could hear. "With everything going on in Germany, I worry."

Dr. Sonnenberg gave a solemn nod. "I too have loved ones I am concerned for. The last I knew, my brother and his family were safe in Switzerland, but I do not know about my sister's family. No one has heard from them since the war began."

They discussed the latest news from Europe as they ate. Near the end of their meal, loud voices rose from across the room.

When Gunther glanced over, he saw members of the Schlageter, including Wolfgang Schmidt, harassing a new internee. The young man—wasn't his name Karl?—was a teacher and offered to give classes in English at the *Schule*, held on the second floor of Building 61, where instruction was conducted by qualified internees on subjects ranging from chemistry to philosophy. Many detainees eagerly signed up for Karl's class, but the group of Nazi supporters did not approve. They declared it traitorous to speak any language other than German, most especially English.

The usual din of conversation in the mess hall grew quiet as the argument escalated.

"You are a disgrace to your family," one of the Schlageter bellowed, standing face to face with Karl. To that young man's credit, he remained where he was rather than backing away. "The Führer himself demands that German citizens speak only our mother language. Why do you disobey our esteemed leader?"

Gunther couldn't hear Karl's low, calm reply, but it clearly infuriated the other man.

Before anyone could stop it from happening, his balled fist slammed into Karl's face. Blood spurted from Karl's nose as he stumbled backwards and landed on his backside.

While the men of the Schlageter laughed and cheered, Dr. Sonnenberg rose from his seat and hurried over to Karl. Gunther followed. Everyone else in the large room stayed where they were, unwilling to put themselves at risk.

"Get away from him, Jew," the furious man yelled when Dr. Sonnenberg knelt beside Karl.

"He needs medical attention," the doctor said. Ignoring the sailor, he took a handkerchief from his pocket and applied it to Karl's bloody nose. That young man seemed dazed by the blow, his eyes unfocused.

"Get your hands off him, Jewish dog." The sailor took a menacing step toward Dr. Sonnenberg, but Gunther put himself between his friend and the angry man.

"We are taking Karl to the hospital." He kept his voice firm and his eyes steady on his opponent. When Wolfgang and another man from the Schlageter approached, Gunther didn't budge.

Dr. Sonnenberg helped Karl to his feet.

The Nazi supporters looked ready to fight, but thankfully Boyd, a border patrolman, arrived on the tense scene, led by one of Karl's students who'd obviously gone for help.

"What's going on?" The armed guard eyed the group. He held a rifle in both hands, ready should anyone make a move. "Why is this man bleeding?"

The sailor who'd slugged Karl narrowed his eyes on Gunther, a clear warning to keep silent. Despite the unspoken threat, Gunther was not going to let him get away with his brutality.

"This man attacked Karl for no reason," Gunther said, identifying the angry sailor. "Everyone here witnessed it."

Boyd glanced around the circle of men, sizing up the situation.

Finally he turned to Gunther. "Take him to the hospital." His attention then landed on the sailor. "You, come with me. The rest of you back away." He raised his rifle, ensuring everyone cooperated.

Gunther and Dr. Sonnenberg got on either side of Karl, with his arms over their shoulders, and carried him from the mess hall. Boyd and the sailor were steps behind. When they turned toward the guardhouse, the sailor shouted at Gunther in German, "You'll regret this!"

Gunther ignored the remark and continued to the hospital. Dr. Ludwig was just leaving the building when they arrived.

"What happened to him?" he asked, studying Karl's swollen, bloody nose. When they told him about the brawl, the man looked annoyed. "Dr. Lipp isn't here, and I am on my way to eat my dinner. Put him in a room. I'll tend to him when I get back."

Irritation washed over Gunther. "He needs attention now."

Dr. Ludwig huffed. "Very well. Sonnenberg, take care of him. If anyone questions why you're here, tell them I authorized it." He turned and left the building.

Gunther and Dr. Sonnenberg looked at each other and shook their heads.

"He certainly believes himself important, does he not?" Dr. Sonnenberg said.

"I'd rather have you tend me, sir," Karl mumbled.

Dr. Sonnenberg nodded. "I am happy to do so, son."

They cleaned Karl's face, but unfortunately there wasn't much Dr. Sonnenberg could do about his broken nose. Only time would heal it.

"Do you want me to try to straighten the bone?" he asked Karl. "It will be painful but will only last a short time."

The young man frowned. "If you don't straighten it, will I look deformed for the rest of my life?"

Dr. Sonnenberg offered a gentle smile. "I can't promise it will look like it did before, but you're a handsome fellow. The girls will still swoon, no matter if your nose is a bit crooked."

Karl chuckled, then cringed, obviously in pain. "Might as well try to straighten it." He gripped the edge of the examination table where he sat. "Go ahead."

Dr. Sonnenberg skillfully pushed the bone into place so quickly, Karl barely had time to let out a yelp. The doctor packed it with gauze, with instructions to remove it once Karl was back in his room and flat on his back.

"You will need to keep ice on it to help with the swelling." Gunther took a bottle of aspirin from a cabinet and poured six tablets into a small envelope. "Take a couple of these to help you sleep tonight," he said, handing the packet to Karl. "Aspirin can cause the blood to thin, so we don't want you to take too many."

"Thank you, both of you," Karl said, a nasal tone to his words. His nose had almost doubled in size. "I don't know why those men are so upset about me teaching English. I am as grateful for my German heritage as they are, but I can't pretend to be proud of our country and its leaders." He looked at Dr. Sonnenberg. "I don't agree with what they are doing to Jews."

Dr. Sonnenberg placed a hand on the young man's shoulder. "Thank you, son."

They bid Karl good night. Gunther disposed of the soiled cloths while Dr. Sonnenberg sterilized the instruments he'd used. It was dark when they made their way back to the dormitory, chatting quietly about the incident.

Neither of them saw the men in the shadows until it was too late.

THIRTY
AVA

CAMP FORREST, TENNESSEE
JULY 1944

I tidied my desk and prepared to leave for the day. A big celebration was planned on base tomorrow, commemorating the independence and freedom we enjoyed in this country. Families of soldiers and staff were invited to enjoy food, games, a parade at noon, and fireworks as soon as the sun went down. While the hospital administration office would be closed, I planned to arrive bright and early and get some work done while it was quiet.

I stifled a yawn and dug in my purse for my car keys.

Now that the hospital received a regular flow of incoming wounded from overseas, my days started early and ended late. Letters and official documents must be typed. Mounds of paperwork needed to be filed. Colonel Foster's schedule kept him on the run, which in turn kept me on the run too. A few weeks ago, he requested I accompany him to meetings throughout the base so I could take notes, declaring it an invaluable help to him. Sometimes the meetings took place after normal work hours, making the days especially long. When that happened, he always insisted we stop at the PX for a sandwich or hamburger before I headed home.

"I can't have you fainting from hunger while you drive back to the farm," he said after the first meeting ended well after dark.

From then on we made a habit of grabbing a bite together and enjoying conversation that had nothing to do with the hospital. He asked questions about the farm and horses, and I learned more about his personal life, including his hope to open a private medical practice after the war. His time in the military was satisfying, but he was ready to settle down somewhere.

I didn't mind the extra hours of work—and the extra pay—but Bren and the other girls teased me about "dates" with my boss. I reminded them I wasn't romantically involved with anyone and had no plans to do so. I'd never mentioned my correspondence with Gunther. His letters were too infrequent, and their lack of emotion convinced me he wanted nothing more than friendship. I'd resigned myself to being a widow for the rest of my life.

"Mrs. Delaney," Colonel Foster said as he came from his office. He looked smart in his dress uniform and spit-shined shoes. "I hate to ask this at such a late hour, but are you free tonight?"

I hoped he didn't have extra work for me to do. A long soak in a hot bath sounded divine. "I was planning to stop at the PX before going home. Gertrude wants to bake an apple pie for tomorrow, but she used her last sugar ration card last week to make Ivy Lee's birthday cake. I thought I'd surprise her."

He nodded. "The reason I ask is, I was to escort Mrs. Isbell to a dinner tonight at Hotel King, but she's feeling under the weather. I would prefer not to arrive alone, considering they've planned for a certain number of guests at the table."

Mrs. Isbell, Tullahoma's wealthiest widow. The older woman

held a vast fortune, inherited from her late husband's thoroughbred horse enterprises, and was known for her philanthropic endeavors. She'd chosen the hospital at Camp Forrest as one of her projects. While the hospital couldn't officially accept financial donations, she'd worked with Colonel Foster over the past year and found many ways to help the patients and staff without bending rules.

"I hear they're serving prime rib," he grinned, obviously trying to bribe me.

My mouth watered just thinking about it. We hadn't had beef in ages, let alone prime rib.

"I'm not exactly dressed for a dinner party." I glanced down at my pencil skirt and plain white blouse. There wouldn't be time to go all the way out to the farm and change.

A sheepish look crossed his face. "When Mrs. Isbell called to cancel, she suggested I take you in her stead. She even offered to let us stop by her home on the way into town so you could borrow one of her daughter's evening gowns."

I blinked. "My goodness, that was generous of her."

"If you'd rather not go, I'll understand."

I heard disappointment in his voice. I knew he didn't attend dinner parties often. Bren speculated it was because he didn't like to go alone and was too much of a gentleman to ask a woman he wasn't interested in romantically to attend with him. The only reason he asked me now was because he'd already accepted the invitation and it would be rude to cancel.

"I'd be happy to attend the dinner with you," I finally said. "Let me call Gertrude and tell her I won't be home until later."

A smile lit his eyes. "Thank you, Mrs. Delaney. I can't tell you how much I appreciate this."

We drove to town in Colonel Foster's military sedan. I'd been to the Isbell estate a handful of times, but the white-columned mansion never ceased to impress.

"I'm glad you're going in my place," she said after a maid led us into a parlor where we found the older woman lounging on a sofa, a blanket over her legs. "I simply don't feel up to a night of mindless conversation and rich food." She waved the maid over. "Clarice will take you upstairs to my daughter's old room. Barbary is married and lives in Nashville now, but she keeps a small wardrobe here. Choose anything you like, my dear."

While Colonel Foster remained in the parlor with Mrs. Isbell, I followed the maid up a grand staircase, down a hall, and into a bedroom that looked like it belonged to a princess. A number of gowns were already laid out on the bed, a rainbow of brilliant colors and lush fabrics. The emerald green immediately drew me. A pair of matching shoes and a lace shawl completed the outfit. Clarice suggested a simple up-twist to my hair and had it expertly fashioned in no time.

When I came downstairs, I couldn't help noticing admiration shining in Colonel Foster's eyes when he stood and came toward me.

"You look lovely, Mrs. Delaney," he said, his voice soft.

"Now, now, you can't use formal titles tonight," Mrs. Isbell said, tsk-tsking. "It must be Ava and Hew, don't you agree, my dear?"

My face heated as Colonel Foster met my gaze, awaiting my answer. "I'm sure that will be fine."

I thanked the woman for loaning me the items and promised to return them the next day. She bid us good night with what could only be described as a mischievous grin.

"I don't believe she's ill," I said once we were back in the car, headed for Hotel King. "I think she just didn't want to go and made up an excuse so your feelings wouldn't be hurt."

Colonel Foster chuckled. "I don't doubt it." He glanced at me. "But I can't deny I'm glad you're here in her place. You really do look beautiful."

"Thank you," I said, suddenly shy.

We arrived at the hotel and were escorted to a private area of the Minors Restaurant where dozens of military officers and elegantly dressed women mingled. I was familiar with most of the men, but their wives and girlfriends looked at me with curious stares.

Thankfully Colonel Foster never left my side. He introduced me as Ava Delaney, nothing more, nothing less, and made a point to include me in conversations. We sat next to each other at dinner, which allowed me to relax and enjoy the delicious food, the likes of which we were unable to get with our ration cards. When the hotel staff shot off a round of fireworks, Colonel Foster offered his arm so I wouldn't stumble on the uneven lawn.

As the party wound down and we prepared to leave, he draped the lace shawl over my shoulders, his hands lingering.

"Thank you for coming with me, Ava. I don't usually enjoy these parties, but I did tonight because of you."

"I had a nice time too." I grinned. "I'll have to thank Mrs. Isbell for pretending to be ill."

A valet brought the colonel's car, and we drove away from the bright hotel lights. The sleepy town of Tullahoma lay quiet beneath a clear, star-studded sky.

"I should take you home. I don't like the idea of you driving by yourself in the dark," he said, concern in his voice.

"I'll be fine. I've driven home in the dark lots of times."

"I apologize for that. I've been selfish with your time and generosity."

Although I couldn't make out his features, I knew he was sincere. "There's no need to apologize. I enjoy my job. It lets me feel as if I'm doing my small part to win the war."

He reached to grasp my hand. "You're truly a gem, Ava Delaney."

The warmth of his fingers sent a shiver up my arm. I didn't remove my hand, and he didn't remove his either. I wasn't sure what was happening, but I was certain of one thing.

I felt a shift in our boss-employee relationship.

And I had no idea what to do about it.

THIRTY-ONE

MATTIE

DELANEY HORSE FARM

DECEMBER 1969

Despite the earth continuing to spin on its axis, my world had come to a crashing halt two days ago.

I had yet to recover.

Mama's staggering revelation that Gunther Schneider was my father left me reeling. I'd stared at her, wordless, while a thousand questions and the terrible consequences of the answers sped through my mind like a stampeding herd of stallions. Dad had arrived upstairs before I found my voice, and Mama put her finger to her lips, an indication she didn't want me to discuss the subject in front of him.

I'd fled from the room.

For the next forty-eight hours my imagination went in a dozen frightening directions, a jumble of shock, fear, and horror.

Did Dad know Mark and I weren't his children? Had Mama become pregnant by the German prisoner and tricked Dad into marrying her? Did Gunther Schneider even know I existed?

I'd been an emotional mess at dinner and excused myself from the table, unable to look Dad in the eye. Nash knew something was wrong, but I couldn't tell him. Not yet. Not until I had all the sordid details.

But Mama took a turn for the worse during the night.

Dad called Dr. Monahan, and an ambulance arrived, its lights flashing in the pitch-black sky, and carried her to the hospital. There, the doctors determined the tumor was pressing on her brain. To relieve the pain, she'd been put on an IV drip of morphine that essentially knocked her out. We stayed at the hospital all day, but visitors weren't allowed to remain overnight with a patient. Neither of us ate the simple dinner Nash had prepared. When I woke up after a night of tossing and turning, I found a note by the coffee percolator informing me Dad had gone to the hospital. Nash would drive me to town when I was ready.

Now, with morning sunshine streaming through the curtains, I sat on Mama's empty bed, numb. No tears. No wails. No clenched fists. Just mind-numbing nothingness.

That's where Nash found me.

"Tell me what's going on, Mattie." He planted himself in the chair next to the bed. "Something happened before your mom was taken to the hospital. Does it have to do with the letters?"

I met his worried gaze. "My entire life has been one big lie," I said before bursting into tears.

He moved to sit on the edge of the mattress and wrapped his arm around me while I sobbed into his chest. He didn't speak but simply held me, his presence and strength the only communication I needed. I don't know how long we stayed like that, but when my weeping finally subsided into hiccups, he stood and returned with a handful of tissues.

I wiped my face, blew my nose, and took a deep, steadying breath. "The night Mama went to the hospital, she told me something . . . shocking." I put my fist to my trembling lips, forcing myself not to break down again.

He didn't ask questions but simply waited until I was able to speak again.

"Mama said Gunther Schneider is—" My voice cracked. I swallowed, hard. "He's Mark's and my father."

The widening of his eyes told me he was as shocked as I felt. "Oh, Mattie. I don't know what to say."

I divulged the details of the brief exchange I'd had with Mama that night, Dad's arrival that interrupted us before I could ask questions, and her apparent desire to keep our conversation secret.

"I don't know what to think, Nash." Despair washed over me. "I've never been close to Dad, but he's always been my father. But now, knowing that he *isn't*, things are starting to make sense."

"Like what?"

"Like why he's always been so distant and quiet. Why he never talks about his family. Why he and Granny Gertrude didn't like each other." I glanced at the picture of Mama and him standing in front of the farmhouse. "Everything I ever believed about myself was false. I have no idea who I am. And now, with Mama so sick, I may never know."

The tears came again. Nash held me, letting me sob until I had nothing left. When the clock downstairs chimed, I realized it was almost noon.

"I should go to the hospital," I said, sniffling. "It's horrible to admit, but I don't want to go. I don't want to see Mama. I don't want to see Dad. I just want to get on a bus or train or plane and go far away from here."

Nash smoothed my hair. "You tried that once." There was no judgement in his voice. Only compassion and honesty. "Sometimes we can't run away from the hard things in life." He turned my face so our gazes met. "I'm here for you, Mattie. I'll go through this with you. You're not alone."

I nodded, unable to tell him how grateful I was to hear that.

We drove to the hospital. Dad met us in the hallway outside Mama's room. I couldn't help but study his face, wondering. When and how had he come into Mama's life? If he wasn't my father, who was he, and why hadn't Mark and I been told the truth?

"Dr. Monahan was just here. Ava's a little better today, but they still have her on morphine." He glanced into the room where my mother lay in a hospital bed, with tubes running beneath the blanket. "I don't think she'll wake up for a while."

He looked and sounded worn-out. While I may not know who he was or how he'd come into our lives, I had no doubt that he loved Mama.

"I'll stay with her," I said. "You should go home and get some rest."

He shook his head. "I can't do that." He glanced at Nash. "I'm sorry to leave you with all the work, but I need to be here."

"I agree," Nash said. "Don't worry about me or anything else at the farm."

I left them discussing care for the injured horse and walked into Mama's room. Her face was pale and swollen, almost unrecognizable. "Oh, Mama," I whispered.

I didn't know what to feel.

Desperation? Grief? Anger?

Why had she lied to me all these years? Why was she dying now when I needed her?

Why didn't God *do* something?

I needed answers, but none came.

I stood there, silent, confused, exhausted.

Dad approached. "Could you help Nash with chores?" He spoke softly, as though he didn't want to wake Mama. "I'll stay until visiting hours end."

I turned to face him. I wanted to blurt out what Mama told me about Gunther Schneider and demand answers. Demand to know his part in the lie. Or was he a victim of her deception, like me? But now wasn't the time or place for that conversation.

"Nash and I will take care of things at home. You take care of Mama." I paused. "And yourself. Eat something."

"I will," he promised.

Nash and I spent the rest of the afternoon doing farm chores. The work helped keep my mind occupied, but Mama's illness and her deception were never far. When the sun began its slow descent, we headed to the house. Jake followed behind, looking as tired as I felt.

"I'll rustle up something for dinner," Nash said. "You go rest or take a bath."

"A soak in the tub does sound good." I held his gaze. "Thank you, Nash. I don't think we could get through all this without you."

He looked thoughtful. "Mark always said I was part of this family. I didn't believe it, even though your parents made me welcome. But I didn't think I deserved anything good. I didn't deserve to belong. At least that's how I felt back then."

"And now?"

His expression softened. "Now I know he was right. You and your folks *are* my family. I'd do anything to make sure you're all taken care of."

His words stayed with me as I sprawled in a tub of hot, sudsy water.

Family.

They came in all shapes and sizes. Some were related by blood. Some weren't. I didn't dispute Nash's belonging here with us. Mark would want his best friend to always feel welcome on the farm.

But what about Dad?

In the past few days, I'd learned that not only was he *not* related to the Delaney family as I'd always believed, but he also wasn't even my real father.

I closed my eyes.

Why, Mama? Why did you keep all this secret?

Unless she rallied, I may not ever have an answer to that question or any of the thousand unknowns regarding Dad and Gunther Schneider.

Nash had ham and cheese omelets ready when I came downstairs.

"This looks good," I said, realizing I hadn't eaten anything all day. My stomach had been in such tight knots, I hadn't been hungry.

We ate in silence for a while before Nash said, "Maybe you should read the rest of the letters from Gunther. They might shed some light on the situation."

I thought of the three remaining envelopes in the shoebox upstairs. When I'd put them away, I'd been confident Gunther Schneider was simply a friend who'd corresponded with Mama during the war.

But now I knew the truth.

He was my biological father.

My stomach churned, and my appetite bolted.

I pushed the plate away, offering Nash a look of apology for not finishing the meal he'd prepared. "I'm afraid to finish reading the letters. I don't even know what to hope might be in them. Mama already admitted Gunther Schneider is my father. Do you know what that means? She wasn't married to him when she became pregnant with Mark and me."

He nodded. "I understand that, but the letters might tell you more of their story."

I blew out a long breath. "I can't believe any of this is happening. First Mark is killed, then Mama is sick. Now I find out that my entire life has been a sham. We're not the happy family I always thought we were. It was all smoke and mirrors, as they say."

Nash placed his hand on top of mine. "Mattie, think about how great your life was growing up. About how much your mom loved you and Mark. About how hard your dad always worked to provide for his family. None of the things you're learning about them now changes any of that." He squeezed my fingers then stood. He stacked our plates and carried them to the sink. "As long as I've known your folks, I've seen what good people they are. Give them a chance to tell you their story before you make a final judgement about things that happened a long time ago."

The truth of his words helped to calm my anxious heart.

I needed to know the entire story. No matter how much it might hurt or frighten me.

I heaved a sigh. "All right. I'll go get the letters."

While Nash cleaned the kitchen, I went upstairs. A glance at Mama's darkened room reminded me that although I was angry with her for keeping her past a secret, I wished she was home, in her own bed.

Nash and I settled on the sofa.

I opened the next letter.

"July 1944. Dear Ava," I began, suddenly struck that I was reading words my father—my *real* father—wrote to my mother from a prison camp in North Dakota.

My throat tightened, and I swallowed hard.

> *I wish I could tell you that I am well, but a terrible thing has happened. Dr. Sonnenberg and I were attacked by—*

The next words were blacked out.

> *I am slowly recovering, but my friend is very ill. He has become like a father to me, and I don't know what I will do*

if he doesn't make it. I have spent many hours praying for Dr. Sonnenberg. He believes in the same God as I do, and our study of the Bible has made him curious about Jesus. He is especially impressed with the writings of the Apostle Paul, a Jewish man like himself. It is my hope we will once again enjoy our theological discussions as soon as he is able.

I think of you often. Memories of our time together are the only joy I have in these long, lonely days.

Yours affectionately,
Gunther Schneider

I stared at the name. "Gunther Schneider," I repeated. "This man, this stranger, is my father."

"He seems like a man of faith." Nash leaned over to read the faded handwriting. "*Memories of our time together are the only joy I have.* It sounds like he cared about your mom. I wonder who attacked him and his friend."

I refolded the yellowed paper and returned it to the envelope. "Maybe the next letter will have more information."

Headlights from a car flashed across the window.

I hurried to look outside. "Dad's home." I glanced at the shoebox, remembering Mama wanted it to remain a secret from him. Until I had more information, I didn't feel I should confront him. Especially not when he'd spent a long day at the hospital with Mama. "I better put this away. We can read the others later."

When I returned downstairs, Dad was in the kitchen, filling the kettle with water. I heard Nash's voice outside, instructing Jake to do his business before turning in for the night.

"How's Mama?" I asked from the doorway.

Dad turned weary eyes to me. "A little better. Dr. Monahan hopes she can come home by the end of the week. She'll need an IV for pain medication though."

He took a cup from the cupboard. "Do you want some tea?"

I shook my head. "I think I'll turn in."

But I didn't move.

I studied him as he placed a teabag in the cup and poured hot water over it. So many questions spun across my mind.

Why had he let Mark and me believe he was our father? Why not tell us the truth? Wouldn't it have been easier than pretending?

He carried the cup to the table and slumped into a chair. He looked beat.

"I'll go to the hospital with you in the morning," I said.

He met my gaze and nodded. "That would be good."

Nash and Jake returned, and I bid them all good night. It wasn't long before I heard Dad come upstairs and close his bedroom door with a soft click. After twenty-something years of marriage, it must be hard to suddenly find yourself all alone.

I rolled onto my side. Tears trickled down my cheek onto the pillow.

How I wished I could turn back time. I'd keep Mark from going to Vietnam, and I'd make Mama see a doctor much sooner than she had. I'd ask Dad questions about his family, and I'd spend time with Granny Gertrude. We'd be a family, but without the secrets, pain, and grief we found ourselves living through now.

My body shook with silent sobs and deep, soul-wrenching regret.

Like a little lost child, I cried myself to sleep.

THIRTY-TWO
GUNTHER

FORT LINCOLN, NORTH DAKOTA
JULY 1944

Gunther stood at the entrance to the hospital and checked his watch for the umpteenth time.

It was nearly noon.

Dr. Lipp had promised to come by after he and his family attended a Sunday morning church service in town to check on Dr. Sonnenberg. That the American doctor would come to the camp on his day off, rather than leave his patient in the care of Dr. Ludwig, spoke of the man's concern for his Jewish colleague. He'd performed emergency surgery on Dr. Sonnenberg to stop internal bleeding the night of the beating, but the injured man remained in critical condition in the weeks following. Now a fever had spiked during the night, and Gunther feared infection.

He returned to the small room at the end of the hall where Dr. Sonnenberg had been since the beating. The older man suffered broken bones during the assault, and his body refused to heal. While Mr. McCoy had the men responsible locked in solitary confinement for thirty days, Gunther didn't believe the punishment severe enough. The sailors should be arrested by the local authorities and tried for attempted murder in a court of law.

"Dr. Sonnenberg?" Gunther said softly.

The older man's eyes fluttered open. "I told you to get some rest," he said, his voice rough from disuse.

"I'll rest when you are better." Gunther settled in the chair next to the bed, noticing that his professor shivered despite the warmth of the room and layers of blankets. "Dr. Lipp will be here soon. You need antibiotics, but no one is willing to administer them without his or Dr. Ludwig's approval. As usual, that clown is sleeping off a night at the canteen and is of no use." He didn't confess he'd tried to sneak a vial of penicillin out of the locked medicine cabinet earlier, but Nurse Roe caught him. She understood his dilemma, but there were rules in place they must follow.

Dr. Sonnenberg grimaced. "I'm afraid it is too late for me," he said, his gaze unwavering. "I can feel my body shutting down."

"I won't listen to that kind of talk. Dr. Lipp is coming, and he'll know what to do."

"If you recall," Dr. Sonnenberg said with a weak smile, "I am a doctor too."

Gunther raised his brow. "And do you let your patients diagnose themselves?"

His mentor chuckled, then groaned. After a time, he said, "I've been thinking about what Paul wrote in his letter to his friend, Timothy, declaring the time for his departure from this world was at hand."

Gunther knew the passage. They'd read it together and had a lively discussion about what Paul meant when he said he'd *fought a good fight*. "He told Timothy he'd finished his course and had kept the faith."

Dr. Sonnenberg's brow furrowed. "Yes, that is the part that confuses me. He was Jewish, as am I, yet the faith he spoke of was not the beliefs he'd been taught from boyhood but were those of a new religion. A belief in Jesus of Nazareth as the long-awaited One." He sighed. "I admit I do not feel the peace Paul experienced when I contemplate the end of my life."

"Then do not do so," Gunther said. "Let us focus on getting you strong and well, then we can discuss the mysteries of life and death while we wait for this infernal war to end."

Dr. Lipp arrived soon after their discussion. He conducted a thorough examination, ending with a grim expression on his face.

"You need not say it, Dr. Lipp," Dr. Sonnenberg said. "I know."

Gunther glanced between the two. "What is it?"

"Sepsis," Dr. Lipp said. "I'll take a blood sample to be certain, but all of the symptoms are presenting."

Gunther stared at the man. He knew the condition was deadly.

Dr. Lipp ordered antibiotics and an IV drip of fluids. Nurse Roe and two other nurses crowded around the bed, tending to Dr. Sonnenberg, while Gunther stood in the corner, helpless.

When the room emptied and it was just the two of them again, he found his mentor's gaze fixed on him.

"Listen to me," he said, his voice raspy and weak. Gunther came forward and took Dr. Sonnenberg's feverish hand. "I am grateful for our time together. You have been like a son to me, Gunther Schneider."

Gunther's eyes filled. "I am not ready to say goodbye. I need you to get better."

Dr. Sonnenberg tightened his grip. "And I need you to be strong. After the war, I want you to finish school and become a doctor."

Gunther nodded, although his heart broke at the thought of losing his mentor.

He stayed with Dr. Sonnenberg through the long night. By daybreak, he knew the end was near.

"I have been thinking," the older man said, his voice barely audible. Gunther grasped his frail hand and leaned close. "If a good Jewish man like Paul was convinced Jesus is the Messiah, I too can believe in him."

Tears clouded Gunther's vision. "Remember what Jesus said to the criminal on the cross next to him?"

Dr. Sonnenberg's entire body relaxed. *"Today shalt thou be with me in paradise."*

A moment later, he was gone.

• • •

After Dr. Sonnenberg died, Gunther withdrew from camp life. He quit his job at the hospital and spent the long, monotonous days in his room reading or walking the fence line by himself. Mr. McCoy didn't assign him a new roommate, for which Gunther was grateful, but his loneliness and depression only increased over time. He didn't bother to shave and seldom took the trouble to bathe. The men in his barracks avoided him, and even the Schlageter had the decency to leave him alone in his grief.

Months passed.

In February, news reached them that Heinz Fengler, the internee who escaped last October, was found in New Orleans. A week later, six-hundred-fifty Japanese internees arrived at Fort Lincoln, transferred from camps in California and New Mexico. Although they were housed in a separate part of the camp, the German internees were abuzz about the new residents.

By the first of April, newspapers predicted Germany and the Third Reich would soon fall. Gunther worried about his mother and brother, praying they'd survive the bombings. On May 1, the shocking news of Hitler's suicide swept through camp. While the Schlageter mourned the death of their Führer, Gunther felt the tiniest shred of hope that the war would truly come to an end.

He woke to bright sunshine and shouting on the eighth day of May.

"The war in Europe is over! It's over!"

Gunther, like the rest of the internees, wondered what this meant for them. While Germany had surrendered, the war against Japan still raged in the Pacific. It could take months or even years to bring that faraway conflict to an end.

No one could have foreseen what took place on August 6 and again on August 9.

News of the atomic bombs quickly spread through camp. Gunther stood in the yard with the other German internees, stunned to learn how many lives were lost. Across the fence, the Japanese internees grieved the horrific destruction in silence. When Japan finally surrendered five days later, the celebrations were subdued. While everyone was grateful the war was finally over, the devastation it had wrought throughout the world was sobering.

Gunther lay in his bunk that night, thinking about Ava.

He hadn't written to her since Dr. Sonnenberg died. Couldn't bear to put the sad news in writing. She hadn't known his friend, and he couldn't expect her to grieve his loss, but she was never far from his thoughts.

What would she do now that the war was over? Already rumors had begun to circulate that camps like Fort Lincoln would eventually close. He guessed the same fate would take place at Camp Forrest, leaving her without a job. Would she stay in Tullahoma? In Tennessee?

A new fear circled his mind.

What if she'd met someone? Was that the reason she'd stopped writing to him?

He glanced at the small desk in the corner, moonlight illuminating a stack of books and Dr. Sonnenberg's fountain pen.

Should he write to her?

He had no news regarding what his future held—when or if he would be released—nor did he know her situation or feelings. But if he didn't try, he would always regret it.

Gunther clicked on the desk lamp. After settling in the chair, he stared at a blank page of paper a long time before he picked up the pen.

My Dearest Ava,

I know it has been some time since I last wrote. There is much to tell of all that has happened, but I will wait to share the details with you in person.

The purpose of this letter is singular.

Ava, I love you. I have from the moment we first met. When I am once again a free man, will you marry me?

I anxiously await your answer.

Yours forever,
Gunther Schneider

The note was short and inadequate, but it expressed the two most important things he wanted her to know. He loved her and wanted her to become his wife. But time and distance were his enemies. Would she believe he was sincere?

His eyes fell on his Bible.

Yes, he thought. He would send the letter tucked between the pages of the Book his *Mutter* gave him. Despite all that had happened, he still believed in God's goodness. Still believed in God's sovereignty.

He would leave his future, and Ava's, in God's hands.

Gunther turned out the light and slept soundly for the first time in months.

THIRTY-THREE

MATTIE

DELANEY HORSE FARM
DECEMBER 1969

Mama came home from the hospital one week before Christmas.

Her homecoming was delayed by setbacks, pain management issues, and a fever that worried Dad more than anything else.

I felt like I'd been in limbo for days, going from the farm to the hospital, only to repeat it again and again. Everything else, including my questions about Gunther Schneider and my roller-coaster emotions, were put on hold while we waited for Mama.

While she lay in the hospital, I'd read to her from *The Cost of Discipleship* by Dietrich Bonhoeffer, the book Mark gave me the night before he left for Vietnam. Bonhoeffer's life was fascinating, and it helped me understand my brother's choices a little better. I still believed both men should have chosen to remain safely with their families rather than risking danger for their beliefs, but I had a new respect for my twin.

The first morning Mama was home, she had a request.

"You need . . . to decorate . . . the house . . . for the holidays," she said, her voice hoarse, and her breath coming in short gasps.

Nurse Bradford was joined by two other nurses, each of whom took a shift, ensuring Mama had round-the-clock care. One of them—I forget her name—had just gone downstairs to get herself a cup of coffee after staying with Mama all night. Dad slept on the sofa despite Nash volunteering to return to the cottage and offering Mark's old room.

"Mama, I don't think any of us are in the mood to celebrate Christmas."

A scowl came to her swollen face. "Christmas . . . is about . . . Jesus . . . not presents. He . . . is why . . . we celebrate."

I knew I would lose this battle. "All right. I'll go to the attic later and look for the decorations."

A soft smile replaced the frown. "That's . . . my girl."

After the nurse returned, I put on a coat and headed outside. A frozen water pipe burst in the barn overnight. While Dad and Nash were busy with repairs, I figured I could help with the horses.

I hadn't gone far when a navy-blue Chevy Chevelle pulled into the yard. An attractive young woman stepped out, her tan hip-length coat lined with brilliant white fur around the collar and cuffs.

"Hello." I walked toward her. "May I help you?"

She chuckled. "It's me, Mattie. Paula."

My mouth gaped. "Paula Allyn?" I couldn't believe the difference in Mark's old girlfriend's appearance. She'd come to his funeral last year, but she'd looked the same as I'd always remembered. Now her hair was bleached blonde instead of brunette, and she wore a thick layer of makeup around her eyes and on her cheeks.

We hugged. "It's good to see you," I said sincerely.

Nash came out of the barn and stopped short when he saw us.

"Nash, look who's here. Paula."

An odd expression crossed his face before he slowly moved forward. "Good to see you, Paula."

She nodded, then sobered when she faced me. "I've been visiting my parents this week, but I wanted to come out before I leave town and tell you how sorry I am about your mom. She was always very kind to me."

"Thank you," I said, my throat thick.

We chatted for several minutes, catching up. Nash was quiet, but I knew he'd run into Paula a time or two since he'd come home, so he probably didn't feel the need to join our conversation.

"I better be going," she said. "It was great to see you again, Mattie. When Nash and I had dinner a couple weeks ago, I was happy to hear you were home."

"Dinner?" I asked, confused.

She cast a shy glance at Nash. "We've only been out a couple times."

I stared at her, suddenly feeling like an idiot for not putting two and two together until now.

She bid us goodbye, with a lingering look at Nash, and climbed into the car and drove away.

Before he could say a word, I turned on him. "You're dating my dead brother's girlfriend?"

He frowned. "It isn't like that, Mattie. We have dinner when she's in town. She's lonely. I was too. We mostly talk about Mark."

I glared at him. "Why couldn't you just be honest with me? Why does everyone in my life feel the need to lie to me?"

"I didn't lie to you, Mattie," he said. "But I didn't think you'd understand. And I see I was right."

"Don't you dare put this on me." A bitter taste filled my mouth. "Mark loved her." I couldn't say more.

I left him standing in the yard and stormed back to the house. The nurse stepped into the hallway when I stomped up the stairs.

"Your mother is resting, dear," she said, rebuke in her tone.

Although I didn't think Mama would hear a freight train if it thundered by, thanks to the morphine, I apologized, tiptoed to my room, and closed the door.

Nash and Paula were dating.

Was I the last person to know? Why would he comfort me, hold me so tenderly, if he had a girlfriend? *Mark's* girlfriend. I'd trusted Nash. Poured my heart out to him.

What a fool I'd been.

I paced the room like a caged lion. I needed to roar and let off some steam.

There was only one way to do that.

I headed to the barn and saddled Mark's horse, True Blue.

In a matter of minutes, we were flying across the land.

• • •

I didn't speak to Nash for three days.

Each time he entered the house, I ignored him and left the room. Dad noticed the tension between us but wisely didn't get involved. I busied myself with putting up Christmas decorations and spending time with Mama, who mostly slept. When she did wake for brief periods, she was incoherent. I'd simply hold her hand and carry on a one-sided conversation about the farm, the horses, the weather, always avoiding topics that could send me to the floor.

Two days before Christmas, however, she slipped into a coma. Dr. Monahan was notified and immediately came out to the farm. After he examined Mama, he called Dad, me, and Nash into the living room. With a somber voice, he told us she most likely wouldn't come out of the coma.

"Ava isn't long for this world, I'm afraid."

I stared at the floor, my jaw clenched, while Dad thanked the doctor for everything he'd done for Mama. After they walked outside, Nash and I sat in silence. Floorboards above us creaked as the nurse moved around upstairs. Sunshine streamed through the curtain. Life carried on, no matter that Mama's was ebbing away.

"I'm sorry, Mattie," Nash said softly. "I love your mom. She's always treated me like a son."

The crack in his voice was my undoing.

My vision blurred, and my annoyance with him fell away. "What will I do without her?" Sobs overtook me.

He stood, pulled me to my feet, and let me weep into his chest. His shoulders shook, and I knew he wept too.

Dad returned, and the three of us sat in the living room, stunned and heartbroken.

"I'll go into town tomorrow morning and make the arrangements," he said, his face ashen. "Pastor Arnold offered to help."

I knew planning Mama's funeral would be a heart-wrenching task. "Do you want me to go with you?"

He shook his head. "One of us should be here." He heaved a sigh and stood. "I think I'll go sit with her a while."

I watched as he left the room, his face drawn and his shoulders bent under the weight of grief. The nurse came downstairs, book in hand, and sat at the kitchen table to read. Nash suggested we put on our coats and move to the porch swing.

After we settled, he sent the bench into motion with his foot, the same way Mark used to do when we sat beside each other. My feet didn't quite reach the porch floor, so I'd let him do all the work.

"I should have told you about Paula," Nash said. When I turned to him, he held my gaze. "I'm not interested in her, Mattie. It was just nice to talk to someone who'd loved Mark as much as I did."

I couldn't find fault with that. "I shouldn't have gotten so angry. It isn't any of my business who you date."

He reached to caress my cheek. "I want it to be your business."

I captured his hand and held it to my face. "I can't make any promises, Nash," I whispered. "Things are so . . ." Tears flooded my eyes.

He nodded. "I know. I'm not asking for any promises . . . yet."

He kissed me then. His lips on mine, warm and gentle. When he pulled away, there were tears in his eyes too.

"Stay here," he said as he stood. "I have an early Christmas present for you."

He walked across the yard to the cottage. When he returned, he carried a large, flat parcel, wrapped in plain brown paper.

"I know Christmas presents aren't important this year, but I already had this ready for you."

He held it while I tore off the paper.

I gasped. "The painting."

His head tilted. "Did you go snooping in the cottage and see this already?"

I gave a slight chuckle. "I wasn't snooping. Mama sent me to find a photo album that belonged to Granny. I saw this in the corner, but you hadn't finished it yet." I studied the image of a horse and a little dark-headed girl, their noses touching. "This is amazing, Nash."

"It's you."

My eyes roamed the canvas, taking in the beautiful, intricate details. A red scarf around the girl's neck. Dark hair untamed, blowing in the breeze.

"Remember the story of the day I first met you?"

I nodded, my gaze fixed on the child in the portrait. "I was riding Midnight Pride."

He sat next to me. "I figure the horse is a combination of Midnight Pride and Moonlight, but the girl is exactly how I remember you."

I turned to face him, stunned, seeing him—*really* seeing

him—for the first time, my heart unexpectedly but wonderfully blown wide open. "I love you, Nash McCallum," I said, laughing and crying at the same time. "I think I always have."

"I love you too, Mattie. I think I always have."

I kissed him then. Passionately. Completely.

With more love than I dreamed possible.

THIRTY-FOUR

AVA

CAMP FORREST, TENNESSEE
AUGUST 1945

Loud, raucous celebrating continued for days after Japan surrendered.

The Camp Forrest band marched down streets while military personnel and civilians alike waved American flags and cheered. Guns and even cannons went off, the sound of freedom rather than war. Only the German POWs who remained in camp wore solemn expressions, their fate, and the fate of their country, unknown.

I could hardly believe the war was over. While I cheered along with everyone else, I couldn't help but wonder what would happen to Gunther now. Would he finally be released and finish his studies? Or would he be sent back to Germany?

I hadn't heard from him in over a year. When I didn't receive a response to my last two letters, I stopped writing to him. I had no way to know if he was still interned at Fort Lincoln or if he'd been transferred to a different camp. When the war in Europe ended, ships once again were free to sail the Atlantic without fear of attack from enemy U-boats. Almost immediately, the government began deporting German POWs and enemy aliens by the thousands, including some from Camp Forrest, shipping the men back to their war-torn fatherland.

I heaved a sigh.

I needed to forget Gunther Schneider. We didn't have a future together. There was no point dwelling on it.

On Saturday afternoon, Gertrude found me in the kitchen brewing a pitcher of iced tea. Her eyes took in my dress and styled hair. "You going out with Colonel Foster?"

"He's coming here," I said.

Hew and I had begun seeing each other socially after the night I accompanied him to the dinner party. I'd wanted to take things slow, and he'd complied. I'd never invited him to the farm before, mainly because there wasn't much privacy with three women living in one house.

But Ivy Lee moved out two days ago. Her colonel was transferred as soon as the war ended, bidding her a hasty farewell. He long ago revealed he was married, but he refused to leave his wife, as he'd promised, which left Ivy Lee in a rage. She'd stormed into the house, packed her belongings, and torn out of the yard a half hour later, bound for California. Gertrude wasn't as upset as I thought she would be, considering how close the two women had become.

"Even though the war is over, I'm surprised she's leaving her top secret job before Camp Forrest is decommissioned," I said as we watched Ivy Lee's car disappear in a cloud of dust.

A sheepish look crossed Gertrude's face. "I guess I can tell you now."

"Tell me what?"

"Ivy Lee didn't have an important job. Not like yours. She worked in the laundry facility."

My mouth gaped. "The laundry?"

We'd both burst into laughter.

Gertrude made herself scarce when Hew arrived. We sat on the porch swing and sipped tea, talking about the atomic bomb, the devastation to countries around the world, the sadness over the millions of lost lives.

Hew set his glass on the small table beside the swing and reached for my hand.

"Ava, it's no secret how I feel about you," he said, his gaze fixed on me. "I love you, and I want to spend the rest of my life with you. We survived a war together. Now it's time to live happily ever after."

When I started to speak, he put his finger to my lips. "Let me finish before you give an answer. I know you don't love me the way I love you. But I also believe if you'll give me a chance, I can make you happy." He took a folded paper from his pocket and handed it to me. It was a real estate brochure for a house in Richmond, Virginia. "My sister and her family live in Richmond. They tell me it's a great place to raise a family. I've decided to open my private practice there."

I stared at the black-and-white drawing of a lovely, two-story brick house. Trees, flowers, and a sidewalk completed the idyllic scene. I envisioned Hew and myself there, with two children running around the yard. Maybe a dog. His sister would become my best friend, and we'd host bridge parties for Hew's doctor friends. It sounded perfect, and I knew instinctively it would be a good life.

My heart thrummed.

I should say yes. I should jump into his arms and ride off into the sunset to live the comfortable, happy life I knew Hew would give me. I'd done that before. Richard had promised me the world, too.

But I couldn't. It wouldn't be fair to me or to Hew.

I handed the paper back to him. "I can't," I whispered, regret mingling with relief as I finally said the words out loud. I should have told him the truth months ago.

He accepted the paper. We sat in awkward silence before he stood.

I looked up and met his gaze. "I'm sorry."

He pulled me to my feet, and we embraced. When we parted, he caressed my face for the last time. "I understand, Ava. I really do."

I watched him drive away.

"He's leaving already?" Gertrude asked from the other side of the screen door.

I suspected she'd eavesdropped on our conversation, but it didn't matter. "Yes, he's gone. He won't be back."

After a moment, she gave a single nod and left me alone.

I stayed where I was, staring at nothing.

My future, it seemed, was here with Gertrude. Now that the war was over and Camp Forrest was scheduled to close, I'd throw myself into raising horses and turn Delaney Farm into a thriving business. I didn't know how we'd manage without help or extra income, but somehow we'd make it work.

I sat on the porch the rest of the afternoon. Dust from an approaching vehicle drew my attention. When it came over the hill, I saw it was the mailman.

The older man climbed from the sedan and held up a package. "For you, Mrs. Delaney. Figured I'd bring it up to the house instead of leaving it in the box. You don't get many packages, so I guessed it might be important."

I descended the porch steps and accepted the parcel.

I nearly dropped it when I saw the return address from North Dakota.

"You all right?" he asked. "I hope it's not bad news."

I shook my head, unable to speak.

I stood in the yard after he drove away, staring at the brown paper-wrapped package with Gunther's name scrawled in the left corner.

So many questions poured into my mind.

Why hadn't he responded to my letters? Had he been released? I prayed the answers were hidden in the parcel.

I tore off the paper to reveal an old book. *Die Bibel.* An envelope poked out between the pages, and I ripped it open.

My Dearest Ava . . .

Tears poured down my cheeks and dropped onto the paper as I read the tender, brief message.

> *I love you. I have from the moment we first met. When I am once again a free man, will you marry me?*

I clutched the book and the letter to my heart and wept.

Gunther was safe. He loved me. He wanted to marry me. His future was still uncertain, but I knew I would wait for him.

No matter how long it took for him to once again be free, I would wait.

THIRTY-FIVE

MATTIE

DELANEY HORSE FARM
DECEMBER 1969

Mama remained lost in unconsciousness throughout the long night.

Dr. Monahan arrived with the sun, but other than some basic instructions for the nurses, nothing changed. He did, however, suggest we talk to Mama as though she were awake.

"Some people believe a comatose patient is still aware of their surroundings."

Dad and I took turns sitting with her. The nurses came and went from the room, giving us privacy but remaining close should we need anything. Near dinnertime, Nurse Bradford came for the night shift. It was Christmas Eve, and I knew it was a sacrifice to be away from her family.

"I'll spend time with them tomorrow." She smoothed Mama's

pale cheek. "I want to be with Ava tonight." Her gentle words touched me.

A car turned into the driveway, followed by a knock on the back door. Dad went to see who it was and soon returned, Nash following behind.

"Pastor Arnold brought us a Christmas feast," Dad said, struggling to keep his composure. "The church ladies organized it. There's turkey, ham, all the fixings."

Nurse Bradford insisted we three enjoy the meal while she stayed with Mama. The food was delicious but none of us had much of an appetite. When we'd eaten all we could, Nash volunteered to clean things up. Dad had nearly dozed off at the table, so I insisted he lie down on the sofa while I went upstairs.

The lights were dim when I quietly entered Mama's room. Nurse Bradford sat next to the bed, reading softly from a Bible.

"*My substance was not hid from thee, when I was made in secret, and curiously wrought in the lowest parts of the earth. Thine eyes did see my substance, yet being unperfect; and in thy book all my members were written, which in continuance were fashioned, when as yet there was none of them.*"

The floorboard creaked under my weight, and she turned to me.

"I was just reading to Ava." She closed the book and stood, motioning for me to take the now empty seat. "Come in, dear."

"What does that passage mean?" I asked once I was settled.

She looked thoughtful. "I believe King David was reminding himself of God's divine plan for humankind."

At my confused look, she continued.

"He writes that there is no place on earth or under the earth or in heaven that we can escape the presence and power of God. He is there, David says, when we're formed in our mother's womb." She laid a gentle hand on my shoulder. "God knows the very moment when we'll take our first breath, and when we'll take our last. He's with Ava, right now, here in this room."

I glanced at Mama's still form. "Do you really believe that?"

"I do. The Bible tells me God is a good Father. Ava is his beloved daughter."

Her simple answer didn't satisfy me, just as they hadn't when I was a girl in Sunday school. "If God is so good, why didn't he heal Mama? Lots of people prayed for her. She prayed." I looked at the nurse. "If this is how he treats his followers, you can count me out."

She didn't look offended. "Our suffering here on earth doesn't mean God isn't good. Jesus himself suffered. Death on a cross is a horrific way to die. God—Emmanuel—went through everything we experience in this life, from birth to death."

I'd never heard it explained that way. "Why would he do that?"

"To save us. From sin. From death. To give us eternal life. Mattie, your mother told me she's ready to meet Jesus. In the life of a believer, our last day on earth is the first day of eternity with God."

I swallowed, hard. "Everything I ever believed about God died when my brother was killed in Vietnam. Now Mama is dying. I don't have any faith left in me."

Compassion filled her face. "You may not believe in God, but he believes in you, Mattie."

She left me alone then.

Tears ran down my face.

I wanted her words to be true. I wanted to believe that God cared about us, but how could I?

I grasped Mama's warm hand. "I don't know if you can hear me or not, but I'm struggling, Mama. I need to know you're going to be all right. I need to know you'll see Mark again."

Dad joined me a short time later. He gazed down at Mama, and the raw grief on his face nearly undid me. He sat on the edge of the mattress, but Mama didn't stir. We didn't speak. It was enough to simply watch and wait. Nurse Bradford checked Mama's vitals every so often. Nash stood like a sentinel outside the door. No one wanted to go to bed.

It was close to midnight when Mama's breathing changed. Instead of the death rattle Dr. Monahan had warned us of, she took full, deep breaths. We were all surprised when her eyes fluttered open.

She muttered something unintelligible, her head moving back and forth on the pillow. After days of watching her simply lie still, the small movement was startling.

Mama kept mumbling, her eyes searching. Finally her focus landed on Dad.

"Gunther," she said, shocking everyone with the clarity of the single word. Her entire body instantly relaxed.

I stared in horror as Dad's face paled. I couldn't imagine the devastation he must feel, hearing his wife call out for her lover on her deathbed.

Nash came and put his arm around me. When our eyes met, I knew he understood.

"Gunther." Mama reached a hand toward Dad.

I held my breath.

Would he leave the room, furious and heartbroken?

"I'm here, Ava," he finally said, his voice thick as he wrapped her hand in both of his. "I'm here, my darling."

My mouth went slack.

THIRTY-SIX

AVA

DELANEY HORSE FARM

OCTOBER 1945

It had been two months since the package bearing Gunther's Bible and his proposal of marriage arrived. I'd immediately written to him, declaring my love for him and my desire to become his wife. Yet day after day passed with no word from him. My greatest fear was that he'd been deported and hadn't been able to get word to me.

There was nothing to do but wait.

Colonel Foster resigned his post after his visit to the farm. I arrived at the office one morning to find a new man in charge. I was disappointed Hew hadn't said goodbye, but I understood. With his departure, I felt free to leave my position too. Bren cried on my last day, but she and the other girls had plans to move to Nashville and share an apartment as soon as the hospital closed. Everyone, it seems, was ready for a new beginning.

A cool October breeze met me as I exited the barn. Dark clouds and the smell of rain warned of an approaching storm. I'd spent the morning cleaning out stalls and preparing for the arrival of a dozen new horses from Camp Forrest. They'd been used for training purposes, but with the Army vacating the enormous cantonment, the animals required a new home. I still wasn't sure who gave my name to the sergeant in charge of the stables, but he said he had orders to contact me and offer the horses to us, free of charge. They'd even transport them out to the farm.

The first drops of rain smacked me as I ran for the house. When I reached the porch, I stopped to inhale the fresh scent. I peered out across the farm to see if the horses in the front pasture had taken shelter from the storm, but instead I found a lone figure walking up the drive in the deluge. We'd put an ad in the paper for a stable hand, and I wondered if it was someone coming to apply for the job. Many people couldn't afford fuel for their vehicles these days, so it wasn't unusual to see someone walking along the roads.

Rain fell harder as the stranger approached. I squinted through the downpour, wondering who would come out to the farm on such a dreary day. He wasn't even wearing a hat.

When he reached the middle of the yard, the man stopped. After a moment, he lifted his hand in the air.

I gasped.

It couldn't be.

"Gunther?"

I don't remember stepping off the porch, but suddenly I was drenched, running through the mud. I didn't stop until I was in his arms.

"Ava, Ava," he said over and over.

When we parted, he held my face between his hands, his eyes drinking me in as rain bathed us. "Did you get my letter? And the Bible?"

I cupped his face, laughing and crying at the same time. "Yes, my darling. I did. I will. I will marry you, Gunther. Today if you want."

He picked me up and swung me around. "I love you, Ava."

When my feet were once again on the ground, I gazed into his beloved face. A face I'd wondered if I would ever see again.

"I love you, Gunther Schneider. Welcome home."

THIRTY-SEVEN

MATTIE

DELANEY HORSE FARM
DECEMBER 1969

Mama never woke up again.

She slipped from this world early Christmas morning while Dad and I held her hands. I didn't get a chance to tell her how much I loved her or how grateful I was that she loved me. Dr. Monahan and Pastor Arnold arrived, bringing calmness and comfort with them. A kindly man from the funeral home took Mama's body away, leaving us bereft of her physical presence forever.

By noon, we'd sent everyone away to celebrate the holiday with their families. The funeral was planned for Sunday afternoon.

Dad, Nash, and I sat in the living room amid the Christmas decorations Mama had insisted I put up. They stood as a stark reminder that the life and breath of our family was gone.

"I know you have questions," Dad said after long minutes passed.

I stared at him. "Questions?" Anger overtook my grief. "Yes, I have questions. Before Mama went to the hospital, she told me someone named Gunther Schneider is my father." My gaze bored into him. "Are *you* Gunther Schneider?"

The name echoed in the silent house.

"Yes." He rubbed his face with both hands before looking at me. "I never wanted you or your brother to know my real name."

"Why not?" I shook my head, baffled. "I read the letters you wrote to Mama during the war. You were a prisoner. Is that why you didn't want us to know?"

His shoulders fell. "I asked her not to give you the letters."

"She said I should know who I was, where I came from, but they only confused me." My voice wavered. "All this time I thought—" I gulped air. "I thought some other man, some stranger, was my father."

I burst into sobs.

Dad rose and came to me. He knelt on the floor and took my hands in his. "No, Mattie," he said, tears running down his face. "I am your father. Me. Gunther Schneider. After the war, I was ashamed of being German. Ashamed of what my countrymen, my own brother, had done. When I was finally released from the internment camp in North Dakota, I was afraid they would change their minds and lock me up again. I couldn't let that happen. I couldn't let them take me away from Ava. From you and Mark."

He was sobbing now too.

When he was able to speak, he continued. "I changed my name after your mother and I married. Kurt is my middle name. Schneider can mean *tailor* in German, so I became Kurt Taylor. Ava said I should not be ashamed of my German heritage, but I am. I refused to pass that shame on to my children. It is a burden I would carry alone."

All I could do was stare at him, trying to process everything he'd shared.

He was German, and he'd been consumed by fear after the war. Whether those fears were rational or not, his choices from that point on were not made from selfishness but for love. Love for Mama. Love for Mark.

Love for me.

The anger and betrayal I'd felt after Mama's revelation evaporated with his astonishing confession. "You wanted to protect us."

Nash stood so Dad could sit on the sofa next to me. While he gripped my hand, he told us about his arrest in New York City, his time at Camp Forrest, and how he and Mama met.

"You were going to be a doctor?" I said, dumbfounded.

"My grandfather in Germany was a doctor, and my *Mutter* wanted me to become one too. She sent me to America when I was eighteen years old."

I gasped, as though someone clicked on the proverbial light bulb in my brain. Suddenly all the puzzle pieces fit.

Without explaining my actions, I ran upstairs. When I returned, I handed the old book from the shoebox to him. "Your mother gave this Bible to you. A German Bible."

A sheen of wetness filled his eyes as he reached for it. He smoothed the cover, tenderly, almost reverently. "I have not held this in many years. I wanted to dispose of it, but Ava insisted on keeping it. *Mutter* gave it to me before I left for America. She was a God-fearing woman."

"What does the inscription say?"

He turned to the first page. "*Für meinen Sohn, Ehre Gott immer. Ich liebe dich, Mutter.* For my son. Honor God always. I love you, Mother."

It felt surreal to hear my father speak German, reading something his mother—my grandmother—wrote years ago when he was a boy in Germany. "Is she still alive?"

Dad shook his head slowly. "I do not know. After the war, I wrote to many people, seeking information. A neighbor told me that my brother had moved *Mutter* to Berlin in 1944. So many people were lost in the bombings. I gave my address to some trusted friends in case she returned to our hometown, but I never heard from any of them."

My heart grieved for the grandmother I never knew. "And your brother? Did he survive the war?"

Shame registered in Dad's eyes. "He survived, but he was arrested by the Allies. Rolf was tried for war crimes and executed in 1947."

I told him about the photograph in the back. Tears filled his eyes when he saw it. "This was taken many years before I left for America. *Mutter* sold the car so I could buy passage on a ship."

He went on to tell us about his time at Fort Lincoln, about Dr. Sonnenberg, and how he gave up on life after his friend was killed.

"The only thing that kept me alive was my love for Ava."

His quiet words crushed me. "I'm sorry," I whispered. "I'm sorry for blaming you for everything. I didn't know. I didn't know you."

We hugged for the first time in years. I couldn't imagine how I'd gone all this time without my father's strong arms around me. I clung to him and wept.

When we parted, he finished the tale, explaining that once he and Mama married, he found refuge on the farm. He avoided going to town, afraid someone would suspect the truth about his German heritage. He'd worked hard to correct his accent, but some words simply wouldn't come out right, no matter how hard he tried. He apologized for not attending school events and church with us, and for leaving most of the parenting to Mama.

"I wasn't the father you and Mark deserved." Regret filled his voice. "But I want you to know I've always been proud to be your dad."

"I wasn't the daughter you and Mama deserved," I said, sniffling.

He reached to touch my cheek. "I love you, Mattie."

"I love you too, Dad."

We turned in early, exhausted from the emotional day. When I entered my room, the shoebox on the desktop drew me.

I had yet to read the last letter from Gunther.

I carefully unfolded it. With amazement, I read the words of love my father wrote to my mother many years ago.

My Dearest Ava . . .

EPILOGUE

MATTIE

DELANEY HORSE FARM

APRIL 1970

Dad, Nash, and I waited in the farmyard, ready to welcome the first official clients to our experimental horse therapy clinic.

After our success with Fred, word spread through the veteran community. We soon had former soldiers arriving, wanting to learn to ride a horse. Men came from as far away as Atlanta, and we'd had to quickly come up with a program and a schedule. Nash contacted the VA hospital for advice, and while they couldn't formally approve the clinic for treatment, the doctor in charge told Nash—*"off the record, of course"*—it sounded fantastic and wished us the best of luck.

Because Granny Gertrude left the farm to Mama, stipulating in her will that it had to pass to Mark or me upon Mama's death, I suddenly found myself the owner of Delaney Horse Farm. Dad didn't mind. He said Gertrude never approved of him, often referring to him as "*that Nazi*," so he was happy for me to inherit the property. A friend of Dr. Monahan's came by in January and bought two of our best horses, giving us enough money to cover Mama's medical bills and put some aside for the future. Moonlight Sky delivered a healthy foal last week—a filly that looked just like her mama—and my mind was already alive with ideas of how to improve the bloodlines of our stock.

After we discussed the idea of a horse therapy clinic, Dad immediately drove to Nashville and came home with a stack of thick medical books. Anatomy. Physical therapy. Psychology. Amputations. I often found him at the kitchen table, studying long into the night.

A few weeks ago, I approached him with his mother's Bible. "Dad," I said, a little hesitant. I wasn't sure what he'd think of my request. "I'd like to learn German. Would you teach me? We could use this for our lessons."

His eyes filled with moisture. "I would like that, Mattie. Your *Großmutter* would be pleased."

Since that day, Dad and I often discussed the Bible passages we read during our German lessons, sorting through all my questions about life, death, and heaven. I found he had as many questions as I did, and although we didn't always agree on theological ideas, the time spent together was healing in ways I never could have imagined. I was pleased when he began to join Nash and me at church on Sundays.

A yellow VW bus pulled into the yard. Dad and Jake walked over to greet Fred and the other wounded warriors. We watched as four men with varying physical limitations piled out of the vehicle. One of them bent to pet Jake, who clearly enjoyed the attention.

"Do you know why Dad wouldn't let Mark and me have a dog when we were growing up?"

Nash tucked me against his side. "Why?"

"Because the guards at the internment camp in North Dakota used dogs to keep the internees in line. Their presence always left him uneasy. Jake is the first dog he's ever trusted."

Nash kissed the top of my head. "War leaves a lot of scars, some you can't see."

"Wouldn't Mark love this? He'd be thrilled to know we were using the farm to help soldiers."

Nash's arm tightened around me. "I know you haven't changed your mind about sending troops to Vietnam, but these guys would never guess it. All they see is someone willing to help. Mark would be proud of you, Mattie."

"I'm proud of him." I looked at Nash. He'd finally gone to see his father last week. They had a long way to go in rebuilding their relationship, but Nash had hope he could get his dad to acknowledge his alcoholism and find help. "I'm proud of you, too, Mr. McCallum."

He turned our backs to the small gathering and stole a kiss. "Let's go ride some horses, Miss Taylor."

"Taylor-Schneider, remember?"

He chuckled. "Martha Ann Taylor-Schneider. That's a mouthful. It'll be better when you shorten it to Mattie McCallum."

I smiled, comfortable with our unhurried plans for the future. "Someday."

We held hands as we made our way to the group. While Nash introduced himself, a young man, with burn scars on his face and missing both hands, approached me. He couldn't be more than twenty years old.

"Who's Mark?" he asked, indicating the sign Nash had carved out of wood and hung above the barn entrance.

I glanced up at it.

Mark's Easy Riders.

Yesterday, I visited my brother's grave and told him all about the clinic. Even though I'd come to believe he was in heaven, I found comfort sitting where his earthly body rested, sharing secrets like we did when we were young. I'd whispered a prayer, asking God to tell Mark how much I missed him and that I looked forward to the day when I was with my wombmate again. I still had a long way to come to terms with Mark's and Mama's deaths and God's purpose in it all, but every day brought me a little closer to the peace of soul I hungered for.

With a genuine smile, I faced the young man.

"Mark was a hero, like you. Let me tell you about him."

A Note from the Author

I'M THE PROUD DAUGHTER of a World War II veteran. My dad was a turret gunner on B-17 bombers—you know, the guy in the tiny little bubble on the belly of the plane!—and flew fifty missions over Europe. Like many veterans, Daddy didn't talk much about what he experienced during the war. Now that I'm older and can better appreciate his sacrifice and service to our country and to the world, I wish I could sit at his knee and listen—really listen—to his stories, but he's been in heaven for many years. Those stories will have to wait.

Yet because of my dad's involvement in the war, I've become a student of the history that took place during those turbulent years when Hitler and the Nazis were determined to rule the world and eradicate the Jewish people. It is unfathomable to me that the same evil mentality that existed then is still prevalent as I'm writing this, as evidenced by the war currently taking place in Israel. Freedom and sacrifice are as relevant today as they were when my dad joined the Army Air Forces in 1942.

Because of my interest in WWII, I was aware of the detainment of Japanese Americans, referred to as enemy aliens. I grew up in Santa Fe, New Mexico, and the location of the former internment camp where Japanese people were held during the war wasn't far from our church. But a lesser-known fact is that Germans and Italians were also detained, with many of them spending time at Camp Forrest in Tullahoma, Tennessee. German POWs were also housed there. Gunther's character, including the way he speaks, his desire to remain in America, and his struggle with how to feel about being German in the shadow of the Nazi regime, is based on research as well as personal experience with German friends. My own roots go back to Germany, so the country and its people hold a special place in my heart.

Camp Forrest was a large military installation built in 1940 after war broke out in Europe. Set on 85,000 acres, the huge cantonment cost $36 million to build. There were over thirteen hundred buildings, with barracks, mess halls, post exchanges, warehouses, administrative offices, officer quarters, a large laundry facility, training facilities, and a two-thousand-patient hospital. Thousands of people—military personnel and civilians alike—passed through Camp Forrest during the war. Today, there isn't much left of the large cantonment. It was dismantled after the war and is now part of the Arnold Air Force Base complex.

The Vietnam War took place when I was a kid. Those were the days of protests, hippies, and political unrest. Although no one in my immediate family went to Vietnam, I do have loved ones and friends who were in the military during this time. It is not lost upon me that their stories could have turned out much like Mark's or Nash's.

I hope *All We Thought We Knew* serves as a reminder that, while war is never best, it is sometimes unavoidable. Our military personnel need our respect, our appreciation, and our prayers.

Acknowledgments

WITHOUT PEOPLE LIKE my dad, uncles, two brothers, and sister-in-law who were willing to serve our country in the military—some during wartime—the freedoms most of us take for granted might not exist. All through the ages, men and women have donned uniforms, taken up arms, and sacrificed for Freedom. To each and every one of them, I offer my profound gratitude. Freedom is never free. It always comes at a cost.

Some heroes don't wear a uniform. My husband of thirty-seven-plus years is one of them. Thank you, Brian, for taking such good care of me and our family. You're my favorite person on the planet. Forever and ever. Amen.

Selfishly, I'm grateful neither of my sons have gone to war, but they are young heroes in the making, nonetheless. Taylor and Austin, my prayer is you will continue to seek God's wisdom and grace as you become husbands and, God willing, fathers. To my brand-new daughters-in-law, Erica and Kaley, you are both answers to this mama's prayers. Genesis 2:22 says, "Then the Lord God made a woman from the rib, and *he brought her to the man*" (emphasis added). I know for certain God brought each of you to my sons, and I'm so happy he did!

Thank you to my family and friends for your unwavering

support and encouragement through the years. My life is richer because you are in it.

I count it a huge blessing to be part of the Tyndale House Publishers family. When I was ten years old, I was given *The Children's Living Bible*, never dreaming that one day the same company who published it would also publish my novels. Thank you to Jan Stob, Karen Watson, Kathy Olson, and the entire Tyndale team for cheering me on and helping me become a better writer. Your trust, your wisdom, and your encouragement mean everything.

Thank you to my agent, Bob Hostetler. I can always count on your good counsel and sound, biblical wisdom, and I'm grateful to have you in my corner.

To each reader, thank you for taking this journey with me. I appreciate you more than you'll ever know.

Ephesians 6:10-17 is an invitation from God to put on our armor and join him in the battle against the evils we see every day in our world. Without the helmet of salvation, offered to us through Jesus' sacrifice on the cross . . . without the body armor of God's righteousness, which is God's approval . . . without the belt of truth, the shield of faith, peace guiding our steps, and the sword of the Spirit, which is God's holy Word . . . we are totally and completely vulnerable against the strategies of the devil and the authorities of the unseen world. But equipped with God's armor, we *can* stand firm, as a soldier going to battle. We *can* be strong in the Lord and in his mighty power. And in the end, when the battle is over, we *will* still be standing firm. I am eternally grateful to be part of his army.

Soli Deo gloria.

Discussion Questions

1. This is a dual timeline novel, with two sets of characters in different time periods. Did you enjoy both stories equally, or did one capture your interest more than the other? At what point were you able to see how the two stories connected? What were some of the clues you noticed?
2. This novel deals with both World War II and the Vietnam War. What are some of the differences in the ways the two wars were generally regarded while they were being fought? What are the similarities? How do you think each war is viewed now, many years later?
3. Were you surprised by any of the historical facts that came out in the story? Have you heard firsthand stories from older friends or family members who lived through either of these wars?
4. Mattie reminds Mark it's possible to speak up for what's right without putting himself in danger, and Mark responds that sometimes, someone has to do the hard things and make sacrifices to make sure the people they care about are safe. Have you ever faced this choice, for yourself or a loved one?

5. After Mattie learns more about Nash's homelife, she feels differently about his decision to go to Vietnam. What are some of the dangers of making judgements without knowing a person's full story? How can we guard against it?

6. Mattie has strong feelings against Nash and others who chose to fight in the Vietnam War, but eventually she realizes the soldiers themselves were not the enemy. What changes her mind?

7. While working at Camp Forrest, Gunther and Ava begin to have feelings for each other, but both are certain there can be no future for them. While many of the barriers that existed in the 1940s have been overcome, what issues can still come between friends or couples today?

8. Mattie blames herself for Mark's death and is surprised to learn that Nash, too, feels responsible. Have you ever blamed yourself for something only to find that someone else feels responsible too? Why is it easy to blame ourselves when something bad happens to us or to the people we love?

9. Mattie recognizes that she always feels better after a horseback ride. Today it's well established that interacting with nature is good for mental health. What are your experiences with this?

10. Mattie says she always had questions about the Bible as a child in Sunday school, and as a young adult, she has even more significant questions. How have your questions about God changed as you've gotten older? Do you find them harder or easier to answer now? Why is it important to be honest about our questions?

About the Author

Michelle Shocklee is the author of several historical novels, including *Count the Nights by Stars*, a *Christianity Today* fiction book award winner, and *Under the Tulip Tree*, a Christy and Selah Awards finalist. Her work has been featured in numerous Chicken Soup for the Soul books, magazines, and blogs. Married to her college sweetheart and the mother of two grown sons, she makes her home in Tennessee, not far from the historical sites she writes about. Visit her online at michelleshocklee.com.